District: Surviving the Zombie Apocalypse

SHAWN CHESSER

ISBN: 978-0-9980683-1-2

CONTENTS

ACKNOWLEDGEMENTS

For Maureen, Raven, and Caden ... I couldn't have done this without your support. Thanks to all of our military, LE and first responders for your service. To the people in the U.K. and elsewhere around the world who have been in touch, thanks for reading! Lieutenant Colonel Michael Offe, thanks for your service as well as your friendship. Shannon Walters, my top *Eagle Eye*, thank you! Larry Eckels, thank you for helping me with some of the military technical stuff. Any missing facts or errors are solely my fault. Beta readers, you rock, and you know who you are. Thanks George Romero for introducing me to zombies. Steve H., thanks for listening. All of my friends and fellows at S@N and Monday Steps On Steele, thanks as well. Lastly, thanks to Bill W. and Dr. Bob … you helped make this possible. I am going to sign up for another 24.

Special thanks to John O'Brien, Mark Tufo, Joe McKinney, Craig DiLouie, Armand Rosamilia, Heath Stallcup, James Cook, Saul Tanpepper, Eric A. Shelman, and David P. Forsyth. I truly appreciate your continued friendship and always invaluable advice. Thanks to Jason Swarr and Straight 8 Custom Photography for the awesome cover. Once again, extra special thanks to Monique Happy for her work editing "District." Mo, as always, you rose to the occasion! Working with you has been a dream come true and nothing but a pleasure. If I have accidentally left anyone out ... I am truly sorry.

***

Edited by Monique Happy Editorial Services
www.moniquehappy.com

Prologue

Three things worked against Sid and Nancy as they traversed the open range fronting the tree- and scrub-covered foothills to their immediate left. First was the temperature, which had buoyed from well below freezing to the mid-fifties in the span of just a couple of hours. Snow-covered and firm underfoot when they'd taken flight from their captors in the dark early morning hours, the grassy expanse stretching out before them, a never-ending canvas of green and brown dotted with stubborn patches of snow, was now sucking mercilessly at their oversized boots and stealing what precious little energy they had built up overnight.

Then there was the problem of the clothing they'd taken from their high-centered Volvo wagon and layered on after they had distanced themselves from the string of headlights approaching from far off north on the nearby state route. Amounting to virtually every stitch of cold weather gear crowding their closets before the outbreak, the once thin and pliable high-dollar items—all either touted as *GORE-TEX® Treated, Thermal Insulated*, or purported to possess *Wind Stopping Technology*—were now heavy with sweat that had them bunching and pinching at the elbows and knees.

Lastly was the throng of dead angling in on them from the direction of the road and, in the process, blocking the way to Nancy's sole objective: Securing anything tangible from the hulk of metal on the road that might help her to remember her dead little boy.

***

Hours earlier, after having abandoned their overloaded car on the state route, Sid and Nancy had hopped the barbed wire fence and fled across a sparkling carpet of white toward the night-enshrouded tree line.

However, once they reached the perceived sanctuary the darkened copse of firs and alders promised, Sid looked back and gasped audibly upon seeing the laser-straight trail of shadowed footprints leading right to their position. Thankfully, Nancy had anticipated the effect the diffuse moonlight would have on the six-inch holes they'd stomped into the recent accumulation and was already, literally and figuratively, one step ahead of her husband. Without uttering a word, her breath coming out in great white plumes, she mouthed: "Follow me," and, grasping his elbow in a firm grip, led him to their left, away from the damning footprints.

After a minute or two spent ducking low branches and fighting through tangles of ankle-grabbing underbrush, the soft yellow glow of approaching headlights crested a hill ahead and began to slow on the stretch of two-lane to their left.

Suddenly, and inexplicably, catching Sid by surprise, Nancy went to ground, dragging him down with her. They lay there for a moment listening to the sounds of engines laboring in four-wheel drive and breathing hard from the exertion of breaking brush along the north/south-running tree line. Then, after the trio of vehicles had passed from right to left on the state route and were drawing near to their inert Volvo, she rose and helped Sid to stand. They gawked for a minute, then, with the vehicles gearing down and their brake lights painting the white stripe of road blood red, Nancy nodded for Sid to follow and started off at low-sprint, leaving cover behind.

Attempting to conceal the evidence of their passage, Nancy stepped only in the shadow of a raised feeder road and led them straight to the hard-to-miss dark oval mouth of a galvanized culvert buried sidelong beneath it.

As the growl of engines softened to an easy idle, Nancy again fell to her hands and knees, taking Sid along for the ride. Together, panting and grunting, the two backed themselves into the drainage pipe and lay there as the *thunk* of doors opening and closing and low murmur of hushed voices carried back to them.

"Thank God they ate the dog," Sid whispered to Nancy as the backlit silhouettes conferred on the shoulder beside the high-clearance vehicles.

"What makes you so sure that was all they ate?" she whispered as the dark forms crouched down and trained rifle muzzles on the Volvo.

Sid stared at her stump, but made no reply. Expecting the imminent braying of hounds finding their trail to shatter the night air, he buried his face in Nancy's parka-clad shoulder and began to weep.

Nancy shushed Sid and then directed him to look to the road where a flashlight beam lanced out to illuminate the burgundy-red Volvo. "It's empty," a voice called out. Then there was cussing. Next, accusations were thrown back and forth for a minute or two. Finally, the voices died to nothing and a half-dozen new beams of blue light painted the field a couple of hundred yards south of their hiding place.

There was a shout, the words garbled, and then a disembodied voice said, "Wait a second. I'll get the cutters and snip the wire."

And someone among the group did just that.

The voices rose in volume and pitch as the group poured through the newly created opening. Nancy clutched Sid's hand as their pursuers fanned out and started heckling and calling them by name. The insults and threats of violence continued as the five women and one man walked the length of the fresh tracks and probed the tree line with their flashlight beams.

Soon the cussing was back as the posse fought the same undergrowth Sid and Nancy had. The futile search lasted an hour and ended in more arguing. Within ten minutes of the searchers giving up on searching the tree line and crunching back through the snow towards their awaiting vehicles, doors were thunking closed and motors were turning over.

After letting the rigs warm up for a spell, the two SUVs pulled slowly around the lone 4x4 pickup and stopped single file in front of the Volvo.

Teeth beginning to chatter, Sid said, "You fooled them."

"No … *we* fooled them," Nancy replied, absentmindedly rubbing her bandaged stump.

As the first tendrils of dawn turned the sky to the west from deep black to a harsh shade of purple, the last vehicle in the small convoy, a squared-off black pickup truck, stopped alongside the Volvo. Without warning a lick of red flame lit up the retreating night and a thunderous report crashed across the countryside.

"There goes the window," Sid exclaimed.

"We'll get another car," Nancy said consolingly.

Sid sighed. "What's *she* doing?" he asked.

As if answering the question, where there had been darkness between the vehicles, a bright red point of light spewing smoke and spark suddenly appeared, illuminating the Swedish wagon in a lava-like red-orange glow.

"A flare," Sid whispered, his already damaged night vision etched further with red tracers as the truck driver swung the sputtering and spitting item lazily back and forth a couple of times before tossing it through the Volvo's newly shot-out driver's side window.

For a long while they remained silent and watched their car burn, their meager belongings—mostly boxes full of memories: curling pictures of their tow-headed boy, the certificate of live birth with his tiny footprints stamped in blue ink, and moldy toddler's clothes Nancy hadn't been able to part with after his death at the hands of the rotting dead—going up with it.

Nancy stared stone-faced. She was cried out. Had been for a long while. Sid, on the other hand, was not. He cried for a long while as tendrils of smoke curled from the smoldering Volvo. And while he did, a driving sleet started up and the snow began to melt.

Thankfully, their combined body heat was trapped in the culvert with them and Sid finally cried himself to sleep.

Nancy spent the next three hours staring at the bloody stump where her dominant hand used to be. The makeshift dressing was holding, but the cauterized wound had begun to seep again, the new yellow and red splotches mingling with the ground-in grass and mud.

After the first hour the sleet turned to a cold, hard driving rain—the water streaming in the culvert making things even more miserable.

Hour two saw the rain slow and the pewter clouds cruise off to the southeast.

By the third hour Nancy still had not heard so much as a single exhaust note from the direction of the state route—south or north. The temperature was also rising quickly, and as a result trees to the left were shedding snow at a quick pace—the thumps startling at first, then welcome as their true source became known. At the end of the three hours, as if a switch had been flicked, the storm had been usurped and to the west was brilliant blue sky as far as the eye could see.

Smiling broadly, Nancy shook Sid, urging him to wake up. Her simple moment of joy was quickly shattered when she looked down and realized that the red slush his hand had been resting in was melted fully, which meant the dead would be thawing out, too—a death warrant for sure, if they didn't find shelter soon.

Feeling the sun warming her face, Nancy told Sid to stay put. After shimmying from the culvert, she commando-crawled a few feet down the ditch in the direction of the road and lay still in the shallow water pooled there. After listening hard for a moment and hearing only a steady dripping and occasional *whoosh-bang* of more snow calving off the tall trees behind her, she rose up slowly, her head barely breaking cover of the ditch, and regarded the dense forest that had saved their lives. It was much closer than she remembered. In the dark the sprint from the forest's edge to the drainage pipe had seemed like a forty-yard dash with lions snapping at their heels. In reality, the lush green wall behind her was less than thirty feet away.

Dead ahead, Nancy's vantage was mostly blocked by long tufts of grass slowly springing back after being knuckled under the snow for a day and a half.

"I'm going to take a better look," she whispered over her shoulder to Sid. He muttered something a little louder than she would've liked, and she winced. Then, rearing up off the ground in a pose never attempted outside of a yoga studio, she got an unobstructed look at the burned-out windowless shell that had been their Volvo. Craning left, then right, she saw only a steaming ribbon of road spooling away from the charred hulk in both directions.

"Clear," she called over her shoulder. Which was a little white lie, because though their pursuers were nowhere to be seen, a small group of undead had keyed in on Sid's plaintive voice and were ambling onto the pasture through the breach in the barbed wire fence. The lie had been enough to get Sid moving and out of the pipe.

In the light of day, Nancy saw that Sid's clothing, like hers, was drenched and sluicing water as he stood. *So much for manufacturer's promises*, she mused, grabbing hold of her man and pulling him stammering and flailing in the general direction of the slow-moving zombies.

"Hell are we going that way for?" he asked, his voice gone hoarse.

"Because everything we had was in that car. *Everything.*"

And by "*everything*" she meant all of her dead son's belongings, some of which she hoped had survived the fire. His favorite spoon, hopefully. Perhaps some of his Hot Wheel cars … at least the metal bodies. Anything tangible to have and to hold would be better than the memories that seemed to get fuzzier around the edges the farther she got from that horrific day in late July when she had lost him.

Chapter 1

Now, slowed by the unlikely combination of mud sucking at their oversized boots and waterlogged fleece and nylon weighing them down like suits of armor, the young couple were no faster than their *new* pursuers—nearly a dozen moaning and hissing dead things all in various stages of decay and undress.

Nancy and Sid trudged a rough semi-circle around the things to get to their car. Once there, they found only ashes and charred skeletal seat frames inside the metal shell that had once contained all of the memories of their past lives.

"Let's go, Nance," Sid urged.

Shaking her head, Nancy pounded on the car's flat roof with her good hand, sending blackened, scaling paint flying in every direction.

"We'll make new memories," Sid called, as he led the slow procession of dead things around the front of the Volvo and away from Nancy.

"Fuck memories," Nancy hissed, as Sid returned, grabbed her elbow, and lead her toward the fence.

"We can't stay on the road. They're coming back … sooner or later."

The dead were hissing and moaning louder than ever as Sid dragged Nancy away from the now low-to-the-ground car.

Sid reached the snipped wire fence and ushered Nancy through. He burned the ten-second lead over the zombies by working feverishly to wind the longest of the rusty strands around a post as a makeshift barrier.

Falling short by less than an inch, Sid gave up and reentered the pasture through the breach and began shedding his leaden layers of clothing the same way he had donned them: on the run.

"Fucking Pineapple Express," he shouted, tugging at a sleeve to extricate his arm. "Thought these kinds of wild weather swings only happened near the ocean."

"Help," Nancy called out, one arm bent at an awkward angle and stuck fast in the sleeve of her goose-down parka.

Sid stopped in his tracks and, as he turned at the waist to regard Nancy, there came a string of hollow popping sounds. In the split second between realizing what the noises were and opening his mouth to tell Nancy to duck, his side vision registered two slender women rising up from the roadside a hundred feet south. In the next beat he was delivering the warning and staring directly at winking muzzles as the two shooters advanced along the state route toward them.

Turning back to help Nancy with her coat, a bullet grazed Sid's cheek, sending him to the ground where suddenly he found himself within arm's reach of an emaciated female cadaver. Drawing in a mouthful of carrion-tinged air, his eyes were drawn from Nancy to the creature's bare feet and on up to its horribly shredded mid-section that, judging by the advanced state of decay the remaining organs had suffered, had been exposed to the full wrath of the elements since the early days of the outbreak.

Hearing Nancy cry out, Sid scrambled backwards on hands and feet toward her.

More bullets scythed overhead, crackling and hissing. Two of the advancing dead fell under the withering fire, landing equidistant between Sid and his wife. Still locked onto Sid like a meat-seeking missile, the female zombie plodded through the sucking mud.

Finally, lamenting the fact that his vision was blurring and he was unable to move faster on his back across the open ground than the undead woman with what amounted to barely bungee cords for core muscles, Sid raised his hands defensively and focused his gaze on the hollow of her neck.

Feeling the sting where a flying fragment of rock or, God forbid, bone shard from one of the fallen zombies had cut a jagged inch-long wound on her shoulder, Nancy extricated her forearm and hand from the sodden sleeve. With the angry noise of bullets flying by her head, she turned toward Sid just in time to see the female zombie's toothy sneer erased by a final long fusillade of gunfire coming from the direction of the state route.

The pasture suddenly went deathly quiet.

Casting her eyes groundward, Nancy waited for the bullets to tear into her and Sid. But none came. Which caused her to wonder why. Reluctantly, she swung her gaze up and around and saw that the other walking corpses had been cut down before they could fully flank her husband, who was now on his hands and knees and surrounded by their bullet-riddled corpses.

From out of sight a familiar, gruff female voice said, "Don't move!"

Nancy could feel the beginnings of an icy ball forming in her gut. She looked at her good right hand and it dawned on her why the dead had been gunned down instead of her and Sid.

"Stand up," the same voice ordered.

Nancy saw black combat boots in her peripheral. Then a long gun barrel, a curl of smoke wafting from it, entered the picture. Finally, she walked her eyes up the woman's quilted snow pants and regarded her silver and turquoise belt buckle which struck her instantly as Native-American-made. It was very ornate. Dozens of light green shards of stone had been fashioned into the shape of a gecko. Zuni in nature, maybe. Nothing bought in a New Mexico gift store, for sure.

She felt the rough leather of a black glove brush the soft flesh under her chin. Then iron fingers gripped her jaw and lifted her head up, forcing her to meet the woman's steely glare.

"Don't take us back there," Nancy said breathlessly, as the noise of engines firing carried from far off down the state route.

"I have no plans of doing anything of the sort," the woman said, grinning wickedly as Sid, already bound at the wrists and ankles with thick plastic zip ties, was thrown to the ground near her muddy boots.

Nancy lowered her gaze and delivered a look to Sid that said: *I love you.* A tick later, in her peripheral vision, she saw the woman gripping her jaw receive a black parcel handed to her by one of the others.

Mercifully, the woman let go of Nancy and in the same motion set the kit on the uneven, soggy ground. Then, with the slow, calculated precision of a Swiss watchmaker, the big hulk of a woman pulled the thick leather cords and unrolled the foot-long item with a practiced underhanded flip.

There was a rattle of metal on metal as the four-foot-long rectangle of treated black leather unfurled. A strong odor of cowhide fought with the stench of the gunned-down corpses.

Sid saw Nancy's rigid body go limp. The fight was gone from her. As was the last shred of dignity their escape had fomented in the strong-willed woman. He craned his neck and regarded the big woman everyone called *Mom.* Though nearly every square inch of her was covered in black leather, it didn't hide the fact that she was morbidly overweight. Her lips curled at the corners, showing off pristine enamel, as she withdrew a wicked-looking knife from a slot amongst the squared-off bone saws and myriad other stainless steel rendering tools.

Sid looked at Nancy and was relieved to see that she had apparently fainted. Which was a good thing, because he would be first to go and wouldn't have to witness what they had in store for her body. And as he steeled himself for the first sting of the butcher's blade, he relived the moment the woman brandishing the knife had severed Nancy's hand and awarded it to the blonde and blue-eyed woman who had captured them at the farmhouse outside of Eden, Utah the day before.

Suddenly a thumb found its way into Sid's eye socket, bringing him back to the present and causing a flash of white hot pain to flood his brain. Next, gloved fingers clamped over his mouth and his head was drawn back, the corded muscles in his neck stretched to their limits.

Through his one good eye, Sid saw the patch of snow below him go red with his steaming blood. A biting metallic odor hit his nose and suddenly there was a strange warmth coursing through his body. In the end there was light. And in that light the faint outline of what had to be his boy, tiny arms outstretched, a knowing smile on his face.

Strange what endorphins could do to a man, was Sid's last thought before the lifelong atheist's wildly flailing arms and kicking feet ceased moving, the mud angel beneath his prostrate corpse truly a work of art.

Chapter 2

Cade Grayson rattled four 200-milligram ibuprofen into his palm, popped them in his mouth and washed them down with a swallow of water. He leaned forward on the folding chair and set his plate and fork on the small table next to the door of the particular Conex container in the subterranean redoubt that had come to be known affectionately by all of its tenants as the "*Grayson Quarters.*" With room enough for a trio of bunkbeds—and not much else—the place was about as close to home as anything Cade had known since fleeing the Graysons' two-story Craftsman in Portland, Oregon on that fateful day in late July when the newly dead began to rise.

"Raven," he called through the open sheet of steel serving as a door. "Time to police up the dishes. And bring your partner in crime with you."

There were footsteps on the plywood floor and suddenly Tran was standing an arm's reach from Cade. Wearing his easy smile, the slight man tucked a graying lock of his dark hair behind an ear and raised a brow.

"What's up, Tran?"

"I'll get your plate."

"Oh no you won't, Tran," Brook Grayson called from her perch on the top bunk of the nearest set of steel Army-issue equipment. "Those girls earned the privilege of ninety days KP."

Cade piped up, "At *least* ninety days. Besides … you did all of the work whipping up dinner for ... twelve?"

"Thirteen, counting you," Tran said, his smile growing wider.

More footsteps approached from down the corridor, out of sight behind Tran.

"Damn fine meal. Venison?" Cade asked.

Tran nodded. "You can thank Daymon for the meat. He bagged it up at the quarry late last night."

Propped up on one elbow, her face lost in the gloom near the ribbed metal ceiling, Brook said, "What was he doing at the quarry?"

Tran shrugged as first Raven, then Sasha—a head taller than the Asian man, on account of her wild thicket of red hair—squeezed past him and edged sideways into the Grayson Quarters. Silently, without making eye contact, the girls took the camp plates and silverware and left the narrow room as they had arrived.

Back pressing the corridor wall, Tran watched them go. When he looked back through the door, he glanced up and met the dark-haired woman's gaze.

"Chilly reception," Brook said. "How's it going topside?"

"It's been real quiet. Heidi and Seth are manning the cameras. A few of the others are gearing up. They're going to use the break in the weather to go foraging north of Woodruff."

Grimacing, Cade leaned forward and snatched his water from the table. "Who all's going?"

Tran shrugged. "I saw Daymon, Lev, and Jamie cleaning weapons. But there were at least six packs on the ground under the Raptor's tailgate."

Since the Raptor was Taryn's ride, Brook cocked her head and asked the obvious, "Taryn and Wilson are going, too?"

Again, Tran shrugged. Then he flashed Cade and Brook an arched brow look. "Anything else?"

"Yes, there is," Brook said. She crawled down from the bunk and approached Tran. Standing toe-to-toe with the man she matched in height and basic build, she whispered, "Me and Cade have placed the girls under a pseudo house arrest until further notice."

With Cade looking on silently, Tran nodded.

Buying a moment to think, Brook adjusted her ball cap. Finally, after meeting Cade's gaze and seeming to have read his mind, she said, "I need you to be our eyes and ears when we're not around. If you see or hear the girls scheming or going near the entrance without one of us—or Wilson, in Sasha's case—you have my permission to detain them."

Face wearing a look of understanding, Tran nodded, then backed away from the door and disappeared down the corridor to the right.

Cade pulled the folding chair nearer to him and adjusted the pillow his still swollen left foot was propped up on. "I hate to do that to the girls. Especially Raven, but pardon the pun on this one, our Bird doesn't have a leg to stand on after that stuff she pulled. Nor does Sasha for instigating."

"Thank God it ended well," Brook noted. "I think Raven may have learned her lesson."

Cade nodded in agreement. "I concur. Raven's following days are over, that's for sure."

"Keep that foot up, Cade Grayson … or this nurse isn't going to sign off on your next mission."

Smiling, Cade said, "I'll just go and get a second opinion."

Brook guffawed. "Glenda Gladson is *not* going to take your side of this matter." Issuing a playful glare, she put her hands on her hips.

"I've got an ace in my hand."

"Duncan?"

Cade nodded.

"He's of sound mind now. He'll do *whatever* his lady friend tells him to do."

Conceding her point, Cade said, "I might just have a little dirt on Old Man."

"Liar."

Cade tried to keep a straight face, but in the end he couldn't lie to Brook. Never had. Never would. So his lips parted with a revealing shit-eating grin.

Brook wagged a finger at her man. "Toes above the nose, Grayson. You're almost there."

"By tomorrow?"

"By tomorrow, do you mean during the day?" Arching a brow, she took a deep breath. "Or tonight at one minute after midnight?"

Cade's game face was back. "Closer to the latter," he replied, flatly.

Exiting the room, Brook shot Cade a no-nonsense look and repeated her earlier admonition. "Toes above the nose, Mr. Grayson."

Smile fading, Cade threw a crisp salute at the closing door and, without missing a beat, rose from the folding chair, testing the ankle.

Good to go, he told himself, the grimace fading along with the resulting stab of pain. However, rather than following *nurse's* orders and getting back under the covers on the bottom bunk and propping his foot up on the tubular metal footboard, he looped around the bunk, unlatched his Pelican gear box, and hinged the lid open.

Instantly the familiar and comforting smell of Hoppe's #9 gun oil filled the air. The grimace returning, he knelt next to the box and, working on a sort of autopilot mode, grabbed his gear and weapons from the box and started in on the time-consuming process of getting each piece of kit ready for his upcoming mission.

Chapter 3

Cade quickly stripped down his pair of Glocks—one a full-sized 17, the other a compact 19—and laid out the pieces neatly on the table. After meticulously cleaning and oiling each individual part, he reassembled the polymer semi-automatic pistols, snugged them in their respective holsters, and placed them on the freshly made bunk beside his trusty M4 carbine.

Next, he unfolded a pair of black pants and blouse—both identical in cut and fit to his MultiCam fatigues—and laid them on the bed by the weapons. Both articles of clothing were fashioned from heavy mil-spec ripstop fabric and had rubberized pads affixed to the knees and elbows.

Drawing a deep breath, he sat back down on the folding chair and, while gently massaging his swollen ankle, quickly went through his mental pre-op to-do list. Gerber sharpened? *Check.* Fresh batteries in the EOTech holographic optic atop his cleaned and oiled M4? *Check.* Suppressor threads cleaned and inspected and can replaced hand-tight onto the barrel? *Check.* Night vision goggles tested and stowed away, powered down? *Check.* Ankle one hundred percent? *Not even close.* However, he figured after the long helo ride east, a little shuteye along the way with a thousand-plus more milligrams of ibuprofen hard at work on the swelling, once they were wheels down he'd be able to stow any residual pain in the same compartment his emotions went in every time he was pulled away from family and friends. Besides, he mused, this wouldn't be the first time getting into the shit with the same chronically bum ankle. To be precise, it'd be the third time, and once the dead came into play—or, more likely in this case, the bullets began to fly—the adrenaline would kick in and, as always, pain would be secondary to completing the mission and coming home in one uninfected piece to his little family.

His routine was battle-tested and had worked before. Why wouldn't it this time? After a millisecond's reflection, the details of the mission started piling on all akimbo, like a game of Tetris lost on the first misplayed game tile. So he willed his own inner voice to forget the question. Ordered it to not even go there. Because if the number of enemy he had seen on the videos beamed by Nash to his laptop the day before were any indication as to what he and the team could be facing downrange, he didn't want to ponder the big picture. Better to take small bites from the enemy. Hit them head on with extreme violence of action, spit them out destroyed and mangled, and move on to the next obstacle. *Best to keep it all compartmentalized;* like his emotions had to remain.

A woman's voice calling his name loudly enough to be heard through the closed metal door ripped him from the battle being waged in his head.

"Cade!"

Heidi?

"Hear you loud and clear," he bellowed back. "Be there in a moment."

Eschewing the crutches, and risking an ass-chewing from Brook if she saw him in the corridors without them, he rose and made his way to the security pod, again testing his *bad wheel's* load-bearing ability.

Upon turning the corner, he was confronted with the blonde who had hollered his name. Heidi's arm was outstretched, a thin black sat-phone clutched in her small hand. On her face was a smile Cade guessed to be derived entirely from the satisfaction she must be feeling from having not missed the incoming call—regardless of who might be waiting on the other end.

Making slow progress toward the offered phone, Cade lifted his brows and whispered, "Who is it?"

Can't be good.

"A woman," Heidi replied, making no effort to lower her voice, thusly completely destroying any chance of Cade buying a few minutes to think by having Heidi tell the caller a little white lie.

Waving Heidi off, Cade mouthed, "Tell her I will call her back," and began a slow backpedal toward his quarters.

"It's Nash, I think," Heidi said, a little louder this time, all the while flashing a *careful what you wish for* smile and pumping the hand holding the phone at Cade—universal semaphore for *take the damn call!*

Hell!

"Nash … oh, good," Cade replied loudly, laying it on thick while at the same time giving Heidi a mild case of stink eye. "Can't wait to hear what she has to say." Definitely a white lie.

Smile fading fast, Heidi relinquished the phone and turned back to the flat-panel. One ear cocked, she feigned intense scrutiny on the feed showing Brook and Duncan in the motor pool conversing with Daymon and Oliver. Someone—probably Jimmy Foley—was working under the Chevy's hood, only his backside showing.

Cade's fingers curled around the phone much tighter than he'd meant them to. Before putting the handset to his ear, he stole a look at the monitor and saw the same scene Heidi was presented with: a good old-fashioned jawing session with Duncan occupying center stage. And that meant good money was on Brook not coming back anytime soon.

"Cade here," he said, turning his back to Heidi.

There was a short delay during which he heard only the usual electronic hiss as his words were bounced up into the stratosphere, relayed through one of the few remaining military satellites and returned to Earth, presumably, at Schriever Air Force Base four hundred and twenty-five miles south by east as the crow flies.

Finally, a female voice said, "*Wyatt* … you avoiding me?"

Effin Jedi mind reader.

"No, Major," Cade lied. "Just collecting my thoughts, that's all. What's up?"

Right to the point. Nash said, "Change of plans."

Cade said nothing. Sweeping his gaze back to the flat-panel monitor, he slid a folding chair out and took a seat.

"We underestimated the enemy's speed of advance. When I finally got real-time satellite reconnaissance back on station, finding them took some time. When we reacquired, we found that they had split in two."

"I watched the drone footage," Cade replied. "Even if it split … it'd be impossible to miss a column of that size. Especially from orbit considering the Key Hole's advanced optics."

"You know we're stretched thin in the recon-sat department. I've got one parked over the California/Nevada border watching the Mountain Warfare Training Center—"

Cade interrupted. "Speaking of Pickel Meadows … how are the Marines there holding up?"

"Like they should be. Captain Swarr and his boys are kicking ass and taking names. They've got the Chinese battalion fractured and on the run. Scattered to the wind like a dried-out dandelion."

"Squirters?" he asked.

"Just the advance element that got by their northern FOB days ago," Nash replied, and went quiet.

On the other end of the line Cade heard his favorite Air Force officer draw in a deep breath. Simultaneously, on the screen in front of Heidi, he picked up movement on the lower right partition.

Nash picked up after a long beat. She said, "I'm guessing your undead PLA recon scouts were some of the first wave. Hell, there were so many beachheads up and down the West Coast, California *and* Oregon, that we're just now getting a handle on how many troops they were able to land. A battalion or two is our best estimate. No doubt the Zs chewed up a good number of them the moment their landing craft hit land."

"But?" Cade said.

"Half to three-quarters of them likely made it inland." Nash went quiet for a few seconds then said, "We are facing an invasion force on American soil. And that's just the tip of the iceberg. The East Coast will be seeing landings in the coming days and we don't have enough active subs or surface ships to interdict all of the PLA Navy vessels in transit. I'm afraid the West Coast is nothing compared to what is coming."

Now Cade went silent as he watched on the screen the woods surrounding the feeder road disgorge an eighteen-wheeler, its squared-off snout and wide cab making the surrounding tree limbs and ground-hugging bushes dance and send airborne the few colorful leaves still clinging to their skeletal branches. As the sun glinted off the gleaming chrome tank riding out back, Cade posed his next question—one that he had been eager to ask for some time.

"What about the Pacific Northwest?"

"You mean Portland, specifically?"

"Saw right through me," Cade admitted. "Yeah … I'm curious to know how Portland is faring. And to a lesser extent Seattle and the coastline from Coos Bay on up to Puget Sound."

"That all?" Nash said, her voice carrying a hint of incredulity. "I thought I sent you footage of Portland prior to you going off to Los Angeles. I did thank you for rescuing my girl … didn't I?"

"The footage of Portland *was* eye-opening," Cade said. *And it worked at getting me back in*, he thought. "But that was all captured before the PLA Navy broke through your pickets. About *the* mission to L.A. Are the FEMA hard drives producing the intel you hoped they would?"

"And then some," she said. "Using the individual logs of the rescue birds coming and going from the Long Beach facility we were able to locate and rescue dozens of surviving HVTs (High Value Targets) before the Chinese Navy made landfall. Consequently, they've been instrumental in getting Springs up and running."

"You knew about the PLA fleet *before* L.A.?"

"It was need-to-know, Wyatt. President's orders. Besides, you, Ari … the *team*. None of you were in any danger. All of us watching from the op center had zero confidence that the lead destroyer's active phased-array radar could pick up Jedi One. *If,* and I mean a helluva longshot *if,* that Ghost Hawk somehow *was* painted, the PLA seaman watching the scope would have thought the blip was a flock of seagulls."

"Flock of seagulls … so says the *chair force* Major sitting in her air-conditioned office *behind* the wire and separated from said destroyer and escorts by eight hundred miles and a formidable mountain range." Instantly Cade regretted his words. And as a result of his not employing his usual *filter* between brain and mouth, there was a long uncomfortable silence, during which he heard that awful eighties new-wave synth-heavy *A Flock of Seagulls* song, *I Ran*, fire up in his head. Meanwhile, on the security monitor, whoever was behind the wheel of the semi-truck had backed it up expertly and left it parked alongside a similar rig containing a full load of LNG—liquefied natural gas—compliments of Alexander Dregan, who had undoubtedly sent this rig and the precious fuel contained within the massive chrome-plated tank.

After a long five-count Nash responded to the criticism in an even voice. "I'm with you and the men every time you go down range. In fact, I lose a chunk of my soul when one of you fall. I'd hoped you knew that by now, Cade."

"I'm sorry. That was a low blow to your upstanding character."

"And if you believe the rumors," Nash quipped, "that was also a direct hit to my family jewels."

If only she knew the true extent of the good-natured ribbing she suffered from the shooters her satellites watched over. Suppressing a chuckle, Cade rose from the chair, phone still pressed to his ear.

Nash went on, "I don't want to say more than I have to over this unsecure line, so I'll have a brief for you when the bird arrives to pick you up."

"And what time will that be?"

Cade looked at Heidi, who was looking at him while he concentrated hard on what Nash had to say.

Seeing Cade glance at his Suunto and his usual stoic expression morph to one revealing a hint of exasperation, Heidi wisely turned her attention back to the action topside. On one partition she saw that the mid-point gate on the feeder road was closed, as it should be. On the two adjacent panels the video feed picked up nothing moving near the camouflaged main gate nor on the length of state route in both directions. *No zombies.* Which was strange, because something as noisy as a fuel-laden semi barreling down the state route usually drew in rotting monsters like moths to a flame. As she scrutinized the video on the middle panes the camera covering the grassy meadow and runway picked up a new development. One that might put her in the middle of whatever the call was about. So, hoping to avoid even a hint of confrontation, she tugged on Cade's tee shirt and stabbed a finger at the monitor.

In the center pane Cade saw that the pow-wow had broken up and people were boarding a trio of pickup trucks—the newly arrived tanker driver among them. He also saw Brook walking towards the camera, which just so happened to be positioned outside the compound entrance twenty feet to his left. Seeing this, he hurriedly finished the call with Nash, thumbed the sat-phone off and put it back up on the shelf—the entire time shooting Heidi a harried look that could only be construed as: *Let's keep this between us.* He hustled back to his quarters.

Heidi began to say something, but was interrupted by a grating of metal on metal that drew her attention to the inky gloom of the nearby foyer. There was a clomping of boots on wood and suddenly Brook's petite frame was filling up one end of the cramped space.

Breathing hard from exertion, Brook locked eyes with Heidi for a half-beat before regarding the trio of sat-phones on the top shelf. She let her gaze linger there briefly, then regarded Heidi.

Wearing a startled look, Heidi blurted, "What?"

"Something you want to tell me?"

A dead giveaway, Heidi's gaze inched up to the satellite phones.

"Who called?" Brook demanded, her hands going to her hips, the left inadvertently settling on her holstered Glock.

Busted. Heidi sighed as she scooped up the phone Cade had just replaced on the shelf. Handing it over her shoulder, she said, "Best if you go into the call log and see for yourself."

"You're a quick study, Heidi." Brook took the phone and thumbed it on. "Plausible deniability. Straight out of Cade's playbook."

Heidi didn't respond. The hole she'd dug herself was already deep enough. And this little attempted cover-up had come just as she seemed to be getting back on the intense woman's good side. Returning her attention to the monitor, she watched the trio of trucks motor away from the center gate. In the ensuing seconds between the three-vehicle convoy slipping from view of the mid-road camera and reappearing on the one trained on the run-up to the main gate, out of the corner of her eye she saw Brook scroll to the call log. There was a second of silence, then Brook was cursing under her breath.

As the convoy pulled close to the main gate, Heidi took her eyes off the monitor and regarded Brook. "Everything good?"

Clearly in need of help staying on her feet, Brook put her left hand on Heidi's shoulder and leaned against the low desk to her right.

Heidi placed her hand atop Brook's. "Still getting the dizzy spells from the antiserum … or is this a result of Nash calling your man again?" She continued to watch the monitor as her new fiancé hopped from the lead vehicle and stalked to the gate, leaving the driver's door wide open.

"A little of both," Brook conceded. "More from the latter, though. It's not like Nash to deliver good news over the phone."

Heidi said, "If it's any consolation, my man is leaving the wire, too."

Brook turned her hand over. She clutched Heidi's hand and looked her in the eye. "Glad we're in the same boat." Forcing a half-smile, she released her grip, turned, and set off for her quarters.

Heidi watched until Brook had disappeared around the corner. Then, when she turned her previously divided attention back to the monitor, she saw dead things congregating outside the gate in twos and threes. In the next beat Daymon was luring the monsters away from the gate, the fence paralleling the road the only thing keeping them at bay.

"Be careful," she said aloud, watching Daymon cull the monsters with swift chops to the head from his trusty green-handled machete.

Outside the door to the Grayson Quarters, Brook paused to collect her thoughts. What was the worst news Nash could have added to the already shitty prospect of having Cade go down range? Have him do so undermanned and without proper air support and terrible rules of engagement? Oh wait, she mused bitterly, that's what he'd been doing those last couple of months on the teams before opting to cycle out and come home to her for good. And, unfortunately, some of that crap had resumed after he'd been drawn back into Desantos' and Nash's orbit. Only this time, she couldn't blame Cade coming home in a body bag on the feckless actions of lawyered-up politicians trying to run a hot war by proxy from walnut-paneled offices thousands of miles away. If something should happen to Cade this time around, she would have nobody to blame but herself. And that was acceptable. Because, Lord knows, the only child was doing what he loved. Moreover, unlike that final year running ops with the teams, he was doing it now for all the right reasons.

Cade's voice carried through the door, reaching Brook's ears in the hall. "You going to come in, or just stand out there and block the light under the door?"

"I'm coming in," Brook called. "Are you decent?"

Still talking through the door, he responded, “Not for long, if I have anything to say about it.”

Chuckling, Brook pushed the door open with her left hand. In the light of the sixty-watt bulb she saw her husband. The gray woolen blanket was covering him from his shins to his waist. His left leg was propped up on the near end of the bunk. Brown liquid eyes tracked her as she closed the door.

“Which news do you want to hear first,” he asked. “The bad or the good?”

“The bad,” Brook answered.

“Better sit.”

She moved to the bunk and sat next to him. “But I want to hear the bad *after* I’ve had my way with you.”

Cade sat up and removed his shirt, exposing chiseled abs and an apocalypse-honed upper body. Reclining, he watched his wife reciprocate, grimacing as the cotton tee shirt cleared her high ponytail.

Right arm hung up in the sleeve, she said, “A little help here?”

“First things first,” Cade said. Sitting up, he snagged the string to the light and tugged. As the room was plunged into total darkness, he wrapped Brook in a bear hug and dragged her into bed with him.

Chapter 4

"Come on," Daymon called from the fence. "I'm going to need some help getting the bodies moved before more of the flesh-bags arrive."

Wilson was already out of the Raptor and edging past Daymon's Chevy. He paused at the passenger door, looked in at Oliver and saw fear in the man's eyes. Disregarding it as a part of their new *normal*, he shook his head subtly and pushed past the undergrowth crowding the road.

Lev jumped from the borrowed F-650 and turned back toward the open door. "Stay, Max," he said to the brindle Australian Shepherd that had adopted Raven and Brook back at Schriever weeks ago. Since coming along with the Graysons on their cross-country trek from Forward Operating Base Bastion on the Colorado border to the Eden compound in rural Utah, the inquisitive canine had taken to every member of the small band of survivors.

Regarding the veteran of the 2004 Iraq invasion with his dual-colored eyes, Max yawned and stayed put, his stub tail thumping a steady cadence on Jamie's thigh.

"He's no dummy, Lev," Jamie said, scratching the dog behind his cropped ears. "Close the door … it's not summer."

After complying fully without acknowledging the brunette's quip, Lev turned his back to the idling F-650 and scanned the road behind the super-sized pickup.

Clear.

"*Checking your six*" is what Cade called the practice that came naturally to Lev, a former 11 Bravo infantryman in the Big Green Machine, as Duncan was fond of calling the United States

Army—past and present. Easy to remember, the lexicon well-known among combat veterans had become popular with the younger Eden survivors. Which was a good thing for a generation brought up with all manner of handheld electronic devices constantly vying for their attention. And save for a couple of recent slip-ups, the handful of civilian members in their rag tag little band seemed to be adopting the practice.

Head on a swivel. No better way to stay alive, that was for sure, Lev reflected. It was standard operating procedure that had seen him come home from the sandbox in one piece, and, so far, a routine that had kept him walking on the right side of the dirt even after a worldwide virus had decimated humanity's ranks.

Arriving at the gate last, Dregan's man, a ruddy-faced fella calling himself Cleo, exited the 4Runner given to him for the return trip to Bear River. Without a word of complaint, he strode past the lined-up vehicles to the state route and pitched in by helping Wilson and Daymon drag the leaking bodies off the road. A half-dozen black trails leading from the front of the open gate to the far ditch told him the men had been making quick work of the grisly task.

Lev bent over and grabbed a female cadaver by the ankles, the skin sloughing off in his hands as he pulled the body across the two-lane. "Where the hell is Oliver?" he said to nobody in particular.

Hitching a thumb over his shoulder, Daymon said, "He pussed out."

After rolling the corpse of a young boy into the ditch with a nudge of his combat boot, Wilson scanned the road in both directions. "Still clear," he observed. "Someone going to tell Oliver he needs to start pulling his weight … or do I have to do it?"

Daymon encircled two thin wrists in one gloved hand and trudged across the road, the dead Z's skull producing a hollow keening as it grated along the asphalt. Unceremoniously, as if he were bucking a bale of hay into a truck, he heaved the shell of a former human atop the others. "Let it go," Daymon said. "I'll get to the bottom of it."

"Straighten him out," Wilson said, glancing toward the vehicles clogging the feeder road. "Or I will."

Lev paused, one hand gripping the wrist of another dead thing, the other, out of habit, resting on the butt of the Beretta riding on his hip. Eyebrows hitching in the middle, he regarded the redhead in the floppy camouflage boonie hat. "I see that someone watered his balls this morning."

"From this point on I'm not letting anything slide," Wilson shot. "Not Sasha's bullshit. Not Oliver's staying in the truck while we do the dirty work. *Nothing.* Fuck sake, even Cleo is getting his hands dirty." Breathing hard, he leaned forward and began dragging a portly corpse toward the ditch where the others were being deposited. Boots scraping the roadway, he fumed inside. Inwardly, in a roundabout way, he was still blaming himself for not keeping his sister in line. While he was away during the recent freak snowstorm, the petulant fourteen-year-old's actions had jeopardized the lives of every person who called the compound home. Never again was he going to worry about hurting anyone's feelings. Pupa into a pissed-off butterfly, if you will.

Daymon walked over to the last of the twice-dead Zs. "Uh, oh," he said, ignoring the leaking body at his feet. "Looks like we missed one." In the ditch, partially obscured by the out of control weeds growing there, was a near skeletal specimen. "First Turn" was what survivors had taken to calling the ones that showed evidence of lots of wear and tear. "Crawler" was what Daymon called the thing he was staring down on.

Meeting Daymon's gaze, the thing hissed and raked its fingernails across the toes of his boots. How the deflating tire sound made it out of the hole passing for a throat escaped him. The noise, however, made the hairs on his arms prick up.

"I'll take care of it," Wilson spat. "You take care of *Oliver*." The man's name rolled off the redhead's tongue dripping with venom.

Daymon shrugged and stepped aside. As he cleaned his machete, aptly nicknamed *Kindness*, on the long grass, he watched Wilson jam a folding knife to the hilt in the crawler's eye socket. Then, after slipping the machete into its scabbard, he rose and regarded Wilson with a hard stare. "I'll figure out what Oliver's deal is," he promised, then turned and stalked off towards the awaiting Chevy, the specter of the looming interrogation already troubling him.

Chapter 5

Daymon waited until they were several miles east on State Route 39 and nearing the quarry feeder road before broaching the subject of Oliver's strange new behavior. Slowing the Chevy a bit on a long straightaway, he drew a deep breath and cast a sidelong glance at the man next to him.

Sensing the change in speed, Oliver shifted in his seat and met Daymon's chilly one-eyed glare. "What?" he asked, straining against the shoulder belt as he squared up with the dreadlocked driver.

Not one to mince words, Daymon said, "What the *fuck* was that back there?"

"What was *what*?"

Facing forward now, Daymon sighed. "The inaction on your part back there at the gate. You stayed in the truck like a little—." Reining in his rising anger, Daymon went silent, tightened his grip on the wheel and steered the nearly new four-by-four pickup through a gentle left-hand sweeper. Trees growing up from the sodden bank on the right side partially shielded the turbid Ogden River from view. To their left, the small mountain the abandoned rock quarry was perched upon rose several hundred feet from the road, partially blocking the watery early morning sun.

"Bitch. That's the word you swallowed, right? Newsflash, Daymon. I'm guilty as charged." His green eyes darkened. "Oliver frickin Gladson is a goddamn fraud who is deathly afraid of living corpses. Have been since the first time I left the Pacific Crest Trail to resupply and saw the dead grocery clerk with his throat torn out walking the aisles and bloodying up his store. So there.

You have it straight out of the horse's mouth. I'm a frickin *coward*."

Daymon's shoulders slumped subtly as the quarry entrance blipped by on the left. Shortly after, on their right, the rectangular sign announcing the feeder road to the long-abandoned Smith mining operation loomed. It had been shot up from behind. Big holes blown right through it that left twisted triangles of sharp metal jutting forward and the words on its face barely recognizable. Daymon made a mental note to himself to ask the others in the trailing vehicles if they remembered the sign being bullet-pocked.

Uncomfortable in the silence permeating the cab, Oliver removed his black stocking cap and ran his hand through the unruly ring of graying hair.

Finally, Daymon said, "What about the early legs of the Pacific Crest Trail in California? With all of those people in Cali surely you had some run-ins with the dead."

"I didn't see anything for days after the outbreak. I had no radio. Wouldn't have gotten good reception where I was anyway. So everything I heard about the dead coming back to life came from trail angels and other through hikers. Needless to say, I was skeptical. So I took it all with a grain of salt and forged ahead."

Seeing something lying across the road a good distance ahead—basically just a horizontal shadow at this point—Daymon flicked his eyes to the mirror to see what kind of following distance Taryn was observing.

As always, the former dirt track racer had her white pickup tucked in tight to his bumper. In fact, she was so close—Nascar drafting close—that he couldn't see the prominent FORD logo on the matte-black grill. Worried that if he stood on the brakes the white Raptor and its young occupants would become the frosting center in a big metal Oreo consisting of the black Chevy up front, and the massive F-650 behind, he tapped his brakes three times to back her off, then slowed to the posted thirty-five. Keeping his eyes glued to the distant roadway obstruction, he said, "All that distance you covered on the roads from Oregon to Utah, how did you go about avoiding the dead?"

"I holed up during the day and travelled at night. Simple as that."

Daymon grunted.

"I had the night vision goggles I took off a dead Oregon National Guardsman. Their roadblock near Mount Hood was a mess. The vehicles were all shot to hell. The bodies, too. Ones that hadn't reanimated and walked away were nearly picked clean by the mountain birds. Hell, Daymon, the guy I took 'em off didn't need 'em anymore."

"I'm not judging you on that," Daymon replied.

Reining the pickup back to a walking speed, he leaned over the wheel to scan both sides of the road for evidence of an ambush: a light glinting from glass or metal. Fresh tire tracks on the shoulder. Out of place bodies. Pools of spent brass or debris that looked as if it had been purposefully placed on the road. Seeing nothing of the sort, he sped up a little and asked, "What about the Ogden pass? And Huntsville? You put down dozens of rotters there. That's not the work of a coward."

Oliver snugged his cap down over his ears. Then, in a flat monotone, said, "Why couldn't the snow have stuck around? I can handle those things if they're not moving. If those hungry, dead eyes aren't flicking around … searching. In Huntsville I was pretending to be Charlton Heston. You know … the Omega Man … fucking with mannequins. That's not courage, though. That's just borderline crazy."

Daymon said nothing. He was focusing on the newly fallen tree. It was resting on the right guardrail and stretched shoulder to shoulder across the road. It was nothing like the monster old-growth numbers he had felled to block 39 west of the compound. This alder was about as big around as a man's thigh, devoid of leaves, and had patches of white bark curling up. It looked diseased, its affected roots likely compromised by the weight of the recent snow and further weakened by the rains that followed.

Voice cracking, Oliver went on. "I was cleaning up Huntsville for my mom. After finding my dad like I did, guts all ripped out; bite marks and all … I figured she was dead for sure. Had become one of them things."

On the console between the two men, the two-way radio began to vibrate.

Ignoring the buzzing, Daymon threw the truck into Park. "And Duncan? Are you two cool yet?"

With no hesitation, Oliver spat, "Fuck Duncan. He'll never replace my dad."

Daymon shot Oliver a sidelong glare as Wilson's voice emanated from the Motorola's tiny speaker. He scooped up the handset and keyed the Talk button. "Keep your pants on, kid," he growled. "And yes … I did see the shot-up sign back there."

"I was wondering about that," Wilson said. "I didn't see any signs of an ambush. You think this tree was cut down on purpose?"

"Roots are showing," Daymon answered. "It was ready to go. All it took was that heavy snow and then all that rain softening the soil. Good thing it didn't fall on the rig Cleo drove over. Would have been a fireball for sure."

Following a short burst of squelch, Jamie entered the conversation. "Our six is clear," she said. "We saw the sign, too. Lev seems to think the holes in the sign are new. No signs of rust, he says." There was a short pause. In the background the F-650's engine rumble could still be heard. "Lev wants to know what you want to do with the tree? You going to take it out with the Stihl? Or should we pull forward and use the winch to drag it off the guardrail?"

"The latter," Daymon acknowledged. "Come around on my left." He released the Talk key and turned to Oliver. "Wilson used to be the skittish one around the dead. A little razzing by his sister led to him trying to force the issue on the way here from Colorado. Nearly got him killed. But it went a long way toward loosening him up around the things."

Oliver scanned the road on his right. He shifted his gaze to the bushes crowding the road on the left. "I'm not going to lie to you," he conceded. "I'm scared as shit out here in the open … in broad daylight."

"A little fear is necessary. Keeps us sharp," Daymon said as the F-650 pulled alongside, casting its shadow on the Chevy. "'Frosty' is what Captain America likes to call the razor's edge he tries to ride. Heard him describe it as the perfect blending of fear and confidence."

"But he's a trained soldier," Oliver noted. "I'm nothing of the sort."

"That trained soldier had to get used to dealing with the living dead just like me and Wilson and the others. Hell, your mom did it. Means you can, too. So just *watch*. Sponge it up. And *learn* from your mistakes."

The sounds of multiple doors opening and closing entered the cab through Oliver's partially rolled-down window. He wiped away a stray tear with the back of his hand.

"Baby steps, my man. Baby steps," Daymon said, shouldering open his door. "Be right back. Lock up if you feel the need." Leaving the truck idling, he closed the door and hustled to join Wilson and Jamie, who were already stretching the winch toward the far shoulder where the tree's top had come to rest.

Chapter 6

After attaching the F-650's winch to the fallen snag, Daymon moved out of the way and stood with Lev, Oliver, and the Kids while Jamie reversed the big truck. There was a puff of gray exhaust that hung low to the road as horsepower and torque combined to get the sixty-foot length of timber moving off of the dented guardrails.

The Ford crouched down on its suspension and the tires chirped as Jamie mashed the pedal.

Finally a ripple went through the timber and the staccato crack of limbs shearing off filled the air. The old *equal and opposite* reaction came into play and the tree tore free from the rail and rolled a few feet toward the assembled group.

One last toe stab to the pedal by Jamie jerked the cable taut and brought the tree parallel with the guard rail on the river side of 39.

As soon as the tree had stopped moving, its bare branches done quivering, Dregan's courier, Cleo, pulled the 4Runner next to the F-650, flashed a mostly toothless grin at Jamie, then motored off down 39 alone.

Seeing this, Daymon merely shrugged and sent Oliver, Wilson, and Taryn off to help Jamie untangle the cable. Once the trio were out of earshot, he turned to Lev and told him all he had just learned about their new friend, Oliver, and how he planned to bring the newest member of the Eden group up to speed.

When Daymon was done saying his piece, Lev shook his head then looked away and watched Taryn help guide the winch cable back into its bumper-mounted housing. Wilson was policing the shattered branches from the road. Meanwhile, Oliver was leaning against the bowed-in guardrail, watching the others work.

Daymon craned his head to get Lev's attention. "What?" he said, palms up, exasperation evident by the tone of his voice. "Look at him. You don't think he needs a fire lit under him?"

Lev fixed his gaze on Daymon. "Not what I was thinking," he said. "It's all coming together. The other day I was wondering why a guy who humped hundreds of miles of countryside to get home didn't look like he'd just ridden a boat across the River Styx. What you just told me also explains the night vision goggles and all of the spare batteries he was carrying. But what you've got planned … it's kind of harsh, don't you think?"

Tucking a dread behind his ear, Daymon said, "Not more so than the alternative. Raven had the last of the antiserum and it's gone now. No telling if Captain America …"

"Remember your *new leaf*?" Lev interrupted.

"Er, yeah," Daymon said rather sheepishly. "As I was saying, there's no telling if Cade is going to return from his next excursion with more of those vials. So … I think an evaluation by fire of our new weakest link isn't too harsh. Especially if it ends up saving lives down the road."

Lev hung his head. "Wilson didn't get that kind of treatment. And he's *finally* turned the corner."

"That transformation has been months in the making."

"Yeah," Lev agreed.

The Raptor suddenly came to life, its 6.2-liter engine rumbling low and steady.

"Well?" Daymon pressed. "It's only every one of our lives at stake. And, as always"—he paused and took a deep breath—"I'll be the bad guy."

"I guess," Lev conceded. "Hell of a baptism, though."

"I won't let it get out of hand. Think of it as a blanket party. That's what you Army guys call that thing you do to initiate the noob privates … right?"

Lev smiled conspiratorially. "Only in the movies." Spinning a finger in the air, he addressed the others. "We're oscar mike. Thirty seconds. Mount 'em up."

A minute later they were in fact *oscar mike*—military speak meaning on the move—and the trees lining 39 were scrolling by, their gnarled reflections creating a hypnotic effect as they juddered bottom-to-top across the three vehicles' bug-spattered windshields.

***

Twenty minutes after clearing the tree from the road, the three pickups were parked side-by-side, Chevy on the left, Raptor in the middle, and the big Ford F-650 taking up the exact spot on the right shoulder where the overturned school bus used to reside. All three vehicles were facing the asphalt confluence where 39 met 16, the state route connecting Bear River in the south with Laketown and scenic Bear Lake near the Utah/Idaho border some thirty miles north by west.

Daymon and Lev had purposefully maneuvered their trucks close enough to the Raptor so that the entire group could chat without broadcasting their intentions to the world on an open radio channel.

Daymon spoke up first. "Seeing as how our friends down south haven't seen hide nor hair of the horde since yesterday, I figure in order to cover as much ground as possible before dark, splitting up is our best bet."

Taryn and Wilson both nodded their approval.

Speaking from a much higher perch, Lev craned his head to make eye contact with the others. "As long as the horde is still down south and we keep the radios on … I don't see why not."

"Me and Oliver will skirt Woodruff on the east side, come around counterclockwise, south to north. Lev, you and Jamie start at the rehab place and work towards the center of town."

"We'll drive to the north edge of Woodruff and start moving back this direction," Taryn said. "Meet you all in the middle near the post office."

"Sounds like a plan," Lev agreed.

Hand tightening on his AR-15's grip, Oliver looked to Daymon. "You sure of this?"

Before Daymon had a chance to answer, the long range handheld CB belched static. A tick later Heidi was asking for Daymon.

"Daymon here. What's up?"

Voice wavering, Oliver said, "The horde is coming. I *knew* it."

Daymon looked sidelong at Oliver and adjusted the volume up a notch.

"Change of plans here at the compound," Heidi said. "Chances are you'll soon be hearing or seeing military aircraft in the vicinity."

Glaring at Oliver, his index finger now held vertical to his lips, Daymon said, "Cade's ride is inbound *already*?"

"You got it," she replied. "Could be that quiet black helicopter or the noisy as hell tilt-rotor thingy. Cade didn't say either way. I didn't ask. He just looked at his big soldier watch and said he's being picked up in the coming hours … whatever that means."

"Shit," Daymon exclaimed. "I was hoping to get something to him before he left." He slapped a palm on the steering wheel, causing Oliver to visibly tense. He glanced to his right and saw Taryn in the driver's seat in the Raptor looking a question his way.

Daymon glanced at his wrist. Realizing he wasn't wearing a watch, he flicked his eyes to the clock on the instrument cluster. Then, after a quick mental calculation, he thumbed the Talk key. "Have someone meet me at the gate in ninety minutes."

Trepidation creeping into her tone, Heidi said, "Will do."

Daymon's gaze landed on the trip computer where he saw the outside temperature indicated in small digital numbers. *Fifty-eight degrees … effin pineapple express.* Shaking his head, he dialed the volume down and handed the CB to Oliver.

"What do you want me to do with this?"

Nodding toward the Raptor, Daymon said, "Have the Kids pass it through to Lev."

Taryn took the radio from Oliver without saying a word.

The CB continued its journey through the Raptor and Wilson deposited it in Lev's outstretched hand. Then, bowing his head to see past Taryn, Wilson whistled to get Daymon's attention. "What's this extra special item on your shopping list?" he asked.

Jaw taking on a granite set, Daymon locked eyes with Wilson. "An amends," he said through clenched teeth. Truth be told, acting on Duncan's advice, swallowing his pride and admitting he was wrong did feel a bit liberating. However, the only child in him was kicking and screaming all the way.

In the F-650, Lev passed the CB to Jamie then turned back to address Wilson. "You think I ought to convince him we should stick together? We can always come back out this way tomorrow."

Wilson shook his head vehemently side-to-side causing the boonie hat strap under his chin to swing like a pendulum. "I want no part of this one. Both Cade and Duncan agreed to Daymon calling the shots on this little excursion."

Lev smiled. Thumbing the Motorola two-way he said, "We're good to go." To his left the black Chevy made a slow sweeping turn onto 16. Taryn moved out next, quickly bringing the race-tuned Raptor up to speed. Lev pulled out last, taking up rear guard on the three-vehicle train.

As agreed upon ahead of time, Daymon took the first right at Back In The Saddle Rehab and drove east on Center Street. Soon, the narrow two-lane entered a shallow depression and the upper story and wood-shingled roof of the rehab place disappeared from view. After a long steady climb out of the dip, the farmhouses near to town gave way to rolling countryside rife with green fields of chest-high alfalfa.

Standing out smack dab in the middle of one of the fields were a pair of prefab homes. A pair of long gravel drives roughly a quarter of a mile apart led up to identical cement parking pads fronting each house.

"Cade's already been through those two," Daymon said, slowing and pointing out the white Xs scrawled on the doors. "He never mentioned marking them up like that, though."

Shrugging off the practice that seemed to make sense in a natural disaster, but not so much in the zombie apocalypse, Daymon pinned the accelerator to make up for lost time.

Soon the two-lane was flanked by trees and the red-brown foothills of the Bear mountains were filling up the windshield.

"Five minutes gone," Oliver noted. "Where are we going?"

"Don't worry," Daymon replied. "I've been here before. Whether or not someone else has since is the make or break."

Oliver fidgeted with the strap on his custom rifle. "When were you there last?"

Letting up on the pedal and steering around a doddering zombie, Daymon said, "Two or three weeks ago."

"By yourself?"

"Yep."

Oliver stared out over the shiny hood at the peaks where residual pockets of snow high up on their flanks reflected the low-hanging sun. "There's no skiing up there," he stated matter-of-factly.

"No shit."

"What are you planning, then?"

Abruptly, Daymon pulled the Chevy to the right. He rattled the transmission into Park and dragged the keys from the ignition. Looking at Oliver, he said in a pleading voice, "Just humor me … *please.*"

Semiautomatic pistol in one hand, keys in the other, Daymon stepped to the road and closed the door at his back.

Oliver actuated the power door locks and then looked on as Daymon approached a weed-choked gate on the opposite side of the road. Interest mounting, Oliver craned and watched the lanky man crouch on the shoulder for a tick before rising and venturing into the knee-high grass growing up through the soft dirt fronting the gate. After a few seconds spent standing before the gate, Daymon pushed it inward and returned to the pickup with a substantial length of chain in hand.

Back behind the wheel and ignoring the quizzical look on Oliver's face, Daymon pulled the pickup across the road and nosed it through the yawning gate.

Taking the chain with him, Daymon hustled back to the gate and secured it with the Schlage padlock—just as he'd left it weeks ago. After looking both directions up and down the road, he returned to the truck displaying the same sense of urgency as when he'd initially approached the gate.

Not a second had passed between the time Daymon's door slammed shut and Oliver's interrogation began. "What the hell are we doing here?"

"You'll see," Daymon answered cryptically as they barreled north on a smooth, paved road flanked by nicely manicured trees and once sculpted hedges clearly in need of a gardener's attention.

Chapter 7

They followed the winding drive in silence until a lone zombie came into view on Oliver's side of the truck. Upon hearing the engine noise, the male first turn instantly snapped its head in their direction and raised its pustule-riddled arms. Head bobbing and seemingly restrained by an invisible hand, the thing marched in place, its bare feet churning the muddy shoulder as it struggled mightily to set foot on the pavement.

"Was *that* here before?"

Daymon snorted. "He's right where I left him. You could say he's on a *stake* out."

"You made him your fuckin' pet?"

"Early warning system is more like it. The simple fact that he's still standing likely means nobody's driven this road since I did last."

Oliver recoiled from his window as the wing mirror came into contact with the zombie's left hand. The solid *thud* was still resonating through the door when the keen of fingernails raking sheet metal started up. Disgusted, he asked, "What'd you do, *stake* its foot to the ground?"

"Not quite," Daymon answered with a soft chuckle. "I tethered the Z *to* a stake. Rope's around his waist. Reaaaall tight. He isn't going anywhere without help."

Warily eyeing the rotting cadaver's shrinking reflection in the side mirror, Oliver said, "You're one sick individual."

"Sick is in the mind of the beholder, my friend."

After a short right-hand bend, a basketball standard and garishly painted basketball court came into view. As the sports court slid by on Daymon's side, a three-story house filled up the entire windshield. It was all wood and stone and framed by the naked boughs of a picket of mature trees planted long ago. Where the drive spilled to a large circular parking pad, the Bear Mountain Range was visible rising up behind the house.

Oliver whistled. "Looks like this McMansion missed the left turn to Aspen."

"Exactly," Daymon said, smiling. "Reminds me of the houses back in Jackson Hole. And that pad there"—he wheeled the truck right and pointed left at a long rectangular area of poured concrete. It was newer, stark white, and stood out from the rest—"is where I found the Winnebago me and Heidi call home. Believe it or not, it was gassed up and ready to go."

"Judging by that cow pasture gate at the road, you'd never know the drive would lead to a house of this caliber."

"Or any house for that matter," Daymon proffered. "And I want to keep it looking that way." He steered the pickup in a big counterclockwise loop and parked it on the herringbone pavers underneath the covered entry adjacent to the front door. "Because one day when the effin dead actually start dying off this will be mine and Heidi's retirement home."

Oliver walked his gaze over the home. It was constructed of wood beams secured with rugged-looking rubbed-bronze iron bands. The roof and gutters were black steel and contrasted nicely with the pale gray stonework running up both sides of the huge wood and iron front door. Numerous gables jutted up through the multi-faceted roof. The windows on each floor were flanked by legitimate storm shutters. Constructed from what looked like louvered steel and mounted to the home on sturdy-looking hinges, the black slabs made the mini mansion look damn formidable from any angle.

After a pregnant pause, Oliver asked, "Whose place is it and where are they? I never heard any of the usual rumors that hit the wire when new money comes putting roots down around here. At least my mom didn't mention it. Which is not like her at all."

"There was nobody home when I was here last," Daymon said. "Looks like it has been shut up since before the shit hit the fan. The junk mail in the recycling bin inside was postmarked well before summer."

"Maybe this was their winter retreat."

"Couldn't think of a better place to store the RV. It's a pretty easy drive to Yellowstone and Grand Teton from here. Both are very beautiful year round. Plus, there's a trailer and four new snowmobiles in the garage."

Oliver craned around. "Where *is* the garage?"

"That's the best part of the place. It's out back and full to the brim with *toys*. Hell, I felt bad leaving the spare 4Runner parked in there with all those big dollar rides." Daymon killed the motor. Grabbing his AR from the backseat, he asked, "Coming or staying?"

Oliver hesitated.

"Because we've got to get back to the compound before hooking up with the others, It'll just be a quick in and out. No sightseeing."

"I'd just slow you down," Oliver replied, looking over his shoulder. "What makes you sure there's nobody already squatting inside?"

"I have a few tricks up my sleeve," Daymon said. "Learned my lesson the hard way in Hanna waking up with a Glock stuck in my face."

"Cade?"

Daymon nodded. "I was slippin' … won't happen again."

Grinning, Oliver said, "And that's why you tea-bagged him at Mom's place."

"Bingo," Daymon said. "And that's why we're here. Be right back. Don't forget to lock 'er up."

Oliver nodded. In fact, the door locks were thunking home before Daymon's boot hit the front stairs. Oliver looked on from the truck as the former BLM firefighter ran his hand around the door jamb and fiddled with the lock and brass handle. After the cursory inspection, Daymon flashed a thumbs-up and set off for the corner of the house closest to the RV parking pad, black AR carbine held at a low ready.

And a poor tea-bagging at that, thought Oliver, walking his gaze in a full three-sixty around the truck. *He didn't even drop his trousers.*

Two miles west of the McMansion, Lev and Jamie were already exiting Back In The Saddle Rehab emptyhanded. The pair of first turns that had been locked inside and wandering freely about the downstairs area were sprawled out on the cement ramp where Jamie had felled them. Just as she'd been conditioned to do since the dead things started walking, the old knock and listen had proven effective.

Once inside, however, everything of use in treating an injury or instrumental to someone on the road to recovery from one had been stripped from the place. Downstairs, papers with pictures of models performing therapeutic exercises littered the floor. They'd found the floor-to-ceiling cabinets all thrown open, the plastic bins once containing the exercise handouts on the floor, some of them in shards as if they had been kicked and then stomped on. Staggered boot prints of varying sizes and with different tread patterns marked up the scattered papers with a reddish-brown mud.

Only office furniture, file cabinets, and the festering corpses of a young mother and her little one occupied the second floor.

In short, humans had picked the place as clean as the birds had the bones of the dozens of corpses sprawled in silent repose in the parking lot and sidewalk alongside the ransacked business.

From the rehab place's elevated back entry, Jamie surveyed the gravel parking lot. "Well that was a bust," she said, throwing the empty day pack over a shoulder.

Standing beside the F-650, Lev cocked his head and looked to his left. A tick later, engine sounds could be heard riding the wind somewhere well north of them.

"Whoever tore up the place," he said, his attention still on the familiar engine growl approaching from the north, "there must have been a whole bunch of 'em."

"Half a dozen, at least," Jamie said. "I counted that many unique shoe prints in there." She nudged the corpse at her feet.

"What's really bugging me is how these two got shut inside after the breathers left."

"Let's hope they aren't evolving," Lev said, brow cocked. "They learn to turn handles and work keys in locks, we are toast."

Jamie fixed Lev with a concerned look.

"Cade and Duncan believe they go through some of the motions they used to. Just not consciously. And that's a theory I can get behind."

Jamie shuddered at the thought of a pistol-wielding corpse. Or worse, a handful of them thwarting a door by a means other than brute force and entering the Eden compound employing stealth and cunning. "You're right. We'd be done so quick if they did evolve."

"I bet the owners of those boots left the door cracked when they left," Lev theorized. "Then the two that were in there barged in and accidently bumped it closed behind them."

Cocking her head toward the engine noise and recognizing it as the throaty growl of the Kids' Raptor, Jamie asked, "You think maybe Dregan and the Bear River folks are responsible for this?"

Lev shook his head. "They agreed to leave the north to us. Besides, those tire tracks in the lot run deep and were definitely made by something much larger than anything of theirs we've seen so far. The wheelbase looks to be a good deal wider than a military Hummer."

"Wider than the Graysons' Ford, too," she observed, glancing away from the chevron-patterned indentations and settling her gaze on the mud-spattered black pickup parked beside the tire tracks in question.

Lev's face tightened. "Yep," he said, exhaling. "Could be a threat to Eden if they get lucky and follow us home like Dregan did Cade."

"Speaking in Cade's defense," Jamie said, "Dregan followed his tire tracks in the snow to Eden."

"Whatever the case," Lev said agreeably. "We still better keep our eyes peeled. And it would be wise for us to stop every once in a while, kill the engines, and listen. The motor stuffed under the hood of the thing that made these tracks is probably diesel and makes a hell of a racket. And that'll carry real well considering this autumn quiet."

After scanning the area one last time from the elevated perch for any rotters backing the F-650 into the lot may have attracted, the pair closed the door and made their way to the vehicle, heads on a swivel and weapons sweeping the lot.

Chapter 8

Head panning side-to-side, Daymon padded around the southwest corner of the multi-story home and struck off north in its shadow. All along the walk the bushes growing up beside the house brushed his right side as he made his way to the red paver drive he knew looped around back between the house and massive garage.

Thirty paces from the front of the house, he found himself facing a structure nearly half the size of the one at his back. Finished in the same stone and exposed timber style as the main residence, the garage rose up two stories and partially eclipsed the Bear Range to the east.

The roll-up doors all passed inspection, as did the dead-bolted door on the garage's far northeast corner.

So far so good, he thought, turning his attention to the main home's covered back porch and half-dozen stairs leading up to it.

The thick welcome mat on the decking in front of the sturdy wood door was just as he had left it: lined up perfectly with the marks he'd scribed with his knife on the deck next to each of its outside corners.

After banging on the door with a closed fist, Daymon waited the requisite half-minute listening for the telltale sounds of the dead: low-in-timbre moaning of the recently turned. Dry hisses of the first turned. Numb knees and shins inadvertently moving furniture around inside. Or, lastly, as Daymon ticked off the seconds in his head, cold dead flesh slamming headlong into the closed door he was about to enter.

Thankfully, none of the above happened. A minute removed from his last words with Oliver, Daymon was working the key in the lock and holding his breath. There was a soft click. Simultaneously, he pushed the door inward and took a wide step to his left, carbine trained on the ever-widening slice in which the home's well-lit mudroom was presented.

He saw the washer and dryer first. Expensive items on pedestals with seemingly a thousand settings and something called "steam finishing." There were a number of high-dollar jackets on pegs. Below the jackets were four different sets of new-looking boots still lined up smallest to largest just as he had arranged them.

Daymon closed the door at his back and ventured into the kitchen, stunted dreads bobbing with each footfall.

With its stainless steel Viking appliances, black granite counters, and bright white woodwork, the modern kitchen could have graced the pages of Architectural Digest. Maybe it had, Daymon mused as he made his way past the jumbo island to the formal dining room where a live-edge plank table in dark wood was arranged horizontally between the kitchen and wide-open family room.

After a quick glance to the grand staircase left of the front entry, Daymon padded across the room to the massive plate glass window looking out over the porch, red brick parking round and black pickup with Oliver still in the passenger seat, head on a swivel, the same as when Daymon had left him there.

***

After making a quick trip upstairs, Daymon returned the way he'd come and was outside the back door with a bulging gym bag in hand, carbine slung over his shoulder, and locking the door with his key.

Still on the porch, he stood still for a moment and looked over both shoulders. Nothing moved. The garage sat quiet, its windows darkened. The picket of trees encircling the rear of the property sighed and shimmied as a light east wind coursed through their upper boughs.

Satisfied he was still alone, he turned back to face his *casa,* squared the mat's corners back up as he'd found them, and took the stairs down two at a time.

***

The quick in and out of Daymon's future home coupled with the sprint back to the truck had burned all of two minutes. Thirty additional seconds went by as he slid behind the wheel, turned the engine over, and nosed the truck south down the winding drive.

In total three minutes were history and Oliver's questions were filling the cab when the gate came into view.

After bringing the truck to a grinding halt a dozen feet from the gate, like a policeman directing traffic, Daymon silenced the yammering by holding his heavily calloused palm in front of Oliver's pasty face.

"Give it a rest until I get us through the gate safely, will ya?"

Still feeling the last vestiges of the cold chill brought on by the keen of the staked-down Z's fingernails raking the driver's side door as they had wheeled past, Daymon shouldered open his door.

From his seat, Oliver shot a sour look at Daymon's back as he stepped from the truck. Stewing internally from the perceived insult, he watched the dreadlocked man crawl up onto the fence's middle rung and give the road ten seconds of scrutiny in either direction before throwing the latch and swinging the gate open.

"Clear?" Oliver asked once Daymon was back behind the wheel and had closed the door.

"For now," Daymon answered. "But there's a rotter a few hundred feet down the road. Must have seen or heard us coming in. And the squeaky gate just got its undivided attention." He rattled the transmission into Drive and wheeled them out onto the road and stopped the Chevy straddling the centerline, its chromed grill aimed at the ambling ghoul. "You want to earn your man card?"

Oliver remained tightlipped.

"C'mon … water your balls. Get out there and kill it face to face."

Still Oliver sat in silence, staring at the approaching corpse.

"This ain't no different than bombing down a double black for the first time, OG. Sure you've got the butterflies. We all still get them now and again. But once you get the tips over the precipice and commit ... survival instinct takes over and edges the fear out. Same as doing a rotter up close and personal. You stab it in the brain. It falls. It's all over. Plus, you'll find there's a certain sense of satisfaction you get from giving it sweet release." He tucked his longest dreads behind his ears and fixed a no-nonsense stare on Oliver.

"Sure it's different, Daymon. Way different. You fuck up on the ski hill and ski patrol'll strap you in the basket and take you to the med hut. Best case scenario you've only sprained something and they give you a pain killer or two. Next thing you know you're in the bar chasing them down with a shot of Rumple Minze."

"Jägermeister ..." Daymon interrupted. "Hell yes. Those were the days."

Oliver made a face then went on, "Worst case scenario: a concussion and broken bones gets you aboard a life flight heading to Ogden or Salt Lake. If I freeze up out there and get bit my mom will kill me. Then, after she kills me, she *will* kill you. Probably with your own blade."

Clucking his tongue, Daymon took his foot off the brake and let the truck roll forward until the creature was broadside with Oliver's door.

Instantly, the thing rushed the door, mashing its face against the window. The clicking noise of its teeth impacting the glass reverberated in the cab, setting Oliver's arm hair standing to attention. Its face was marred by circular bite marks oozing a viscous yellow liquid. One eye was missing, and the optic nerve—or at least what looked like one to Oliver—snaked from the puckered opening and rested limply on one sunken cheek.

Casting his gaze downward, he saw that the female creature's flaccid breasts bore punctures and scratches, likely from encountering brambles and branches while traipsing the countryside in search of prey.

"No water is getting near these balls," Oliver stated, inching away from the window, the seatbelt crossing his body suddenly going taut.

Renewing its efforts at trying to eat the meat through the rapidly clouding passenger side glass, the thing opened its maw wider and planted its maggot-riddled tongue where Oliver's face had been.

"Look at that thing," Daymon said. "You want her to slip you some of that? I could punch the window down and let you touch it."

The monster was palming the window now, bony fingers splayed out like gnarled tree roots. It tilted its head and, almost as if it could sense the fear radiating off of the fresh meat, shot a confused dog's look straight at Oliver.

"You better go now if you want to make it to the compound and back within the hour," Oliver said, throwing a visible shudder.

"Don't worry," Daymon said. "We'll make it."

Turning away from the persistent abomination, Oliver showed Daymon his watch. "That's only forty some-odd minutes. How are you going to make that happen?"

"Like this," Daymon shot, simultaneously releasing the brake, matting the pedal, and steering into the rotter. "I'm going to drive it like I stole it."

Chapter 9

Taryn was holding the creature at bay—barely. Still, the thing had been able to snake one arm through the four-inch-wide gap between door and jamb and had gotten hold of a fistful of the nineteen-year-old's fleece jacket.

"Hurry up, Wilson!" she hollered across the parking lot. "Damn thing got the jump on me!"

Unable to see the true gravity of his fiancée's situation, he tucked his carbine to his shoulder and called back, "Why don't you just step away from the door and I'll pop it when it comes on out?"

Taryn was straining mightily, her shoulder mashed against the door, all hundred-and-five pounds of her small frame invested fully in the life-and-death struggle. "I can't. It's got ahold of me," she said. "If you're going to be my husband, Wilson … you have to *jump* when I say *jump*!"

And he did. Not literally, though. However, even before he had followed through on the first powerful stride towards the fix-it shop's front door, he had spun the carbine out of the way, letting it hang on its sling at his back. The easier to handle Beretta semi-auto pistol had cleared its holster and was in his fist as he halved the distance to the short, unkempt hedges fronting the combination stairs/wheelchair ramp.

To Wilson, as he ran headlong for the stairs with the carbine thumping steadily against his backside, time seemed to slow down, allowing him to see that the looming, vertical rectangle of white Taryn was crouched before was stickered over with certificates promising A+ Customer Satisfaction, ensuring AAA Accreditation, and trumpeting Chamber of Commerce

Membership Since 1982. All minutiae to the twenty-year-old considering the first and only true love of his life was in imminent danger. And as his adrenaline-affected vision began to narrow, he shifted focus from the big picture to the gnarled fingers beginning to find purchase on the tightly braided shock of hair hanging down the back of Taryn's camouflage jacket.

He cleared the trio of cement stairs in one bound and added all hundred-and-seventy-some-odd pounds of mostly wiry muscle to the effort. But it was too late, for the thing had quickly transitioned its grip from Taryn's jacket to her long ponytail and was reeling her head toward the shadowy opening which, inexplicably, was beginning to widen instead of narrow as it should given the added weight.

Reacting to the sudden sight of his girl's head snapping back, Wilson disengaged the Beretta's safety and, without thought of the consequences, thrust his right arm into the narrow opening. After twisting his wrist and bending his elbow to get the muzzle pointed to where he envisioned the thing's head to be behind the windowless steel-door, he squeezed off half a dozen rounds to no good effect.

Slumping backward, her knees beginning to buckle, Taryn slipped her knife from its sheath and motioned with her eyes to the arm dragging her down.

Instantly getting her message, Wilson accepted the offered knife with his free hand while loosing the remaining four rounds from the Beretta at the shadowy shapes inside the darkened store.

Seeing Wilson going for her twisted hair with the black Tanto-style blade, Taryn drew a breath and in a choked voice blurted, "The wrist. Cut the tendons. That'll make it let go of me."

Having been in a nearly identical predicament himself, albeit with the offending appendage sans the attached reanimated corpse, Wilson had every reason to sympathize. So he hacked away with the razor-sharp blade, slicing a trio of inch-deep furrows across the pallid swath of skin on the Z's upturned forearm.

On the third pass of the Cold Steel blade the Z's fingers snapped open and a thin tendril of sticky black fluid painted a crazy pattern on the cement all around Wilson's boots.

Freed from the cold hand's grip, Taryn drew her pistol and crabbed sideways from the door. "Let it come," she hissed at Wilson, her eyes never leaving the ever-widening crack between door and jamb.

Ears still ringing from his own weapon discharging so near to his head, Wilson relied on his minimal lip-reading skills, complying only when he realized what Taryn had in mind.

"Let 'em come," she urged, eyes dark with anger.

Wilson eased his weight from the door and backpedaled to his left, taking up station partway down the wheelchair ramp.

Naturally, with the weight of the monster—or monsters—still pressing out on it, the door flung wide open, hitting the outside wall with a bang.

Painted by the intruding slice of white sunlight, the sneering creature looked more ghost than living dead. Eyes panning left and right, it remained rooted, seemingly stuck making a decision as to which morsel looked the most appetizing. Then, as quickly as the rotten male cadaver had filled up the door, several pale arms snaked around both sides of his body.

The Beretta in Taryn's small fist bucked twice. The first 9mm slug cut the air just to the right of the zombie's left ear and hit a wire rack containing pamphlets, sending it spinning slowly clockwise and a spritz of shredded glossy paper airborne. The natural rise of the discharging pistol combined with a slight flinch brought on by the first sharp report sent the second bullet high and left of the first. Which was a welcome yet unintended consequence that saw the speeding missile careen sidelong off the bridge of the thing's nose and embark on an exploratory mission of the inside of its cranium. There was no explosion of brain, bone, and hair as Taryn had expected. Instead, the strangely silent first turn's head snapped back and its body instantly followed that same trajectory to the floor.

Already having slapped a fresh magazine into the Beretta, Wilson was pleading for Taryn to get off the landing when a pair of first turns suddenly spilled through the doorway, clambering over the twice-dead corpse. Numb fingers swiped the air a yard in front of Taryn, but, inexplicably, the long- dead duo stopped their forward surge just one footstep beyond the door's threshold.

"What the eff?" Wilson exclaimed, lowering his weapon.

"You've got to see this to believe it," Taryn said, massaging her scalp and slowly distancing herself from the curled fingers kneading the airspace to her fore.

Chapter 10

The familiar abandoned school bus in the roadside ditch was a yellow blur as the new Chevy fishtailed through the slight S turn where Center crossed 16 and became State Route 39.

In the passenger seat, Oliver was beginning to think he was about to live out a scene from Bullitt or Gone In 60 Seconds. And as the realization settled in that the man driving the pickup was not a trained driver, let alone a stuntman, he began to wonder if *live out* was the proper way of framing the upcoming experience. The prospect of Daymon taking a corner too fast and leaving them alive and trapped in the crushed hulk and easy prey for the walking dead was almost too much for him.

Glancing sidelong at his passenger, whose right hand was curled around the grab bar, Daymon snickered and applied more gas, throwing the truck hard through a left-hand sweeper. "You need to barf, Oliver?" he asked. "'Cause if you do, it better not be in the gym bag."

"What's in the bag that's so damn important?" Oliver queried through tightly clenched teeth.

Daymon began, "A couple of things for Cade, a couple of things for Duncan, and a couple or twenty things for Raven and Sasha."

"What?" Oliver pressed.

Tongue firmly planted in cheek, he said, "If I told you what's inside the bag, I'd have to kill you."

"It better not be full of effin Snickers bars and six packs of Diet Coke. 'Cause if it is …" Oliver made a play of grabbing for his carbine. "I just might kill you."

Near simultaneously—or so it seemed on account of how fast Daymon was driving—the lower mine and upper quarry entrances both flashed by. The former had come into view first off the left-hand side. Then, a tick later, the brush-covered road snaking up the mountainside was in the rearview and growing smaller by the second.

Woodruff

The fix-it shop was a handful of blocks east of Main Street and only two long country blocks south of Woodruff's northern boundary. Set back from the two-lane and fronted by a large gravel lot, the once-white cinderblock garage was now mottled gray from what Taryn guessed to be several decades' worth of seasonal change. Rain, wind, and no doubt an inordinate amount of the white stuff that had just recently come and gone had taken its toll on the swaybacked structure. From the ground to roughly waist-level on Taryn, furry green moss clung tenaciously to the red brick foundation.

She was leaning against the Raptor's fender and looking in the general direction of Main when she first heard the engine sounds approaching from the south. That Wilson had just hailed the others to come and offer their opinion on what they had found inside the shop led her to believe it could only be the Graysons' F-650. And that initial assumption moved closer to one hundred percent in her mind when the vehicle was near enough for her to discern the unique exhaust note. Still, trained ear or not, and the times being what they were, she shouldered her carbine and aimed the business end at the nearest intersection where the vehicle in question was sure to emerge.

Across the lot, Wilson was standing behind the rusted-out shell of an old Studebaker pickup and aiming his carbine at the intersection. Should their assumption be false, from where he and Taryn had positioned themselves, any evasive maneuver the vehicle should undertake would expose both the driver and passenger to a shallow crossfire from the pair of AR-15s.

Better to be safe than sorry was what the older folks were always preaching. And after the ambush in Huntsville, the Kids had been more than happy to take that advice to heart.

North and southbound traffic was regulated at the intersection by a pair of stop signs. To the left, a late-model import sitting on four flat tires and a waist-high white picket fence fronting a two-story house partially blocked the vehicle's approach on Main from view. However, once the matte-black bumper and massive grill broke the plane, there was no mistaking the vehicle for anything but the towering Ford.

Peering through the 3x magnifier atop his carbine, Wilson confirmed the two in the truck were indeed Jamie and Lev. "Clear," he called out, still training the muzzle on the passenger door.

"Copy," Taryn said, setting the rotters in the doorway off on a new round of try-to-climb-over-each-other which sent the rest of the automotive brochures spilling onto the ground outside the entry.

Lowering his carbine, Wilson smiled and approached the Ford with one hand raised in greeting.

Once her window had powered down completely, Jamie asked, "Whatcha got?"

"Follow me," Wilson said, setting off for the short stack of stairs to his right.

Jamie exited the idling truck, one hand holding a boxy pistol, the other resting on the handle of her sheathed flat-black war tomahawk.

Wilson and Lev formed up behind the women and followed them up the wheelchair ramp fronting the building.

Disregarding the unruly pair of zombies stalled out in the doorway, Taryn stopped and knelt next to the gaunt first turn. "I walked right into a trap," she said, turning the twice-dead corpse over so that its neck faced the others. With the angled tip of her Tanto, she pointed to the gaping wound where an Adam's Apple should have been. "All three of these have been … for lack of a better word, *silenced.* It's as if someone took out their voice boxes

… or damaged their vocal cords so badly they've been rendered mute."

"That's why we bang on doors *first*," Lev said.

Coming to Taryn's aid, Wilson said, "She did. Three or four times." He moved closer to her and squared up to Lev.

"I waited the full ten-count before trying the door, too," Taryn added, her eyes flicking from Jamie to Lev. "Look here." She probed the creature's left ear with the knife. Where there should have been the usual canal and raised cartilage inside, there was now just a hole roughly the circumference of a dime. It had well-defined edges and was partially filled in with crusted blood black as marrow.

Jamie asked, "Is it the same on the other side?"

Grimacing, Taryn grabbed the shock of dirty hair atop the corpse's head and turned it over. Same thing. A neatly bored hole crusted over with some kind of dried fluid.

The other two monsters continued battering themselves against the doorframe, teeth bared in silent snarls. Both had puckered bullet wounds peppering their torsos.

"Those holes aren't the work of hungry larvae," Lev said. "Someone's used them for target practice." He took a step toward the doorway and craned to see the handiwork up close. Quickly determined that the bullet wounds looked new. And like the rotter at his feet, these two had had their ears drilled out and their throats operated on.

"So what's keeping them in check?" Jamie asked.

"Let's find out." Lev drew a knife from a scabbard on his hip. He set his right foot forward and leaned in like a fencer, jabbing the dagger hilt deep into the eye of the corpse on his right. Instantly an awful-smelling liquid seeped from the punctured orb and the shirtless Z collapsed vertically into a heap, bony knees twisted Indian-style, sharp elbows and knobby vertebra straining against pale, parchment-thin skin.

After dispatching the other Omega-infected monster in the same manner as the last, Lev stepped over the tangled corpses and into the inky gloom.

A handful of seconds after entering the bowels of the auto garage, Lev emerged with the knife sheathed on his hip and a long, silver length of what looked to be a plastic jump rope coiled around one fist.

"Did these two get tangled up in that?" Wilson asked, crunching his boonie hat down over his red mane.

Lev shook his head. "Nope … same story inside there as the rehab place. Someone picked the place clean. They didn't stop there, however. They left these two tethered to a four-by-four support beam with this plastic-coated wire." He deposited the end he'd been holding atop the corpses. "These two were left with just enough leash to allow them to almost reach the door … *but* not enough for them to wander too far away from it."

Jamie said, "Whoever did this wanted them to be close enough to react to the light when the door opened. Fuckers wanted us to get our faces chewed off the second we set foot inside."

"Precisely," Lev agreed. "This old boy," he pointed to the one that had reached the door first. "He slipped his tether when the skin and flesh sloughed off his ankle and foot."

"First turns," Wilson said, covering his mouth and nose against the stench. "I don't think I'll ever get used to looking at 'em."

"Why booby trap this place? And how'd they do it without getting bit themselves?" Obviously annoyed, Taryn hitched her camouflage coat sleeves up, exposing the scaly dragons and sneering skulls inked in black on her forearms. "I almost bought the farm," she said, voice wavering subtly.

"They plucked them out of the wild when it was still snowing … or at least still below freezing," Jamie theorized. "Pretty easy to do whatever it took to silence them and then run a power drill into their ears when they're not squirming and trying to take a bite out of you." She moved closer to Taryn, went up to her tiptoes and gently inspected the young woman's scalp.

"How bad is it?" Taryn asked in a near whisper.

"Not so bad. It could stand a little splash of hydrogen peroxide, though." Jamie looked the younger woman in the eye and her voice took on a motherly tone. "First that crispy thing at the Shell station the other day. Now this? Girl … you have got to be more careful. Especially when entering automotive garages." Flashing a smile of relief, Jamie turned to face the guys.

Lev suddenly went still and met the others' eyes one at a time. Body rigid, he rose from his haunches and swept his gaze over their surroundings. After a quick glance at his watch, he stated, "I don't like this one bit. Too much organization went into preparing this. I'm going to call this in to the compound." He cast a glance up the street. Panned his gaze left to an expanse of overgrown yard seemingly split by the shadow cast by the steeple atop a nearby church. "Then I think we should head back to the post office a little early. Clear it of dead and wait for Daymon and Oliver to get back. Once they return we can all decide where we go from there."

Heads nodded all around as Lev retrieved the CB from the F-650 and placed the call. Then, once he had finished filling Cade in on their findings, he used the two-way to hail Daymon and did the same. Finished, Lev followed Jamie and the Kids to their waiting vehicles. Finally, less than ten minutes after the Kids arrived in the Raptor, the pair of engines roared to life, and the two-truck convoy wheeled from the gravel lot at a slow roll heading west toward Main Street, the F-650 in the lead.

***

The watcher took a final drag on the unfiltered cigarette and grimaced at the stale aftertaste it left in her mouth. Blowing the pungent smoke out through her nose, she blindly stubbed the butt out on the windowsill and shifted in her chair to get the blood flowing back into her numb backside. The binoculars pressed to her eyes were trained on the group of four standing beside a pair of vehicles parked on the gravel lot three blocks to the west.

The redheaded guy in the camouflage hat and the fresh-faced girl with the ponytail who had arrived alone minutes earlier were doing most of the talking. Judging by the group's fairly relaxed body language as they stood in a ragged circle conversing amongst themselves, the girl with the ponytail who had initially entered the auto body shop alone had inexplicably avoided becoming lunch for the *purged*. The less-than-urgent response her friends in the big black truck had displayed while responding to the scene, and that nobody down there was breaking out a first aid kit, all but confirmed to the watcher that she wouldn't be collecting anything as a result.

Part of her was happy the girl had survived her brush with death. But the fleeting emotion wasn't fueled by any kind of empathy she harbored for the brunette. It was selfish and self-centered and born from the knowledge that the long wait for the victim or victims to finalize their purge and eventually stagger off in search of prey was not going to happen. But more so than that, the fact that the brunette and her redhead friend were still *pure* and not scavenging claimed territory alone as the watcher had initially reported, spared her momentarily from going through their personal effects—a necessary task that always dredged up painful memories from the time before the *purged* had risen to usurp the unbelievers.

Shuddering at the prospect of eventually having to again relive that *old-life* moment when all she had held dear had been violently stripped from her, the watcher panned the binoculars left of the group and scrutinized their vehicles. Sure they were probably full of supplies, their tanks holding precious fuel, but the mere thought of siphoning them instantly turned her stomach. Smacking her lips, she screwed up her face as a Pavlovian response reminded her how awful it would taste in her mouth. Though the cigarettes left behind after the purge were barely palatable, and what she was required to do sexually to Mom and others in order to acquire them even worse, she lit up another and inhaled deeply.

Down the street the small group of *uncleansed*—the term Mom had bestowed upon those not like them who had survived the purge—entered their vehicles two-by-two, closed their doors in unison, and motored off the way they had come.

Two-by-two, thought the watcher, smiling as the figure of speech brought back yesterday's lesson of Noah and Mom's mention of the space ark being constructed for the *Enlightened*.

Still smiling dumbly and in her mind already light years from a slowly dying Earth, she set the binoculars aside, scooped up the CB radio, and called in to report what she had just witnessed.

After listening to the soothing, slightly robotic voice on the other end instruct her exactly what to do next, the watcher lowered the volume on the handheld CB and then wiggled her knife from the sill where she had stabbed it when the white truck had so rudely interrupted her *work*.

She set the radio down on the wood floor, leaving a garnet trace of her own blood on the light ash surface. Then, picking up where she had left off, she finished the final flourish on the descending serif of the ornate capital R that she'd already spent the better part of an hour carving into the painted windowsill.

She drew in a deep breath and exhaled slowly while moving her head left-to-right along the length of the dirty windowsill.

Even before the fine wood shavings had floated all the way to the floor to be absorbed into the blood spattered around her crossed legs, she was attacking the next letter in the chosen one's name with the quiet vigor and precision of a Buddhist monk laboring over a sand mandala.

Chapter 11

"Drive it like I stole it" was still cycling through Oliver's mind when Daymon came upon a straightaway, sped up exponentially, and inexplicably took one hand off the wheel in order to answer the warbling two-way radio.

"Daymon," he answered, matter-of-factly, as if the fallen leaves from the skeletal trees weren't blazing by in spurts of red and orange and brown.

The speaker hissed white noise for a second then a voice said, "Lev here. We have an *issue.*"

Daymon was about to ask "*What kind of issue?*" but before he could get a word in Lev was spilling all about the zombie booby trap and the feelings of being watched he'd experienced outside the fix-it place.

Preparing to brake for a corner rushing at them, Daymon said, "You sure?" and passed the radio off to a near hyperventilating Oliver.

"Near a hundred percent sure," Lev answered. "By the way … Cade was none too happy we split up."

Silence on the other end.

Surprised that Daymon wasn't pissed because of the disclosure, Lev said, "We'll be waiting at the post office. What's your ETA?"

Daymon took his eyes from the road for a second. "Tell him we'll be turning onto 16 in twenty-five minutes … give or take."

Hands trembling, Oliver keyed Talk, passed on the message, and signed off.

Once again matting the pedal on the next to last straightaway before the curving arc of 39 fronting the compound feeder,

Daymon looked sidelong at his passenger and said, "Hail the compound and ask whoever is watching the road for a SITREP."

Oliver drew a deep cleansing breath, raised Seth on the radio and, without fanfare, relayed the message.

Another burst of static emanated from the tiny speaker. With a trace of levity in the delivery, Seth said, "You're clear at the road. A special welcoming party will be waiting to receive your *secret* delivery."

Still in the dark about what the oversized gym bag on the floor contained, Oliver handed the radio back to the crazy driver.

***

Listening in on the conversation through the ear bud stuck in his right ear, Cade shouldered his M4 and aimed the barrel east down the road at the distant corner. Through the EOTech 3X magnifier, he saw the Chevy round the bend and slow a bit. Tucking the collapsible stock tighter to his shoulder, drawing a deep breath, and exhaling slowly brought the front windshield and cab into sharp focus.

Willing himself back into mission mode, Cade catalogued in his mind what he was seeing through the optics. *Two bodies. One passenger: Caucasian male. Driver: African American male. Confidence is high these are the principals.* He thumbed the switch on the foregrip and flashed the oncoming truck three times with the high-lumen weapon-mounted tactical light.

Seeing the signal, Daymon hailed Seth. "Who's waiting at the gate?"

"Cade," Seth replied at once.

"Oh shit," Daymon replied. "This could get weird."

One of Cade's eyebrows hitched up as he lowered the M4's muzzle toward the ground. Wondering what the Eden compound's mercurial former firefighter had up his sleeve, he stepped from behind the blind and raised a gloved hand in greeting.

"I see him," came Daymon's voice over the open channel.

The Chevy came to a stop a yard from Cade's knees, lurched a bit as the transmission was disengaged, and then the body rolled a bit on the chassis when Daymon stepped to the road. In the dreadlocked man's hand was the black gym bag with the words WEST HIGH PANTHERS - SALT LAKE CITY, UTAH silkscreened in red on its sides.

Cade hefted the bag. "Heavy." He set it on the road and tugged the zipper. Peering at the contents, he said, "You came all this way to give me these before I left?"

"Hell, you've been known to wear armor fashioned from magazines. Those are no different. Besides, I might need to borrow your muscle *and* your truck before winter really gets a-poppin'."

Cade zippered the bag and shot Daymon a look that implored the man to elaborate.

"I found a place. Not far from the crossroads. Real secluded and secure."

"Aboveground, I assume."

Daymon smiled. "Oh, is it ever."

"What exactly do you need me and the truck for? You can't have much that needs moving."

"I was pulling your leg." Daymon glanced at the Chevy. The window was down now and Oliver was waving to get his attention.

Daymon regarded Cade and added, "In the old world. Before all this dead people walking around bullshit … didn't you effin hate it when people asked you to help 'em move?"

"Not if it was a friend who was asking."

"What am I to you?"

"I would help you move, Daymon"

"I'm going to get all misty-eyed here," Daymon said. "Hope I don't break down and bawl."

"Better not," Cade said, motioning in the direction of the black domes. "Foley fixed the audio on those things. Seth probably hears everything we're saying."

In his ear Cade heard Seth chuckle and confirm that he could hear what was being said, but wasn't really *retaining* any of it.

Though the volume on the radio in Daymon's pocket was dialed down to 5, he still heard Seth's admission. Flipping the black dome the bird, he said, "Be safe out there, Cade. Wherever *there* is this time." He nodded and winked conspiratorially. "Can you give me a hint?"

Cade smiled. "If I did I'd have to kill you."

"Can you at least bring me back a half-shirt or a shot glass or something?"

"Copy that," Cade said offering a fist bump. "I have to get back. My ride's due here any minute."

"And I gotta see what OG wants."

Cade shouldered the bulging bag. Looking Daymon in the eye, he asked, "Is Oliver as advertised out there?"

"He's about average," Daymon lied. "Still got a lot to learn, though."

"Don't we all," Cade replied.

"Oh, I almost forgot." Daymon's lips curled into a half-smile. He fished the pair of aviator-style glasses from an inside pocket where they'd been since he plucked them off the dresser inside Casa De Daymon twenty-five minutes ago. "Along with the other stuff, give these to Old Man."

Cade took them in hand, inspected the thickness of the lenses, and noted the fine bi-focal lines. Shifting his gaze to Daymon, he said, "These just might do the trick. I have to admit I'll miss the Elton John look."

"The others are waiting at the post office," Oliver called from the truck.

Daymon looked at his watch. "He's right. We gotta go."

"Be careful," Cade repeated. "You all better stick together. Strength in numbers … and all that. Whoever is responsible for that trap means business."

"You know me," Daymon replied, as he turned to the truck. "I'm always *frosty*."

Cade patted the bag. "Thanks again for these."

"My pleasure," said Daymon.

Cade slung his rifle, then retreated behind the camouflage gate and was lost from view.

***

Back inside the truck, Daymon clicked on his seatbelt and squared up to Oliver. Stared at him for a long five-count.

Oliver shifted nervously in his seat. Finally he asked, "What?"

"You're watering your balls right now. First deadhead we come upon you're getting out and doing it up close and personal. Ask me why."

"What?"

"No, why," Daymon hissed.

"Why?"

Daymon rolled the Chevy into the first leg of a three-point turn. Once he was finished reversing across both lanes and had the truck pointing east, he said, "Because I just lied for you and I don't know why."

Oliver was speechless and still gawking at Daymon when his head was whipped into the seatback from the brisk and sudden acceleration.

***

Fifteen minutes after leaving the compound feeder road behind, Oliver was staring off into the forest and spotted a slow-moving matte-black object. He watched it quickly grow larger as it moved south to north, skimming a copse of alders far off in the distance before being blocked from view by the pickup's B-pillar. By the time he craned around and peered out the back window to reacquire the mysterious craft, there was nothing in the sky save for scattered clouds pierced with stray bars of golden sunlight.

Facing back forward, Oliver said, "You see that?"

Eyes never leaving the road, Daymon said, "What … Bigfoot?"

Oliver frowned. "No, *dickhead*." Gesturing in the direction of the truck's right rear wheel, he said, "I saw something big and black flying real low over those treetops."

"Like a stealth fighter jet or something?" Daymon replied, chuckling at the visual Oliver's words conjured.

"No. There was more to it than just fuselage. There was lots of movement going on."

"Are you just trying to distract me from finding you a rotter to dispatch?"

"No. I saw what I saw."

Just then two things happened. First, still locked on Channel 10-1, the radio crackled to life and Cade was alerting Seth that his ride to Springs was inbound to the clearing. Then, as the Chevy rounded a sweeping left-hander, Daymon said, "Speak of the Devil," and standing there in the center of 39 adjacent to the quarry entrance was a male walker. It looked fresh. Full of face and carrying about a buck eighty, the thing looked like a lost hunter. Only Daymon knew better. Hunters had rifles. This guy did not. And hunters wore either safety orange or some type of camo. This guy was stripped down to just his skivvies and had about a hundred red welts crisscrossing his pallid chest and extremities.

"There you go, Oliver. That one is tailor-made for you. Set up just like they instruct folks how to overcome their fear of public speaking."

"How's that?"

"They say to imagine the audience sitting there in their undies. Calms the nerves, they say." He applied more brake and the Chevy's nose dipped slightly. "There you go. Nothing to be nervous about."

Oliver said nothing.

Daymon pulled the truck diagonal to the centerline.

Down the embankment off the Chevy's right flank, the Ogden River rushing by sounded like morning freeway traffic.

Hearing the engine noise rising over the nearby river, the zombie turned and showed interest in the truck.

"Take Kindness," Daymon said. "She hasn't eaten much today. You feed her good and I'll feel better about fibbing to

Cade about you." He threw the automatic locks off and fixed his gaze on Oliver.

"If I don't?"

Daymon closed his eyes. "Get out."

"If I don't?" repeated Oliver, the machete wavering in his hand.

Opening his eyes, Daymon said, "Then you're dead to me. Literally. Get out … *now*."

Chapter 12

Cade was nosing the borrowed Dodge pickup in next to the Eden group's lone Humvee when he felt a sudden change in the air pressure. His ears popped first. Then, as if he'd been transplanted a second heart, a subtle throbbing began in his chest.

Standing directly in front of his white Dodge Ram, Duncan bent over and pretended to inspect the truck's grill and bumper.

"There's no new scratches on your baby," Cade said, stepping out of the truck, arms full with the M4 and oversized bag. "A little help here?"

Still feigning the auto-rental-return inspection routine as he looped around to the driver's side, Duncan stopped mid-stride and shifted his gaze skyward as a colossal shadow darkened the clearing.

Cade watched his friend walk right into the Dodge's wing mirror, bending it back on its breakaway mount.

Spewing a couple of expletives and rubbing his bicep, Duncan took his eyes from the helicopter orbiting high overhead and looked a question at Cade.

After a brief glance at the helo, Cade determined that the pilot of the exotic-looking craft was conducting a thorough recon of the landing zone before committing to a final approach.

"That's my ride," he said nonchalantly as he tossed the bag on the ground lengthwise in front of his boots. Crouching next to the bag, he drew the zipper back and pulled out several retail packages of Halloween-sized candy bars. "For the girls," he growled at Duncan, who was already reaching for them. Next, he removed six boxes of shotgun shells, placing them on the crushed grass.

"I've got plenty of those," Duncan said. "But thanks all the same. The candy, though …"

Cade shot a quick glance skyward. Saw the unknown to him twin-rotor helicopter still orbiting high up. His first thought when the bird had come on station was that he was in for a long, slow ride to Springs aboard a lumbering Chinook MH-47. Now he wasn't so sure as the black silhouette began a final descent.

"Raven and Sasha get the candy. You, my friend, may have shells," Cade said, shifting his gaze back to Duncan, who had crouched next to him. "But you don't have one of these." He pulled a black shotgun from the bag. It was fitted with an EOTech holographic sight, folding stock, and had a vertical front grip attached below the squared-off forestock.

Duncan's eyes went wide behind his Elton John-esque glasses. "You shouldn't have," he gushed, already fingering the black stub of a shotgun. He examined the barrel. "Flash suppressor. Nice." Turned it over in his hands, noting the AK-47-style selector arm. Stamped just forward of the selector was a white S for *Safe* and a red F denoting *Fire*. And jutting from the same side in front of the embossed letters was the weapon's charging handle—a hook-shaped metal lever an inch or so long. All in all, it wasn't much longer than the shotgun he usually carried. And—bells and whistles notwithstanding—didn't look any more complicated at first glance.

"I didn't," Cade conceded. "Daymon did. Consider this Saiga 12 an olive branch. He said he'll explain it to you later." He reached back into the bag and it lost most of its shape when he withdrew a trio of black, boxy magazines and a pair of bulky, circular-shaped items. He patted the former, which were substantially larger than an M4 magazine and had a more pronounced forward curve to them. "These are ten-round 12-gauge mags." He pointed to the others. "And those two drum magazines hold twenty shells apiece of the same."

"This beast is semi-automatic?"

Cade nodded. "Pull the trigger until she's empty."

Duncan whistled. "Makes the old Street Sweeper shotgun look like a baby Derringer."

"That dog *will* bark," Cade agreed. He zipped up the bag and rose, grimacing as his left ankle took most of his weight.

Using the truck's muddy rear tire for support, Duncan also rose. "Time for you to go, mi amigo."

Cade nodded even as he was waving Brook and Raven over from the shadow of Daymon's Winnebago where they had been standing.

Glenda and Heidi remained where they were, sitting side-by-side on the RV's folding stairs.

"Couldn't sit this one out," Cade said, glancing at the helo just as it was settling on its landing gear dead center on the dirt airstrip. Even with a hundred-plus-yards separation, the rotor wash made the branches overhead dance and clack together. "Not after what I saw on the video Nash sent."

Duncan nodded, one hand holding his Stetson on his head. "Never thought I'd see the day foreign troops set boots on our shores."

Cade was about to respond, but was rocked sideways as first Raven hit his legs like a mini linebacker, then Brook wrapped him up in a one-armed hug and planted goodbye kisses on his cheek. He returned the affection, whispering in Brook's ear then hefting Raven off her feet to give her one of his trademark bear hugs. Blinking the mist from his eyes, he set his daughter down and plucked his rucksack from the ground near the Humvee where he'd left it earlier. He shrugged the ruck on and checked that the spare mags were in place in the pouches on his MOLLE vest. Lastly, he scooped up his M4 and the nearly empty Panther's bag and stood to attention, fighting valiantly to hold back the tears forming in his eyes.

After nodding toward the bagged Hershey's bars, he shifted his gaze to Raven and Brook, blinked fast a couple of times and mouthed, "Love you." Before the emotion of the moment got the better of him, he quickly turned toward the helo whose rear ramp was just beginning to motor down.

In passing, Duncan looked the man clad in all black up and down. He said, "Be careful out there, Jim Phelps," clearly a reference to the special agent from Mission Impossible. Then, loud enough to carry over the thrum of the distant chopper, the grizzled Vietnam veteran hollered, "Peter Graves has nothing on you, Wyatt," and began humming the unmistakable theme song.

"I must be getting old timers," Cade said, turning back and withdrawing the aviator shades from a pocket. "These are from your buddy, too."

Smiling, Duncan swapped the old glasses with the new. He spun a circle, declaring them damn near perfect once he was facing Cade again.

"They're you, Old Man," Cade declared and was on the move again.

Though there was no need to duck his head under the matte-black chopper's madly spinning rear rotor blades, Cade put a hand on his helmet and bent low at the waist anyway. *Old habits really do die hard.*

A compact fireplug of a man clad in MultiCam fatigues soiled with dirt and who-knows-what-else greeted Cade at the ramp. Taking the sports bag from Cade's gloved hand, the crew chief, whose nametape read Spielman, directed him to a seat just inside the canted ramp.

Cade squinted and stumbled as a boot caught on the foreign surface underfoot. Eyes still adjusting to the abrupt switch from the flat, unforgiving light outside to the chopper's dim interior, he took the seat Spielman had pointed to, quickly adjusted his rifle on his chest, and slipped the safety harness over his shoulders and hips. Clicking the black buckle together over his sternum, he let his eyes roam the helo's long, narrow cabin.

There were two lumps partially blocking the aisle a few feet to his left. There were also several seated forms, still just silhouettes thanks to his compromised vision. He counted six seated shapes to his left, and four more he assumed were looking back at him from across the aisle. As the hydraulic piston to his right went to work drawing the ramp closed, his vision slowly began to improve.

Letting his helmet rest on the bulkhead behind him, Cade opened and closed his eyes rapidly half a dozen times. Finished blinking the dust from his vision, he cast his gaze around the cabin and found the inside of the craft belied everything he had expected. Whereas the outside was very similar to the Ghost Hawk in appearance and attitude—a mashup of angles and soft curves all wrapped by what had to be radar-absorbing materials—the troop compartment of this bird had none of the same accoutrements. There were no flip-down flat-panel monitors that he could see. If there was a way to communicate with the aircrew, he could see no jacks to plug into. It appeared that the technology bomb that had seemingly exploded and coated the insides of the Jedi Ride he was used to being ferried around in had missed this bird entirely.

The sliver of light atop the rear door faded to black and the hydraulic whine ceased. As the engines spooled up with a different kind of whine—a satisfying sound that meant they would soon be underway—once again Cade felt the pressure worm its way into his ear canals and take up station deep in his chest. The sensation coincided with his stomach going south as the helo launched under what seemed like full power. Strangely, however, the rotor *thwop* didn't reach anything close to the crescendo created by this craft's nearly fifty-year-old predecessor. Nor was the same vibration present. Transmitted through the bulkhead pressing his back, he *could* feel the turbines and mechanicals at work, but smooth as silk in comparison to the CH-47 "Shithook" as Duncan fondly called the venerable workhorse of Army Aviation.

With the rear ramp closed, Cade got a whiff of the air inside the hulking bus-sized helo. It stank of stale sweat, gunpowder, and JP-8 jet fuel, all ensconced in the ever-present sickly-sweet pong of death. Once the crew chief made his way fore and took a seat beside a flush squared-off window that was within arm's reach of the internally stowed minigun, Cade scrutinized the now fully-defined forms across the aisle from him. They were, to a man, stripped down to just their Crye Precision MultiCam combat shirts and like-colored camouflage pants. Sweat stains marked the wicking fabric where their vests and rucksacks had been riding over their Crye tops. Their MOLLE load-bearing gear—pouches empty of magazines—sat in an unruly pile on the cabin floor near the ramp. He let his eyes pause on the patches affixed by hook-and-loop tape to their dirt- and blood-soiled uniforms and discovered he was sitting amongst a chalk of Rangers from the Army's storied 75th Regiment which he proudly hailed from. *Hooah*, he thought, pride welling in his chest.

The feeling quickly faded and his heart grew heavy when his eyes fell on the two lumps to his left and realized they were draped with flags. Likely fallen fellow Rangers.

A gloved hand had worked its way out from under one of the flags. It vibrated subtly against the floor as if the soldier it was attached to was still alive. But he wasn't. Of that Cade was certain. For where his head tented the flag up there was a deep, almost blackish red stain that had spread into a Rorschach-like pattern with edges much like the chopper's—rounded where gravity had dragged it down the corpse's cheeks, and jagged where runners had soaked across the upturned profile. In places on the dead soldier's chest, the "stars and bars" were stained crimson.

No body bags.

That didn't speak well of the outcome of whatever battle they were returning from.

Once the chopper attained level flight and had picked up speed, the SOAR crew chief named Spielman worked his way aft from the hip gun with a flight helmet in hand and a grim look parked on his bearded face.

The helmet was thrust in Cade's face.

No umbrage was taken. Cade was aware his black fatigues bore no rank, unit insignia or any of the other markings to denote who he was and where he'd been. Even if the crew chief or any of the other men had met him before or knew of him, the nearly full beard obscuring his face negated the possibility they would know who he was right here and now. And that was just fine in Cade Grayson's book.

"Thank you," he mouthed, taking the helmet and quickly peeling off his low-profile tactical model.

Staff Sergeant Spielman said nothing. He stood gripping a strap near his head and gently swaying along with the rest of the *customers* aboard the Night Stalker bird.

Cade snugged the helmet on. It was a perfect fit. Shrugging and staring up at Spielman, he mouthed, "How does this plug in?"

"It's Bluetooth-enabled," Spielman mouthed back, no emotion conveyed at all. His eyes were hidden behind the lowered visor. "It'll come on-line in a second or two."

The first words Cade had understood by reading the staff sergeant's lips. The last sentence he heard loud and clear through the headset built into the helmet. He was adjusting the boom mic near his mouth when he heard other voices: the first belonging to the aircrew flying the chopper. Then a tick later the response to their query for the weather conditions in Colorado Springs came through not crisp and clean, but with a series of clicks and chirps before and after suggesting it was an encrypted transmission delivered via an overhead communications satellite.

Hearing the all-business SITREP from one of the pilots up front and then the prompt reply from the 50th Space Wing in Schriever told Cade he was not only able to hear the crew chief, but he was also plugged into the shipwide coms and would be privy to everything going on behind the scenes. Which was a good thing seeing as how he was the black sheep—figuratively and literally—aboard the chopper. Whether the crew chief was aware how the helmet comms were configured was no concern of Cade's. That he might be treading where he was not supposed to could be debated later if it came to that. So, not wanting to tip his hand and give up the chance to learn more than just what he could see with his own eyes from his window seat in the stealth helo, he fixed his gaze on the visor where he guessed Spielman's eyes to be and mouthed, "Copy that."

Spielman merely grunted and then strode back to his seat beside the retracted minigun.

The Rangers, most with their eyes closed, some staring off into space, didn't let on if they had witnessed the exchange with Spielman or not. And as the crew chief stalked around the shrouded bodies, saluting them as he did, Cade put himself in their boots. He imagined that if he had just gone through the same kind of hell these Rangers had, he'd also find little joy in diverting to pick up what—just going on his black uniform and specialized gear—had to be a CIA spook who'd gotten himself in too deep.

Burying their fallen was atop the to-do list, no doubt. Followed closely by hot chow and some shut eye before the next battle waged against an enemy that was now coming at them from all points of the compass.

So, with nothing to do on the four-hundred-mile flight but let his senses soak up every bit of available intel, he craned over his shoulder to watch the country awash with the colors of fall flash below the low-flying chopper and listened in on the constant chatter between the pilots up front and Schriever Air Force Base, presumably his first stop on what was going to be a long trip Back East.

Chapter 13

Oliver had remained rooted in place for three long minutes before Daymon repeated his ultimatum. This time the words had come out slow and even without a trace of anger.

The steady *tic … tic … tic* of the creature's splintered, blood-soiled nails drumming the glass off his right cheek was sending tremors of fear coursing through Oliver's body.

"Sink or swim," Daymon repeated. Hoss was on his mind now. The anger he'd felt after being trapped in the sweltering farmhouse attic in Hanna, Utah was as well. He could hear the moans of the dead. The scratching of nails digging into once ornate wallpaper and lathe and plaster. The home's old bones creaking under the weight of all those cold, jostling bodies. "Do it with the knife."

Without warning, in one fluid movement, Daymon leaned across the seat, worked the door latch and put all of his weight and upper body strength into one solid lunge that started the big creature on a clumsy arms-flailing backpedal away from Oliver's window.

"What the hell?" Oliver rasped, even as his seatbelt was retracting over his shoulder and Daymon's follow-through forearm shiver was sliding him out the door.

"Sink or swim."

Now on his knees on the roadway, Oliver heard the door suck shut at his back and the pneumatic *thunk* of the door locks slamming home.

"You'll thank me for this later," came Daymon's muffled voice through the glass at his back.

If I survive.

Having regained its already compromised balance, the long-dead rotter fixed his unblinking eyes on a just-rising Oliver and found another gear in its forward shuffle.

Bent at the waist, the folding knife held in front of him at an upward angle, Oliver moved to his right and backpedaled to create a little separation and some time to think.

Daymon rooted silently for Oliver as he and the dead thing did a slow roundabout dance a dozen feet off his right shoulder. Slowly but surely the monster was advancing and Oliver was checking his retreat, no doubt steeling himself for a last stand.

Hand poised over the horn and ready to give a sharp attention-getting blast should the rotter get the upper hand, Daymon craned to follow the action in the side mirror. He truly wanted the man to survive the encounter. To lay the first brick of the foundation he would need to survive going forward. Hell, even the Kids were rising to the occasion. Why shouldn't this crack shot have to as well? After all, thought Daymon. As the saying goes: You're only as strong as your weakest link. And right now that link was being exposed to the crucible necessary to strengthen it to the level of the others.

The anger he was feeling over Oliver's reluctance to get his hands dirty was in danger of growing to that of the hatred he felt toward the imbecile of a lawyer who had gotten him and Cade trapped in the attic in Hanna.

"Come on, Oliver!" Daymon shouted. "Water them already!"

And he did. The lunge caught both Daymon and the undead man flat-footed—the latter literally as the knife flashed on an upward arc and became buried hilt deep in the thing's right eye socket, displacing one clouded blue eye and sending the atrophied corpse on a one-way trip to the gray, oil-streaked asphalt.

In the cab Daymon did two things simultaneously. First he let out the air trapped in his lungs. Then he honked out a little ditty to voice his approval.

Seven short toots.

Shave and a haircut … two bits.

He unlocked Oliver's door.

The door opened with a creak and Oliver slid into the seat. Handing the knife back handle first, he said, "Thank you."

"You don't want to stab me with that thing? Give me the Omega? Hell, I'd want to if I was you."

Oliver shook his head. A slow side to side wag. "After letting you all think I was some kind of mountain man gun-toting John J. Rambo … I had it coming."

"I was ready to save your ass if I had to," Daymon admitted. "Hand was on the horn. Big ol' Bubba would have broken his neck to see the cause. You could have gotten away from that lumbering rotter … no problem."

Silence in the cab.

Daymon carefully cleaned his blade on a paper napkin. Tossing the soiled item out the window, he said, "So how'd it feel?"

"Too real."

"How so."

"I looked him in the eyes first."

Daymon clucked his tongue. "I made that same mistake early on. Did it again recently when I killed a man up in Idaho. Put an arrow in his throat and watched the light leave his eyes as he gargled his own blood."

Oliver shuddered. "I'm not there yet. Can't say I ever will be."

Daymon locked the doors, selected Drive, and started the truck rolling east past the pair of quarry feeder roads. "Then this won't be the last time one of us snips your umbilical. Takes your training wheels off and gives you a good downhill shove. Winds up your—"

"I get your drift," Oliver said. "I aim to make you all proud. Don't worry."

"I never worry," Daymon replied, eyes on the two-lane. "I cut the necessary firebreaks. Make sure the fire can't jump the lines. Same concept that was just on display here."

"Like tough love," Oliver stated, hands reeling in his carbine's sling.

Daymon shook his head, making the stunted dreads quiver. "Nope. That was more like the old saying … *an ounce of prevention—*," he began.

Clicking his seatbelt home, Oliver finished, "*—is worth a pound of cure.*"

"Bingo," Daymon said, slowing the truck and taking them left at the 39/16 juncture. "Now that that's settled, get one of the others on the horn and tell them not to shoot … it's just us."

Saying nothing, Oliver scooped up the Motorola two-way and hailed the others.

Chapter 14

Mostly out of respect for the dead, but also because he felt like an interloper sitting in his relatively clean black uniform alongside the battle-weary Rangers, Cade peered out the porthole window, dividing his attention between the direction the watery sun was tracking behind the clouds and the distant buttes scrolling by on the helo's port side. During the first few minutes of flight a handful of things he had been expecting to happen never came to fruition. For one, after lifting off from the compound's grass strip the helo remained in low-level flight, gaining altitude only to clear the tallest of trees or hillocks while following the Ogden River nearly due east—not quite nap of the earth maneuvering, but damn close based on Cade's experience. The constant altitude and speed corrections surely weren't good for fuel consumption, but to keep the helicopter hidden from any hostile radar that may be painting the skies along the flight path, the tactics were golden.

The flightpath itself was the second thing that had been niggling at him. Whereas Colorado Springs was almost due southeast of the compound, based on both the sun's position—roughly eleven o'clock in relation to the speeding craft's nose—the first leg of the journey had them tacking substantially more to the north. And further adding to the mystery, once the helo reached the north/south running stripe of highway he knew to be 16, the craft banked sharply to starboard causing the bodies on board—both living and dead—to loll and strain against the restraints holding them in place.

The pilot held the new southerly course and kept their altitude at what looked to Cade to be a constant five hundred feet above ground level. Which at times caused the road below to seemingly rise up toward the helo from where it followed the natural contours of the earth and then fall back down and run flat and true where fenced-in fields and scrub-dotted range dominated on both sides.

A short while after the banking turn, a two-story farmhouse complete with a hulking red barn and tubular silo appeared below Cade's port-side vantage. And going off of second-hand descriptions of Ray and Helen's place, the structures, snaking dirt drive, and sloped grazing area, when all taken into consideration, left him no doubt he was looking at the elderly couple's defunct alpaca ranch.

Shortly after the Thagon place was lost from view Cade felt the craft slow considerably and list slowly to port, the unexpected maneuver pressing him into his seat and causing some of the Rangers who weren't sleeping to crane around and look out windows of their own.

We're going to buzz Bear River, thought Cade. No sooner had the words dissipated from his mind than they were spoken by the pilot. He also heard Dregan and Judge Pomeroy's names uttered in the same breath as the air crew debated the merits and risks of the low fly-by meant solely to add an exclamation mark to the message already delivered by Major Freda Nash via satellite phone the day before.

Nash, he thought. *You wily son-of-a-gun.* A move like this was just her style.

The next-gen Chinook orbited above the Bear River compound, scribing an elongated oval disturbance in the low-lying cloud cover.

Like the Rangers, all who were now alert and craning toward the windows, Cade was pressing his nose to the Plexiglas and taking in everything he could see on the ground. There was an orchard of skeletal trees north of town, a dirt road cutting through their uniformly spaced ranks. Guard towers, partially hidden behind the tallest of the trees, rose up from all four corners of the makeshift cement wall ringing the entire enclave.

Interspersed between copses of small and medium-sized trees growing up inside the wall were dozens of homes. Most sat on large plats of land and appeared to have been built decades ago. The small pockets of one- and two-story dwellings on the northern periphery were obviously of newer construction, most erected around circular cul-de-sacs and facing each other, while others were laid out in a grid pattern with narrow paved streets running neatly between them.

There were static vehicles parked here and there on the streets and nearly every home had a vehicle or two nosed into the driveway against closed garages.

West of town, the lengthening grass between the highway and wall was host to dozens of Zs. A handful could be seen lurching along muddy trails beaten into the low-lying pastures. Dozens more were pressing their chests futilely against the wall ingeniously constructed from dozens of twenty-foot-tall highway noise deterrent partitions. No way anything less than a full-blown horde of thousands was getting inside those walls, he surmised. On one hand he kind of envied the setup. It was like most of the forward operating bases he'd occasionally run ops from in the 'Stan, only supersized. However, the walled-in town, blessed with good fields of fire and nicely elevated platforms from which to engage enemies both dead and alive, was way too close to the road for his liking. Against a determined sizable force composed of armed breathers it would only be defensible if you had dedicated operators in the towers and more shooters positioned in the upper stories of the tallest homes near the walls.

Too many possible weak links amongst the reported two-hundred-plus individuals calling the place home.

Midway through the first pass, people began filing out of the homes and some of the businesses in the center of town. They stood on the main drag, side streets and handful of muddy alleyways crisscrossing the older part of Bear River.

Cade saw pale faces peering up expectantly. The helo's faint shadow rippled over the town center causing him to imagine what the former Salt Lake County Circuit Court Judge the message was meant for must be thinking at this very moment. Was he sitting in *chambers* in denial and trying to decide how he was going to keep his hold on power? Or had he already done the President's bidding as relayed by Nash during the phone call and handed the reins of town security back to Alexander Dregan?

While only time would tell on the latter, Cade knew the message the menacing chopper's eerily thwopping blades and deployed minigun barrels delivered went a long way toward discouraging the Judge of attempting the former.

After the second pass over Bear River, the helo dropped back down to near nap of the earth flight and Cade heard the twin turbines overhead spool up and begin whining like a pair of pissed-off banshees.

He watched the school bus blocking the town's south entrance grow smaller and eventually become a dull yellow pinprick bracketed by slate gray squares the size of Lego bricks. Down below, the State Highway tracking south rippled left and right and up and down like a roller coaster. Soon the *where* that this new course was taking them dawned on him, but not the *why*. Which was nothing new in his line of work. For the real mission began *when* he reached Springs and had his butt in a seat in Nash's office for the pre-mission face-to-face she had requested via the video beamed to his laptop days ago.

That she had been cryptic with her delivery when making the request didn't sit well with him. When taking into account the fact that the entire overture for him to undertake another mission had come in the form of packets of information not only encrypted by the 50th Space Wing's computers upon transmission, but also routed through one of the remaining super secure military satellites before being beamed to the portable dish he'd attached to his rugged laptop, sitting well was a bit of an understatement. In fact, he was damn scared. For if what she had to tell him held the kind of dire information making the face-to-face necessary, he knew said information would be nothing less than life changing. *Or*—he thought to himself while focusing on a string of static cars, their burned-out hulks contrasting sharply with the gray stripe of road they looked to have been fused to—*potentially world-altering if things could possibly get worse in my little corner of it.*

Chapter 15

The crushed gravel squelched under tire as Daymon steered the Chevy pickup onto the Woodruff Post Office parking lot. The truck lurched and took a sudden lean to the right before leveling out.

"Jeez," he said, stopping two car-lengths short of the glass double-doors being pawed at by a handful of rotters.

"Yeah," chimed Oliver. "Where in the hell did all of those things come from? And why haven't the others put them down yet?"

"The pusbags aren't what I was *Jeezin'* about."

"What's the problem then?" Oliver asked, hefting his AR and racking a round into the chamber.

"Did these cheap Woodruff mofos *ever* repave anything? You'd think for the United States post office they'd skim a couple of hundred off the annual hootenanny fund and hire a fly by night paving outfit to slap a couple of inches of fresh blacktop down. Or at the very least scrape some gravel off what passes for sidewalks at this end of town and fill in the frickin' Marianas Trench that just jacked up my lower lumbar."

That's the burr under his saddle? thought Oliver, as he gave his rifle a onceover. Safety on? *Check*. Stock collapsed to the last stop? *Check*. He blew some dust off the scope lens and shot a sheepish look at Daymon that said: *I'm ready as I'll ever be.*

Daymon sighed, killed the motor, and put the truck into Park.

"What do you have in mind?" Oliver stammered, his hands nearly as shaky as his voice.

Knowing the others had to be close by because the Raptor and F-650 were sitting a dozen yards away and splashing long shadows across the entry and lower partitions of the building's painted-over windows, Daymon said, "Get them on the radio."

Hands steadied somewhat, Oliver thumbed the Talk button and said, "Anyone there?"

"Good copy," Lev said, almost instantly.

Thinking the others were inside and had been watching as he pulled in, Daymon said, "Ask them what's up with the welcoming party."

In the thirty seconds since the Chevy had taken station on the frost-heaved blacktop, the dozen or so zombies had given up their silent vigil at the glass double-doors and cut the distance to the truck in half.

After delivering Daymon's message, Oliver inched away from his door and threw his gaze to the lock post, which to his relief was in the down position. Then, fearing Daymon might again forcibly eject him with just a knife to take on the advancing mob, he screwed up his courage and tried beating the dreadlocked man to the punch—or shove, whichever the case may be. "Are we going to …"

Oliver's question was cut off by the burst of white noise preceding Lev saying, "You're late."

"Give me that," Daymon said, snatching the Motorola from Oliver's hand. He thumbed the Talk button and let the radio hover near his lips for a long three-count as he reined in the rising anger. Finally, after consulting the clock on the dash and doing the math in his head, he said, "We're only twenty minutes late. I had to stop and give Oliver here an impromptu training session."

"Well, better late than *never*," Lev answered. "We tried you on the two-way but you must have been out of range. So I used the CB and got Seth, who said you'd already come and gone from the compound. That was thirty minutes ago … we were real close to fighting our way out of here to come looking for you."

"I'm sorry," Daymon said, the sincerity in his voice coming through loud and clear on Lev's end. "But I have to ask … why didn't you guys have a plan B?"

"We *did*," Lev said, sounding annoyed. "Then we came to find both of the doors to the loading dock chained and locked from the *inside*."

"And the bolt cutters are in my truck," Daymon said slowly. "Sorry again, bro. To make it up to you, we'll take care of these things out here."

Kindness slid from her sheath with a distinct rasp and Daymon was kneeing his door open even before the Motorola had stopped spinning on the center tray where he'd chucked it.

Seeing the man act without any kind of warning, Oliver drew in a lungful of the carrion-polluted air infiltrating the cab and reluctantly cracked his own door an inch.

Most of the Zs were already vectoring for the driver's side when Daymon stepped onto the lot. The noise from his door slamming shut behind him got the attention of the remaining ghouls, causing them to leave Oliver a clear path out of the cab.

Seeing that he was all alone on his side of the truck, Oliver flicked the AR's selector to Fire, went into a low crouch, and looped around the right front fender. Barrel slowly tracking with his eyes, he crabbed past the grill and rose over the left front fender just in time to see Daymon's scything right-handed swing relieve a rotter of its head.

Feeling a rising tide of panic gripping him, Oliver planted his elbows on the hood and lined the carbine up with a female rotter flanking Daymon from the blindside. Finger tensing on the trigger, he was about to fire when the dreadlocked dervish spun and delivered a backhanded chop from Kindness that relieved a second and third zombie of the tops of their skulls.

Momentarily stunned by the vicious effectiveness of the razor-sharp, yet utilitarian blade, Oliver inadvertently relaxed his trigger finger. Which was a good thing, because in his peripheral he saw Taryn in the open doorway flapping her arms up and down as if attempting to fly away under her own power. In the next beat, she held a finger vertically to her lips and mouthed, "Don't shoot."

Message received. And not a moment too soon. Whereas the sound of gunfire had no effect on zombies stopped in their tracks due to freezing temperatures, it had just dawned on Oliver that the crash of even one gunshot would echo and travel for blocks, bringing around more of the same currently encircling Daymon.

Seeing Taryn draw her black blade from the scabbard on her hip and fully expecting her, Wilson, and the others filling up the doorway to come running to Daymon's aid, Oliver released the breath trapped in his lungs and let his hands go slack on the AR.

Expectations shattered by what happened next, Oliver found himself with a snap decision to make. Either bend down to retrieve the black blade skittering and spinning across the blacktop toward him. Or go against Taryn's admonition and risk drawing a horde by bringing the carbine into the fight against the remaining dead.

In the end he found himself acting without really thinking. Instead of going into a crouch and plucking the noisily jangling piece of metal off the ground before it came to a complete stop, he spared himself diced fingertips by trapping it under his boot prior to scooping it up. Next—as if being directed by some power outside of himself—he bent at the waist and sprinted toward the clutch of dead with the Tanto-style blade clutched firmly in his right hand.

The only thing Oliver felt when he plunged the borrowed blade into the nearest rotter's concave right temple was the jagged tips of its previously broken ribs poking him in the gut. Trying to ignore the awful sound of Kindness sinking into flesh and bone to his left, Oliver crabbed right, moving on to his next *victim.*

***

"Daymon was right about him," Taryn said, peering over her shoulder at the rest of the group crowding the doorway at her back. "He's definitely a *swimmer.*" When she turned back around Oliver had already used her blade to send two more former humans to a final death.

Meanwhile, a few feet beyond the knife-wielding Gladson, Daymon was backed up against a wall of unkempt topiary and swinging Kindness head-high into the advancing picket of death.

Hissing, "Back off," he wiped a thin rope of something slimy from where it had landed on his neck and bulled backward through the dense, chest-high shrubs, eventually making it all the way through to the sidewalk on the opposite side.

Fixated solely on the meat barely a yard to their fore, the mindless automatons tried to follow Daymon into the bushes and became bogged down by the grabbing branches.

Smiling at the sight of so many zombies marching in place and getting nowhere for their efforts, Daymon met Oliver's gaze over the hedges. "Get over here and finish them," he said, eyes bugged to get the point across.

Having been wedged in the doorway next to the others and finding it more difficult by the second to stay out of the way—as Daymon had requested earlier when he first spoke of doing something such as this—Lev could take no more of being a spectator to Oliver's upper level survival course. First off, he didn't think the man was capable of a two-on-one encounter with a Z, let alone a forced four-on-one melee, especially after what Daymon had told him about the man. Cowardice and dishonesty notwithstanding, he couldn't stand by and let the guy die right here in front of him. No way he could sleep with that kind of death gnawing on his conscience.

As if reading Lev's mind, Max emitted a low growl and squeezed his snout past Wilson's leg.

Telling the Shepherd to "Stay," Lev edged past the Kids, pulled his blade from its scabbard and set off across the parking lot. But it was all for naught, because one stride into his *charge of the light brigade*, he saw Oliver handle the first of the remaining Zs with a short but efficient thrust of the Tanto. And before the rotter was crumbling to the ground, its brain scrambled by the intrusion of cold steel through cranial bone, the compact, balding man had moved on to the threat to his immediate left. Then, three strides into his rescue mission, Lev saw Daymon mouthing

"Stay back," while pointing at the post office with the tip of his blood-streaked machete.

Unaware that Jamie was on his heels, Lev stopped abruptly, causing a two-person pileup that was at once jarring and enjoyable on account of whose flesh was pressing hard against his. "Looks like he's got it handled," he whispered at about the same time Oliver was withdrawing the bloodied blade from the third trapped creature's temple and squaring up with the last of them.

"And then some," Jamie said, backpedaling and drawing Lev toward the post office door with her.

***

Winded and with nerve endings afire from the surge of adrenaline the likes of which he hadn't experienced since bombing down Powder Mountain high as a kite a couple of days ago, Oliver shot Daymon a death look and wrapped his free hand around the fourth zombie's scrawny neck. Still staring at the man who thirty minutes ago had kicked him from the safety of a truck and into a one-on-one confrontation paling in comparison to this, he tightened his grip and drew the rotter's snapping teeth close to his face.

"Is this what you wanted?" Oliver shouted, the spittle flying from his mouth landing on the pallid face just inches from his own. The vein on his temple was engorged and throbbing wildly. "Because all I have to do is let go and I'll be out of your hair."

Daymon shook his head, causing the spiky dreads to move in accordance. "Not my goal," he shouted. "I just wanted to light a fire under you. Show you what you were capable of."

Oliver's arm was growing tired now. Still, not wanting to show any sign of weakness, he held on as if his life depended on it. And it did. Bicep burning with fatigue, he asked, "What about the stunt you pulled back by the quarry … kicking me out of the truck?"

Daymon recognized the signs of exhaustion setting in. Sweat beading on the man's brow. A slight tremor beginning to show in his left arm. "First step in the interview process. Had to happen."

"And this?" Oliver hissed.

"Consider it your graduation party."

A thin sheen of sweat had formed on Oliver's upper lip.

Daymon leaned over the hedge. Sharp branches gouged his arm, chest, and stomach. Focusing on a spot behind the Z's ear, he raised the machete to deliver a short downward killing stroke.

In the next beat, making lethal intervention unnecessary on Daymon's part, Oliver positioned the business end of the Tanto horizontally an inch from the zombie's face, then, inexplicably, released his grip on its throat.

Newton's Third Law kicked in.

First, the zombie's toes found purchase on the rough pavement. Then, gravity, inertia, and an unyielding desire to take a bite of the meat that was so tantalizingly close sealed the zombie's fate when it lunged forward and swallowed steel.

No sensation of pain or taste transferred through long-dead nerves and taste buds as the Tanto split the thing's swollen tongue in two. The *tink* of steel on brittle teeth was also lost as the angular tip made contact and redirected the blade up and through the ghoul's soft palate, which was especially pliable due to several weeks' worth of decay.

Instantly the scrabbling feet went still and the grimy fingers that had found their way into Oliver's open mouth went limp and slithered out. Releasing his grip on both the knife and the rotter's throat, Oliver stepped back and let the hedges have the corpse.

"Shish. Ka. Bob," Daymon bellowed. "I didn't think you had it in you."

With friends like these, thought Oliver, back aching mightily from holding off the beast from hell.

From out of nowhere Lev and Jamie appeared by Oliver's side and whisked him away from the killing field.

"There's more coming from the north," Wilson called from the doorway.

"I'm on it," Taryn said, stalking toward the fallen Z to retrieve her blade.

Jamie fixed a glare on Daymon. "What the hell was all that?" she asked heatedly, redness spreading about her cheeks and neck.

"Your man co-signed this blanket party," Daymon said matter-of-factly. "Which went *way* better than expected, if I don't say so myself." He broke eye contact with Jamie and leveled his gaze on Lev. "You agree?"

Oliver hiked his shirt up to inspect where the thing's broken ribs had raked against his own.

"I *did* co-sign exposing him to the dead," Lev said. "And based on what Daymon told me earlier, I thought Oliver needed it. But that four-on-one crap was a little over the top in my opinion."

Jamie went to one knee and proceeded to give Oliver's back and sides a thorough onceover.

Grimacing from Jamie's gentle probing, Oliver waved to the others. "Hello … I'm alive," he said. "*Oliver* is standing right here even as you talk about him as if he was invisible."

"You're good here," Jamie said. "There's no broken skin."

Oliver sighed and thanked her. Then, as if a switch was flicked, his jaw clenched and he swung his gaze back to Lev and Daymon. "I let the first one slide," he hissed at Daymon. "You two may have had your reasons for conspiring and doing what you did. But I'll let you know here and now"—he wagged a finger, mostly in Daymon's direction—"you're not going to get away with this ever again."

Crossing his arms, Daymon said, "You've got a long way to go before you're one of us."

There was a long moment during which nobody spoke.

Oliver shifted from foot-to-foot and walked his gaze from Daymon to Lev to Jamie, where he paused and said, "You, of all people. You went along with it once it started."

Jamie said nothing. She looked down at the tomahawk hanging from her waist and fiddled with the worn leather wrapping the handle.

"And you," Oliver said, singling out Wilson, who was returning with Taryn after having helped her dispatch the pair of curious rotters. "You just stood there and did nothing. If it wasn't for Taryn sliding me her knife, I would have been toast."

Wilson opened his mouth to speak, but Taryn beat him to it. "In hindsight, I probably shouldn't have done that." She wiped her blade with the scrap of tee shirt taken off one of the corpses.

"Why?" Oliver asked.

"Because the time may come when you really do find yourself all alone and get jumped by a much larger group of rotters."

"She would know," Wilson said. "She's the queen of opening Pandora's Box on herself."

Taryn elbowed Wilson in the ribs. Regarding Oliver, she said, "I'm happy you're still with us and all … it's just that I'm afraid I may have just prolonged the inevitable."

Daymon approached Oliver. He towered over the man by nearly a head's height. "Everything Taryn just said is on point. You were going to go to guns right away. That would have drawn more rotters to us. Heaven forbid there's a horde of any size nearby."

Nodding in agreement, Lev said, "You still have a lot to learn and very little time in which to do so. No telling when the horde will be back."

Coming off the adrenaline high, Oliver was blindsided by a wave of exhaustion the likes of which he had never felt before. As a result, he nearly lost his legs and leaned hard against the Chevy, his bodyweight making the door panel pop inward. Fully expecting Daymon to react to the affront on his rig, he shoved off the pickup and began to apologize.

"Don't worry about it," Daymon said with a dismissive wave. "I stole it … remember?"

Everyone, save for Oliver, looked quizzically at the dreadlocked man.

"Long story best told around a campfire," said Daymon. "Saddle up. I want to see this place where Taryn almost bought the farm."

Chapter 16

Duncan's frame nearly filled up the security pod. He brushed the hanging bulb aside and retrieved a slim black Thuraya satellite phone from the shelf littered with spare long range CBs and multi-channel two-way radios recently supplied to the group by one of Dregan's faithful scavengers. He thumbed the Power button and saw the little screen flare to life. It was bright in the dim environs. Nearly more so than the sixty-watt bulb dangling between him and Brook.

"When did Nash say I should call the Judge?" he asked, leaning sideways and looking down to meet her gaze.

"Initially she wanted it placed fifteen minutes after Cade's ride launched. Then she mumbled something about letting "reality sink in" and changed it to forty-five minutes." She consulted her watch and regained eye contact. "And that's about where we're at. Apparently whatever she had in mind has sufficiently sunk in. Might as well get it over with." She tapped the legal pad on the plywood sheet serving as a desktop.

"What do I say?" he asked, scooping up the pad and adjusting his newly acquired aviator-style glasses.

"Nash was pretty cryptic in her message. Why don't you just wing it? You're fairly adept at that."

Duncan sighed and directed his gaze to Heidi, who had been sitting quietly and intently eyeing the verbal ping pong match. He began to punch in the digits and paused after the area code. "You sure you don't want to do it? You handled the Dregan guy like a pro litigator. Said all the right things that needed to be said. You know … *just the facts, ma'am.*"

Brook said nothing. Just shook her head and shot a questioning look at Heidi.

Heidi shrugged and settled an equally quizzical gaze on Duncan.

"Joe Friday. You ladies never heard of him? Just the facts …"

"Put the call through," Brook insisted.

"I thought Nash said the person in charge here should place the call."

"Exactly." Brook's hands settled on her hips. Her eyes narrowed to slits.

"That scowl worked on Dregan," he said, looking down at the pad. "And damn it to hell it's working on me." Without further pause, he tapped out the remaining digits and put the phone to his ear. There was a hiss as the sat-phone searched for a high-orbiting military satellite to shake hands with. A tick later there were a couple of audible clicks and the electronic trill was assaulting his ear.

While Heidi and Brook looked on expectantly, Tran and Foley showed up from outside and filled up the front entry anteroom.

"We've got a full house," Duncan mouthed. He was getting hot standing near the hanging bulb and had started to sweat.

After eight rings a man identifying himself as Judge Pomeroy answered. And just as Duncan had already imagined, the Judge sounded aristocratic in his tone and delivery.

"Charlie Hammond, that's who," Duncan lied, walking his eyes over the others until settling back on Brook and shrugging at his use of a fake name. Inside his guts were churning at the sound of the name that had rolled off his lips. It was a name he hadn't uttered since the first days of the zombie apocalypse. The name of a friend whom he had lost to a freak accident on a deserted street in outer southeast Portland, Oregon, but hadn't actually died until an hour later when he put a Colt Model 1911 in his mouth and pulled the trigger. Why he had blurted out that name, he hadn't a clue. But he had to live with it and improvise, because the Judge had demanded to know who had so rudely interrupted him and there was no way to reel it in now.

"I'm Central Intelligence Agency," he said. Another lie. "I report directly to President Valerie Clay … your boss, in a roundabout way." He went quiet and glanced at Foley and Tran, who were both doing the puzzled-dog-look head-cocked-to-one-side thing.

Ball's in your court.

After a long uncomfortable silence, the tinny sound of a voice talking rapid-fire emanated from the Thuraya's earpiece.

"I know the helicopter has already left your airspace. But do know that we still have satellites at our disposal. We *will* be watching. And Judge, you so much as argue with the man about whom he deputizes … or give him grief for commandeering one of your bailiffs for guard duty, we'll be back with a dozen black helicopters and a company of Army Rangers. Things will get sorted. Are we clear?"

There were a few seconds of silence followed by the same Alvin the Chipmunk voice coming from the phone.

Duncan ended the call and took a deep breath. "I told so many lies in that one conversation, I'm sure I'm going to hell."

"As if we all aren't already," Heidi quipped.

Moving aside to let Tran and Foley by, Brook asked, "Well … what did his Honor have to say?"

"Nothing after I announced who I was. It was so quiet on his end I bet you could've heard a mouse pissin' on cotton if you were in the room with him."

Brook's eyebrows arched.

A soft chuckle escaped Foley's mouth. "I'm stealing that one," he stated, sounding extremely unapologetic.

Duncan nodded. "Then the Judge said his men were freaked out because the helo that picked up Cade did a couple of low and slow racetrack orbits over his fiefdom. That's when I hinted that there were more black helicopters where that one came from."

"And his reaction?" Brook asked.

"Priceless," Duncan answered, resisting the urge to cackle. "He started to stammer. Not just a one- or two-syllable trip of the tongue. No … old Judge Pomeroy was doing the Porky Pig motorboat routine. I'm sure the phone's mouthpiece was getting a spit bath. And he continued to do so every time he tried to speak after I delivered the threat. I bet if he wasn't planning on it … he soon will be in *full* compliance." Duncan smiled, obviously pleased with his improvisational performance.

Brook grimaced and began to massage her shoulder, kneading the scar tissue through her Army tee shirt. Composing herself, she rolled her shoulder, stretching the muscles there and said, "Don't collect your Oscar just yet, Duncan. Now you have to call Dregan."

North Woodruff

The short drive north to East 100 Street was uneventful. Along the way, the three-vehicle convoy passed by the larger fix-it shop which had suffered major damage due to the migrating horde. The hedges bordering the walk parallel to Main Street had been trampled and were brown and long dead. The rollup doors fronting the building were battered and bowed inward, the porthole-style windows devoid of all but the smallest shards of glass. A handful of older model cars in various stages of disrepair had been displaced from the lined parking spots by the moving crush of dead and now rested sidelong across the garage bay doors.

Across the street from the fix-it place, both the telephone poles lining the street and a once regal Cadillac sedan had failed to escape the wrath of the unstoppable biomass. The former—for as far as the eye could see—had been forced away from the road at crazy angles. Some of the power poles had come to rest against the upper branches of trees lining the road, their multiple black lines inexorably intertwined with the upper boughs. A pair of poles near the end of town were canted so much so that their upper T bars had skewered one building's entire run of second-story windows.

Daymon wheeled the Chevy onto the lot first, leaving it broadside with the body shop and Oliver staring at the closed front door from the passenger seat. Taryn pulled the Raptor in next, careful to leave it pointed at the curb cut west of the lot. And as if there wasn't enough American iron taking up space on the body and frame shop's lot, Lev parked the F-650 beside the Raptor with the sidewalk running under the rig lengthwise and its oversized driver's side tires resting partially on the street.

All three engines cut out near simultaneously and the six-person foraging party plus dog emerged from their respective vehicles. Doors thunked closed and the group made their way to the closed door in pairs, Max growling low, hackles standing to attention.

Less than ten minutes after rejoining the others at the post office, Daymon found himself standing in front of the body shop door with the rest of the group forming a rough semicircle off his right shoulder.

"You sure everything inside is *all the way* dead?" he asked Taryn.

She said, "As dead as a few nine-millimeter slugs'll get them."

Daymon kicked a spent shell, sending it skittering away into the parking lot. He flashed a wan smile and withdrew Kindness from her scabbard. He stepped back a foot or so and, holding the machete blade vertical to the door, tapped the garish-hued handle against the brushed-nickel doorknob.

No sound came from within the building.

"Looks like they didn't come back and rearm the trap," Wilson said, trying to lighten the mood and failing horribly at it.

"Not funny," Taryn said, shooting him a look that could only be interpreted as: *You're sleeping alone tonight, buddy boy.* Then she looked at Daymon and nodded an affirmative. "All three are shot in the head dead."

Brandishing Kindness one-handed, Daymon grasped the knob. "Well, here goes nothing then," he said, giving it a solid tug.

Nothing rushed him. The trio of cadavers were sprawled just inside the door where they'd fallen. Even truly dead, the sight of them all trussed up and what it all meant sent a chill tracing his spine. He peered into the gloom and saw that the shelves in the front retail area were mostly stripped clean. Only items useful for minor at-home body repair remained. Which made sense to Daymon. No reason to Bondo a dinged fender with the pickings for a new vehicle so plentiful.

Returning his attention to the three dead bodies, he shuffled by the nearest and went to one knee, careful to avoid the pooling fluids. He probed the areas of their necks where some kind of organs had been removed, then focused his attention on the cables affixed to their ankles. Whoever had prepared them had probably spent some time in the military or a trade where being thorough and precise was expected. There was no way these bonds were coming loose without help from the living.

He shuddered again at the thought of being in the rotter's place. Had Taryn and Wilson not come along when they had, the former humans may have remained inside until they eventually rotted away to nothing. Hell on Earth until the bitter end as muscle, sinew and, eventually, the brain putrefied inside the skull. At least that was what he was pinning his hopes on. For if these things never decayed to the point that they stopped roaming, convincing Heidi to move from Eden to his secret place was little more than a pipe dream.

"You thinking what I'm thinking?" asked Lev.

Daymon grabbed the counter on his right and rose, his boots slipping on the fluids and shredded papers scattered underfoot. Standing by the counter, his face in the shadows, he met Oliver's gaze then went face to face until finally locking eyes with Lev. "I'm not so sure that silencing these things was the only motive for removing everything inside of there that they did. I didn't pay attention during Biology 101, but I'm pretty sure that all they had to do to silence them was saw through their vocal cords."

Taryn asked, "What *was* their motive then?"

Singling out Taryn and Wilson, he said, "Do you two remember hearing Cade and Brook mention a bunch of civilians back at Schriever being infected on purpose?"

"There was an outbreak inside the wire while we were there," Wilson recalled. "Something about a terrorist injecting them with Omega-tainted saliva—"

"Ah," Taryn interrupted. "I overheard Annie or Brook … not sure which one of them … talking about the saliva being milked from glands harvested from the dead."

"Bingo," Daymon said, sliding Kindness back into her sheath.

Lev rested a hand on his pistol. "So what does it all mean?"

Daymon edged past the others without commenting and urged them to follow. Once he reached the street beyond the parking lot and sidewalk, he gazed westward at the pair of zombies that hadn't been there a couple of minutes ago. Lured from wherever they had been lurking when the noisy vehicles returned, they were now trudging their way toward the body shop in the slow arm-swinging shuffle indicative of first turns. Beyond the ratty road-worn pair of Zs was a long country block with static cars edged up to the curb and trash strewn about the sidewalks and single-lane drive. On the far corner of the block stood a single-level ranch-style home, its lot overgrown with weeds and grass. And backstopping the entire apocalyptic scene was a continuous left-to-right run of low rolling mounds of scrub- and pine-covered red dirt. Though far from mountains, the wave-looking geological features deposited there by ancient glacial movement still mostly obscured the verdant Wasatch-Cache National Forest from view.

"The attack at Schriever?" Lev prompted.

After turning a one-eighty and peering down the street for a long three-count, Daymon pointed to a whitewashed church and two-story house sharing the fenced-in lot due east of it. Regarding the others, he said, “Let’s go on a little hike and I’ll tell you what I know.”

Chapter 17

A handful of minutes after the Stealth Chinook pulled out of the slow menacing orbit over Bear River, Cade knew there was no way Colorado Springs was its next destination. For one thing, the sun remained in relatively the same position as it had been since the first course correction that saw them follow 16 and ultimately arrive over the small town. Albeit sitting a little higher in the sky, the sun was still parked off the helo's port side at roughly eleven o' clock to the nose and barely showing through the veil of high clouds. That they were heading mostly south now versus southeast was a given. That the Rangers and crew chief didn't seem concerned they weren't tracking on more of an easterly heading led Cade to believe the waypoints had been set in long ago and the place they'd ultimately be landing was familiar to everyone aboard.

***

Now, forty-five minutes later, the helo, call sign Nomad One-One, a nugget of info Cade had gleaned from eavesdropping on the pilot's chatter, was bleeding both altitude and airspeed.

Even as the ground rushed by outside the window at a dizzying clip, the rotor noise and turbine whine seemed to have diminished. On the sage-dotted tan and ochre desert floor, cacti, tumbleweeds, and scattered islands of upthrust, snow-crusted red rock blipped by. Now and again on a distant road paralleling their flight path, the sun glinting off dusty chrome and glass would draw Cade's attention to colorful knots of stalled-out cars. Some were small caravans piled high with worldly goods and most likely had been stranded due to mechanical failure or lack of fuel. Others were victims to major pileups, the vehicles involved forever locked in embraces of twisted metal or burned to shells where they had come to rest. With first responders suffering the brunt of the casualties those first hours of the outbreak, it came as no surprise to Cade that nobody had come with tanker trucks full of water and brandishing jaws of life to extricate the victims—some of which still sat inside, dim silhouettes thrashing around in reaction to the passing helo.

Cade had been transfixed on the scenery outside his window and was caught completely unaware when the bottom suddenly fell out from under him. One second there was gravity pressing him into his fold-down seat. In the next—having just learned the hard way that the desert floor was actually the top of a red rock mesa—he found himself momentarily weightless with the horizon outside seeming to rear up as the helicopter dove over the unseen precipice.

Collecting his stomach from his throat, Cade swallowed hard and swept his gaze around the cabin just as the helo leveled and turned hard to starboard. Unlike the sudden drop, the turn came as one fluid motion that had the crew chief and everyone aboard pressed hard into their seats.

"Gonna puke?" mouthed Spielman.

Cade didn't afford him the satisfaction of an answer. No way he was earning a *puker* patch today. If Ari throwing him around in the Ghost Hawk hadn't earned him one, there was nothing the Night Stalker pilot at the controls of this exotic craft could do to make him succumb.

After wiping the bead of sweat from his upper lip, Cade craned around and resumed watching the dead world blip by. A tick later the pilot said, "Bastion Actual, Nomad One-One … how copy?"

Bastion replied at once. "Good copy, Nomad. Bastion Actual requesting a SITREP."

"Bastion Actual, we are conducting a standoff flyby of GJR and will continue west. Incoming with two KIA. Clear us a spot at the table."

Simultaneously, there was silence in Cade's flight helmet and off the port side a small city he recognized came into view. Just like he remembered it from before: whole neighborhoods on its periphery were completely razed by fire. Grand Junction Regional—a place both he and Taryn knew all too well—sat silent and somber off the craft's nose. On the near side of the medium-sized airport, throngs of zombies—just clusters of small black dots from this distance—patrolled the runways and tarmacs with impunity.

A different voice sounded in Cade's helmet: "*I'm picking up zero heat signatures.*" Cade assumed it to be the co-pilot in the left-hand seat operating an infrared camera and relaying his observation to the pilot in the right-hand seat. And he had a good idea why the low-level flight was necessary, even this close to a United States military outpost. Though the Chinese Special Forces scouts he had come across in Huntsville had been infected, it wasn't outside of the realm of possibility that there were more of them out there who may be armed with FN-6 MANPADs (Man Portable Air-Defense Systems), China's newest lightweight shoulder-fired surface-to-air missiles. Similar to the U.S.-supplied Stinger missiles the Afghani Mujahedeen employed against Russia's heavily armored MI-24 Hind helicopters with such ruthless efficiency, the FN-6 packed more than enough punch to knock down this bird. So if low-level-flight and the occasional stomach-churning maneuver associated with it was deemed necessary to stave off even the most remote possibility of facing one of the lethal weapons, Cade was all for it.

"*Copy that,*" came the reply in Cade's headset from some soldier in charge back at Forward Operating Base Bastion. The voice was gravelly and accented, therefore not his old friend and mentor Greg Beeson, who last he heard was still in charge of the lonely outpost.

Minutes after giving Grand Junction Regional the promised flyby, Nomad One-One overflew the small unincorporated town of Loma and continued on a die-straight westerly heading that saw the dead towns of Loma, Fruita, and Mack, Colorado slide by underneath the helo.

Nearly straddling the border with Utah and a short drive from FOB Bastion, Mack was where he and the Kids had liberated the Ford Raptor from the vehicle lift inside the 4x4 shop. Mack was also where Cade had come across the two-story Craftsman so closely resembling his childhood home back in Portland. The long dormant memories that brief in and out had dredged up had stuck with him for some time. And though from where he sat he couldn't pick out the particular house that had momentarily transported him back to a time before all of this madness had begun, he knew the place was down there somewhere, just as he had left it: quiet, dark, and longing for the family whose uneaten breakfast still sat forlornly on the table nestled in the little eating nook.

With the melancholy from revisiting that day still wending its way through his head and heart, FOB Bastion—formerly Mack Mesa Municipal Airport—was creeping into view at the forward edge of his small window.

No longer a lonely and hastily thrown together outpost, Bastion's south side had swallowed up untold acres of flat land and now bordered Interstate 70, the four-lane running east all the way to Colorado, Springs and west all the way to Cove Fort, Utah.

Seeing the surprise in Cade's narrowed eyes, or perhaps having seen countless other returnees gape at the changes, Sergeant Spielman said, "She's come a long way, hasn't she."

Cade looked the length of the helo, nodded, and flashed a quick thumbs-up.

The crew chief was right. Once a postage-stamp-parcel of land—by airport standards—Bastion now rivaled GJR in both size and complexity. Judging by the aircraft and support vehicles scattered about the base periphery, the place probably had the ability to sustain round-the-clock combat operations if needs be.

The Rangers' body language told Cade they'd already been-there and done that where FOB Bastion was concerned. The ones who were still awake remained stoic—holding that thousand-yard stare Cade was all too familiar with on whatever they'd been looking at when Spielman offered up his inane observation. *Small talk.* Cade despised it, for the most part. There was a time and place, but not here with two dead Rangers lying on the cabin floor.

Still, to a man, the Ranger chalk didn't seem fazed.

So Cade saw no reason to share his bitter feelings about the matter with the SOAR load master. Which was a good thing. Because the unease over being kept in the dark by Nash was beginning to push at the edges of the vacuum in his mind where he kept all of those type of emotions bottled up. And the second that seal got breached, the offending party was going to wish they hadn't gone there.

The helo suddenly popped over a stand of trees and buzzed a football-field-sized grave containing thousands of grotesquely twisted corpses.

Cade crossed himself and returned his gaze to the looming base. The closer the helicopter got, the taller the fence surrounding Bastion seemed. Might have been the extra rolls of razor wire added to the top that gave the illusion, but Cade couldn't be certain. One other thing that stood out starkly since he'd been here last was the addition of a half-dozen *real* guard towers. The sturdy twenty-foot-tall items had taken the place of the sheet-plywood and two-by-four treehouse-gone-wrong-looking jobs that Beeson's boys had thrown up in haste around the tiny airstrip those first days.

To be honest, the place now had the look and feel of some of the more secure FOBs Cade had had the displeasure of passing time in during his multiple stints in the Sandbox.

In his ear, Cade heard the same gravelly voice give directions on where to land to the SOAR pilots up front.

In response, Nomad One-One swung around the east entrance, overflew the interstate and entered the base airspace from the south, low and slow. Splitting the two perimeter guard towers like a goalpost, the helo's flat underbelly cleared the top roll of razor wire, flared, and Cade heard the muted sounds of something mechanical at work underfoot. Next there was a series of *thunks* immediately followed by a slight ripple through the cabin floor as the bird's tricycle-style landing gear locked into place. Then, running strangely quiet, the helo covered the next hundred yards to the designated landing pad at a slow, level crawl barely a dozen feet off the cement apron.

This kind of approach was far different from how Ari would have brought them in. However, Cade had a feeling the sudden reduction in airspeed was to keep the craft's rotor wash from sandblasting the contingent of soldiers he knew must be waiting for them. And he concluded after mulling it over for half a beat, the sudden halving of the engine and rotor noise was a direct result of the bigger helo sharing the same blade design and turbine exhaust routing technologies as the smaller Ghost Hawk.

Fifty yards from the flight line, the ochre, dust-covered ground gave way to black asphalt marked by painted symbols and numbers whose meaning only an aviator could fully grasp.

Then the pilot changed course starboard a few degrees and the welcoming party Cade had imagined came into view outside his window. Standing shoulder-to-shoulder to an Army chaplain and just beyond the reach of the wind-whipped haze was his old friend and commander of FOB Bastion, Major Greg Beeson. Both men wore Army-issue MultiCam fatigues, the only difference being that the man of the cloth actually had the sacred cloth draping his shoulders. Beeson had one hand clamped down on his cover, while the chaplain wore nothing on his bald head, but both of his hands were currently employed at keeping the camouflage stole from whipping his face.

Behind and to the right of the major and chaplain was a group of soldiers clad in the same fatigues and also standing at attention, no doubt an honor detail hastily assembled for the morbid task of whisking the fallen Rangers from the arriving bird to receive their last rights and then a proper burial.

Just as the helicopter settled softly on its gear atop a bright yellow circle and rolled forward a couple of yards, Cade picked out a particular shape sitting amongst the lined-up helicopters behind the welcoming party. It was angular and black and seemed to devour the sun's rays rather than reflect them.

Simultaneously the hulking craft he was in came to a complete halt and the turbines spooled down, rendering the rotor blades whisper-quiet. A tick later, getting the attention of all aboard, a hydraulic hiss filled the cabin and the rear ramp parted from the airframe, letting in a wide bar of white sunlight and a gut-churning blast of heated air tinged with kerosene and the sickly-sweet stench of rotting bodies.

Cade waited for the honor guard to come aboard. Once the flag-draped bodies were removed from the cabin floor, the rest of the Rangers, who to a man were moving like the walking dead, filed out into the light with hands clutching weapons and full rucksacks weighting them down.

The last man in the procession, a blond staff sergeant with a bull neck and a wide angular face, stopped for a tick and regarded the man in black.

Lips set into a thin line, Cade merely held the man's gaze. He'd been there before and most certainly would be sometime in the coming days. There were no words he could offer the Ranger that would help the man reconcile whatever he had recently gone through, so he remained silent and seated.

The crew chief came forward with Cade's duffle bag and dropped it on the seat next to him.

After what amounted to a two-second staring contest, the Ranger shuffled off into the square of light and disappeared from view.

The crew chief followed the Ranger aft and returned with Cade's ruck and weapon. Placing the gear on the seat, he asked, "What's in the jock bag?"

Cade said nothing. He had hoped to keep anybody from seeing what Daymon had gone out of his way to procure for him.

"Understood," Spielman intoned. "Beeson knows you're here, but won't be able to receive you. Your ride is hot. She's number four down the flight line."

Go directly to Springs, Cade thought. *Do not pass Go, do not collect $200*. In reality, all he wanted from his old friend and mentor was to be able to pick the man's brain. Find out how far inland the foreign invaders had come. Any little piece of intel he could forward on to Eden would have been better than none. But that was a moot point now, because the second the crew chief had passed along the little nugget of bad news, he remembered he didn't have a sat-phone on his person in the first place.

Chapter 18

Although the angular black craft had projected the same sense of menace as the old MI-24 Hind attack helicopters Alexander Dregan was most familiar with, he hadn't the slightest clue as to what make or model the helicopter was that had paid Bear River a wholly unexpected visit forty-five minutes ago. However, he was aware that anybody who had been watching the craft as it lumbered overhead—in this case the town's entire population along with several dozen equally interested zombies lurking just outside the walls—would have had to have been blind to have not seen the low-speed, low-altitude orbits for exactly what they were. Someone was sending the denizens of Bear River a message in a very real and in-your-face way. And judging by the muted gray markings on the craft's upswept tail, that someone had the ear of the United States Army. That the landing gear remained inside the craft's fuselage told him whoever was sending the message had no intention of landing on Main Street and delivering it via uniformed emissary.

Seeing the multi-barrel miniguns protruding from both sides of the craft during the entire three-minute show of force had added some extra emphasis to the message. It was as if the business end of a rifle was being trained on each and every person looking skyward.

You've been warned, Judge Pomeroy, Dregan had thought at the time. Now he was wondering why in the hell the effusive former Salt Lake City judge hadn't come calling to discuss the aerial intrusion. Surely he wasn't tired of micromanaging every bit of minutiae of day-to-day survival as he'd been wont to do since his admission to Bear River a few short weeks ago.

All of Dregan's wondering ceased the second the satellite phone in his jacket pocket emitted its shrill electronic peal. There was no way the helicopter flyby and this out-of-the-blue call from his new friends to the west—the only number he'd sought fit to program into the phone—could *not* be connected. So he fished the slim black device from a pocket without bothering to squint and try to read the small words on the illuminated screen and thumbed the green Talk key.

"Hello," he said, more guttural grunt than spoken word.

"Dregan?"

He recognized the voice on the other end. Like his, it had a unique inflection. But instead of sharing his Slavic accent, this man named Duncan spoke with a pronounced Southern drawl.

"Da," he said. Then quickly correcting himself, added, "Yes ... this is Dregan."

"Duncan here. I bet you're wondering who was responsible for springing the surprise airshow on y'all."

"I *know* who was responsible," Dregan answered. "The helicopter had U.S. Army markings. If I had to guess, I'd say it belonged to the 160th SOAR."

"Well I'll be dipped in shit," Duncan said. "You an aviator, Dregan?"

Though he wasn't a pilot, Dregan sidestepped the question. "Before all of this I liked to watch the History Channel. Back when it actually ran programs having to do with *history*. Not shows about hunting antiques or digging gold mines."

Duncan said, "Me too. Sure miss the ol' boob tube. Anyway ... that was—"

"—a message for the Judge," Dregan finished. "And almost an hour later the nosy pig has yet to come over and sniff for truffles." He looked out over the backyard and saw his boy, Peter, toying with the blue tarps covering the military vehicles parked underneath the fir tree dwarfing the nearby run of cement freeway barriers.

"If he does," Duncan said, drawing the words out, "give him that phone of yours and tell him to call the number stored under 2 in the speed dial."

After a moment of silence, Dregan said, "There is only one number stored in this phone."

"In a second there will be two." There was a rustling of paper on the other end. "Ya there?"

"Yes."

"You have something to write with?"

"One moment."

Roughly thirty miles away, Duncan heard Dregan put the handset down. Muffled by distance, he heard what sounded like drawers being opened and then soft cursing filtered over the connection. A few seconds ensued and there was a prolonged bout of coughing. It was loud and phlegm-addled. Someone hawked and spit and then the accented voice was back. "Go on."

After rattling off a string of numbers that began with a Colorado area code, Duncan said, "Program that into your phone. If the Judge comes to you with his panties in a wad, don't say a thing. Just power that bad boy on, find that number on speed dial, and give the old boy the handset."

"Then what? Who will be on the other end?"

"Just sit back and watch hilarity ensue as our robed friend gets taken down a peg or two."

There was another prolonged coughing fit on Dregan's end. Finally he asked, "By whom?" The question was followed by a steady wheezing.

"The President herself," Duncan answered, a happy tone to his voice.

Stunned silence on the other end.

"You okay, friend?"

"No. I am not," Dregan conceded flatly.

"Take your time and compose yourself. Because as farfetched as it sounds … I'm not blowing smoke up your ass."

After a few wet, laughter-infused rasps, Dregan said, "The cancer isn't down there. I suspect it is in the lungs."

Grimacing at his choice of words, and not sure what to say after the sudden revelation, Duncan simply changed the subject. As if the big "C" had never been broached, he said, "Cade has the President's ear. You did the right thing the other day. And since then everything we've seen leads us … and in a roundabout way, President Clay, to believe Bear River would be better served as it was founded—with you running the show and men whom you appoint handling security. So long as you leave interpreting the rule of law as it is in the books to the Judge, everything should run smoothly. At least as smooth as a damn near frontier town can considering the circumstances."

"When he gets over the bug that's going around here, I'll deputize my boy, Greg. We have no doctors or medicine strong enough to beat back what's going around, let alone what I have. Eventually I will succumb to this." He swallowed hard. "Gregory will carry on for me."

Seeing as how Gregory was the son who had been bitten and consequently saved by Raven's dose of antiserum, Duncan didn't think it kosher to ask for particulars concerning the *bug.*

After a short silence, Dregan added, "We'll be fair, as always."

"That's what Cade figured you'd say. He's a pretty good judge of character."

"Judge," Dregan said and began laughing. "I shall do my best."

Duncan cackled at his unintentional funny. Once he'd composed himself, he said, "Call us if you need *anything.*"

"Your people saved my boy's life. You may call us if *you* need anything."

What we have here is a regular old lovefest, thought Duncan as he agreed to agree with the man. Knowing full well that there was nothing anyone could do to combat the big "C," even considering the combined six decades of nursing know-how sitting on folding chairs in the nearby clearing, he simply said, "Take care of yourself."

"Da," Dregan answered, and the line went dead.

"Everyone is off the hook," Duncan called out. "The dreaded call has been made."

"Get off your pity pot and get over here," Glenda ordered. "I've got a crick in my neck from you spooning with me all night."

Seeing as how Raven had already set the precedent, her small hands kneading the hardened scar tissue between her mom's shoulders, there was nothing Duncan could do or say to shirk the duty. So, putting his game face on, he stuck his tongue out at a smirking Raven, made a show of cracking his knuckles and, under the watchful gaze of Foley, Seth, and Tran, trudged grudgingly, hand in hand with Glenda, toward the coveted patch of sunny ground in the center of the clearing.

Chapter 19

The watcher was still hunched over and carving on the sill when the growly white pickup truck returned. When she looked up she saw that it was trailing two similar vehicles, both painted black as night. Blood still weeping from the wounds on her hand, she set the knife aside and began to suck hungrily at her fingers. Craning her head fully to the right, she pressed her cheek to the glass and tracked the convoy with her eyes, watching intently as all three vehicles turned left off of 100 and wheeled onto the body shop parking lot. Eyes narrowing, she muttered something unintelligible as the pickups came to a halt parked three abreast, the largest among them on the left and rudely blocking the sidewalk. Then she noted how they were arranged color-wise, the two black trucks bookending the white. *Like turkey and Swiss on rye. Or better yet,* she thought, her stomach growling loudly, *a Double Stuff Oreo cookie.* Of which she sometimes still dreamed, and was forbidden from consuming. In fact, *all* sweets and junk food were off limits to everyone but Adrian, who apparently needed them for the arcane rituals that kept the Purged at bay.

Mother liked rituals.

And sacrifices.

She smiled and breathed deeply. In her head was Mother's gruff voice again: *We all make sacrifices. All for One. One for All.*

The truck's doors opened wide and out spilled four men and three women. A mix of old and young. One black and five Caucasians.

The watcher was still milking the cuts on her hand of salty goodness when the brindle-colored dog emerged from the big black truck.

A thick rope of drool, pink with blood and wholly unexpected, sluiced from the corner of her mouth. She wiped her lips dry with the back of her hand as she watched the looters follow the dog up to the closed door. The dog sat while the looters conferred.

She scooped up her radio and powered it on. Once the initial burst of white noise had subsided, she clicked the Talk key twice and waited.

The wait was short.

"Yes," came the all-too-familiar voice.

The watcher depressed the Talk key. "They're back," she reported.

A one-word order was delivered by the person on the other end. Same strained rasping voice: *Observe.* Then, every bit abrupt as the delivery, the connection cut out.

She lowered the volume and shoved the radio into her vest pocket. Eyes never leaving the dog, she shrugged on a ratty canvas daypack, and without warning her salivary glands kicked into overdrive and her mouth began to fill again.

So she spat in a corner and focused her attention solely on the looters, who were still in a huddle and conversing animatedly, seemingly oblivious to the pair of Purged shuffling their way.

After a moment's contemplation, during which the younger girl and the redhead man both seemed to be arguing with the dreadlocked man, the latter of the three turned around and banged on the shop door with a green-handled machete.

Good luck with that, dummy, the watcher thought, drying her lips on her shirt sleeve. *The kids already released them … forever.* Suddenly, causing her to start visibly, the watcher's stomach emitted a low, wet rumble that went on for a couple of seconds. Oh how she wanted something to eat. *Anything. Hell,* she thought, embarrassed the nasty habit hadn't died with the Purge, *a cigarette always numbs the hunger.*

So she rattled the last bent Marlboro from the pack, which she wadded up and chucked across the room. When she looked back down the street, the body shop door was wide open and the dreadlocked man was squatting and inspecting the dead things Ratchet had left tethered together inside the shop.

Consider it a warning, Ratchet had muttered as she cleared the stoop of snow so that the door would swing wide enough to allow the inert, cold-affected bodies passage. *Like marking our territory,* she had added with a mirthless grin as she had gone about doing whatever it was that she did to them prior to setting their leashes and shutting them inside.

The watcher had been real proud of herself that day. The old her would have been begging for details. Nagging Ratchet until she snapped and hit her. It had been that way with her biological dad and grandpa and seemingly every boyfriend she ever had up until Pocatello fell and the ones who hadn't fled the city became affected by the Purge and came back meaner than ever.

Nope.

Nosiree … she hadn't even thought to ask Ratchet what she used the scalpels and bone saws and bolt cutters for. Details now were none of her concern. As the title implied, Watchers were supposed to be seen and not heard. Get out of the way and observe. Whenever Mother repeated that mantra, the watcher heard her grandad's voice: *You make a better door than a window, Iris.* It was *his* mantra whenever she stood too close to the old console television, blocking his view of the Lawrence Welk Show or Hee Haw or Live from the Grand Ole Opry.

One day, thought Iris, blocking out the memories of the abuse she had suffered during the previous five decades she now referred to as her *old life*, I *will* be trusted to *do.*

Again Mother's harsh voice echoed from deep inside Iris's brain where only she could hear. *Do unto others as they would do unto you*, it reminded.

When the looters had finally tired of inspecting the fallen Purged, they shoved the bodies back into the gloom, closed the door, and then made their way to the road with the Shepherd in tow and sniffing the air and ground all around. They stopped dead-center in the middle of the road in a loose knot. After half a beat, Iris saw the dreadlocked man step away from the others and stare westward, down the length of the road. Then he spun a slow one-eighty and rejoined the group, where he immediately pointed up the road, seemingly straight at the window her face was mashed against.

She drew back from the light spill and swallowed hard. "No way he could have spotted me up here," she told herself.

She put her sliced fingers in her mouth and admired her handiwork for a beat.

ADRIAN.

The N is perfect.

She was done.

When she eased forward and peered out the window, the group was a block and a half west of her position and marching up the sidewalk. Head craned to the left, the dreadlocked man was walking and pointing. Was he still focusing on her window? Or was he eyeing the church? From Iris's vantage, she couldn't tell. However, the dog was a more immediate threat. It was running free, ears perked and stub tail wagging furiously. Ranging a few yards ahead of the looters, it would stop periodically to sniff the tires of the cars edged up against the far curb before knifing off through the grass growing window-high beside them.

Now marching beside the dreadlocked man was a tanned thirty-something. He was clad head-to-toe in camouflage consisting mostly of dark greens and browns and patterned like trees. The two brunette women walking in the center of the group were also swathed in camouflage. The older wore the same dark woodland theme as the man to her fore, while the tanned and tattooed woman's garb sported a much tighter pattern made up of lighter shades of tan and green.

Bringing up the rear of the slow-moving cluster was a slim, younger man whose shock of red hair seemed to be trying to escape from under his rumpled, floppy-brimmed camouflage hat. And walking in the redhead's shadow was a shorter, balding man. He moved like a cat in the company of feral dogs, pensive, eyes darting and head constantly moving, as if on a swivel.

Suddenly the group stopped at the bottom of the church steps. *Go. Do it*, Iris thought, envisioning herself setting a trap of her own one day. A smile creased her face at the mere thought of graduating from *Watcher* to *Doer.*

Then her imaginary house of cards came tumbling down.

Chapter 20
Forward Operating Base Bastion
Mack, Colorado

As soon as Cade heard the words, "*Your ride is hot. She's number four down the flight line*" roll off the crew chief's tongue, he had shouldered his ruck and weapon and hustled past the Rangers and base personnel assembled in the receiving line, the so-called *jock bag* banging against his hip. In passing he had caught Beeson's eye and acknowledged the slight nod from the commander with one of his own. With a slight limp evident in his gait, Cade hustled past a pair of Little Bird helicopters and an MH-60 Black Hawk, all undergoing inspection by their respective aircrew.

Once he reached the outer edge of the Ghost Hawk's rotor wash, he put a hand atop his tactical bump helmet and, ignoring the dangling straps and buckles whipping against his throat, ducked and trudged headlong into the black craft's buffeting down-blast. Barely five feet from his waiting ride and squinting hard against the fine grit being thrown about by its wildly spinning rotor blades, Cade saw the co-pilot flashing him a thumbs-up and a wide grin. The hulking form behind the welcoming gesture was the same African-American aviator who had co-piloted the craft during the Los Angeles mission some three and a half weeks prior. Before he'd had a chance to return the man's greeting, the port side door slid open and a second man he recognized from the same mission leaped to the tarmac. In the next beat Cade was being relieved of his rifle and gym bag by the SOAR crew chief and a glove-clad hand of one of the customers inside the helo gripped his and hauled him inside.

As Cade strapped into a port-side seat aft of the crew chief/door gunner whose nametape read *Skipper*, a sleek black flight helmet was thrust into his lap by his old friend Captain Javier "Lowrider" Lopez.

"Plug it in," mouthed the stocky, Hispanic Delta Force shooter, pointing to his own helmet and then a nearby jack as if that might somehow expedite Cade's compliance.

Cade reached over his shoulder and plugged in. As he swung back to face Lopez, he took inventory of the craft's occupants. Up front in the right-hand seat, visor sparkling with sun glint, was Ari Silver, an exceptional SOAR aviator and obviously the commander of Jedi One-One — assuming that was the name the higher-ups had assigned the ship for this particular mission.

Already strapped in across the aisle from Cade was President Valerie Clay's former head of security, Adam Cross. With his blond locks, blue eyes, and clean-shaven face, he looked more Malibu surfer boy than the tough-as-nails former Navy SEAL that he was. Cade's nod was greeted by a smile that exposed a picket of unnaturally white teeth.

Adjusting his well-worn blue ball cap, *McP's Irish Pub* emblazoned on it in gold stitching, Cross said, "Captain Grayson, Delta operator emeritus. How's it hanging, brother?"

Cade flashed a thumbs-up. "Still inhabiting the correct side of the dirt—"

"And possessing a heartbeat and respiration," finished Ari, his voice able to be heard in everyone's headsets via the shipwide comms.

Cade cracked a smile. "Jedi driver Ari Silver," he said. "Thought that was you up there punching buttons and pulling levers."

"Welcome aboard, Wyatt," said the heavily muscled African-American chief warrant officer in the left-seat, a smile blooming below the lowered visor.

"Pleasure's all mine, Haynes," Cade answered. "Do I have a couple of minutes to adjust my slip before you and Ari resume your never-ending attempt at pinning a puker patch on me?"

"Adjust away," Ari said, suppressing a laugh.

"Wheels up in five," Haynes warned, his voice deep and unmistakable even through the onboard comms.

Wasting no time, and under the watchful eye of Lopez and Cross, Cade unzipped the gym bag and spilled its contents on the floor. He arranged the items in a row by his feet. Next, he drew his Gerber combat dagger and carefully sliced through the laces on both of his tan desert boots. He sheathed the Gerber then slipped the worn items off his feet and nudged them out of sight under his seat. He scooped up the black plastic-and-Velcro stirrup-looking contraptions Daymon had liberated from "*the sporting goods room*" at the place he hoped to call home one day. Sensing all eyes on him, Cade slipped a heel into each brace and tugged and adjusted the nylon rear straps until the built-in pivot points were positioned comfortably over each protruding ankle bone while still leaving him an acceptable range of motion front to back. The topmost strap was wider than the rear and wrapped around his lower leg below the calf. He cinched both ankle braces down tight and tested them for fit.

Good to go.

Sensing the turbines spooling up, Cade glanced toward the cockpit and noticed Ari inputting waypoints on the wide touchscreen display stretching the cockpit between him and Haynes. Swinging his gaze around he saw Lopez and Cross eyeballing him. A grin was parked on Lopez's face, while Cross was nodding, a knowing look clearly evident on his.

Unable to curb his curiosity, Lopez asked, "What the eff are those and where did you get them?"

"Says *Active Ankles* right here on the strap," Cade answered glibly. "A friend gave them to me earlier today."

Not wanting Ari to hear him, Lopez closed a fist around his boom microphone and mouthed, "Still wobbly from the Draper crash?"

Cade nodded. Grabbed up the pair of well-worn size 9 Danner boots he'd pulled from the bag and began working the laces loose. "Same friend got me these, too," he said, heading off the next line of questioning.

Satisfied, Lopez sank into his seat and tightened his safety harness.

"Two mikes," Haynes said.

"I did both ankles *real bad* playing hoops at Venice Beach," Cross intoned. "They've never really fully healed. No idea how I made it through BUDs on them."

Grinning, Lopez said, "Because you're shit hot and high speed, Cross."

Smiling inwardly, Cade tucked his black pants legs into the dark brown boots, cinched the laces and bloused the cuffs. After wiggling his toes and rolling each ankle in a tight little clockwise circle, he silently deemed himself mission capable.

"One mike," called Haynes.

Now occupying the seat beside the stowed minigun to Cade's left, the SOAR crew chief named Skipper—obviously having let his personal grooming go since the L.A. mission—stroked his graying billy-goat beard with one gloved hand. He seemed completely at ease, letting his helmeted head loll against the bulkhead as the craft launched off the tarmac behind a growing turbine growl and accompanied by the unusual harmonic vibration that supplanted a normal helo's hurricane-like rotor noise.

Cade heard Ari speaking with the tower as the Ghost Hawk continued to climb and spin to port. Outside his window, FOB Bastion's flight line slowly rotated from sight and he was afforded a bird's eye view of Mack Mesa Municipal's old parking lot and transient receiving area. The lot was full of military vehicles wearing both desert tan and the much darker woodland camouflage schemes. Rising up atop the building's officer's quarters was a two-story plywood and plate-glass addition bristling with half a dozen antennas. On the far corner of the cobbled-together control tower, a bright orange wind sock hung listless in the still, high-desert air.

Beyond the sprawling parking lot ringed by prefab trailers and a liberal amount of fencing and what looked like ten-foot-wide by ten-deep trenches, soldiers in hazmat suits were going about the grim task of removing the previous night's accumulation of twice-dead corpses.

"She's always under siege," Cross offered, peering out his starboard window. "Has been since the day the first Chinooks landed."

Shifting his attention to Lopez and Cross, and noticing their newish-looking uniforms, Cade quipped, "You two clean up nicely."

Lopez rested his chin on the butt of his rifle. "Should have seen us an hour ago."

Deadpan, Cross added, "Yep. It's amazing what a couple of passes over the old ball sack with a warm washcloth will do for a fella."

Cade felt the helo nose down and pick up speed. Compared to the bus-like ride of the Stealth Chinook, the Ghost Hawk was a Ferrari—super nimble and peppy. Maybe the weeks spent on the ground had skewed his perception of speed—especially when it had come to the bigger helicopter's performance. At any rate, it appeared they would arrive at Colorado Springs sooner as a direct result of switching birds. Shifting his gaze from the tilting horizon over Cross's shoulder, he locked eyes with Lopez and asked, "What have you been up to?"

"Me and Cross were in your neck of the woods," Lopez said. "Poking around the Wasatch Front."

Cade perked up. "Did you recon Salt Lake?"

Lopez nodded. "Started out in Wendover, Nevada. It straddles the border with Utah. Buried some listening devices there on Interstate 80. The Zs can't help but follow it straight across the salt flats to Salt Lake, which is teeming with them."

"Did you two come across PLA scout soldiers in Nevada?"

Cross nodded. "We were expecting contact."

"Praying for it," added Lopez, eyes narrowing.

"President Clay sent out a pre-recorded pep talk. Everyone at Bastion watched it. Your name came up, Wyatt. Something about finding foreign soldiers on our soil … as far east as Ogden."

"Huntsville," Cade said. He glanced at Skipper, who didn't seem interested in the conversation. If he was, it didn't show. The crew chief's eyes were hidden behind a smoked visor, and his helmeted head, facing the port-side hip window, was constantly panning in small little increments, presumably between the ground and horizon. "I came across two PLA special operations scouts."

Cross asked, "Were they riding dirt bikes?"

Cade nodded. He looked at Lopez, then, settling his gaze back on Cross, said, "They were dismounts. Already dead and turned. They were wearing—"

Suddenly the Ghost Hawk slowed considerably and, as if it wasn't already skimming the weeds, halved the distance to the ground and began a tight counterclockwise orbit.

"Bastion, Jedi One-One. We've got a large group of Zs moving south on State Route 65," Ari said, his voice carrying over the shipwide comms.

After Bastion came back with a terse "Copy that," Haynes relayed the estimated size of the horde followed by their current GPS coordinates, direction of travel, and estimated speed.

Lopez fixed his gaze on Cade. "Per Beeson's orders, more than a thousand roamers on the open range warrants a Screamer drop."

"Working one up," Ari answered back.

Regarding Cross with a look of confusion, Cade mouthed, "Screamer?"

After stabbing two splayed fingers at his own eyes, Cross pointed to Skipper and mouthed, "Watch this."

Chapter 21

For reasons unknown—a gut feeling, perhaps—Daymon put one toe on the lowest stair leading up to the faded white Catholic church then did an about-face, saying, "Let's clear the caretaker's house first."

Without a word of protest, the others followed him up the sidewalk to the next stack of cement stairs.

As if privy to some kind of insider information, Max had already continued on past the church steps and was nose deep into the bushes at the base of the stairs leading up to the Old-Colonial-style house rising up from an elevated parcel of land barely a hundred feet east of the church.

Stopping beside Max, Daymon looked up at the house, first focusing his attention on the windowed gables up high, then walking his gaze over the ground-level windows which were all completely shrouded by dark-colored drapes.

"Front door or back?" Lev asked, drawing his semiautomatic.

Eyeing the overgrown front porch and stairs, Oliver said, "I just spent dang near three months bushwhacking the Pacific Crest Trail. I vote we try the back door first."

"I miss this kind of work," Daymon replied, pulling Kindness from its sheath and telling the others to stand back.

More than three months removed from human intervention and growing crazily over the slender handrail, the cat-pee-smelling bushes looked to be a formidable opponent to reaching the front door. However, after a few minutes of hard work, Daymon had cut a three-foot-wide path up the first rise of stairs and was bulling through the grabbing vines overtaking the whitewashed front porch.

"Not quite the same as cutting a firebreak," he called down from the porch landing. "But it sure brought back some memories." He moved his blade slowly left to right, cutting the air in front of the front door. Brought it close to his face and inspected the cobwebs and bug husks clinging to it. A big fat spider—Brown Recluse he guessed—darted along the blade's spine and dropped off to the weathered floorboards, scurrying between his boots before he could stomp it flat.

"Spider," Taryn squawked, flapping her tatted arms and doing a little dance on the stairs.

"Dead spider," Jamie declared, bringing her combat boot down hard and leaving behind a messy arachnid pancake.

Calling up from where he was standing on the first run of debris-strewn stairs, Wilson said, "All those webs didn't just accumulate over two days' time. Brings back bad memories of the inside of Ray and Helen's old barn."

Daymon wiped the webs off on his pants and sheathed the blade. "And what does it tell us, boys and girls?"

Approaching the door, Lev said, "It tells *me* that nobody's come or gone through this particular entry for quite some time."

Wilson said, "And that means the place probably isn't booby-trapped."

"Bang on it anyway," Taryn said, eyes narrowing. "Real hard. And be careful when you open it—"

"I won't make the same mistake you did," Daymon interrupted. "What's that for you now, Taryn? Two botched entries this week?"

Taryn smirked and thrust her left arm in front of him, fist closed. Then, under the watchful gaze of all present, she moved her right fist in a slow clockwise circle next to the left. And moving even slower than her hand was working the imaginary crank, her middle finger extended until it was standing at attention and delivering Daymon a nonverbal, albeit very clear message.

Daymon stuck his tongue out at Taryn then turned to join Lev at the door.

Like the church, the paint on the squat two-story house was weathered and scaling off, even on the walls semi-protected from the elements by the porch roof. The door was windowless and appeared to have been hewn from a single slab of oak. A lattice made of brass covered a small peek-a-boo door inset at eye level. A sheen of dust pocked by raindrop strikes covered the horizontal porch rails and door.

Daymon paused for a beat, raised his hand, and looked to Lev for approval.

As if saying, *Better you than me,* Lev stepped back and nodded.

So, doing Taryn's bidding, Daymon delivered three sharp, rapid-fire blows dead center on the door with his closed fist.

Bang! Bang! Bang!

He listened hard. Heard nothing but shallow breathing behind him.

"Again," Taryn insisted.

"Says the girl who just flipped off the entry person," Daymon said, repeating the process.

Bang! Bang! Bang!

Nothing.

Growling low, hairs on his back raised, Max sidled up onto the porch.

"Stay frosty," Daymon warned, just before rearing back and delivering a bone-jarring front kick to the spot on the door just inches below the tarnished brass knob.

Max yelped and there was a sharp crack of wood as the jamb failed and the door rocketed inward on its hinges. A half-beat later there was a dull thud and puff of fine white powder as the knob punched a hole into the lathe and plaster foyer wall.

***

Forty feet from where the breaking and entering was about to begin, the door leading to the back stoop was clicking shut.

Breathing hard, Iris crouched down on the top step and fumbled around the door jamb, feeling for the filament-like fishing line Ratchet had left dangling there. Hearing the rapid-fire knocking coming from inside the house, she wrapped the leader up in her hand, then, cautiously, so as to not disturb Ratchet's surprise, held the line loosely and turned a one-eighty on the short stack of stairs until she was facing the door.

The second volley of knocks came just as she was wrapping the leader line around the eyehook screwed knee-high into the hinge-side doorjamb.

Finished with her task, she leaped off the steps and sprinted straight to the rickety picket fence, leaving a trail of trampled grass in her wake. After making sure none of the Purged were lying in wait for her, she scrambled over the fence and went to ground beside a natural barrier of brambles that extended north to a low bluff a dozen yards beyond the picket fence.

Just as Iris was beginning to camouflage her large frame with the pre-positioned pile of soggy, month's old grass clippings, the looters breached the front door. Though muffled by interior walls and separated by a long hallway and at least thirty feet of additional open ground, the sound of cracking wood was unmistakable in the infinite quiet of the new world.

***

As a result of Newton's Third Law, Daymon had involuntarily backpedaled three feet from the threshold even before the door had completed half of its inward swing. By the time the brass knob was making its perfect round hole in the interior wall, he had regained his balance and was conducting a quick visual inventory of the foyer and rooms beyond. Seeing there were no rotters with carved-out voice boxes waiting to pounce, he stepped over the threshold, halting the door on its return swing with his left forearm. Pistol drawn, he peeled off to his right, muzzle moving in unison with his gaze, and quickly called back, telling the others the living room was clear.

Berettas drawn, Lev and Jamie entered the house on Daymon's heels. Lev swung to the left to clear the dining room, while Jamie continued straight down the narrow hall dividing the house in two.

"Left is clear," Lev called as he threw open the drapes, fully illuminating the butler's pantry and kitchen beyond it.

"Found the stairs," Jamie called from the rear of the house. "And I smell cigarette smoke." She cast a quick glance out the window over the sink. "Nobody out back." She tested the knob. "Back door's locked, too."

After waving Oliver, Taryn, and Wilson inside, Daymon stared Max in the eye, telling him to sit.

Putting a finger vertical to his lips, Daymon closed the door softly behind them, forcing it shut despite the damaged jamb. "Follow," he said over his shoulder and struck out down the hall to reunite with Jamie and Lev.

After a twenty-foot-run down the middle of the house, the hall spilled him into the kitchen. It was done in a classic farmhouse style, appointed with white cupboards, all yawning open and fully cleaned out. The fridge was pushed up against an inner wall. Its doors were closed. Still, the seal had failed and a stinking sludge had accumulated around its base. No telling what was inside the thing, Daymon thought, throwing a shiver.

Coming to a large butcher-block-topped island, Daymon halted and spun a circle. For a house this size, the kitchen was massive, encompassing nearly a quarter of the downstairs footprint.

Having just emerged from the adjoining butler's pantry, Lev padded to the door leading to the backyard and peered out the window.

Daymon swung his gaze right and spied Jamie standing at the base of a short rise of stairs, gun drawn and holding a finger to her lips.

Getting the hint, Wilson crossed the kitchen diagonally and joined Lev by the back door.

Oliver and Taryn stood rooted in the kitchen doorway, the former, back turned and peering down the hall at the compromised front door.

"Hear anything?" Daymon whispered.

Jamie shook her head. Leveling her pistol, she scaled the half-dozen steps and paused on the landing where the entire run made a ninety-degree turn to the right.

Daymon whistled softly to get Jamie's attention. "Wait for me," he whispered. Looking back at the others, he motioned Taryn over.

"You want me to go upstairs, too?" Taryn whispered.

Daymon nodded and stepped aside to let her pass. "Wilson, you watch the back door," he said, still whispering. "Oliver, anyone comes a knockin', dead or alive, shoot first and ask questions later."

Oliver and Wilson both nodded in agreement.

Daymon called Lev over with a nod and started off to his right toward the stairwell. Before scaling the stairs, just to be safe, he went to the door underneath the stairs and tried the handle, finding it unlocked. Figuring it for a small powder room, he yanked the door open and found only a threadbare coat on a hanger and a pair of galoshes arranged side-by-side on the floor. Propped in the back corner was an oversized golf umbrella and a golf club which, based on its short shaft and mostly open face, he figured was probably a 9 iron.

Feeling sheepish, Daymon closed the closet door and mounted the stairs.

With Jamie in the lead and Lev bringing up the rear, the four Eden survivors made their way to the second floor, stepping only on the sides of each tread to keep the squeaking of loose boards to a minimum.

At the second landing where the stairs twisted to the right again, Jamie halted to point out pea-sized drops of blood. She swiped at one with her toe and visibly stiffened at the sight of the crimson arc left behind. "Still wet," she mouthed to Daymon before mounting the final run of stairs.

Mirroring the main floor, a long hall split the upstairs in half. Two doorways on each side led to bedrooms, presumably. The smell of smoke here was much stronger than it had been in the kitchen.

Communicating with hand gestures and nods, the group moved on down the hall, Taryn and Daymon taking the two doors on the left, while Lev and Jamie approached the doors on the right.

Taryn poked her head into the nearest room and found only a dust-covered wood floor and four bare walls. The door on the small closet to her left hung open, the high shelf and hanger bar both bare. Sunlight splashed the walls, and just outside the east-facing window was a mature oak tree, its bare branches nearly touching the house.

The second door Daymon opened was to a bathroom instead of a coat closet. After a cursory glance revealed a clawfoot tub, pedestal sink and toilet, the latter bone dry and sporting a rust-orange waterline, he turned and looked down the hall to where the others had assembled.

Jamie shook her head, causing her carbine to swing on its sling. "Three empty rooms," she announced, acting as spokesperson for the others.

Nodding agreeably, Lev said, "We crapped out. Nothing of use here. Time to move on."

"The blood, though," Jamie said, pointing at the floor. "It ends right here."

"And the smoke," Taryn said, her nose crinkling. "Someone was here and we spooked them."

"I agree," Daymon said, his gaze suddenly walking up the wall and settling on the ceiling above their heads where he saw cut marks. They were maybe an eighth of an inch thick and ran two feet across on the ends and four on the sides paralleling the walls. A rubber T-shaped handle was nestled into a four-inch-wide cutout on the end nearest the stairs. He pointed to the find, then put a finger to his lips. "Let's go," he said, voice booming. "Nothing here." He turned and clomped on down the hall alone and then made a lot more noise going down the stairs by himself.

In the kitchen, Daymon quietly told Wilson about their find and told him to keep doing what he was doing.

Moving to the front of the house, Daymon found Oliver gripping his carbine tight and standing tall with his back to the bashed-in door. On the shorter man's face was a look the former BLM firefighter knew all too well. Oliver Gladson was scared shitless and it showed.

"What is it?"

Oliver drew in a deep breath. "Max was growling on the porch."

"And?"

"I looked out the window."

"And?"

"That pair of rotters down by the intersection—"

"Yes," Daymon interrupted. "What about them?"

"They're at the bottom of the stairs now," Oliver stammered.

"Don't worry. It'll be the second coming of you know who before they reach the porch. *If* they do reach the porch. Relax."

"What if they *do* make it to the porch before we're done in here?"

"Simple, Oliver. If Max can't handle them, you'll have to step in." Daymon opened the door. "You got our six, Max?"

The dog just stared at the creatures fumbling around at the bottom of the two flights.

"Sorry, Max," Daymon said, slamming the door for effect. Stabbing a thumb at the ceiling while speaking softly in Oliver's direction, he added, "We think we have ourselves a Goldilocks wannabe upstairs. Just stay here. Keep your eyes open and be quiet. Max can handle himself around those things."

Before Oliver could protest or fire off a second barrage of questions, Daymon was padding quietly down the hall.

***

It took Daymon a full three minutes to scale the stairs with any semblance of stealth. Then, a full five minutes after leaving Jamie, Taryn, and Lev alone upstairs, he was heel and toeing it down the hall and looking a question their way.

"Nothing moved up there," Taryn whispered. "I think you're right about us spooking them. Whoever left the blood trail did so on their way *out*."

Chapter 22

The answer to Cade's mouthed question about the Screamer came three long minutes after he posed it.

Ari continued the slow clockwise orbit over the undead horde, drawing them along all the while tightening the circle until the helo was at a steady hover just a hundred feet above the multitudes of pale faces leering expectantly skyward.

Once the monsters were packed in tight a good distance from the state route and anything the Screamer might get trapped underneath, Ari came in over the comms. "Half-moon-shaped clump of sage. Taking her down close."

"Copy that," replied Skipper, turning away from the window through which he'd been observing the creatures' movements. He hastily unhooked a safety line from the bulkhead, then secured one end of the three-foot-long cable to a waist-high anchor point a few inches left of the minigun. He clicked the carabiner on the other end of the lifeline to the D-ring on his flight gear. While the port-side door slid aft, letting in the pong of death and decay, he retrieved a gear bag from the nylon webbing, securing it to the front bulkhead. From the bulging bag came a round, grapefruit-sized device painted in bright safety orange. The sphere had two black panels the size of a pack of Wrigley's gum inset one to a side. Running vertically between the shiny panels, the letters "SCRMR" had been stenciled in black. No doubt an Army acronym, Cade thought. Then, as the helo slowed and fell into a steady hover a few feet off the deck, Skipper opened one of the panels on the device and began fiddling with its internal workings. A tick later he snapped the panel shut and instantly a shrill scream emitted from inside the orb. It was high-pitched and warbling, the kind of death knell Cade had heard coming from the mouths of way too many real people as they died at the hands of the Zs. The hair-raising keening was also loud enough to trump the muffled helicopter turbines and rotor blades and eerily enough came across to Cade as authentic, not a special effect created by a computer in some sound studio. Which then made him wonder how the ten seconds of audio filled with the sounds of some anonymous person's intense suffering had been captured in the first place.

Pushing the morbid line of questioning from his mind, he looked at Lopez and said, "What does SCRMR stand for?"

"Self-contained … rolling—"

Cutting Lopez off, the usually quiet crew chief said, "I've forgotten what the M and R stand for, but that doesn't matter. I'll tell you all about it." As the Ghost Hawk made a final hundred-yard sideslip maneuver away from the auto-choked state route, Skipper held the device at eye-level. "The panels are the latest generation of mini solar collectors. Inside this baby is the battery pack and motion sensor. If I'm not mistaken, it's some kind of a jury-rigged mercury switch that starts it making that noise." Then, like a short, old, and melanin-deficient version of a Harlem Globetrotter, Skipper rolled the Screamer in his hands and spun it on one gloved finger like a mini basketball. "That it's round makes it nearly impossible for the Zs to accidentally crush it."

"I've seen a group of them chase one as it rolled around the ground screaming bloody murder," Lopez interjected, a half-smile curling his lips. "Damn if it didn't look like a bunch of drunks chasing a beach ball."

"The Zs are one hundred yards off port and turning back," warned Haynes, craning hard over his left shoulder, voice all business.

Skipper glanced out the door, then went on, "The scream is on a timed loop. Ten seconds on, fifty off."

Crunching numbers in his head, Cade figured he had just north of thirty seconds until the sphincter-puckering noise again assaulted his ears. With Eden and the coming winter in mind, he asked, "Is it waterproofed?"

"Can't take one in the pool with you," Skipper said, as the vibration from the Ghost's landing gear motoring into place transited the bulkhead under his feet. "So far we haven't had one fail from getting rained or snowed on. We lost one down by Green River recently. My theory … the effin Zs kicked it under a vehicle and with no sun to charge it the battery eventually died."

"They've acquired us again," Haynes intoned. "Ninety-five yards and closing."

"They're persistent bastards, aren't they," Cade stated, seeing the distant biomass halt and pause for a beat, a slow rippling action that preceded them turning their heads in unison and fixing all eyes on the dust-shrouded helo just as it touched down softly.

Skipper nodded at that. "If they think they have something trapped they'll stick around for awhile. But more and more," he said, as he reached out and rolled the device into a wiry shock of ankle-high scrub brush, "if they don't get a kill or hear anything that tells them prey is nearby, they're going to move on. We've been seeing them herding up and staying in constant motion for days and weeks."

"Hunting the living," Ari said over the comms. "In mega hordes, Wyatt. Like that million Z march we witnessed during the Castle Rock mission."

"*Witnessed?*" Skipper said, hitting a switch on the bulkhead that started the side door powering shut. "With all due respect, sir. I think you mean *decimated*."

After validating the statement with a thumbs-up directed at his long-standing crew chief, Ari said, "Wheels up," and there was a brief whirring sound followed by a solid clunk as the landing gear rotated back inside the airframe and seated into place. A tick later there was a soft thud as the radar-absorbent panels covering the gear wells locked down. An increasing turbine roar was quickly quelled by the side door seating. Finally, Cade felt his stomach roil as Ari powered the helo vertically off the desert floor and banked hard to port, lining the nose up with the distant Rocky Mountains.

Addressing Cade, Skipper said, "Beeson's come to the conclusion that it's better to be proactive. Catch the Zs in groups small enough that a couple of truckloads of Pikers can roll in and neutralize them on the spot. Leave the bodies for the elements to take care of."

Though Cade had a good idea what Skipper meant, he still felt compelled to ask. "Pikers?"

"They're the poor bastards among the volunteers who happen to draw the short straw. Playing piker means you get to ride exposed in back of whatever vehicles are available—usually deuce and a halfs. Driving the rigs, I hear, isn't a choice assignment, either. They do the old Pied Piper thing by either leading them in a straight line and letting the pikers do their job from the rear. Or, if they're out in the open I've heard of them driving around the herd in a big circle … three or four trucks and a dozen pikers. Pretty effective, but finding the Screamer under all of the corpses afterward tends to be a bit of a bitch."

"Wash. Rinse. Repeat," Cade said.

"Yep. They don't look it, but they're real durable," replied Skipper, casting his gaze on the herd which was already packing in tight around the Screamer. "We scoop 'em up and dust them off then go find the next manageable pack of deadheads and start all over. Record stands at an estimated six thousand Zs culled in one day."

Cade nodded. "Saves on ammo, that's for damn sure."

"We're still not making much of a dent in their numbers," Cross said soberly.

"Every dead *demonio* is a step in the right direction," Lopez said, crossing himself.

A silence filled the cabin as the helo nosed down slightly and picked up speed.

Bracing against the maneuver, Cade heard Ari talking to someone at Schriever. He looked across the aisle and saw that both Cross and Lopez had their arms crossed similarly over their load-bearing gear. Already Agent Cross was chin down and eyes closed, his head bobbing with the motion of the ship. Now and again his face would brush the butt of his SCAR rifle trapped between his legs, causing him to start and mumble something, the words "Zs" the only thing intelligible.

Face aimed skyward, the tactical helmet framing his closed, vein-snaked eyelids, Lopez started to snore.

"Couple of regular Sleeping Beauties we got here," Skipper noted.

Cade nodded. Then, following advice Desantos had offered up so long ago, something to the effect of, *"You're Army. You have to sleep when you can get it,"* he wrapped his arms around his M4, shut his eyes, and thought about his girls.

Chapter 23

The first warning sign of the impending claustrophobic attack struck Daymon the moment he had spotted the overhead door and came to realize where it led. Instantly, his throat had clenched tight and his mouth had gone dry as a piece of day-old toast.

Standing rooted for an additional ten minutes with the knowledge of what had to be done bouncing around in his brain had whipped his guts into a churning mess. And while the second hand on the clock in his mind had proceeded ahead on its steady metronomic march to the decided-upon time, the putrid smells and wails of the dead he'd endured for hours while trapped in the farmhouse attic with Cade and Hoss came rushing back to him with mind-numbing clarity.

Now, the agreed-upon time having slipped into the past with not so much as one attic board creaking overhead, Daymon shook his head to clear the haunting visions and looked at the others. "I don't think anyone's sleeping in *my* bed, Baby Bear."

Jamie smirked and asked, "So how do you suggest we get the thing open without a chair to stand on?"

Lev edged close to Daymon. He intertwined his fingers into a stirrup and leaned forward, offering the man a leg up.

Daymon's dreads bobbed as he shook his head and waved Lev off. Squaring up to the attic access hatch, he withdrew Kindness, reached up and started probing the edges of the flush panel with the long blade. Getting nowhere with that tactic, he pried at the rubber T handle with the machete's rounded tip. Finally, after a little effort and with his craned neck beginning to ache, one side of the handle popped out and it freefell eye-level to him before the orange cord securing it to the door snapped taut and arrested its fall.

"I got it," Taryn said, grabbing for the handle.

Beating her to the punch, Daymon snatched the handle from midair. "Everyone stand back."

Once the other three had backed down the hallway, he yanked down on the cord and stepped clear.

The hatch was spring-loaded and swung down with ease, the bi-fold ladder extending downward and stopping a foot shy of the floor with a resonant *bang*.

As if expecting a flurry of gunfire or guillotine to come scything from the attic entry, the four inched forward, necks bent at unnatural angles and guns aimed at the dimly lit portal.

"It's all yours," Lev said.

Swallowing hard, Daymon whipped his head back and forth. Then, as if they'd never gone away, all of the usual symptoms of a mounting claustrophobic attack were back. Dry mouth. Tight throat. Racing heart. And worst of all, the cold sweats started. "Hell no! I'm not going up there," he said, taking a step back from the ladder.

"I'm small," Jamie said. "I'll do it."

She put a hand on Taryn's forearm. It was far from smooth. On the contrary, though they were fully healed, the dragons, skulls, and skeletons tattooed on the teen's arm—sleeve style, Jamie thought it was called—were basically just scar tissue: raised and welt-like. "I'll go first. You follow me," Jamie said, starting up the ladder.

"Be careful," Lev called. In fact, he wanted to pull her from the ladder and go in her stead, but knew that wouldn't fly. Like Taryn, Jamie was strong of will and didn't take *no* for an answer. So he didn't push it. He simply watched her disappear into the gloom.

There was no medieval executioner's blade awaiting. Bullets didn't cut his girl to ribbons. And most comforting of all was Jamie calling down and saying she was all alone up there and urging everyone to join her.

Everyone wasn't joining Jamie upstairs.

Taryn holstered her weapon and monkeyed up the creaky ladder.

Swinging his M4 around to his back, Lev climbed the stairs and disappeared into the attic.

Daymon grabbed a rung and stared up into the dark, listening as the others described what they were seeing.

Jamie first noticed the stench of cigarette smoke hanging in the air. Because the four gables, each facing a different point of the compass, were built into the roof pitch, the attic was much smaller than she had expected. The attic itself was maybe three or four hundred square feet, max. The roof was angled so that one could only stand erect near the center of the storage area. Cobwebs clung to everything at eye level. Open-topped boxes filled with dusty books, mostly old leather-bound bibles and hymnals, were pushed against the sloped roof. And piercing the plywood sheeting overhead, rusty nails protruded into the space at crazy angles.

"Careful," Jamie warned, putting a hand on Taryn's shoulder while pointing out the nails. "One already nicked me."

Taryn bent at the waist and made her way to the east-facing window. "Just cobwebs over here," she said, staring out the window at a tangle of gnarled branches.

Staying on his hands and knees, Lev made his way to the west-facing window. The first thing that struck him was the fresh wood shavings piled on the floor below the sill. Even competing with the other odors, the faint smell of newly carved attic-cured old growth reminded him of high school wood shop.

Oddly, the name ADRIAN that he found carved into the sill brought back memories of art class. The letters were scribed with care. They weren't cursive nor connected in any way. They were of an old-school font, yet fancy all the same. Then he saw the blood intermixed with the wood shavings and called out his find. Two plus two just became four in his mind. When combined with the blood trail downstairs, the spongy mess on the floor here told him that the person responsible for both had been watching them. He also concluded that the culprit or culprits' exit had been hasty. Then the probability that they might still be nearby, or perhaps going for reinforcements, hit him broadside.

"Tell Wilson and Oliver to ratchet up their alert level," he called out loudly enough so that Daymon would hear. "The bleeder was spying on us and rabbited when we crashed the place."

"Copy that," Daymon replied.

Hearing Daymon clomp down the hall, Lev peered out the window. He could see the body shop parking lot where they had parked their vehicles. Nothing was amiss, or so it seemed. However, due to the steep viewing angle from the rooftop dormer, he could only see the top two-thirds of their trucks. So there was no real way of telling if their tires had been slashed or whether any other kind of booby traps had been set.

"Check this out," Jamie called, her voice carrying from the front of the attic where mounds of winter clothing, no doubt donated to the church and awaiting distribution before the outbreak, sat crowding the south-facing dormer.

"Looks like your lady has found a clue," Taryn said.

***

Downstairs, Daymon stood beside Wilson, both of them staring at the back yard through the rectangular window inset into the back door.

"It was locked when Jamie got to it," Wilson stated.

"Doesn't mean a thing," Daymon said.

"I know," Wilson whispered. "I think I saw something moving over there … beyond the fence." He nodded and then traced his finger on the glass. "See that?"

"See what?" Daymon asked, a hint of irritation creeping into his tone.

"The trail in the grass. It's like the game trails around Eden."

"I saw it earlier," Daymon admitted. "Figured it was just made by some nosy rotters. But seeing as how the front porch was covered with cobwebs when we got here, it's pretty obvious that when we banged on the door our bleeder came running down here and squirted out the back."

"Think they're gone?"

"I'd put money on it," Daymon said in a low voice. "Would you stick around?"

Wilson shook his head no.

"I wouldn't either. My guess is the movement you saw was likely just the wind bending the grass."

"Or someone beating feet," Wilson proffered.

Daymon made no reply. He just continued staring at the overgrown backyard.

The sound of heavy footfalls filtered down the hall a tick before Oliver, breathing hard and wild-eyed, burst into the kitchen babbling about rotters on the porch.

"—and they're turning the doorknob," he added, gesturing toward the perceived threat with his rifle muzzle.

"Take a breath," Daymon ordered. "Is the door locked?"

Oliver nodded an affirmative. "Deadbolt was good, so I threw it."

"Do rotters use keys to open doors?"

Oliver shook his head side to side, then ran a shaky hand through his hair.

"Then what's the problem? There's only two of them … right?"

"I haven't looked recently."

"Some help you are. Follow me." Daymon led Oliver down the hall. At the foyer he told Oliver to wait while he split off and made a beeline for the living room window.

"Well?" Oliver called out.

"We're good," was Daymon's reply as he turned and padded back down the hall toward the kitchen. "Keep doing what you're doing. But check the front stoop now and again, will ya?"

Oliver nodded. "The handle … it's still moving."

Nearly to the kitchen, Daymon slowed his gait and turned toward the front door. "I'll fill you in on that piece of the puzzle before you go out to put them down." He didn't wait for the argument. Instead, he turned back to face the kitchen and saw that Wilson had thrown the lock and was pulling the back door inward. About to admonish the redhead for going outside without backup, he instead broke into a full sprint, holstering his pistol midway through the first long stride.

Hearing the rapid clomp of boot heels striking hardwood, Wilson spun around midstep and raised his arms in a defensive posture. Which did nothing to soften the blow from Daymon's two-hundred-pound frame as it struck him chest-high and lifted him off his feet. Then, while the air escaped his lungs with a hollow *whoosh*, Wilson witnessed three things happen near simultaneously, seemingly in slow motion. First he saw the door jambs and kitchen cabinets fly by in his peripheral as inertia from the sidelong tackle set his body spinning on axis and tilting horizontal to the floor. Once fully airborne, his gaze went to Daymon's contorted face, then moved on to the unlit porch light atop the door frame, and finally saw some unknown foreign object scything the air above both of their heads.

Though possessing a fair amount of give due to the recent snow and rain, the ground still was unforgiving when Wilson's sudden and unexpected meeting with it stole what little air remained in his lungs. Consequently, a fraction of a second later when Daymon's full weight came crashing down on Wilson's fully prostrate body, there was nothing left in the lungs to purge, so instead his stomach gave up its contents, fully and also without warning.

Timing being everything for the second instance within the span of a couple of heartbeats, Daymon rolled off of Wilson a half-beat shy of being splashed by what remained of the younger man's breakfast. And as he lay there in the crushed grass listening to Wilson retch, he stared past his boots and saw the four-foot-long section of tree trunk that had just missed them swinging pendulum-like outside the back door. Barely bigger around than his wrist, the length of aspen was shot through with a couple dozen of what looked to be six-inch-long 60-penny nails.

"That was close," Daymon said, as Oliver came skidding to a halt, his body nearly filling up the door frame.

"What the eff?" Oliver mouthed as he reached out to arrest the contraption.

"Back off," Daymon bellowed.

With a quizzical look settling on his face, Oliver did as he was told, both hands going up in mock surrender.

"How'd you know?" Wilson asked, his words coming out barely above a whisper.

"When I saw there were no cobwebs across the back porch I started thinking that whoever left the rotters in the body shop may have more tricks up their sleeve."

"But how did you *know*?" Wilson asked, wiping the bile from his lips. "What made you drop everything and just act?"

"I saw you about to go through the door alone. At that point, seeing as how we already have a pair of Zs at the front door, I was a little concerned … *and* a little pissed-off." Daymon bit his tongue and hung his head. "Good thing my eyes are better than Old Man's … I spotted the twine stretched across the door frame when you pulled the door toward you. And luckily for you I ran track in high school."

"You gotta see this," Oliver called from the back porch.

Daymon rose and helped Wilson to his feet. "Anything broken?" he asked.

"I'll be sore tomorrow," Wilson answered. "But thanks to you there will be a tomorrow." He slapped the taller man on the back and together they scaled the back stairs.

Chapter 24

Daymon was down on one knee at the top of the stairs inspecting the sprung trap, which at this point was no longer caroming off the door jambs and had come to rest blocking the doorway. Twine looped through metal eyehooks screwed into the door header kept the medieval-looking contraption suspended roughly knee-high to the shortest person in the group. A third length of twine that had triggered the trap now lay in a loose coil on the rectangular cement landing where a door mat would normally be.

Daymon took the slack length of twine in hand and followed it up the door frame to where it passed through a series of metal eye hooks identical to the ones securing the trap to the top header. Near the top of the frame, a knot stuck fast in the final eyehook had arrested the twine's travel.

"Check this out," Oliver said, pointing to one of the spikes.

Daymon called for Lev to join him outside. He moved out of the way as Lev stepped over the inert trap. Finally, after making room for the former soldier on the cement landing, he said, "Aside from a pretty elaborate shin sticker, what else am I supposed to be seeing, Oliver?"

"This," Oliver replied, pointing to one of the spikes protruding from the tree trunk on his side of the doorway. "There's a moist bit of flesh skewered on this one. And more on these, here … and here." He lifted the trap to afford Daymon, Wilson, and Lev a clear view. "I'd bet this is what came out of Tom, Dick, and Harriet down at the body shop."

"From their necks?" Taryn asked, peering over Oliver's shoulder.

"Yep."

"Motherfuckers *were* harvesting salivary glands," Daymon said, his short dreads keeping time with his bobbing head. "That's some devious shit right there." He cast a furtive glance over his shoulder. "Whoever set this when they left didn't want to kill any of us right away. Hell, this thing is so light it probably wouldn't have killed *Raven* if she had sprung it."

"When I was in Iraq, a staff sergeant leading our fire team liked to remind us before going out on patrol that a wounded man took more resources to bring in than a dead one."

"So he wanted you to die instead of getting injured?" Wilson asked.

Lev stared at Wilson for a long second. "No, dumbass. He didn't want any of us to get injured. That's what this is here for. One of us gets infected and doesn't realize it. Brings it home as a slow burn and then he or she turns and infects a few more of us. *That's* some devious shit."

Wilson stepped up to Lev. Glared at him for a second. "Take it back. The dumbass comment. Take it back."

Lev merely shrugged.

Wilson shoved him in the sternum, knocking him off the short run of stairs.

Reacting instantly, Lev found his balance and threw a looping right that missed Wilson's nose by a whisker. "You watered those balls alright," he said, as Daymon leaped down and pulled him away.

"Name calling? That's a first for you," Wilson said, eyes narrowing.

Daymon stood facing Lev. "Stand down," he said, moving his body to keep the shorter man from making eye contact with the redhead crowding him from behind.

Thinking *boys will be boys*, Jamie looked on indifferently.

Aiming to defuse the situation, Taryn poked her head out the doorway. Staring daggers at Lev, she said, "I found this in the attic," She handed the empty cigarette pack to Oliver, who in turn passed it between the taut twine to Daymon.

"So what if the bleeder was a smoker?" Daymon said, inspecting the crumpled wrapper. "We already knew that by the stink in there."

"Look inside the wrapper," she said as Lev and Wilson seemed to forget about their beef and edged closer to see the item in Daymon's palm.

Daymon inspected the pack closer and fished a worn book of matches from the crinkled cellophane sleeve. He spent a moment turning it over in his hand and reading the words encircling a catchy logo. "These came from The Lodge Motel in Bear River. A long time ago, from the looks of it. So what?"

"Take a closer look," Taryn said.

He read the small print on the cover again front and back. "I stand corrected," he said. "These came from Bear *Lake.*"

Crouching next to Oliver and looking directly at Daymon, who had professed to have fought fires all over the west, Taryn said, "OK … so we all know where Bear River is. Can either one of you enlighten us as to where *Bear Lake* is."

"Enlighten you? Hell no … I'm going to take you there," said Daymon. "Stand back." He rose and pulled a folding knife from a cargo pocket. After thumbing the knife open, he cut the trap down. Being sure to stay clear of the Omega-infected spikes, he took hold of all three lengths of severed twine and carried the trap to the nearby fence and tossed it into the brambles on the other side.

"What now?" Lev asked.

"Check the fence for signs of our squirter."

"All the noise the trap made, if they were still hanging around I'm sure we'd have already started taking incoming fire."

"Humor me while Oliver takes care of the heavy lifting," Daymon said. He pointed at Wilson. "You initiated the physical contact with your *friend.* Time to apologize."

"But he called me a—," Wilson stammered.

"Sticks and stones," Daymon said, cutting him off and folding his arms across his chest.

Reluctantly, Wilson made a quiet amends.

"Apology accepted," Lev said as he headed off toward the fence line. "Sorry I swung on you."

"Doesn't that feel better?" Daymon said, directing the question at Wilson.

Wilson nodded and struck off after Lev.

Daymon turned back toward the door. "Oliver … *come on down*," he said, trying to impart a little Price is Right-like enthusiasm into the request. "I want to show you something."

Daymon led Oliver to the side fence he had spotted earlier from the sidewalk. He ran the folding knife across the rust-scaled wrought iron and began to whistle softly.

After a few seconds the sound of clumsy footsteps on wooden steps filtered around to the side of the house. A tick after the noises subsided, the bushes at the front corner of the house shimmied and branches cracked as the two rotters from the front stoop crashed their way through. Maws already pistoning open and closed on imagined flesh, they hissed and moaned and staggered toward the waist-high fence.

Daymon handed over his folding knife, blade already locked open. "What's the easiest way to deal with these fuckers? I'll give you a hint: I've put down hundreds of them this way."

"Wait until they're trapped on the fence, then stick them in the eye."

"Now we're cooking with gas, Oliver." Daymon chuckled and stepped back from the fence. "We'll make a stone cold killer out of you yet."

The monsters hit the fence at a full shamble, causing the old iron to keen and groan and the entire ten-foot run to lean inward a few degrees.

Breathing through his nose and about to retch from the stench, Oliver thrust the locked blade into the male rotter's eye socket, dropping the snarling beast vertically as if a trapdoor had been opened beneath it. The sudden second-death and subsequent instantaneous failure of everything keeping the two-hundred-pounder upright couldn't have been timed any worse. For when the thing collapsed and was impaled on the spikes atop the fence, it pitched forward, the dead weight causing the entire run of fence to cant forward and stop at roughly a sixty-degree angle.

Damnit, Oliver thought, seeing the law of unintended consequences unfolding before his very eyes as the female rotter hit the fence and started the evenly spaced concrete footings to rise up from the soggy earth. To keep from being pinned to the ground by hundred-year-old iron, and who knew how many pounds of dead flesh, Oliver stepped forward and braced the fence with his left hip. Keeping free of the female's snapping teeth, he grabbed a handful of greasy hair and drew her thrashing head toward his leveled blade.

"Not like that," Daymon blurted, rushing to his aid. "You're likely to get bit."

Grimacing, Oliver said, "I can't stomach stabbing them through the skull."

Daymon shored the fence with his thigh, grabbed a fistful of hair, and then pushed down on the back of the flailing monster's head. After getting Oliver's undivided attention, he stabbed an index finger at the nape of its neck. "Right where the spine goes into the skull is where you want to do it," he said. "There will be a little grating of bone and such. But nothing like when you do them in the temple or through the skull cap." Finished delivering today's lesson on how to effectively kill the undead 101, he pulled harder on the creature's long auburn locks and increased the downward pressure on its skull with his other hand.

After a little probing with the tip of the borrowed blade, Oliver found the sweet spot between the C1 and C2 vertebra and put his weight behind the single thrust. As promised, there was a cold-shiver-inducing grating of steel on bone, but nothing akin to what Oliver had felt and heard when Daymon forced him to put down the rotters earlier.

Muted golf claps sounded from behind Daymon and Oliver as they let the female rotter down to the long grass.

Daymon let go of the thing's hair then turned towards the others and smiled sheepishly. "Did any of you learn anything from today's lesson?"

Taryn and Jamie shook their heads, the former nearly pushed to the point of rolling up another middle finger for Daymon.

Ignoring the quip, Lev said, "There's nothing I can see by the fence. The trail in the grass continues west then goes cold."

"As I suspected," Daymon said. "I would have run, too, once I got an eyeful of this motley crew."

"What next?" asked Wilson. "Are we going to investigate Bear Lake today or continue searching this booby-trap-infested town?"

"Bear Lake," Daymon said. "I figure we can catch up with our Peeping Tom if we get going now. All in favor, hands up."

"Five for, one abstaining," Lev said after a quick head count.

Sounding a little irritated, Daymon said, "Come on, Oliver. Water your—"

"Balls," Wilson finished. "Go with the flow, dude. I used to be afraid of *guns*. Shotguns, pistols, rifles … you name it, I wanted nothing to do with them."

"And look at him now," Daymon intoned. "He's a stone cold killer. And you've officially been overruled, Oliver. Let's go back through the house."

Scaling the steps, Daymon paused and looked over the rigging used to suspend the spike-laden trunk off to the side of the door. Then he turned slowly, regarded Taryn and then settled his gaze on Wilson. "When you two get back to the Raptor, you better check the backseat for a stowaway."

"What are you talking about?" Wilson asked, taking off his boonie hat and rolling it up, then nervously throttling it two-handed.

Looking up from the bottom step, Taryn added, "Who do you think snuck a ride with us?"

Knowing where Daymon was going with this, Lev smiled and simultaneously fielded Jamie and Oliver's confused looks with a dramatic shrug.

"I figure since you two *both* almost bought the farm today, old Mr. Murphy has got to be tagging along with you."

Wilson said nothing. He scrunched his hat down and brushed past Daymon, following the others into the house.

Shaking her head at the tough love Daymon seemed gleeful to be dishing out, Taryn let her thoughts on the subject be known by cranking up another middle finger for the man, then swung it to her right and targeted a retreating Lev with it for a brief second.

"Relax," Daymon said, wearing a shit-eating grin. "I'm not picking on you. You just became the next victim of my equal opportunity ball busting. I still got both of your backs." Lowering his voice on the outside chance their watcher was still nearby, he called ahead to Lev. "Fire up the handheld CB and call Eden. Tell 'em where we are and what we found … or didn't find. Then let whomever it concerns know that we're pushing north."

"With friends like these," Taryn muttered, watching Daymon reenter the house with a certain spring in his step.

"Daymon's a ball buster of the highest order," Oliver said quietly. "Just be grateful you're not our *weakest link*."

***

Iris was rising up from the mound of grass clippings at the same moment in time that the dreadlocked man was tackling the redhead. While their hurtling bodies were clearing the steps on the way to a hard landing, she was edging into the dark shadows on the periphery of the overgrown bramble patch.

Feeling every bit the *doer* for the first time in a long time, she defied standing orders and stayed in the gloom long enough to see the tripwire snag on one of the men's boots. Then, fingering the gold cross on the chain around her neck, she risked death at her own hand by remaining rooted long enough to see the slipknot dissolve and gravity take hold of Ratchet's tainted trap. At first it had moved achingly slow. The first few degrees of the arc seeming to take half a heartbeat. In the second half of that perceived pause it picked up speed and scythed the air where the men had been, failing in its sole purpose: to infect living flesh.

With Mother's final words echoing in her head, Iris rose and crept west toward the church, being mindful to keep her movement steady and fluid-like—as she'd been taught. With the harried voices of the two luckiest men in the world rising above the sound her soft footfalls made crossing the carpet of rotting leaves beneath the skeletal oak, she decided the bad news wouldn't make it into her report. Then, as she padded across the lengthening shadow of the church's steeple on her way to the caretaker's outbuilding, she pulled out the radio and placed the requisite call.

Chapter 25

Sleep had come to Cade in the form of a half-dozen little two- and three-minute cat naps that were regularly being interrupted by Ari's constant course corrections. The first few times he had been jostled awake and stole a peek out the window he saw mostly open range and the occasional low-rolling tree-dotted hill. The latter couple of times Cade had cast his gaze at the ground, the cover had changed from the sage and cactus that had dominated the high desert terrain in and around Grand Junction, Mack, and Mesa, Colorado to a more alpine mix of green pines and firs, from which white peaks jutted. In the low spots, the occasional snow-covered meadow or deep-blue jewel-like lake flashed by.

By the time Cade had opened his eyes for good—an hour and a half after leaving Bastion, according to his Suunto—the Ghost Hawk had already skirted a number of peaks, overflown lush green national forests and was once again flying low level on an easterly heading that he figured would take them through a pass in the southern tip of the Rocky Mountain Range and eventually deliver them to Colorado Springs.

Returning his attention to the cabin, Cade saw Skipper still parked by the minigun. The crew chief's visor was retracted and his eyes were constantly on the move, probing the scrolling terrain with an intensity dulled by neither time nor distance. Across the aisle from Skipper, Cross and Lopez were both awake. Apparently sensing him stir, the operators perked up and both flashed him a thumbs-up.

"Getting close," Skipper said. "Keep your eyes peeled, gentlemen. Springs ain't what she used to be."

Hearing this, Cade rubbed his eyes and stretched his arms toward the cabin roof. Feeling the dull ache returning to his left ankle despite the new Danners and athletic braces, he fished into a pocket and brought out the half-full bottle of Ibuprofen. *Vitamin M*, he thought. *Said to cure a grunt of everything from sore muscles to a sucking chest wound.* Knowing full well Brook wouldn't approve of him exceeding the maximum recommended dosage, he still rattled six of the tiny Motrin into his palm and swallowed them dry. Seeing Lopez watching him hawklike, he capped the bottle and lobbed it across the cabin to him.

"Turnaround should be quick," Ari said over the comms. "Whipper is going to top us up with everything we need."

"I'll make doubly sure we get a full complement of flares," Skipper intoned. "And a full loadout for the mini."

"Copy that," Ari said, "I never doubted you, Skip. You keep talking so much and we're going to have to think up a new handle for you."

Cade studied Skipper while digging into his own memory for the crew chief's *current* nickname. Suddenly, in his mind's eye he was back outside the Three Palms in Los Angeles and clambering aboard the Ghost Hawk with Zs closing in from all sides. Soon to be the very fortunate recipient of a lifesaving exfil, he recalled how the minigun's electric motor whined as shells spilled onto the hot pavement. He remembered seeing Skipper then, filling up the door, visor covering his eyes, jaw with a granite set to it. No words accompanied the crew chief's death dealing. For that matter, the man had spoken sparingly the entire ride to and from Los Angeles. Then Cade remembered Ari calling the man *Doctor Silence.* Fitting then, that was for damn sure. Now, however, not so much.

"President Clay, Colonel Shrill, Major Nash, and one of the newly appointed Joint Chiefs will be waiting in the TOC for you gentlemen," Ari said, breaking Cade's train of thought. "There will be a Cushman and driver waiting for you three when we arrive."

Airman Davis, no doubt, thought Cade.

"After the briefing I suggest you all grab some chow," continued Ari. "Whipper and his crew are going to give Elvira a quick once-over, so I gather you'll have an hour, give or take, to get squared away."

"Copy that," Lopez said. "Sounds to me like you're saying we have time for a four-course meal and then a quick round of golf."

"Only nine holes," Haynes shot. "You set foot on the back nine and you're walking to the District."

Cross whistled. "Washington D.C. My old stomping grounds. I. Can't. Wait."

Remembering the mission to the White House to collect the football containing the codes to the United States' nuclear arsenal, Lopez shivered and said, "She's not the senorita you used to know, mi amigo. All of the snakes are dead and walking upright now."

"Once a zombie, always a zombie," Ari quipped. "Speaking of Zs. We're crossing the Continental Divide. Keep your eyes peeled, fellas. The walkers are real thick on the east side of the Rockies. They seem to collect in pockets and then get stalled out for a while when they hit the *wall* so to speak. You might even see a mega horde ranging around the east slope."

Cade asked, "So the megas aren't sticking to the roads like they were early on?"

"Damn things aren't as predictable in their travels as they once were."

Explains their prolonged absence from the state route from Woodruff to Bear River and beyond, Cade thought. He said, "What about Springs? Are the lights really on?"

Ari chuckled as the helicopter slowed and yawed right to negotiate a treed canyon leading up to a massive peak. "You'll see, Wyatt. You'll see."

Staring out his window at the Douglas Firs whipping by at danger-close range, Cross said, "I couldn't believe my eyes at first. How many survivors call Springs home now?"

Again, Haynes broke in. "A few thousand if you count all of the soldiers taking R and R between combat deployments."

Between combat deployments, thought Cade, dumbstruck. Though he longed to know more about what changes had taken place in the days and weeks since he'd been gone from Schriever, he decided to wait and see it with his own eyes from the air. There was also that sit-down requested by Nash herself during which he figured he could mine her for dirt on all of the particulars that he could think of between now and then.

At the top of the peak, Ari nudged the nose over hard and skimmed the treetops and rock-covered mountain flank with just feet separating the tree tops from the helo's smooth underbelly. After a few seconds traveling at that nose down pitch Cade felt his body pressed down into his seat as the helo leveled out and its forward momentum increased greatly.

"Thank you for flying Night Stalker Airways," Ari said over the comms. "Jedi One-One will be wheels down at Schriever Air Force Base whenever in the hell we get there. The current temperature on the ground is nippy with periods of intermittent rain and sleet expected during your stay."

"No golf," Cross muttered.

"No sunbathing," Lopez quipped.

"I need to visit the armorer," Cade said soberly.

"Don't be a buzzkill, Wyatt," Ari barked over the comms. "While we're en route there will be plenty of time to load mags and oil your piece."

Everyone aboard chuckled at that.

"We need to focus on the mission. The farther east we go, the more Zs there will be. Just saying a certain level of frostiness needs to be attained and then maintained."

"We don't even know *why* President Clay wants us to go back to D.C. yet. It could be a cakewalk mission like the Long Beach—." Ari drew a sharp breath. Recalling that the Delta team had lost a shooter there to a freak Z bite, he instantly regretted the comment. The soldier had been a real solid shooter named Lasseigne. New to the team, he got swarmed and didn't realize he was dead until they were airborne. Still, that was no reason to forget the man, Ari thought. There was no excuse *ever* to forget *any* of the dozens of good men he knew who had fallen to Omega since the dead began to walk. But there was a tiny silver lining to Kelly "Lasagna" Lasseigne's death. For unlike Maddox's death at the hands of the Zs back at Grand Junction Regional, Lasagna was buried back at Schriever, not MIA somewhere in the middle of the Colorado high desert.

"Yeah, right," Cade answered, "a cakewalk. In case you forgot … a soldier died there. A good man named Lasseigne. It's going to be nothing of the sort. We all saw the same satellite footage of the area in and around D.C. … didn't we?"

Heads nodded all around.

"I take back what I said about Long Beach. And no slight was intended." There was a moment of strained silence as the helo popped up and rode over the uneven top of a copse of trees. "However, in my defense," Ari continued, the craft now back to level flight, "what I meant to say and failed miserably is that this one is going to be *nothing* like the last six missions Nash has sent us on. There's a good chance we're going to have *air cover*."

"Predators from Creech?" Cade asked.

"Nope," Ari said. "The long knives are coming out. Take my word for it."

Lopez grimaced and grabbed for his stomach. "From where?" he asked, the sudden, sharp pain beginning to subside.

"A-10s owned the skies over the MWTC for hours," Ari said. "Those Marine aviators chewed up the PLA armor real good."

"What about aerial refueling?" Cade said, the memory of two dangerous hot-refuels conducted on a Z-choked runway in Grand Junction still fresh in his mind. And though he had already reconciled Hicks' death, he again relived the haunting vision of his fellow Delta operator falling in total silence before disappearing under the crushing tangle of dozens of ravenous dead.

"A given, now," Ari answered.

Cade shifted in his seat to look groundward. Seeing a road suddenly appear along their flight path, he said, "Has Whipper *really* gotten his act together? Or is he still patching his birds together with bubblegum and bailing wire?"

"Don't you worry," Ari said behind a soft chuckle. "The fear of God you placed in that man is still firmly rooted. I'm convinced he sees your face and that wicked dagger of yours every time he hears that a Night Stalker bird is comin' a callin'."

Cross nodded.

Lopez smirked, then nodded. "It's kind of funny seeing a man of his rank jump as high as he does. Hell, he even cleans the windows and kicks the tires before we head out."

"I wouldn't be surprised that after the man sees you he ups the ante. I bet he'll go full on Oil Can Henry Premium Service and haul a vacuum inside this bird and tidy her up—"

"Hey Wyatt," Ari said, "see if you can scare Whipper into cleaning the inside of all the windows. Then tell him we're not leaving until you see a Vanillorama air freshener tree hanging from my rearview mirror."

"I hate vanilla," proffered Haynes. "Strippers smell like vanilla. My ex-wife started stripping a couple of months before she left me. I hate glitter, too. She brought it home on her vanilla-body-spray-smelling-self every night." He chuckled sadly at the thought.

"I'm learning more and more about you every day, Haynes," Ari said. "Narrowed it down to boxers yesterday."

"And we learned that Haynes is a *boob* man the day before that," Skipper stated glibly.

An incoming call from Schriever's TOC (Tactical Operations Center) interrupted the banter.

Cade listened to the female voice in his ear tell Jedi One-One and any other air assets on the net to be on the lookout for an enemy patrol spotted by a group of survivors passing through Pueblo the day before.

"How many PLA?' Ari asked, even as he was autonomously taking an evasive maneuver by quickly halving the Ghost Hawk's altitude.

Sensing the craft dip, Cade began to relive the bird strike and consequent crash that killed friends and left one of the gen-3 Jedi rides a smoldering wreck in a church graveyard outside of Draper, South Dakota. The verdant ground cover was rushing up and then the window was filled with a scrub-dotted expanse of flat land shot with all the colors one usually associated with the planet Mars: reds and oranges set in a patchwork fashion held together by veins of mineral a strange, muted ochre-yellow.

"Two armed personnel riding motorcycles," said the disembodied voice.

Risking a tongue-lashing from the aircraft commander, Cade asked, "Were they both men and were they wearing uniforms?"

"Schriever, Jedi One-One," Ari said, his voice a little strained. "That's one of my Delta Boys talking over the open channel. Wyatt's a captain, so I trust he's good to be in the loop on this matter."

The Schriever controller—a captain herself—drew a sharp breath that registered loud and clear in everyone's headsets. "Negative, Captain Grayson. But that's about all the detail we could ferret out of the couple who reported seeing them."

Changing their tactics, Cade thought before saying, "Thank you, Captain Jensen. Good to hear your voice again."

"Enough back patting," Ari said. Then, as the comms went deathly silent, two things wholly unexpected happened. First, a shrill electronic tone indicating the helo's sensors had just detected a missile launch filled the cabin and sounded in everyone's headsets. Next, as Ari banked One-One hard to port, the distinctive staccato *whooshing* of multiple countermeasure flares popping aft and underfoot reverberated through the cabin.

A fraction of a second after the Ghost Hawk began taking evasive maneuvers, Lopez groaned once and doubled over as far as his safety harness would allow.

Chapter 26

After a cursory search for the person or persons using the rectory as an observation post turned up nothing, the group moved west across the expanse of grass between the church and priest's residence.

"Come on," Oliver urged. "We gotta see what's inside the church. I bet there's a ton of canned food and stuff in there."

"He's got a point," Lev said. "People in small towns like this had a little more time to prepare for the infected onslaught than the poor bastards in and around Salt Lake."

"Or Denver," Wilson added.

"Grand Junction wasn't pretty, either," Taryn said. "I watched all of the videos posted to my Facebook by all my friends." She swallowed hard then added, "And those posts stopped going up real quick. Still had them saved though. In a way they kept me going while I waited in that airport office. Gave me hope … resolve. If I didn't get out of there, who was going to tell their story? Remember them going forward?" Her words trailed off and she began to sob.

Wilson drew her in and held her tight as Daymon stopped before the church stairs, looking up at the stained glass windows and peeling paint. The doors were sturdy and looked as if they had been shut tight by the last person to leave—or perhaps, more troubling, by those still closed up inside. On the door was a sign that read SERVICES CANCELLED UNTIL FURTHER NOTICE.

Face screwed up as if he was working on solving a big dilemma in his head, Daymon placed one foot on the cement stairs.

Sidling up next Daymon, Oliver read the sign aloud then looked sidelong at his tormentor. "What are *you* afraid of?" he asked, his tone imparting a hint of accusation.

Those five words—or perhaps what they implied—set off a chain reaction in Daymon that had been arrested since he first set eyes on the attic access panel in the house next door.

"I'm afraid of nothing," he hissed, staring daggers at the shorter man. Speaking real low and slow, he added, "I just don't like enclosed spaces. That's all. End of story."

Oliver raised his hands and backed away. "Sorry, man. We've put exactly zero cans of food in our trucks. Our supply run isn't looking too good. Just saying, though. Plus, I bet there's really high ceilings inside the church."

"And effing spiders," Taryn said.

Sitting on the sidewalk, his stub tail thumping a hollow rhythm, Max growled, seemingly in agreement with Taryn that the only good spiders were of the deceased variety.

Jamie placed a reassuring hand on the younger woman's tatted arm. "I'll stomp 'em for you." She smiled and cast her gaze down the road towards where they had left their trucks. "We've got *rotters*," she whispered, her smile fading and the war tomahawk suddenly appearing in her gloved hand.

Instinctively, all heads swiveled to see half a dozen emaciated first turns of indeterminable gender approaching from the west.

"They don't see us," Daymon said, crouching down by the stairs.

"Yet," Lev added, going to a knee beside a dirty Pontiac ravaged by rust and plastered with dried-on leaves.

Then, almost in unison, everyone who was still standing made themselves small and looked for cover.

Max scurried under the nearest car.

Oliver slipped behind the hedges bracketing the stairs.

Using the tall grass on the parking strip as a blind, Taryn and Wilson both went to one knee on the sidewalk.

As soon as Jamie had spotted the dead things shuffling uphill toward them, swaying and lurching and mainly keeping to the center of the street, she had uttered the warning and also gone to ground next to the Pontiac.

Now, a couple of seconds later, Jamie was duck-walking past Lev, one hand tracing the side of the Pontiac, the other moving the tomahawk in a slow and menacing clockwise circle. She made it to the car's A-pillar and was about to rise up and deal with the interlopers when, over the long, gently sloping hood, she witnessed the rotters inexplicably perform a clumsy left-hand turn and strike off to the north, hissing and moaning, the lot of them in full-on hunt mode.

"Let them go," Daymon said as he rose and watched the procession cut in front of the trucks. He scaled the steps hesitantly and tracked their movement along the near side of the body shop until they were lost from sight.

"Think they're following our bleeder?" Lev asked.

"Could be a dog," Taryn said quietly, craning under the car to get a look at Max. "If it is, our guy doesn't seem concerned."

Wilson climbed the stairs. He braced himself by placing a hand on Daymon's shoulder then extended fully, craning to see for himself. "They're gone now. Doubt it was a dog," he stated. "I haven't seen one since we left Bastion."

"You have a point," she answered. "Are we checking the church out or not?"

Sweeping Taryn aside with one arm, Lev scaled the steps and formed up behind Wilson, carbine readied, the previous altercation seemingly forgotten.

Without warning the others, Daymon pounded on the dark wood panel inset into one of the massive doors.

Meanwhile a thin finger of clouds scudded in front of the sun, casting a dark shadow over the church and causing the stained glass windows, which a moment prior had shone with all the colors of the rainbow, to take on a dark foreboding shade of gray.

Seeing the all-purpose weatherproof carpeting at his feet suddenly bathed in shadow, Daymon whipped around and, half-expecting to see another spiked tree trunk barreling for his head, shot a wide-eyed glance skyward.

Nothing. He saw only Wilson and Lev a handful of feet away and shooting strange looks at him. Thankful he hadn't become a human pincushion, he flipped the clouds the bird and assailed the door with another barrage of knocks.

Taryn called up the stairs, "Anybody home?"

Daymon pressed his ear to the door and listened hard. Hearing nothing, he came away, looked at the others and shook his head. "I think it's clear. Plus, there's no X on the door like there was at the rehab place and most of the farmhouses up Center Street."

Lev grabbed Daymon's arm. "Could be more of the silenced rotters inside. Best be careful."

Daymon drew Kindness from her sheath, put one hand on the door pull, and pressed his thumb on the latch release. Feeling some give, he turned his head and body sideways and said, "It's unlocked. I'm going to throw it open and backpedal like hell."

Lev moved a few steps to his right. After shooing Wilson off the landing, he clicked off the safety and shouldered his rifle. Training it on the vertical seam between the double-doors, he raised a brow and said, "Ready."

The door was indeed unlocked and the paper affixed to it fluttered and tore away when Daymon heaved the left side open. Then, keeping his promise, he leaped backwards, spinning a one-eighty in the process. By the time he was turned around and had cleared the midpoint of the stairs—all of a half-second later—two things dawned on him. First, he was acutely aware that cold dead hands were not grabbing at his body. Second, he felt a breeze down below and saw that to a person the others were staring at his crotch, wide-eyed and grinning.

As his boots hit the lawn beside the stairs and Lev still hadn't opened fire with the suppressed carbine, Daymon looked down and saw the cherry on his embarrassment sundae—an unbuttoned fly and his manhood hanging out for all to see.

"Damn," Jamie said, eyes tearing up with mirth. "It's true what they say." All eyes instantly turned to her; Daymon's, understandably, slowly narrowed to dark slits.

"Do tell," Oliver said, barely able to contain himself.

"If the barn door's left open … the *hog* will get out," Lev said, his gaze locked on the darkened foyer to his fore.

Blushing, Daymon turned to face the church and put his business away—this time *remembering* to button his camouflage ACU bottoms. Finished, he scaled the stairs, wariness showing in each step taking him closer to the yawning door.

"With Kindness in hand, and you flying away from the door like it was electrified … I must admit," Jamie said, wiping away a tear. "I was starting to worry that you'd have nothing left to take home to Heidi."

"Very funny," Daymon said, craning around the door jamb, Kindness clutched in one fist and blindly working the right-side door with his free hand. "So funny I forgot to laugh. But you know what?"

Humoring him, Jamie said, "Lay it on me."

"I didn't get mad."

"Your Ritalin is kicking in, huh?" Wilson ribbed.

Shooting Wilson a sour look, Daymon crossed the threshold. Just as he set foot inside the foyer where the ceiling was low and empty coat closets flanked him left and right, a myriad of vivid colors splashed the floor and pews and lit up the gloomy aisle stretching away from him.

After drawing in a deep breath and exhaling sharply, he felt his knees giving out on him.

Chapter 27

The missile lock-on warning continued to bleat as Cade braced against the evasive actions taken by the aircrew. In his earpiece he heard Ari breathing hard. "Heat seeker identified," the SOAR aviator said, a millisecond before the craft vibrated from another volley of flares being dispensed. He also recognized Haynes' voice as the left seater calmly informed the TOC controller of their situation and current position.

After hearing Captain Jensen reassure the aircrew that search and rescue birds were on the flight line, fully fueled and spooling up, Cade tightened his flight harness to one notch past tourniquet and ran through his mind what he'd do if they did indeed meet terra firma in a sudden and jarring manner. *No*, he thought as the mottled blue-gray horizon slipped from view and the flat ochre ground filled up every starboard window fore to aft, *sudden and jarring* was too benign a term. Instantaneous and explosive was more like it, and if that should come to pass, he decided the straps biting into his shoulders and hips were most likely going to relieve him of an appendage or two upon impact, not save his life as intended.

As the characteristic *whoosh* of the last round of flares ejecting from the wildly jinking helo faded, abruptly the burnished pewter sky was filling up the port-side windows.

In the middle of the high-G serpentine roll Cade noticed a look of worry park itself on Cross's face. And during that same snapshot in time it also registered to him that Lopez's arms and legs were floating weightless and the Hispanic operator's normally tanned face had gone ashen.

"We have a medical emergency back here," Cade barked into the boom mic, only to find that his audio had apparently been muted. To his left, Skipper was readying the minigun and talking into his boom mic, lips moving a mile a minute, whatever he was saying also going unheard by Cade. A tick after the speeding craft regained level flight, the door concealing the minigun parted vertically down the center, the two jagged edged halves sucking inward and folding neatly inside the fuselage, one to Skipper's right, the other seating flat against the forward crew-door pillar off of Cade's left shoulder.

Cold wind invaded the cabin. It seemed to have an effect on Lopez. His lips, previously pursed and purple, had regained some color and were moving.

Bellowing to be heard over the escalating turbine whine, Cade said, "Lopez, hang in—," only to have his words suddenly drowned out by the deafening buzz-saw-like ripping sound of the minigun belching hot lead. Hundreds of rounds—if not a thousand—poured down onto whatever or whomever Doctor Silence was targeting. In his ear Cade suddenly heard Haynes calling out the range and direction of travel of some kind of vehicle he was tracking visually.

Back in the loop, thought Cade as the minigun roared again. A shorter burst. One second versus three.

Skipper said flatly, "Two tangos down. Still panning. Give me some distance."

In response to the request the helo climbed swiftly and began a tight orbit over the high desert landscape it had nearly become one with.

Now aware of Lopez's plight, Cross unbuckled and took a knee in front of the Delta captain. He ripped off his gloves and checked the stricken man's neck for a carotid pulse. Simultaneously, he flashed Cade a reassuring thumbs-up with one hand and patted Lopez's cheek with the other, getting an immediate result.

"What's going on?" Cade asked at the top of his voice.

Suddenly lucid, Lopez jabbed a finger at his right lower abdomen.

Pressing his thumb firmly on the location Lopez had pointed to earned Cross a face full of hot, runny bile. Lopez continued to spew yellowish liquid even as Cross recoiled and dragged his forearm across his face.

"Earned my Puker Patch," Lopez wheezed. "And my gut's on fire for it."

"Do you still have an appendix?" asked Cross.

Offering Cross a camo bandana with a sheepish, embarrassed look on his face, Lopez said, "As far as I know."

"You'd know if you already lost it," Cross said. "My little sis had hers burst on her when we were kids. Same deal. She was in serious pain. Had the tender abdomen. Then the puking"—he took the bandana and dabbed at his face and neck—"the non-stop puking. Only she never painted me with it."

"My bad," Lopez said.

Cade had been watching Cross tend to Lopez. In his left side vision he saw Skipper rotate the minigun's barrel vertical to the sky and haul it back a few inches and lock it in place inside the cabin. The smell of gun smoke hit his nose. Then he sensed the weapons bay door begin to move and craned and watched the two parts come together and snug flat. All told, the weapon's initial deployment took six seconds or so. Retracting it back into place burned about eight. Not too bad a turnaround to keep a low radar signature. But it didn't amount to shit—as they had all just learned the hard way—if you flew anywhere near a determined foe brandishing a MANPAD antiaircraft weapon outfitted with heat seekers. Murphy was back and Cade didn't like it one bit.

"Taking her down," Ari said flatly. "We're almost smack dab between two decent-sized towns. Stay frosty, boys … there's bound to be dead roaming the area."

"Copy that," Cade said.

Cross retook his seat and fastened his lap belt. He met Cade's eyes and motioned at Lopez. "He needs a doctor, ASAP."

"Appendix?" Cade said.

Cross nodded.

Cade shook his head and cursed under his breath. Just as he began wondering who was going to fill Lopez's spot, he felt the usual underfoot clunk and vibration of the belly doors opening. A tick later came the reassuring whirr of the landing gear motoring into the down position.

"Ohhh my," Ari deadpanned. "Looks like Skipper made us a street pizza."

Having a good idea what Ari was alluding to, Cade focused on the rising finger of oily smoke outside the port windows and waited for the reassuring bump of the bird's wheels kissing earth.

Chapter 28

Even from the front of the foyer, peering across the color-dappled sanctuary to the altar beyond, Daymon knew he was looking at a horror he hoped to never see again. All at once a host of emotionally charged memories were dredged up from deep recesses in his brain and came flooding back, jumping synapses at nearly light speed. Jaw hinging open in a silent scream, he crashed to his knees, eyes locked dead ahead, as if praying to the very sight that had seemingly stricken him down. Excited voices filled the low-ceilinged entry at his back and hands were grabbing his arms in an attempt to steady him.

Daymon noticed all of these things on the periphery of consciousness, but ignored the stimuli, for the sight at the end of the aisle had instantaneously transported him back to Jackson, Wyoming and, though he was physically still in Woodruff, Utah, in his head he was again walking the blacktop on the Highway to Hell—Ian Bishop's mile-long spectacle meant to remind town folk what would happen to them if they tried to defect from the so-called capital of Robert Christian's New America. "Examples" is what Bishop had called the dozens of people he had caught trying to escape Jackson. And *examples* is what they had become, all of them suffering a slow death to a combination of injury, shock, and exposure before finally becoming fodder for the opportunist raptors.

"Heidi is OK," someone said into his ear. "You called out for her as you collapsed. She's not in danger. She's right here."

A gloved hand brushed back Daymon's dreads and the long range CB radio was pressed to his ear. Though his soon-to-be wife's high-pitched voice emanated from the speaker, he still seemed oblivious to his surroundings.

Seeing Daymon's obvious hesitation, Lev pushed forward and kneeled in front of him, making a point of blocking the sight that had presumably triggered his friend's *episode*. He stared into the man's eyes and saw a sort of primal fear in them.

Taryn leaned forward. "Is *he* going to be OK?" she asked, concern evident in her tone.

Lev shook his head side-to-side and shrugged, semaphore for *I haven't a clue*. Then, momentarily breaking eye contact with Daymon, he motioned Oliver and Jamie forward. After watching them squeeze through the crowded foyer, he met Oliver's eyes and tapped a knuckle on the man's slung carbine. "Run to the trucks and get a first aid kit. And make it quick."

Without complaint nor hesitation, Oliver unslung his rifle and disappeared into the gloom.

Lev turned his attention to Jamie. Meeting her eyes, he hooked a thumb over his shoulder. "*Finish* that thing."

She nodded and started a slow pirouette to her right.

Lev reached out and gripped her forearm gently. "Stay frosty," he said in a low voice. "There may be more traps."

Jamie nodded and started down the center aisle, trying her best to ignore the little voice inside her head urging her to take a second look at the crucified skeletal remains. Two steps down the aisle, the voice won out. So she paused between the second to last pews and looked it head to toe. It proved to be a thing from her childhood nightmares, only she wasn't at Disneyland and these bones weren't bleached white and lying on a make-believe pirate-infested Caribbean Island. Nope. This zombie skeleton was twitching now, the few remaining muscles snaking up its neck moving the grinning skull up and down as if it was agreeing with something or, partially doubled-up the way it was, perhaps laughing at the punchline of a joke only it was privy to. Betting on the former, Jamie flicked her eyes to its chest cavity where, save for knobby vertebrae and a nest of what she thought were corded core muscles, nothing resembling an internal organ remained.

Continuing the visual inspection, she dropped her gaze to the flaccid white penis dangling from a ribbon of skin someone had gone to the trouble of tying to what she guessed had been his pubic bone. Moving on to his lower extremities, she saw shiny scraps of dried flesh and sinew still clinging to blood-reddened femur, fibula, and tibia bones. Calling forth every last ounce of willpower she possessed, the hardened survivor tore her eyes from its perfectly preserved feet and the metal rod pinning them to the post and began sweeping the floor for tripwires or anything else that looked out of place. Fully aware of the jaundiced, lifeless eyes still tracking her, she completed her slow procession to the raised dais where the crudely fashioned cross had been erected—proud of herself for not having stolen a third look along the way.

The floor below the dais was shiny where more than one person's spilt blood had dried to black. The stench up close proved to be nearly unbearable.

Breathing through her nose, her usually husky voice nasal and high-pitched, Jamie said, "The aisle is clear of traps."

At the sound of Jamie's voice, the abomination shuddered excitedly, its bony knees and exposed ribs creating a grating sound as they rubbed together.

Lev threw a visible shudder. He squeezed Daymon's shoulder and whispered, "Hang in there." Then, looking around, he hissed, "Where the eff is Oliver?"

Chapter 29

Once Jedi One-One was wheels down on the snow-dotted plat of high desert, Cade hastily shed his safety harness and stood, M4 carbine in hand.

"I'll cover your egress," Skipper said, grabbing a carbine of his own. He slapped the operator on the shoulder and hauled the port-side cabin door open.

Still kneeling before Lopez, Cross looked up and met Cade's gaze. "You go," he said forcefully. "I'll keep an eye on him."

Cade nodded in agreement and unplugged the flight helmet from the comms jack. Then, for the sake of expediency, he deployed the smoked visor to keep his eyes safe from flying debris and exited the helo without swapping helmets. M4 at a low ready, he ran towards the smoking wreckage, head ducked under the imaginary reach of the near invisible rotor blades.

The wreckage was both organic and mechanical in nature and was scattered over a bullet-tilled patch of desert roughly two dozen yards in diameter. The smoke Cade had spotted from inside the Ghost Hawk was coming from a nearby copse of trees where a number of small fires in the damp underbrush struggled to stay lit.

Ari was right. Skipper had indeed turned something into "street pizza." The previously human organic matter was mostly pulped flesh and bone splashed in two long frothy red trails bisecting the epicenter of the churned-up topsoil. The two largest pieces, both limbless torsos, still wore Kevlar vests, the ceramic bullet-resistant plates fractured in dozens of small pieces after having taken direct hits from the speeding 7.62x51mm projectiles.

A severed head, eyes open and staring, lay near one of the torsos. It still wore a knockoff tactical-style helmet, nylon chin straps still snugged tightly underneath the intact jawbone. A several-days-old growth of dark facial hair meant at least one of the dead had been a man. Though he scanned the area, the second head was nowhere to be seen.

Of the mechanical wreckage, the biggest pieces were nearly identical: two large billets of polished metal sprouting milled fins, colorful wires, and black rubber hosing. The items in question were still bolted to frames made of snaking black metal tubes all bent at crazy angles. *Motorcycle*, Cade thought at once. Then he counted four spoked rims that had been scattered to all points of the compass. One was still attached to a pair of long-travel forks, the plastic dustcovers and exposed metal rattle canned in a dark camouflage scheme. Another front wheel—also hastily painted—was a good distance to his left and partially obscured by a clutch of inert tumbleweeds. The two rear rims were a ways uphill from Cade and had come to rest a few feet apart beside shin-high piles of dirty, days-old snow. All four rims were still wrapped in knobby off-road tires. Like the two bodies and the motorcycle chassis, all four tires had been shredded by Skipper's superior marksmanship.

Motorcycles, he thought. *Plural.*

Ignoring the metallic stink of freshly spilt blood and the bloated ropes of greasy-looking intestine spilling from the rent-open abdomen, he took a knee next to the nearest torso and manhandled it around until what he guessed to be the chest was facing skyward. After loosening the vest's Velcro straps, a quick inspection underneath the jagged plates produced a thin diary, an envelope full of some official-looking documents, and a host of laminated topographical maps of the Western United States. Tucked away inside an intact chest pouch was a slim Chinese-manufactured satellite phone. In another was a handful of flash-cards featuring rudimentary pictograms and their corresponding warnings all written in Chinese and pertaining to situations relevant only in a modern day Z-infested theater of war.

On the first card was a nicely rendered drawing of a man, arms up and rifle at his feet. Though the hieroglyphic-like Chinese characters meant nothing to Cade, the image instantly brought to mind one word: *surrender.*

The next flashcard featured a distressed-looking woman with exaggerated red bite marks running up one outstretched arm. Again, the delicate vertical writing meant nothing to him. The image, however, all but screamed: *infected.*

And none too surprising to Cade: The documents, diaries, and weapons he had hurriedly policed up were very similar to the items he and Duncan had taken from the undead Chinese Special Forces scouts outside of Huntsville only a couple of days ago. However, somewhat startling was the stark realization that these MANPAD-armed PLA SF soldiers were less than a hundred miles west of Colorado Springs.

Sensing eyes on him, Cade sidestepped the rising smoke and peered west down the length of the unnamed two-lane. Roughly a mile distant, judging by their stilted gait and that they were loping along on the centerline in a loose knot, he realized a handful of dead were onto them and shambling his way.

Damn, he thought as he turned back to face Jedi One-One. *The persistent rotten bastards are everywhere now. Even on a lonely stretch of road in the metaphorical shadows of the majestic Rocky Mountains.*

As the weary operator covered the distance from the scene of carnage to the awaiting helo, arms filled with items stripped from the enemy and his own slung M4 banging against his back, he noticed the matte-black bird suddenly go light and bouncy on her gear—a dead giveaway that Ari was eager to spool power, pull pitch, and get them all the hell out of Dodge.

Chapter 30

Causing everyone save for Daymon to turn in unison, the door to the outside creaked and the curtain divider fluttered. At the head of the aisle, having just returned from the vehicles, Oliver emerged through the curtains, breathing hard and carrying a red nylon first-aid kit. He unzipped the kit and from a plain-looking box the size of a cigarette pack he fished out a couple of white fabric-wrapped capsules and passed them off to Lev.

There was a soft crunching sound followed instantly by a heady eye-watering blast of ammonia when Lev rolled both capsules between his thumb and forefinger. Turning his head away, he waved his closed fist directly underneath Daymon's nose.

One pass was all it took to snap the former BLM firefighter back to the present. He leaned to his left to see around the pistol hanging off of Lev's right hip.

Sure enough, he hadn't been seeing things. The reanimated skeleton *was* affixed to a giant cross that was sure as hell not a fixture original to the church. Still gawking at the surreal spectacle, he accepted a hand up from Lev and thanked him for bringing him back from his shock-induced stupor.

"You would have done the same for me," Lev said, setting off down the aisle toward Jamie, who was angling in to finish the job started by the people who had skinned and flayed the poor man.

Head still spinning ever so slightly, Daymon stopped shy of the raised carpeted platform and took a deep, steadying breath. "Shit," he said, exhaling. "First sight of this one took me right back to a place I *never* wanted to revisit."

"I won't even ask," Jamie said. "Damn good to see you're back with us, though." War tomahawk in hand, she turned and, going up on her tippy toes, took one wide arcing swing at the Z's gently bobbing skull. The blow was a perfect "one-timer" as she'd heard Cade call a single bullet-saving Z kill. There was a loud *crack* and the living skeleton's upper body went limp, all with little energy expended on Jamie's part. Furthermore, the sound made by steel cleaving bone meant a bullet was saved for a "rainy day," the new catch phrase being bandied about Eden. Rainy and snowy days were coming, which made these last-minute runs outside the wire all the more necessary.

Daymon bobbed like a boxer to avoid a hurtling sliver of hair-covered bone. Raising a brow at the close call, he looked over his shoulder towards the foyer, where Wilson, Taryn, and a panting Max were filling up the doorway. The thick burgundy-colored curtains used to seal off the sanctuary during mass crowded them on both sides, blocking the view behind. For a half-beat Daymon entertained the idea of asking where Oliver was, then thought better of it. *Sink or swim. He'll be the better for it.*

Swinging his gaze forward, Daymon ignored the slumped creature and instead focused on the cross. The upright was a four-by-four post with a substantial amount of cured concrete still clinging to the end resting on the dais. Dried clods of dirt had cleaved off the medicine-ball-sized plug of cement and lay scattered about the floor behind the polished wood pulpit. Some of the clods were flattened into irregular circles that bore distinct prints from some kind of footwear with lug soles.

Seeing Oliver join the others now forming a rough half-circle around him, Daymon cocked his head and stared at the writing on the wall above the cross. Scrawled in a barely legible hand and likely with the crucified man's own blood was the question: WHO THE FUCK IS THE WICKED?

Bracketing the query on all four corners were sets of words and numbers. All four of what could only be Bible verses were scribbled with the same kindergarten-like sloppiness.

"What the eff?" Daymon said, crossing his arms.

"I have no idea what to make of the question," Jamie said. "But those are—"

Finishing for her, Oliver said, "Bible verses."

Without consulting each other, Wilson and Taryn moved quietly between the pews and returned with three Bibles apiece.

"Great minds …" Lev said. "Gimme one of those."

Taryn handed Lev and Jamie their own King James.

After distributing his extras to Oliver and Daymon, Wilson cracked his. Flicking his eyes to the numbers on the wall, he began leafing through the parchment-like pages.

"Let's see … Galatians 5:15, where are you?" He flipped pages for a moment then cleared his throat and began to read. "But if ye bite and devour one another, take heed that ye be not consumed one of another."

Taryn said, "Top right corner. Acts 15:29. That ye abstain from meats obtained to idols, and from blood, and from things strangled, and from fornication: from which if ye keep yourselves, ye shall do well. Fare ye well." She made a face and looked a question at Wilson, who simply shrugged and continued thumbing through the Bible.

Daymon sat down hard on the front pew. "This one is heavy duty. 1 Peter 5:8." He drew a breath and went on. "Be sober, be vigilant; because your adversary the Devil, as a roaring lion, walketh about, seeking whom he may devour …" He went quiet, eyes parked on the butchered Z.

"I've got the last one," Jamie said.

Imitating an English barrister, Daymon lowered his voice and said, "Please cede the floor to the lady from Eden."

"Salt Lake," she corrected. "Revelation 22:13. I an Alpha and *Omega*, the beginning and the *end*, the first and the *last*. Now that's come creepy, cryptic shit. Whoever did all of this"—with one arm, she made a sweeping motion at the wall—"I want nothing to do with them."

"Too late," Wilson said, soberly. "We're hip deep in it. All of it."

"Weather's probably going to be mild again tomorrow," Daymon said, still staring at the whole surreal scene. "I say we go back to Eden and regroup. Pick Duncan and Glenda's brains. She might know more about Bear Lake. At the least we can consult an atlas and see what we're looking at."

"Looking at?" Oliver sneered. "We're *looking at* twenty more miles of zombie-infested road between here and Bear Lake. All the while we have to be on the lookout for psycho killers who just so happen to enjoy setting up Omega-tainted traps. That's all. What could go wrong?"

Rising off the pew, Daymon said, "That's the attitude we're *not* looking for. Keep thinking that way, Oliver, and you're going to end up like *him*." Then, as if he hadn't just been kneeling there a few minutes ago in a near catatonic state, he strode down the aisle, seemingly without a care in the world.

Eden Compound

"Brook," bellowed Heidi, "a man from Bear River wants to talk to you."

Two turns away, behind the closed door of the Graysons' quarters, Raven slid off the lower bunk and tossed her mom a tee shirt several sizes too big for the petite woman.

"Does your back feel any better, Mom?"

After rising up from her stomach with no attempt to cover herself, Brook spun around on the bunk and planted her feet on the wood floor. "I hate to say it, honey, but the pain is worse now than ever. Thank you, though. I appreciate all the massages you, Sasha, and Glenda are lavishing on me. You especially are getting way better at it. I ought to call you fingers of steel or something like it."

Pouting a little, Raven said, "No thanks … that sounds like a wrestler's name."

"Like Nacho Libre," Brook said, suppressing a smile and wondering fleetingly what had become of Jack Black after the shit hit the fan in Los Angeles.

With a blank look on her face, Raven ignored the reference to Mexican food and said, "What *do* you think will make your back feel better?"

"Just time, I suppose, sweetie. Just time." Brook doubled over as a coughing fit gripped her.

Raven rose from the bed, face a mask of concern.

Wiping a rope of spittle from her lip, Brook faked a half-smile and straightened out the shirt. Forgoing her only bra, which three months into the apocalypse was threadbare and mostly just wire and straps, she shrugged on the shirt and rose gingerly. Then, hiding the true amount of pain she was experiencing, a seven or eight on the scale of one to ten she used to query her patients with, she grabbed her gun belt and headed off toward the security pod.

"Brook!" Heidi called again, her voice echoing off the low metal ceilings.

"I'm coming. I'm coming," Brook said. "Keep your—." She bit her tongue. Figuratively, of course. No reason to say the wrong thing and risk setting Heidi off again. The woman *was* even-keeling it at the moment. She'd found her baseline with the meds and most of the credit went to Cade for having scavenged them. No longer was the twenty-something sequestering herself belowground. Lately she had been venturing topside without any sweet-talking from Daymon. She'd even come so far from the dark place she'd been languishing in to have managed two consecutive nights topside with him in the purloined RV. Or "Love Shack" as she'd heard Duncan refer to it as.

Reaffixing the fake smile, Brook rounded the corner and calmly asked the young blonde who from Bear River needed her on the phone this instant.

"Alexander," Heidi said, balancing the sat-phone on her palm.

Baseline my ass, Brook thought as she received the slim black Thuraya. *You spoke too soon, Mrs. Grayson.*

"This is Brook," she said.

After offering up a few pleasantries, which Brook reciprocated, Dregan got down to brass tacks. "Have you or your people been by Ray and Helen's place? You know, the stubborn elderly couple."

"No, we haven't." Recalling the aid she and the kids had received from the couple, she grew concerned. "You think they're in danger?"

"They've always answered their radio," Dregan said. "I didn't want to have to, but I'll stir up some volunteers and go have a look."

Listening intently, Heidi sat back in her chair and fixed her gaze on Brook.

Alarm creeping into her voice, Brook asked, "Is the horde back in the area? We've got people outside the wire. North, actually."

"No, no, no. We haven't seen them since before the snow fell," Dregan said, then started coughing, the fit lasting a few seconds. "I just didn't want to waste fuel to do what a radio could. Though growing scarce, batteries are still easier to come by than fuel."

Not in our neck of the woods, Brook thought. "I'll call Daymon and have them go to the Thagon farm and see what's up."

More coughing on Dregan's end.

Heidi furrowed her brows. "Is he OK?" she mouthed.

Brook grimaced as a lightning bolt of pain shot out from the scarring where the Z had bitten her. "Do *you* need anything, Dregan?"

"No, Brook, my bones have already been thrown and come up snake eyes. It's just a matter of time before the cancer takes me. It's Gregory I'm concerned about. He's not doing so well."

"The sutures aren't holding?"

"They're fine. He's up and about," Dregan said. "But the infection, it's back. In his lungs, though."

"Sounds like the flu. Or walking pneumonia. He *was* out in the elements for some time."

"There's a bug going around Bear River," Dregan conceded. "So you know, we've doubled the dose of antibiotics Glenda provided. We'll have to wait and see if it helps."

"No," she blurted. "The antibiotics are to knock down whatever bugs the rotter may have introduced into your son's system when it took a bite out of him. They do not work on viral infections. Period."

Silence on Dregan's end.

After doing the math in her head, Brook said, "This means you now have less than a week's worth left."

"You are correct, Brook." Dregan said. "So begs the question … will I outlast the remaining pills?"

"Don't go there," Brook said. "I'll see what we have here that we can part with. If we have any narcotics … for your pain, I'll see that you get those as well."

Dregan thanked Brook and reassured her that Eden would be the first to know when the rotters made their return visit.

Brook thumbed off the satellite phone and swapped it for the long range CB. Raising the group outside the wire, she relayed the information regarding the Thagons' radio silence as well as Dregan's confirmation that there'd been no recent sightings of the migrating horde.

Chapter 31

Immediately after launching off the rocky, snow-crusted soil adjacent to the blood-spattered kill zone, Ari had spun the Ghost Hawk around in a tight one-eighty and resumed their near laser-straight flight path towards Colorado Springs. Before the gear had snugged into place in the belly of the bird, a thick blanket of silence had descended upon the once jovial atmosphere inside Jedi One-One.

Now, thirty minutes removed from the close call with the Chinese FN-6 surface to air missile, Cade could see the red rock spires of Garden of the Gods on the distant horizon. Illuminated by the late afternoon sun, the National Park bordering the southwest edge of Colorado Springs was one of the prettiest places he had ever seen, though admittedly, each time he'd made its acquaintance, it had been from altitude and through the thick Plexiglas window of one type of aircraft or another.

Beyond the reddish ochre expanse, downtown Colorado Springs was bookended to the south by 14,113-foot-tall Pikes Peak. And just as downtown Los Angeles had appeared clear as day over the horizon weeks earlier, the pollutant-free air here also let him make out the city's sparsely appointed skyline from twenty miles out.

By Los Angeles, or even Denver standards, the buildings in Springs were stunted. Roughly a dozen high-rises between twelve and twenty-two stories rose up from the city center. Dozens more smaller buildings, nearly all of them less than ten stories, were scattered around the periphery of the taller standouts.

In just a handful of minutes the helo had drawn to within two miles of the darkened city. By this time Lopez was sitting up straight and at times grimacing and groaning softly. It was also when Cade first spotted the vast wall undulating across the landscape's natural contours. Constructed from what appeared to be hundreds of cement freeway noise barriers, the type of which bracketed nearly every metropolitan stretch of road nationwide, the impressive feat of engineering lent the impression that the modern structures the wall encircled had been dropped there through some manipulation of time and space.

The metal and glass stronghold throwing off the westering sun appeared to be in the clutches of a giant sleeping snake, its rigid cement spine made up of hundreds of individual panels that ran in straight lines on the west and east perimeters and arced gracefully where they met on the north and south ends. Modern meets medieval; the juxtaposition was stunning.

Seeing Cade craning his head to make the most of the limited viewing angle afforded by the small porthole-style window, Cross said, "You're looking at miles and miles of unbroken twenty-foot-tall cement wall. Wherever possible, the engineers fortified the interior with dirt berms. In the places where it runs over cement or blacktop they resorted to driving ten-foot steel rods into the ground to shore it up. They finished their work at Schriever weeks ago. I've no idea how many panels that took them to complete. Stripped most of it from the interstates north of Castle Rock and southwest of Denver and Aurora. Smaller panels sourced from Yoder and south near Pueblo were used to shore up Schriever and Cheyenne's fences."

The helicopter banked softly to port and Cade felt the airspeed increase. A half-beat later, Ari said, "The engineers have drawn up plans to stretch the south perimeter to Carson in the next week or so. Eventually they will have the north perimeter moved all the way up to the Air Force Academy."

"Wow," Cade said, eyes glued to the city below. "Any idea why the engineers didn't just use the 25 and 21 as natural borders on the east and west?"

"The overpasses and side streets were a pain in the ass to deal with. President Clay figured that as long as we were taking back the city, we might as well take it all the way to Garden of the Gods and maybe even Schriever sometime next year."

"*We* ... damn easy call for her to make from deep inside Cheyenne Mountain," Cade said, incredulous. "What Gaines, his 10th group and the 4th ID all started, the sacrifices that they made going door to door clearing the living dead, was no small feat."

"She's a good leader," Cross said.

"I get that," Cade said. "That's a lot of work in a short amount of time. I just hope she gives them a break ... that's all. Maybe do the extension once the temperature drops and stays low for a stretch."

"If we waited for Mother Nature to green-light the expansion," Ari added. "We may never get it finished."

Skipper looked away from the window. He said, "Captain Grayson, you know about the Kansas mega horde?"

"I saw footage of it," Cade conceded. "I can appreciate the desire to create as much inside-the-wire real estate as possible." Always the realist, he shook his head and added, "Whether it's going to stand up to the sheer size of that horde of migrating corpses—Schriever included—only time will tell."

Atop some of the downtown buildings Cade could make out forms milling about. Collars were turned up against the coming chill, and the unmistakable silhouettes of the long guns they carried told him they were providing overwatch should the Zs somehow breach the walls or, God forbid, an outbreak occur inside the wire. From the way they carried themselves, moving about beside the low parapets instead of staying in place, conserving their energy and letting their eyes and high-powered optics do the leg work, he was near certain civilians were still shouldering a good deal of the security load. It struck him as a kind of neighborhood watch on steroids. *Better than nothing*, he mused. Lord knew the soldiers were stretched thin executing President Clay's bold new plan of which he was sure to learn more about within the hour. Maybe more than he wanted to know. Because if she was sending him and the team to the place he was thinking, it was more than likely they'd be right in the middle of the biggest pincer movement ever attempted by *any* standing army. Between the proverbial rock and a hard place, with the "rock" being the reconstituted combined forces of the United States and the "hard place" a mega horde consisting of twice the number of Zs that had marched out of Denver.

Finally, as the Ghost Hawk pulled out of orbit and set off east again, towards Schriever less than twenty miles distant, Cross addressed the elephant in the room. Looking directly at Cade, he said, "If Lopez is suffering from what I think he is—"

"I'm not dead yet," Lopez interrupted. "So don't talk about me in my presence as if I am."

Cade smiled.

"Forgive me," Cross said, addressing Lopez directly. "If for some reason you're not mission capable, who's running this op?"

Grimacing, Lopez gestured toward Cade.

Cade leaned back and rested his helmet on the bulkhead. He studied the panels and conduits snaking overhead.

"OK," Cross said, agreeably, staring at Cade now. "If Wyatt is taking point … which I'm totally onboard with"—he shifted his gaze to Lopez—"who's going to take *your* place?"

"Axelrod," Lopez answered.

"Sure would make the long flight more enjoyable," Ari interjected over the comms. "Plus … he has a good outlook on life."

"Axe is a pain in the ass," Skipper said. "And I have a hard time understanding him."

"Cause you're half hillbilly," said Haynes ahead of a loud cackle.

Intrigued, Cade took his eyes off the cabin ceiling and slowly settled his gaze on Lopez, who was again doubled over and wheezing softly. "So we have Griffin, who's as solid as they come," he said. "Besides Doctor Silence here needing a Queen's English Rosetta Stone to understand Axelrod, what's wrong with the guy?"

Skipper didn't humor Cade with a response. He kept staring out the port side, his eyes flitting over the ground below as the helo banked to port and began to slow.

Lopez shook his head while holding up one vertical finger.

Taking the gesture as a sign Lopez needed a second to compose himself, Cade posed the same question to Cross, minus the Rosetta Stone quip.

Cross said, "There's nothing wrong with Axe. And I understand him just fine. Just the usual lift for elevator. Lorry for truck. Bonnet for hood—"

Cade said, "I get the picture. The man's capabilities?"

"I've run a handful of ops with him over the last couple of weeks. Mostly setting out seismic sensors and the like," Cross said. "Oh … there was a snatch and grab, too."

Cade looked a question at the blond operator.

"A couple of guys who were loyal to Robert Christian," he answered. "Someone at Schriever scanning the shortwave bands picked them up. After figuring out they weren't who they said they were, we went in and rolled them up. Dumbasses thought they could hide in Vail … right under our noses. We discovered some documents suggesting more of Christian and Bishop's gang survived the fall of Jackson."

If Cade was concerned about the revelation, he didn't let on. Remaining stone-faced, he asked, "What about Axe?"

"He's not one of us," Cross divulged. "He's SAS. Axelrod was on a training swap at Bragg when Omega broke."

"And that's a problem, why?" Cade said.

"I'll vouch for him," Lopez said.

"That's good enough for me, then," Cade replied. "But you better not be tapping out yet, Lopez. Don't you want to see what the docs have to say?"

Lopez shook his head. Sweat beads rolled off his brow, down his nose and cheeks. After swaying there for a tick they fell to his uniform blouse and cascaded from the semi-waterproof camouflage fabric. "I've taken a bullet and kept on going," he said. "This is different. I feel like I've got an alien spawn clawing its way outta me."

Not liking what he was hearing, Cade turned his head and stared at the large hangars and dozens of aircraft parked along the flight line southwest of Schriever proper.

Chapter 32

Daymon had received the call on the CB while sitting by himself in the cab of his Chevy. As Brook asked him to check in on the Thagons, he watched the rest of the group conversing in the parking lot as they waited for Max to do his business in the tall grass alongside the body shop.

Once Brook was finished with her update, Daymon filled her in on their findings, leaving out how close they'd actually come to losing Wilson and Taryn. However, as he talked up his idea of pushing farther north tomorrow to pay Bear Lake a visit, he noticed that Oliver had somehow disengaged from the discussion and was partially hidden from view by the Raptor, clouds of blue-gray smoke rising intermittently.

"Pushing north kind of depends upon what you find at the farm," Brook replied. "Sounds like we're dealing with some breathers who don't play nice and have no desire to share what's still out there."

"We're dealing with something evil here," Daymon reiterated, visions of the crucified in Jackson worming their way back into his skull.

"How about we talk it over at dinner tonight? Take a vote … is that acceptable?"

Daymon said nothing.

"You there?" Brook asked and turned her back to Heidi, whose expression had gone through so many changes in a minute's time that it was creeping her out.

Finally, Daymon said, "Yeah, I'm still here, Brook." There was another short pause. "You know the weather window is closing. We can't let a couple of close calls scare us from what we need to do to get through winter. I'm sure Cade would be thinking like I am if he were there."

"I get that," Brook said. Then, parroting Cade, she added, "Let's wargame it thoroughly first. That's what Cade would recommend if he were here."

"Touché," Daymon said. "We'll roll by the farm and check on them. Since they know Taryn and Wilson, I figure I'll let them run point. Me … I'd probably just scare them."

"Don't sell yourself short, Daymon. I don't think everyone sees you as you see yourself." Cringing inwardly and pissed at herself for not employing the filter between her brain and mouth, she turned slowly to gauge Heidi's response.

Daymon made no immediate reply. And thankfully, when Brook's gaze landed on Heidi the younger woman was nodding enthusiastically and flashing both thumbs up.

Brook bugged her eyes and jabbed a thumb of her own at the CCTV monitor.

Message received, Heidi turned her attention back to her main task.

"Did I succeed in driving you away this time?"

"I'm *still* here," he said. "Just watching Oliver get high, that's all."

"High?"

"Hitting the weed. Boy's on edge … like his shoes have eggshells for soles."

"Oh," Brook exclaimed. "Is he driving?"

Daymon chuckled. "Not today."

"See you in a bit, then," Brook said. "I'll try the Thagons on the sat-phone. If I don't call you back you can assume I didn't raise them and proceed as planned."

"Copy that," Daymon replied. "And Brook …"

"Yes?"

"Remember the definition of *assume*?"

Despite the pain behind her eyes and stiffness in her right arm, Brook smiled and keyed the Talk button one last time. "Touché," she said and set the CB aside.

Following through with her promises, Brook called the Thagons and let the ring tone drone on for a few seconds. *Nothing.* Crestfallen and fearing the worst, she ended the call. Before placing the phone on the shelf, she jacked the ringer volume all the way up and set the phone in front of the monitor. A very effective way of telling Heidi to stay vigilant, without having to engage the woman.

Chapter 33

After skirting the airspace over downtown Springs, Ari steered the Ghost Hawk wide right to make an approach to Schriever from the south. Flying low and slow, the black helo crossed the fence line over the corner of Schriever where Mike Desantos was buried, her angular nose aimed for the painted tarmac near the southernmost hangar of a long row of identical gray structures.

Referring to the dozen or so football-field-sized rectangles of freshly disturbed desert they had overflown moments before crossing the wire, Cade asked, "Those mass graves back there … were those full of dead Zs from the Springs cleanup or was I looking at the final resting spot of the casualties from the Pueblo migration?"

Cross arched a brow and said, "How'd you—"

Interrupting, Ari looked over his shoulder and said, "That's classified, Wyatt. The whole debacle just goes to show that even presidents are not immune to the law of unintended consequences."

Cross reached over and tapped Cade's shoulder. Covering his boom mic, he asked, "How'd you hear about it?"

Also covering his mic, Cade said, "Saw it on a video Nash sent me. All those survivors caught outside the wall … how many? And why no intel? Someone should have known they were coming toward Springs with ten thousand ravenous Zs hot on their heels."

"That was before we started the sensor program," Cross said. "After the close call with the Denver horde, President Clay earmarked all available resources to the building of the wall. I see it as her version of the space race, only with vastly different ramifications if her promised three-week completion fell short. Hell, Cade, the speech she gave rallied troops and civilians alike."

"How long *did* it take?"

"With the help of the 4th Infantry Division, Eckels and his men worked around the clock and got the job done in eighteen days."

"Impressive," Cade said, his tone softening. "Eckels is the first lieutenant who stopped the first wave of Zs coming up from Pueblo, correct?"

Cross nodded. "Bottom line, what happened outside the wall that day couldn't be helped." He went quiet and looked out the window at the freshly paved apron flashing by.

Having been listening to the conversation, Skipper caught Cade's eye and nodded agreeably. Then the familiar sound of the landing gear motoring down interrupted the solemn moment.

Once the gear locked into place, Cross reestablished eye contact with Cade and finished answering the question. "Had President Clay known ahead of time, she still wouldn't have had the engineers breach the south wall. It was either six hundred deaths on her conscience, or, if she made the call to breach the wall to let them inside … maybe thousands." He pinched the bridge of his nose, grimacing at the images on the footage he'd seen. Which was the same four-minute clip Cade had alluded to. In his mind's eye he saw the shooters on the wall euthanizing American citizens by the scores. He remembered vividly the licks of orange flame lancing the still dawn air. Twenty-eight 10th Group shooters following inexplicable orders, thirteen of them now dead by suicide. He could almost hear the screams of the people as they fought off the dead and tried in vain to scrabble up the rough concrete walls. Finally, firm in the belief that his old boss had done the right thing, he added, "Clay's call was the right call. Those graves you saw contain only the remains of the horde. The Pueblo dead are buried in the Garden of the Gods in view of the tallest spires. We just skirted the park's south end. You would have been able to see it clearly on your—"

"I saw it," Cade said as the helo settled onto the apron with a slight jounce. "That place is almost as fitting a final resting place as Mike's." He deftly removed his safety harness and crossed the cabin to the window next to the stowed starboard-side minigun. Peering out, he locked his gaze on the battered yellow door at the bottom right corner of the closest hangar—roughly seventy-five yards distant. From past experience, Cade knew that the man responsible for every aviation asset on base, First Sergeant Whipper, called the cramped room behind that yellow door his office. And damn if that yellow door didn't fly open and a short man in coveralls—full head of wispy white hair blown about by the rotor wash—didn't charge across the tarmac before Ari'd even had a chance to power down the helo's turbines.

Then, from around the right side of the hangar where the humongous tracked doors were opened wide, a Humvee painted desert tan and configured as an ambulance cut the corner at speed and accelerated, its low, rectangular snout aimed straight for the Ghost Hawk.

Skipper hauled open the starboard door, letting the fifty degree outside air in.

As Cade helped Cross get Lopez turned around toward the starboard-side door, he stole another glance and watched the Humvee, lights ablaze, quickly overtake Whipper and skid to a complete stop just outside of the helo's rotor cone.

Perched atop the squat vehicle was a box-shaped cab over-shell, the ubiquitous red cross on white background painted on its slab sides. In unison with the Ghost Hawk's side door opening, both of the ambulance's doors flew open and out jumped two airmen wearing camouflage ABUs. One of them lugging a bulky box, the airmen broke into a sprint and reached the open door ahead of Sergeant Whipper.

With a brisk wind biting his exposed skin, Cade helped Lopez to his back on the floor and gave his good friend a fist bump. "I'll drop by the infirmary after I jaw with Nash."

Cade saw Lopez's smile morph to a grimace as the airmen brushed him aside as if he didn't exist. Then, as he spoke to Cross about Lopez's symptoms, the airman removed the Hispanic operator's MOLLE gear and peeled off his Crye shirt.

"Hey amigo," Lopez said, wincing as the airman pressed the stethoscope to his exposed chest. "Give the pretty lady a sloppy wet kiss for me."

"Roger that," Cade said. He looked at Cross and nodded toward the approaching Cushman. "You coming?"

The rotors overhead had slowed to a crawl, the turbine noise and steady *thwop* silenced. "Go," Lopez insisted. "If the demonios ain't got me yet … my own *pinche* appendix isn't going to do me in."

Cross grabbed his MP7 and rucksack. "Suit yourself, Lowrider. Better not be expecting flowers."

"A tee shirt from a D.C. gift shop will do," he said with a soft chuckle. "Now go. That's an order."

"You heard the man," Cade said as he hopped aboard the Cushman driven by an airman he knew all too well. "Time waits for no man."

"Who said that?" Cross asked, tossing his gear into the back of the modified golf cart.

"I did," Cade said, putting his gear in atop Cross's. "Actually, I'm just parroting what my wife liked to say to my daughter on school days."

"To the TOC?" Airman Davis asked.

"Major Nash's office for me," Cade replied. "I'll ride to the TOC with her from there."

Turning up his collar against the chill, Cross said, "Mess hall for me. Has the food gotten any better here?"

"You'd be amazed," Davis replied, giving the Cushman pedal. "A lot of things have changed around here."

And as if to punctuate the younger man's statement, a quartet of slate gray A-10 Thunderbolts crossed Schriever proper from the east. The heavily armored ground attack jets banked hard to the south, showing off their dual, rear-mounted turbofans and long, narrow wings.

Things sure have, thought Cade as the vehicle picked up speed.

Chapter 34

The feeder road between State Route 16 and the Thagon home seemed more rutted than before. There were exposed rocks and deep muddy channels that kept grabbing the Raptor's oversized off-road tires. If Taryn had to make a guess, her money would be on the couple having been visited by not one—but an army of vehicles. As she turned the corner where before there had been a rusted old piece of farm equipment, the truck's forward progress was impeded by a twenty-foot-wide channel running diagonally across the muddy drive.

Taryn brought the pickup to a halt with the front wheels perched on the leading edge of the foot-deep washout.

"What do you want to do?" Wilson asked.

"Assess the situation from here, I guess."

She peered over the wheel at the house and barn. The former was two stories. The paint was white and weathered. An immense wraparound porch ambled away to the left and right from the centrally located front door. The screen door was closed and the wooden door behind it appeared intact. A couple dozen yards off the Raptor's passenger side the red barn loomed, its doors still secured with the same padlock and chain that Ray had employed to incarcerate them while Brook had played emissary inside the house.

Wilson removed his floppy hat and ruffled his rowdy shock of hair. "I don't see anything moving."

"Neither do I," Taryn said quietly. "Not from here."

Just then Daymon hailed them from the road. "I can see you. Why'd you stop?"

Wilson keyed the Talk button. "There's a washout here. The road's rutted as hell, too. Ray's blue pickup is here."

"And?" Daymon asked.

"The place looks deserted. I'm not liking what I'm seeing," Wilson conceded. "It reminds me of the Bates house."

Sitting in his Chevy, Daymon looked at Oliver for help and received only a glassy-eyed stare in return. After a half-beat of that he said, "Kathy Bates?"

"*Norman*," Lev called over the open channel. "You know … as in *the* Norman Bates from the movie Psycho?"

Daymon consulted his rearview and saw Jamie in the passenger seat of the F-650. She was laughing and next to her Lev was pretending to bang his head on the steering wheel. So he keyed the Talk button. Held it down for a long couple of seconds contemplating what he wanted to say. Finally, he just spoke his mind. "Sorry, *dick*," he said. "I wasn't big on horror when I was a kid. Still ain't. Hell, every second goes by nowadays makes me feel as if I'm starring in my own horror flick."

Lev came on and started to apologize only to be cut short when Wilson announced that he and Taryn were going to drive across the washout.

Softly cursing Freddy Krueger and Michael Myers under his breath, Daymon gazed uphill and watched as the Raptor started to roll forward. He saw it dip down into the wash, lurch drunkenly back and forth a few times, then rocket up the other side as if the substantial crossing was little more than a parking lot speedbump.

"Nicely done," Daymon said. "You just going to run right up and knock on the door, Red?"

Wilson came back on. "We sure aren't going to pull up front and honk," he shot back. "That'd just draw out any rotters that are nearby."

Making a visual tour of his mirrors for said rotters, Daymon thought: *As if that growling V8 hasn't already.*

***

In the Raptor, Taryn jockeyed the rig around the gravel parking pad and parked it diagonal to the porch, leaving the tailgate facing the front of the old house. In response to the confused look settling on Wilson's face, she set the emergency brake and said, "In case we have to leave in a hurry."

"Good call." Wilson handed her the Motorola and unholstered his Beretta. After confirming the chamber held a live round, he shouldered open his door.

"Be careful," Taryn said, placing a hand on his thigh. "Check for traps."

"Copy that." He gave her a peck on the cheek that morphed into a passionate kiss.

Looking him in the eyes, Taryn repeated herself, but slower this time. "Be … careful, Wilson."

"Checking for traps," he answered as he stepped onto the muddy drive and shut the door behind him. Hearing the locks *thunk*, he wrapped around behind the idling truck and skidded to a halt in front of the short stack of steps.

Blood. Not just a drop or two, either. It looked as if something or someone had gotten cut real deep and started to bleed out here. He'd seen it before. Only that instance, a gusher caused by a horrific Z bite, which had led to Phillip's death and subsequent turn. And much like that pool of drying blood up in the clearing by the compound, this mess at his feet was pretty substantial.

He stood rooted, head down. Saw his reflection staring back at him. Behind his reflection, high clouds scudded across the sky.

No need to be quiet now, he concluded.

He sidestepped the pooled blood and scaled the steps, thumbing back the hammer on his pistol. From his vantage on the front porch he noticed that the blinds were closed and there was no light spilling from within. Wincing as it screeched loudly, he pulled the screen door open. *No need for a burglar alarm with this thing*, he thought, raising a hand to pound on the sturdy oak door. After delivering a pair of sharp raps which nobody answered, he doubled down and pounded with his fist.

Hearing what he thought to be a soft shuffling from behind the door, he took a step back.

From her seat in the Raptor, Taryn had watched Wilson scale the steps and approach the door. She had started when the screen door emitted that cringeworthy sound. Then she had cringed as her man delivered the first flurry of knocks. The rest, however, because it had happened so quickly, had been but a blur to her. One moment Wilson was banging on the door. In the next the door was swinging inward and he was being dragged inside, the barrel of some kind of rifle pressed hard against his neck.

"Fuck, fuck, fuck," Taryn chanted, fumbling simultaneously to draw her Beretta and depress the Talk button on the Motorola. But before she could accomplish either critical task there was a gaping muzzle of some kind of assault rifle tapping gently on the passenger side glass. And peering over the black rifle was a face she vaguely recognized.

Woodruff

Ignoring the spiders and cobwebs and bird droppings, Iris pressed her shoulder against the weathered wood four-by-four beam and craned to see around the big brass bell. Once she determined the looters weren't circling back, that they hadn't seen her and were trying some ruse to get her out into the open, she increased the volume on the long range CB radio and clicked the Transmit button two times.

After a long stretch of uneasy silence, a woman said, "Speak."

"They're gone," Iris said. "I'm in the steeple now."

"Are they really gone … or just moved on?" the voice asked.

"Gone," Iris whispered. "They drove off in the same vehicles they came here in. I went to Main and tracked them nearly to the end of our town. After they made the junction I'm fairly certain they continued south."

"Were any of them injured?"

"No," Iris answered, sadness in her tone. "All six of them made it out of the parochial house. They fought with a couple of the Purged then went straight to their vehicles. I checked their vehicles out while they were dealing with the husks … nothing. No supplies at all. But they do have a *dog*."

"A *dog*?" the voice asked, sounding very interested. "A big breed?"

"No. It was an Australian Shepherd. Male, I think. Multi-colored eyes. Pretty coat," Iris said, her salivary glands acting up again. "Wherever these looters call home, it's got to be nice. They're all pretty clean. Their trucks appear to be running well. Looks to me like they're eating well, too. One of them is borderline obese."

"Perfect," said the voice. "Keep watching. They'll be back."

Chapter 35
Naval Station Norfolk, Norfolk, Virginia

Situated at the southern tip of the peninsula known as Sewell's Point and near the mouth of the open ocean saltwater port of Hampton Roads, Naval Station Norfolk, once home to north of seventy warships and more than one hundred aircraft, was now deathly quiet and seemingly deserted, its miles of wharfs, piers, and dock space completely overrun by jiangshi.

From the roomy confines of the guided missile cruiser *Lanzhou's* high-tech bridge, Rear Admiral of the People's Liberation Army Navy, Chan Qi, watched his PLA Special Forces team returning from their final recon mission of the day. Bundled up against the late October chill, four of the five-man team huddled low in the rigid inflatable boat, their upper bodies bouncing in unison with each new swell the tiny craft blasted through. The soldier manning the tiller, Captain Kai Zhen, was the only exception. Like any good leader he remained upright, determined to not let any obstacle, whether man-made or whipped up by nature, get the better of him. Receiving a face full of white chop sent airborne by the boat's buffeting bow, Zhen simply shook his head, remained ramrod straight, and steered the RIB for the looming destroyer's angular gray fantail.

Once the returning team disappeared from view below the starboard gunwale, Qi turned and addressed the sailor standing silently off his right shoulder.

"Corporal Meng," he barked in Mandarin. "See to it that the team goes directly to the briefing room and begins their after-action report. I want the drone footage downloaded to a tablet and brought to me here at once."

The corporal saluted smartly, but remained rooted.

Grimacing, the flag officer returned Meng's salute and made a shooing motion to his least favorite subordinate. Sadly, Vice Admiral Li Chen, whom Admiral Qi had been grooming to one day take over for him—when the time came of course, and only if the powerful in the party were agreeable to the recommendation—had been victim of a surprise *jiangshi* attack just days after the idiot scientists let their deadly virus escape their supposedly impenetrable underground facility. In fact, the spread of the unnamed virus via the jiangshi it created was so fast and severe that Qi was amazed he'd been able to muster enough sailors and soldiers necessary to make this bold mission possible. Reaching the United States mainland had seemed like a dream three weeks prior. And though the outbreak had made the Chinese Navy's plans to outnumber the U.S. in combat surface ships and become a true "blue water" navy by 2020 unreachable, that plan was moot now, because a number of skirmishes, mainly initiated by U.S. and Chinese hunter-killer submarines acting autonomously, had sent the bulk of both countries' navies to the ocean floor while stand-off surface-to-surface cruise missile attacks had rendered a sizeable number of the remaining fleets' ships nothing but scorched shells drifting bodies of water worldwide. Acting on final use-them-or-lose-them orders issued by the heads of both dying nations the moment it had become evident long range communications were compromised to the point that they could no longer be relied upon, both nations had cut their subs loose to do what they did best: run silent and deep while awaiting new orders.

Just knowing that those ghostly quiet American submarines were still out there gave Qi pause, especially during these rare moments of silence on his usually bustling bridge. Feeling a cold chill trace his spine, Qi studied the choppy water off the bow, at times double-taking at shadows he was certain represented a raised enemy periscope.

"Corporal Meng, where is my tablet?" he bellowed, startling his entire bridge crew.

Regrettably, Admiral Qi reflected, the *Chunming*, a next generation Lanzhou guided missile destroyer he had been slated to command, sat in dry-dock at Changxiandao Jiangnan Naval Yard with only her keel laid and a handful of propulsion system components fully installed. In addition to *Chunming*, three aircraft carriers and dozens of other warships in various states of build rusted away ashore or in dry-dock, their completion an impossibility due to the far-reaching effects of a man-made virus.

The speed at which the world's once mighty nations had fallen took everyone by surprise. That the ruling class initiated this face-saving plan after seeding the virus on the U.S. mainland was truly baffling to Qi. But orders were orders. And his orders were to plant evidence of the virus' creation. Evidence, electronic and physical, that pointed directly to the U.S. government as the true culprit behind the worldwide spread of the aptly named Omega virus. And to make the allegations stick, boots on the ground were necessary. Which was what dozens of PLA Special Forces recon teams deployed from various ports all up and down the West Coast were currently up to.

Qi wondered who would be left to write the history books. Who did the leaders ensconced deep in their bunkers need to impress? And most importantly: Why? The billion walking dead back home didn't care who made them what they were. The peasants and city folk left to fight for survival in the face of such long odds didn't care, either. God? If there was one, He or She or It didn't seem to care.

So what was the real reasoning behind this new program of westward expansion? To colonize the wide open spaces in the center of the country? To enslave America's survivors and put them to work growing food for his people here, on their own soil, where the weather was temperate and the growing season long?

Ultimately, Qi decided, three hundred million bodies—most of them infected—would be less of a mountain to summit than the billion jiangshi currently ravaging the motherland.

Still mulling over what his mission would mean in the grand scheme of things, he cast his gaze along the nearby seawall.

Standing three deep and wavering like wheat before the harvest, the monsters pressing the chest-high safety barrier were emitting a noise similar to the mental image they had initially evoked. Most were Caucasian, their round eyes lifeless black orbs. Some brown- and black-skinned corpses milled in among the encroaching throng. Unlike the undead crowd that had seen the remnants of Qi's South Fleet off under a snow-laden sky so many weeks and hard-won nautical miles ago, scanning the faces of the hissing assemblage here failed to produce one similar to his own. Not an Asian man, woman, or child among them that he could see. Which was a good thing. Because in his experience, it was always easier to kill someone, or in this instance, some*thing* that looked vastly different than one's self.

Looking off the *Lanzhou's* starboard-side, Qi marveled at the number of seemingly still seaworthy vessels caught in port during the outbreak. There were oilers, supply ships, and, probably bound for a scrapyard somewhere, a trio of older frigates whose class he couldn't immediately place. Around the bend north of his flotilla were the piers used to berth both aircraft carriers in port for resupply turnarounds and those loitering temporarily before steaming to Newport News shipyards for refitting or repairs. From the looks of the pair of massive superstructures breaking up the skyline, two of the United State Navy's aircraft carriers were still berthed at Piers 12 and 14 when the virus was let loose.

Looming over the piers to his right, a dozen other ghost ships languished. Straining against taut mooring lines, the Arleigh-Burke-class destroyer and handful of tender ships and tugs all appeared to be trying to escape the watchful phalanx of jiangshi that had been accumulating near their bows since dawn.

Approaching footsteps drew Qi's attention back to the bridge and task at hand. Expecting to see Corporal Meng thrusting the P88—a Chinese copy of Apple's iPad—in his face, he instead encountered Captain Zhen, all six-foot-two of him soaking wet and still wearing his watch cap and comms gear.

"Zhen," the admiral said, his tone softer than it had been with Meng and the bridge crew. "You wish to brief me in person?"

With a none-too-happy look parked on his wind-burned angular face, Zhen grunted an affirmative. "Captain's quarters? Or the officer's canteen?" he asked, the frown dissolving.

"My quarters," replied Qi, observing the captain's reddened face suddenly light up. "I will have the tablet delivered to me there. And while we wait"—he smiled wide, showing off a mouthful of perfectly straight teeth—"we shall have some warm *baijiu*."

Now there was a twinkle in Zhen's eyes to go along with the slow-to-form smile.

"After you," Zhen said, happy with his decision to dismiss the chattering corporal and take matters into his own hands.

***

Admiral Qi's quarters was a two-hundred-square-foot rectangle jam-packed with a single bed, faux-wood-laminated combination table/desk, two narrow chairs with red and gold padding and, tucked underneath the starboard-facing porthole, a microwave and miniature refrigerator.

In all reality, Zhen thought as he took it all in, Qi's berth was about the same size as the efficiencies the working class back home lived in. Blocks of high-rises full of similar living spaces dominated the cities where the pollution-spewing factories were located.

"Sit," Qi insisted.

Zhen removed his black watch cap and did as he was told.

There was a knock at the door.

Zhen ruffled his close-cropped graying hair which was the only indicator that he was nearer to forty than thirty as his unlined face and chiseled physique would suggest.

Qi removed two shot glasses from a desk drawer. After placing one on the table before Zhen and the other in front of his empty chair, he put the opaque bottle he was holding into the microwave and pressed the button marked Warm. While the tiny oven hummed away, he squeezed by the table and opened the narrow door leading out to the corridor beyond. Without uttering a word, he received the P88 tablet from Corporal Meng and closed the door in his face.

Qi deposited the tablet in the center of the table. He took the bottle of grain liquor from the microwave, sat down across from Zhen and, with a flourish learned from years of rubbing shoulders with China's elite, poured a finger's worth of the spirits into each shot glass.

"Ganbei," he said, raising his glass.

"Ganbei," Zhen repeated, touching his glass to Qi's. Fully expecting to have to stifle a grimace, Zhen tilted his head back and downed the warm liquor. Instead, taken aback at how smooth the admiral's offering was, he nodded and complimented Qi on his selection.

"Three thousand U.S. dollars before—"

"The jiangshi arose," Zhen finished. He produced a cigar from his uniform pocket and placed it before Qi. "Cuban. It was a gift from a cadre I trained before all of this. It's yours now."

Qi took the cigar. Then, without so much as offering an insincere thank you or giving the cigar a cursory glance, he set it aside and said curtly, "The pier and beyond. Tell me your findings."

Shaking his head, Zhen said, "Sadly, Admiral Qi, we cannot go inland here."

"The Americans came ashore in Normandy under withering fire. Why can't *we* make landfall here, Captain?"

Zhen picked up the tablet. He swiped and tapped then spun it around to face Qi, a grainy full color video already playing on it. The hundreds of dead framed in the shot were small because the footage was taken by a remotely controlled unmanned aerial vehicle. "*Jiangshi* are everywhere," the Special Forces captain pointed out. "And there are more of them in the city than you see here in the shipyards. We are lucky here. The stink of death hits like a fist as you get ashore where it has become trapped by the warehouses and office buildings."

"As it did in Beijing," Qi said indifferently. "What about the nearby interstates?"

Lips pursed, Zhen shook his head. "Barely passable. Unmoving vehicles and monsters everywhere. You will see in a moment."

"Decadent pigs," Qi said, slapping the tabletop. "Rumor had it that even the young children had automobiles."

"That's a stretch, Admiral. However, it would seem as if every adult had one." Zhen frowned and slid his shot glass forward for a refill.

Ignoring the gesture, Qi kept his gaze locked to the video playing on the tablet. Once the screen went dark, he asked, "What do you propose, Captain?"

"We steam up the Chesapeake," Zhen replied. "Annapolis Military Academy is close to our objective. School was not in session when America fell to the dead. If we make landfall there we can continue onward overland and pick our ingress route from among many. If this small city of two hundred and forty thousand is any indication of the odds we'll be facing on land, docking in Baltimore would be suicide."

Qi steepled his fingers. After a moment's contemplation, he said, "I've already ruled that out. The estuary is too narrow for my liking. The entire cruise we will be vulnerable to attack from all sides."

"With all due respect, Admiral. Protocol says we must monitor the airwaves for enemy radio traffic at all times." Zhen folded his arms across his chest. "Surely you've picked up numerous radio transmissions by American units in the area. Which would explain the quick dismissal of my proposal, no?"

More steepling and contemplation occurred on Qi's side of the table.

Zhen helped himself to another measure of the still warm baijiu. *What can the admiral do*? he thought as he reached across the table to refill Qi's glass. *Run me up the mast*? *Send me home?*

Qi nodded. Voice even, he said, "It's silent out there. Which is why I'm hesitant to chance bringing the oilers, auxiliaries, and landing ships. Perhaps we should recon first with the *Lanzhou*."

"And leave the rest of the fleet here like unguarded sheep? I'm certain that if there was enemy activity in Norfolk or beyond, your warship's sophisticated suite of sensors would have already picked up something."

Qi set his jaw. Peering out the porthole, his face seemed to go slack. He picked up the direct line to the bridge and said two words: "Drop anchor."

Though he couldn't hear what was being said on the other end, Zhen still watched with feigned interest as Qi listened to the commander on the bridge.

"Yes," Qi said. "We stay the night here. Put fresh bodies on the bridge and tell the others to sleep and be ready to throw lines at 0300." He hung up the phone and looked Zhen square in the face. "If you ever disrespect me like that again, Captain, I *will* have you fed to the jiangshi."

Zhen's lips were twin white lines. He stood at attention and saw his reflection in the seated admiral's shiny bald pate.

"Ready your vehicles and weapons and then rest your men, Captain Zhen. We will make landfall at first light and then go into the heart of decadence as saviors in the eyes of her remaining populace."

Salutes were exchanged and Qi ushered the captain out ahead of him. "I hope your assessment is correct, young Captain. For if it is not, all of those days spent on the open sea will have been wasted."

Zhen merely nodded and, with the sound of the door closing at his back, stalked off in the opposite direction of the elitist, Communist-Party-loving ingrate.

Chapter 36

Davis left Cade at the entrance to the building housing Nash's new office. A stone's throw from the TOC, her new one-level digs reminded him of his dentist's office back home. With its gently-pitched roof, multi-paned windows and horizontal metal siding, the place looked as if it had been designed in the late eighties when aesthetics of government facilities were, at best, an afterthought.

The pair of doors out front were mostly glass and locked. He pushed the doorbell button next to the jamb and got no results. So he knocked until an interior door sucked in and the diminutive major poked her head out.

Expecting Nash's face to light up like it always did when any of the boys her satellites followed into battle graced her doorstep, instead Cade saw her swallow hard and take a few tentative first steps across what looked to be some kind of waiting room designed to hold two dozen people and appointed with nearly twice as many magazines all stacked haphazardly on low wooden tables.

Nash wove her way through the two-dozen chairs arranged like a big S with one of the magazine-laden tables at their center. Muttering an apology, she threw the lock and ushered Cade in from the cold.

"Major," he said, offering up a cursory salute.

"Save that crap for someone else's daily affirmation," she said, locking the doors behind them.

Not quite sure where this was coming from, Cade put his hands at his sides. "You wanted to chat before the pre-mission briefing?" he asked, his tone conveying the concern he was feeling.

"Come," she said, pointing him into her office, which at first glance appeared three times the size of her previous one.

Instantly it struck Cade that he hadn't once been in Nash's office—at least here at Schriever—when the AC unit wasn't cranked so high that his nipples could cut glass. In fact, it was warmer inside her central office than the childrearing magazine graveyard he had just been ushered through.

Nash closed the door and stood staring up at him. She was wearing a long-sleeved shirt that looked to have been taken straight out of the Air Force Academy gift shop. The official flying eagle image was emblazoned on it in silver and gave him the impression someone had painted a crude target on her chest. She wore the same camouflage ABU pants as the emergency personnel. Tucked into her black boots and bloused to perfection, the contrast the two articles of clothing presented was telling: part civilian soccer mom and part soldier.

She said, matter-of-factly, "I hear you had a close call with a PLA missile on your way here."

"Nothing Ari and his aircrew couldn't handle." He let his gaze roam the plaques on the wall as Nash circled around behind her desk.

Seeing the Delta operator inspecting her inner sanctum, which was painted in muted pastels and walled in on one side by half a dozen four-drawer, steel filing cabinets, Nash said, "This used to be the family services building. Although I would benefit from both these days, I got rid of the anger management and AA pamphlets when I moved in."

Duncan's recent successes in that arena on his mind, Cade said, "Lots of people could benefit from those kind of pamphlets." Steering the conversation to the Eden survivors, he gave the Cliff's Notes version of how they were sitting going into winter. When he began to shower Nash with thanks for giving his family the antiserum injectors that had recently saved Brook and

Gregory's lives, the woman made a face and raised a hand, stopping him mid-sentence.

"Sit," she said, motioning at the modern chrome and leather chair sitting front and center before her white ash desk. Pulling her rolling chair from the knee well and dragging it across the carpeted floor, she added, "We're both going to have to be sitting for what I need to tell you." She parked her leather high-backed chair beside her desk, sat down hard and swiveled it so that she faced him at a slight angle.

Cade's mind raced, trying to determine what piece of information might be so dire in nature that he needed to be sitting to hear it.

Nash said, "We're finding that the antiserum for Omega isn't all it's cracked up to be." There was a pregnant pause. "What we thought was shaking out at a roughly fifty-percent success rate early on has dropped off to half of that."

"Better than the alternative," Cade said pragmatically. "Before Taryn found the doctor's thumb drive a Z bite meant certain death. Now it doesn't. If you ask me, I'd rather put a revolver with just one round in the chamber to my head than one with a full cylinder. And I'm pretty damn sure anyone else finding themselves staring down a fate like Desantos suffered would be singing the same tune."

"Me too, Cade. But what I'm trying to tell you is that even the patients the antiserum worked on initially are starting to show side effects. Some of the early trial survivors have died of complications we're attributing to Omega's introduction into the system."

"What about antibiotics? That's usually the go to where viruses are concerned, right?"

Nash shook her head. "Antibiotics work on infection."

"Some of these early survivors … did they turn after they died?"

"The doctors are in the habit of destroying *everyone's* brain. It's become routine no matter the cause of death. Call it superstition. I don't know."

"I hope you've changed that practice on the previously infected."

"New protocols are in place," Nash said. She grimaced and added, "However, a week ago a soldier from the 4th ID who was infected weeks ago and saved by the antiserum—." There was a long pause. "He just up and died."

"And?"

Nash shook her head. A slow, sad, side-to-side wag.

Incredulous, Cade asked, "They didn't take him to the morgue. Open him up and see why?"

The major shook her head. "They didn't know to."

Cade saw her hands begin to tremble. He looked her in the eyes and saw they were misted over.

Nash swallowed hard and said, "There were a whole bunch of dropped balls. To the doctors it appeared as if he'd died of a heart attack. IT folks are in high demand elsewhere. Means the hospital staff are all still charting on paper. And this soldier's chart was misplaced by someone. So they put him aside and started in on a civilian who had been crushed by a mishandled section of freeway barrier."

Seeing where this was going, Cade leaned back against the leather chair-back.

Nearly crying now, Nash said, "The previously fit thirty-eight-year-old soldier reanimated on the gurney *after* showing a near full recovery from his bite wound." Another pregnant pause. "And the antiserum he had been saved with came from the same batch as Brook's."

The last sentence hit Cade like a gut punch.

"Brook is on the road to a full recovery. I'm sure of it," he said, trying to ignore the niggling sensation that he might be lying to himself.

Sensing a widening channel of denial concerning Cade's perception of the ramifications of what she'd just divulged and, though she was certain that nothing she would say or do could divert the human missile once he'd been launched, Nash still said what was on her mind. "I totally understand if you want to get on the next bird to Bastion. I would expect no less." She quickly dried her eyes on her sleeve and met his gaze.

Seeing the look of concern parked on the usually stoic Air Force officer's face, Cade said, "Thanks for the heads up, Freda. But I'm a big boy. And Brook, she's a nurse. She'll catch anything strange going on inside her own body. And if she already had suspected something was up, she would have said something to me about it."

"How can you be certain she'll know what it means? This is all uncharted territory."

Cade said nothing.

"I think you should tell her," Nash pressed. "It's the right thing to do for all parties involved. For Raven, especially." She dug in her desk drawer and came out with a pair of satellite phones complete with power cords and the factory-provided paperwork. "These are charged. You asked for them last time we spoke."

"I'll take them," Cade said, ignoring the timing. "We gave up one of the others so we could keep in touch with our new allies in Bear River." Feigning a smile, he handed back the warranty information. "No need for this."

Nash took the papers and tossed them on her desk. "The phones come with a couple of conditions," she added.

Cade arched a brow. "Everything with you comes with at least one."

Nash's expression didn't change.

He asked, "What are your conditions?"

"You have to tell Brook and at least one other person at Eden who you can trust about the 4th ID soldier."

"And let them draw their own conclusions?"

Nash nodded.

Steering the conversation away from this new curveball served up by Mr. Murphy, Cade said, "New office. Springs walled in and Z free. Seems like things are changing real quickly in your neck of the woods."

"Things are changing all over the United States. We are starting to hear from communities like Bear River that are springing up all over the country. And around here," she said, drying her eyes on her sleeve again, "up until now, with the some of the Joint Chiefs recovered and bending the President's ear on matters of the military, I've been left to my own devices. Kind of set adrift, if you will."

"We're lucky to have gotten a healthy Tommy 'Two Guns' McTiernan back in the fold. He *is* the man, Freda. He's Devil Dog through and through. Be glad he's running the show now. Besides, you've been assigned to head this one up."

"Still makes me feel like the kid who gets picked last at recess."

"So how have you been earning your pay?" Cade asked.

"I just send the sats where I'm told and the imagery is piped directly to Cheyenne where I understand IT folks have been working round the clock to upgrade and EMP-shield the computer servers." She looked at the clock on the wall. "We better be getting to the TOC."

"I've got an idea where we're going," Cade said, before divulging the where and why and then, finally, how he'd come to the conclusion.

"The Long Beach mission played a big part," Nash conceded. "Eavesdropping on Ari and Haynes during the flight over from Bastion … that's dirty pool."

"By any means necessary," Cade said flatly.

Eyes still glistening, Nash said, "Very perceptive. You know we can't let the PLA get there first. They've already made landfall once. You'll see all of the latest satellite imagery at the briefing. Short of Pearl Harbor, these are the boldest moves an enemy of the United States has ever taken against her. They know we are severely hamstrung and that's emboldened them. We have very few pilots and to a person they are exhausted and, pardon the metaphor—flying on fumes just like their aircraft. Air and ground resupply missions are still ongoing, however, not with a frequency that'd make me comfortable. The latter have suffered huge rates of attrition. And where the flights in and out of Schriever and Carson were practically nonstop in August and September"—she shook her head—"the pace of air operations here in October has slowed to a trickle."

"Mother Nature?" Cade said.

Nodding, Nash answered, "She's a bitch. We've had one major snow event here that grounded everything. Without the necessary number of weather sats to keep us connected to NOAA's ground-based observatories, high-atmosphere weather balloons, and the picket of buoys deployed in territorial waters, there's no way for the TOC to accurately predict what kind of conditions our air assets are likely to face when they do go out."

"If the Farmer's Almanac is anywhere close to right in its prediction for this winter we're going to be snowed in at Eden and you're going to be hard pressed to get birds in the air in order to watch your flanks, let alone keep tabs on the enemy and Zs migrating the warmer climes."

"Way too many variables to worry about now," Nash conceded, just as the phone on her desk emitted an electronic warble.

Nash snatched the handset off the cradle, announced herself and then listened intently for a handful of seconds. Without saying a word, she ended the call and replaced the handset.

"Lopez?"

She said nothing.

"It's bad, isn't it?"

She nodded again. "Ruptured appendix. He's in surgery as we speak."

Knowing that likely meant he was leading the mission, Cade hung his head and said a silent prayer for Lopez and the men he was about to take down range with him.

"The TOC awaits," Nash said. "And after the briefing see about having Davis outfit you with everything you're going to need … starting with a proper set of fatigues."

Recalling Duncan's quip, he said, "What … you don't like the Mission Impossible look?"

"It is slimming on you, Wyatt. But if you're going to be leading a team into battle ..."

Confirmation, he thought. "Copy that," he said, thumbing on the sat phone and dialing a number from memory.

Pursing her lips, Nash rose from her chair.

"Go ahead without me," Cade said, thumb hovering over the illuminated Talk button.

With Brook and Raven and Cade occupying her thoughts, Nash padded from the office, leaving the man alone to make what she guessed to be the toughest phone call of his life.

Chapter 37

Wilson had been taken completely by surprise when the front door suddenly swung away from him. To make matters worse, he had also been leaning forward and about to apply a technique he'd seen Cade employ to gain entry through a locked door when the human silhouette materialized in the very point in space the door used to be. With all of his weight in the middle of transferring off his back foot and into the forward kick, he was left totally vulnerable to whatever bad intentions the armed person had in store for him.

As he pitched forward, a gnarled hand slick with what smelled like blood grabbed his gun hand and pressure was applied to the rifle, causing the sharp iron sight atop the slender barrel to cut into his neck. At the same time the camouflage boonie hat slid backward off his head and settled softly between his shoulder blades, its fall arrested by the leather chinstrap.

Furious at himself for succumbing to the same fate that had already befallen Taryn two times now, he began pleading for the shadowy figure to let go of him.

***

Behind the wheel of the Raptor, Taryn had given up on her bid to snatch the radio and call down to Daymon for help. Instead, she powered down her window and thrust her face and both arms through the opening. "It's me," she said. "Taryn, from the compound west of here." She watched the face at the end of the AR-style carbine go slack for a quick second. Then the woman brandishing the gun raised her cheek off the stock and glanced at the tattoos encircling Taryn's forearms. When the woman finally flicked her gaze back to Taryn's face, the blank look was gone and in its place one of full recognition.

"Ohhhh, you're Brook's friend," Helen said, sweeping the rifle's muzzle toward the muddy ground. "I didn't recognize you at first."

No shit, Taryn thought, exhaling sharply. She flashed a fake smile and rested her crossed arms on the window channel.

"Ray," Helen screeched. "It's just those nice kids from Huntsville way."

***

Inside the house Wilson was already on his knees. Following the old man's barked orders, he had placed his hands behind his head and interlaced his fingers. Then, though most of the shrill pronouncement from outside was lost on him, he made out the words *Ray* and *Huntsville*, which when put together with the grizzled face of the gray-haired oldster were the best two words he'd heard all day.

Keeping the rifle trained on the redheaded kid's chest, Ray cupped a hand to one ear and bellowed, "What was that, honey?"

"Ray," Wilson said slowly, making sure to keep his hands up. "Your wife …" inexplicably his brain locked up.

"*Helen?*" the man said.

"Yes," Wilson said, nodding, his eyes gone wide. "Helen was just letting you know I'm ... I mean, *we* are the kids from down the road." Paraphrasing, sure. Still, it worked. Because Ray lowered the bolt-action rifle and motioned for him to stand.

Thinking he may have soiled himself, or at the very least sharted and baptized his newest pair of tighty whities, Wilson lowered his hands to his waist and took a deep breath. Ignoring the strange slickness between his butt cheeks, he extended a hand and reintroduced himself to Ray Thagon.

***

Seeing the exchange inside the foyer ending peacefully via her side mirror, Taryn opened her door and jumped down from the pickup.

Walking arm-in-arm with Helen, she sidestepped the blood when the woman pointed it out.

"Ray got a rabbit in his trap," Helen said. "Won't you two stay for dinner? You can call your friends up from the road, so long as they're good people like you and Brook."

Explains the blood. Taryn said, "That's nice of you," as she helped the woman negotiate the stairs. "But we've got to get home before it gets dark."

"You sure?" Helen said, fixing her watery eyes on Taryn. "It's a real *big* jackrabbit. Lots of him to go around."

"Positive." Taryn smiled—a sincere one this time.

"Why the unannounced visit?"

Wilson stepped onto the porch ahead of Ray.

Taryn noticed at once that Wilson's face was much whiter than usual. He looked anemic. Ghostly, even. He was also wringing his boonie hat nervously in both hands, which left wildly corkscrewing hair exposed for all to see.

Taryn winked at her man, then turned toward Helen. "Dregan was concerned because he couldn't get ahold of you two on the CB radio."

"So he sent all of you over here from Huntsville? What a lazybones. Bear River is just a stone's throw south of us."

"It was nothing," Taryn replied. "We were already in Woodruff anyway."

Wilson regarded Ray. "Do you *need* batteries for the radio?"

Ray propped his rifle next to the door. Removed his felt hat and stuffed the ratty red number into his back pocket. Running a hand through his wiry, silver hair, he said, "We have plenty of supplies upstairs. Batteries galore, in fact. It's just that it's hard for us to remember to turn it on every day at noon like Dregan wants. Heck, I don't know what time of day it is at any given time. I'm just happy when I wake up in the morning and come to find I'm still among the living."

"I'm happy you wake up every morning," Helen said. She moved closer and grasped Ray's hand.

Wilson caught Taryn's eye and they shared a conspiratorial wink.

"Let's go inside," Helen urged. "It's cold out here."

"I need to call Daymon," Taryn said, raising the Motorola to her mouth. Leaving out the dinner invitation, she explained the radio silence to the others in the trucks on the road, making it clear that the Thagons were fine and needed nothing.

"Good," Daymon said, his voice tired-sounding over the radio. "Duncan just called from the compound. Said Tran and the girls already have dinner started. And for some reason Brook's calling for a group meeting after dinner."

"Go ahead and get the rigs turned around," Taryn said. "We're on our way."

Wilson wet his sleeve in his mouth then dabbed at the scrape on his neck.

"Sorry," Ray said. "But you were about to kick in my door."

"No biggie," Wilson said. "It could've been worse."

"Thanks for your dinner invitation," Taryn said. "But we have to head back." She wanted to mention the booby-trapped buildings and horrific scene in the church before leaving, but thought better of it. Besides, the couple were the ones who told Brook about the bandits up north.

"The washout was no problem for our rig," Wilson said, hooking a thumb over his shoulder at the muddy pickup. "But it looks as if yours might be stuck on this side of the highway. I could get a few guys together and we could come back and fill it in for you."

"Don't bother," Ray said. "The creek behind the house does that every time a big snow accumulation melts off that rapidly. I've got a tractor outfitted with a grader attachment inside the barn. If I fill it in now, I'll just be doing it again come spring. We'll be fine. If we don't see you again before the real snow arrives, we'll see you when it's gone."

Wilson shook Ray's hand and then accepted a bear hug from Helen.

After hugging both of the Thagons, Taryn leaped over the pooled blood and took her place behind the wheel of the Raptor.

"Our rig," Wilson muttered. He nodded to the old couple, crushed his hat over his hair, and stalked around the rig's mud-spattered tailgate.

Chapter 38

Having spent a few minutes pacing the hall outside the TOC, Cade tucked the sat-phone into a pocket with the other, put his game face on, and pushed through the door.

Major Freda Nash was on the elevated stage and already five minutes into the PowerPoint presentation when she saw Cade enter the rectangular low-ceilinged room through the door at her twelve o'clock. At once she noticed the grim look on his face.

Seeing Nash look away from the sixty-inch plasma-display at the front of the room, he met her eyes, nodded, then let his gaze roam, taking a quick inventory of the room. There was a whisper of warm air coming in from overhead vents. Overriding that was a subtle humming that emanated from the dozens of desktop computers scattered about the room, their processors no doubt crunching information vital to the coming mission. And sitting at those computer stations were a dozen airmen, their attention mainly directed at the oversized computer monitors perched on the edges of their individual desks.

Two long rows of folding chairs were set up at the front of the room. And directly in front of Cade, crowding the hard-working 50th Space Wing personnel from behind, were an additional two-dozen folding chairs. Arranged in a semicircle, most of the chairs were occupied by a mixture of aviators and Army Rangers. Off Cade's right shoulder was the rest of his patchwork Delta team. Without a word, he padded to his right and sat down on an unoccupied folding chair next to a bearded man he recognized from the Los Angeles mission. The former SEAL Team 6 operator William Griffin—or Griff for short—had proven himself highly capable on that mission. That he had come up through the teams alongside Adam Cross and had numerous deployments in all of the hell holes on earth showed in the way he charged hard and fast at every obstacle they had come up against in the City of Angels. And that he was still alive, albeit a little bushier of beard, came as no surprise to Cade.

To Griff's right was Cross, six-foot-four, blond hair and blue-eyed and standing out starkly amongst the other operators. The muscled soldier to Cross's right was nearly as tan as the Ken-Doll-looking Delta shooter. However, the man's hair was long and dark and currently tied up into a neat pony tail kept in check by a sand-colored beret. Affixed to the deflated-looking hat was the hard-to-miss Special Air Service badge emblazoned with a downward-pointing winged Excalibur wreathed in flames. Cade's eyes moved over the uniform, instantly pegging it as standard-issue British Army in Multi-Terrain Pattern, which, like the MultiCam worn by Delta, was basically a subdued version of the United States Army's woodland camouflage pattern featuring more tan than dark green. Then he saw the black-stitched chevrons identifying the man as a sergeant.

Seeing Cade eyeballing him, the shooter, whose nametape read *Axelrod,* blew the last chance of fitting any kind of stereotype befitting a Brit by flashing a picket of straight, white teeth.

Without acknowledging Cade, nor the hangdog look on his face, Nash continued droning on about waypoints to target, aerial refueling timelines, standoff reaction-and-rescue forces and then wrapped up the aviation logistics segment of the briefing with a slide filled with the most up-to-date weather predictions which contained very little detail, upper atmosphere wind speed and direction the most glaring omissions.

"I've provided to you all of the intel I'm privy to," she said, singling out the aviators and their crewmembers seated mostly in the front two rows. "Any new information that comes in from ground observers or other aircraft near your flight paths will be relayed to you en route."

One of the airmen near Nash rose and passed her a slip of paper, which she quickly read and pocketed.

"Our esteemed colleague who just entered missed the beginning of my presentation. For the sake of time I'd normally single Captain Cade Grayson out after the briefing; however, since I just learned one of the SOAR birds is temporarily grounded due to a mechanical problem, I figure I'll go over it again."

The aviators up front groaned.

Turning in his seat, Ari wadded up a sheet of legal pad and tossed it toward Cade in the back row.

Face still a stony mask, Cade watched the paper ball arc over an airman's head and land at his feet.

"Always coming up short," he mouthed to the glaring Night Stalker.

Bellowing to be heard over the rising murmurs and small talk, Major Nash said, "Gentlemen. May I have the floor back?"

A hush quickly descended over the room, leaving audible only the soft taps of fingers striking keyboards and the whirring of fans hard at work cooling the tower computers.

"Thank you," Nash said. "I'm not really going to bore all of you again with that PowerPoint. Air assets, you are free to go. Don't clean the canteen out. The shooters need to eat, too."

A happy-sounding murmur made rounds of the room. Then the sound of chair legs scraping carpet. Finally, the room went quiet again as the group bottlenecked near the door.

Nash waited until all nineteen men and women, aircrew for six separate aircraft, filed out the door at the rear of the TOC.

Once the last man was through the door and it had snicked shut, the diminutive major settled her gaze on Cade, then cleared her throat.

"As you all know, the United States was nearly decapitated three short months ago thanks to the Chinese seeding Washington D.C. with the Omega Virus. Although they didn't entirely nullify our command-and-control with that first blow, their agents did succeed in infecting enough alpha specimens in the District and a dozen other cities to send the members of government who survived the initial outbreak scrabbling to get out of harm's way." She paused to sip a water.

In his mind's eye, Cade saw the politicians represented by hundreds of spindly cockroaches fleeing the light across a filthy kitchen floor that was Washington D.C.

"Bear with me, gentlemen," she said, still looking solely at Cade. "I'm nearly finished." She capped the bottle and set it aside. "And as we all know," she went on, "those initial victims, when combined with man's natural inclination to not believe the unbelievable, or, normalcy bias if you will, led to the start of the massive rate of infection that has us where we are today: clawing our way back from the brink of extinction. And as if those first despicable acts of war committed by a trading partner professing to be our ally wasn't enough, thousands of her PLA troops have landed on our shores and as we speak are making a steady march inland."

Cross leaned in front of Griff. "We're all caught up now, Wyatt. Hope you had a good reason for being tardy."

His jaw taking a granite set, Cade pressed hard into his chair-back and restrained himself from saying or doing anything he'd likely regret.

Chapter 39

"Hurry up," said Oliver, watching the trees flash by outside his partially opened window. "I don't want to get caught outside the wire in the dark without my armor and night vision goggles."

"It's pretty obvious to me you were never a Boy Scout," Daymon said, as he slowed the Chevy to negotiate a near hairpin turn just beyond the quarry entrance.

"Yes I was. Made Tenderfoot and got bored with it. Either that or Scouting got in the way of skiing."

"Doesn't show," Daymon said. "A Boy Scout is supposed to always be prepared."

"You're not perfect. You wouldn't go up into that attic. And you know what else, Daymon?" He removed his stocking cap and raked his fingers through his thinning hair. "A leader is supposed to lead from the front, not the rear."

Feeling a vein in his temple begin to throb, Daymon flicked his eyes to the rearview where he saw the mud-streaked Raptor on his bumper. Behind the Raptor was the hulking black F-650 driven by Lev. Having used the distraction to calm down a bit, he parked his gaze straight down 39 and said, "This is about getting *you* ready … not analyzing *me*. Besides, I'm effin claustrophobic. There, I said it. I *hate* enclosed spaces. My mouth went dry, breathing became a chore, and my heart started banging like a jackhammer the moment I set eyes on the attic opening. Are you happy now?"

"I never get satisfaction out of someone else's discomfort," Oliver admitted. "But I do feel a bit of vindication knowing some kind of fear has a hold over you. That there's a chink in *your* armor."

"Hold over me …" Daymon said, speaking real slowly. "Chink in my armor," he muttered under his breath as a pair of zombies showed up on the centerline near the next right-hand bend in the state route. He tapped the brakes to warn the others and began to slow down.

"What are you going to do?"

"I'm not going to push you out again, if that's what you're worried about."

"I'm not worried," Oliver said through clenched teeth.

Daymon chuckled. *Your eyes contradict your words.*

He said, "You survived the first time I made you walk the plank. No reason to tempt fate by doing *that* again."

"Pull over," Oliver hissed, snatching Kindness off the seat before Daymon could react.

"Careful you don't get the blade lodged in one of their skulls. It'll be pretty hard to get it out if you do."

"Any pointers, then?"

"Follow through," Daymon said. Seeing that Taryn had taken his cue and was lagging back, he sped ahead another hundred feet or so and braked hard broadside to the pair of first turns, roughly the same age at death. Daymon figured the pair could have been a couple in life. She had been wearing denim shorts and a shirt bearing the words *Property of Yellowstone* on her last normal day on earth. Now torn in dozens of places, the once-white shirt no longer hid her midriff from prying eyes. Red at the edges and oozing yellow pus and insect larvae, numerous welts crisscrossed the expanse of pallid dermis north of her grimy navel. Presumably once mid-thigh items, the faded blue shorts had become crusted with dried blood and rode up in all the wrong places.

Likely the cause of infection, purple-ringed divots where mouth-sized hunks of flesh had been rent ran up and down both arms.

The male had suffered horrendous wounds and massive blood loss fending off his attackers. Now dead and sans several fingers and nearly all of the skin, muscle, and underlying tissue on both sides of his neck, the thirty-something cadaver plodded alongside the female, matching her step for step and dry-throaty-rasp for dry-throaty-rasp.

'Til death do us part, thought Daymon as Oliver slithered out the door and slammed it behind him. *Be careful what you wish for.*

The death dance on 39 lasted much longer than it should have, with Oliver plodding in a never-ending semicircle before finally parting both of the rotters' heads from their bodies.

Shouting out his open window, Daymon said, "You made the mess, you clean up the mess." He watched Oliver kick the heads, eyes and jaws still moving, across the road where they rolled under the guardrail and plunged to their final resting place on the north bank of the Ogden River. Though he felt bad seeing the slightly overweight man struggling to drag the corpses off the road, Daymon remained behind the wheel.

"What's the holdup?" Wilson asked over the two-way radio.

Daymon ignored the voice emanating from his pants pocket. He was busy tracking Oliver across the two-lane and kept his gaze locked on the man until he opened the door and climbed aboard. Remaining silent, Daymon shifted the Chevy into Drive and started them rolling west toward the setting sun.

Oliver buckled in. Having already wiped the machete clean on the female Z's jean shorts, he snugged Kindness home into its sheath and placed it atop the center console. Fixing a gaze on Daymon, he said, "Well?"

"A deep, dark hole in the ground, last I checked."

"That it is. So, how did I do?"

On the final straightaway before the compound entrance Daymon slowed considerably. He remained silent as 39 arced gently into a slight uphill climb. Finally, as he brought the pickup to a complete stop beside the hidden entry, he spoke up. "Still a work in progress, I'm afraid." He shifted the truck into Park. Squaring up with Oliver, he added in a low, menacing voice, "I watched you getting high at the fix-it shop. That does not happen outside the wire … ever!"

Oliver's eyes went wide. "Says the guy who blazed up with me on the ski hill the other day."

"The rotters were not a threat that day. Quit trying to make your baptism by fire about *me*."

Speechless, Oliver shook his head slowly side to side.

Daymon went on. "Smoking when you need to be sharp is the least of your problems. Your playing up your prowess against the dead could have gotten any number of us killed. If you lie to me or anyone else again—." He went quiet. Figured he'd let Oliver's active imagination finish the threat for him. Probably way worse than anything he could conjure up.

***

Five minutes after Oliver had received his final warning, all three trucks were barreling down the final quarter-mile of feeder road with the outer and inner gates closed and locked behind them.

Daymon slowed to walking speed prior to entering the clearing, swung a wide looping turn and nosed the Chevy in next to Duncan's white Dodge pickup. As he set the brake and silenced the engine, his attention was drawn to the activity near his RV. Under its deployed metal awning, Tran stood before a pair of stainless-steel propane-fired barbecue grills. Moving what was likely venison around one grill with the fork in his left hand, while at the same time busy flipping what looked like potatoes on the opposite with the pair of tongs in his right, Tran's culinary performance was more Benihana chef than backyard burger flipper.

Raven and Sasha were huddled together under a blanket on one of the folding chaise lounges that had been secreted in a cubby beneath the RV. On a folding chair set up next to the girls, dressed for an arctic storm in a wool-lined jacket and matching boots, Glenda was opening cans of something with a handheld opener.

"We got back just in time," Oliver said, shouldering open his door. "Suddenly my appetite has returned."

Chapter 40
Schriever AFB
3:01 p.m. Mountain Standard Time 4:01 p.m. Central 5:01 p.m. Eastern

After the lengthy aircrew briefing, which consisted of handing out call signs, going over building diagrams, and explaining why certain ingress and egress points had been selected, Nash started a color image moving on the largest of the five displays behind her.

It was obvious from the angle that the image was recorded by a satellite holding a fairly steady position over the target. Though it was captured from an incredible distance overhead, the detail was exquisite. The beltway running around the nation's dead capital was choked with cars and teeming with dead. So many dead traveled the expressways and tollways that a channel was created between the vehicles. Cade had seen what the unyielding forward march of a mega herd could do. Firetrucks and tractor trailers were nothing against the surge of frigid flesh. The passenger cars and trucks and their human cargo fleeing D.C. had fared no better than their counterparts fleeing Denver.

"It's total gridlock for five miles in every direction," Nash said, sounding like a person indifferently narrating a public service announcement meant to get people out of their cars and onto public transportation. "Belowground is more of the same. Panicked engineers trying to flee stations filling up with newly turned citizens pancaked their engines into stalled-out train cars. Metrorail likely won't be running again in my lifetime."

The image on screen flickered and suddenly Cade was staring at the target building. The same structure he'd seen from the air during a joint services training mission years ago. It was all reflective glass and nearly cube-shaped.

"The lone road leading into and out of the target will have to be secured before Anvil Team enters the building. Which can't happen until the grounds around Building Alpha are cleared of Zs."

The satellite capturing the footage was clearly moving away from the target. Suddenly its optics zoomed in a few stops and the situation on the ground was crystal clear.

Rarely did Cade's heart skip a beat. However, this was one of those times. That the previous had happened ten minutes prior when Nash broke the news about the antiserum's newly discovered propensity for failure was not lost on the operator. The reason for this particular cardiac gymnastic move was milling around the building's west and north perimeter in real-time on the HD monitor. The dead things were packed in so tightly to the building that they'd snapped off fixed bollards and pushed massive planters, a handful of cars, and dozens of what looked to be two-thousand-pound Jersey barriers up against the building's glittering lower façade.

Dozens more Jersey barriers were scattered like gray Lego blocks about the cement plaza and vast expanse of dying or dead grass. Most were toppled on their sides, the yards-long dark gouges trailing them in the soil a testament to the sheer numbers of dead that had been there during what had to be a long siege which the incredibly patient Zs most likely won. *Time waits for no man*, Cade thought as the camera lens miles above the once great state of Maryland panned over the hundreds of vehicles sitting idle in the multi-acre lots. And to add insult to injury that was the near total destruction of the once-beautiful adjoining landscaping, hundreds of Zs, their shadows long and gangly in the late evening sun, trooped about among the gleaming sea of glass and metal with seemingly no rhyme or reason to their movements.

Nash hit a button on her wand and the screen went dark. "That, gentlemen, is going to be a tough nut to crack."

Cade sensed movement in his right side vision. He swallowed hard and took his eyes off the darkened monitor, the image of the Zs packed in like sardines burned indelibly into his mind. It was the SAS operator beside Cross who had raised his hand. *So polite, the British*, Cade thought.

"Yes," Nash said. "What is it, Nigel?"

In unison, Cade, Griff, and Cross shifted in their chairs and stared at Axelrod.

"With all due respect, ma'am," he said with a full-blown accent not much unlike Agent 007 of movie fame. "Is there a reason we can't infil via the roof?"

"Good question," Nash said, parking her arms on the podium before her. "And that reason is—"

"That campus held forty thousand people on a normal day," Cade said, stealing the major's thunder. "The building you're looking at was probably home to a couple thousand of them. Even on a Saturday I'd guess the skeleton crew would consist of a thousand or more."

"Bingo," said Nash, drawing the operator's attention her way.

"There have got to be twice that many autos in the surrounding lots," Nigel pressed. "Which would explain the crush of dead things bandying on about the grounds. Which begs the question, ma'am … how do we get infilled by helo and sneak in on the ground floor?"

Nash pushed off the podium and walked around front of it. "I'll throw a question back at you, Nigel. Would you rather fight your way through sixteen floors of who knows how many undead government employees, or six?"

Simultaneously, Cade, Griff, and Cross said, "Six," and looked to Sergeant Axelrod for a reaction.

"Settled," said the SAS shooter, folding his arms across his chest.

For most of the engagement the Rangers had remained silent, to a man watching the conversation as if it were a tennis match, heads craning back and forth, eyes landing on the officer in charge of the briefing, then falling back to the team that would be going inside the belly of the beast.

Finally, a forty-something Ranger with an impeccably cut high-and-tight haircut cleared his throat.

Nash craned to see his nametape. "Yes, Lieutenant Nolen, what is it?"

"You set us down ahead of the D-Boys and we'll clear 'em a path through those things," he said, brimming with confidence and the usual can-do-attitude Rangers are known for. "We'll breach a hole all the way to Hades for them if needs be."

"I have no doubt about that, Lieutenant," Nash said. "But we're going to need you and your men to watch the team's six. The mechanical problems Whipper is dealing with have changed the timeline so that it appears we'll be cutting it much closer to the bone than we'd planned. You can breach a hole to Hades and send the PLA there if you make contact."

Causing Cade to smile for the first time since bad news darkened his doorstep, a chorus of "Hooahs" filled the room.

Once the cheers died out, Nash shushed the residual murmur.

"I don't care how you eventually get inside the target. Just know that we have intel from captured PLA personnel that leads us to believe they are also trying to get to Target Alpha. If they beat us there they'll be able to access the same cell tower records that helped us find Two Guns and a host of other high level government officials who went dark early on. We've been busy running rescue ops since the Long Beach Port mission, but have barely made a dent in the list of survivors found on the hard drives your team rescued.

"If the PLA are able to breach the system, download the data, and break the encryption they'll be privy to the exact location of every one of our people who went to ground after the fall. If we don't succeed tomorrow, gentlemen, the Chinese, though their motives aren't entirely clear, will likely begin a slow war of attrition akin to a systematic series of amputations that I'm certain will ultimately deliver them here to our door."

After pausing to let that sink in, Nash wrapped up the briefing by going over the finer points of entering the target building from the ground level. Next, she handed out diagrams of the half-dozen subfloors underneath the building. Finally, before releasing the twenty-eight men to assault the mess hall, she said, "And gentlemen, I'll leave you with this … the monkey wrench I know you've all been waiting for. You may come into contact with survivors somewhere in the bowels of the building. How many? I have no idea. Who? I have no idea. We are not in contact with them. However, someone has been keeping the lights on and the servers humming along down there. Which is a good thing, because if you do come across them, your job of downloading terabytes of information should go off without a hitch. Questions?"

Just the soft tap-tap-tap of fingers striking computer keyboards.

"OK," she said, stepping away from the podium. "Bravo and Charlie Teams are dismissed."

Cade remained seated until the Rangers filed out. While he waited, he folded the handouts and tucked them away in a pocket. Once the cacophony of voices died down, he leaned forward, extended his hand, and introduced himself to Nigel Axelrod.

"Pleasure's all mine, mate," the SAS sergeant said. "Everybody calls me Axe."

"Grayson or Wyatt works for me," Cade said. "Are you the computer specialist Major Nash alluded to?"

"That'd be me," Griff said, working his fingers through his beard. "Nigel does locks real good. Almost as good as Lopez."

Cade shot Griff a raised brow look. "Why didn't you let on during the L.A. mission?"

"Just following the don't ask, don't tell," Griff said with a wink. "You didn't ask … so I didn't tell. Anyway, figured anyone with a pulse could pull hard drives and police up memory sticks, thumb drives and the like."

"And we did … losing Lasagna in the process."

"I was out there shooting alongside the man," said Griff. "He got the short straw. Sucks. But it couldn't be helped."

"When it's your time …" Cross said agreeably, "it's your time."

"He's in Valhalla waiting for us," Axe stated. Then, turning the direction of the conversation back to the mission, added, "Is she pulling our bell-ends? Ground level entry … really?"

Cross plucked his MP7 off the floor next to him and rose from his chair. "Wyatt, you should know."

Cade said, "She's not pulling anything."

"Not good," said Cross. "Because Axe here hates the *Zeds*—his special name for them—almost as much as Lopez does."

Nash put a hand on Axe's shoulder, causing him to jump. Looking up at him, she said, "If I was pulling your … *bell-end*, you'd damn well be aware of it, Axelrod." She smiled. "But if you men want to fight through twenty or more security checkpoints and breach three times as many doors on your way to the prize… go ahead. You have Ari deposit you on the roof and when you get stuck after going down three of four floors"—her smile broadened—"you can call your Ranger QRF force. Have them go in on the ground and come save your butts."

"Ground floor," Cade, Griff, and Cross said nearly in unison.

Sensing the major's need to talk to Cade, Griff rose and elbowed both Cross and Axe. "C'mon' my little surfer twins. Chow awaits."

Leaving Nash and Cade alone, Cross, Axe and Griff filed out of the room behind a handful of 50th Space Wing personnel.

Nash watched the light from the hall diminish and once the door sucked shut sat on the chair next to Cade.

"How'd she take it?"

"As expected," Cade replied. "With a stiff upper lip."

Nash sighed. "Figured as much. It's not a death sentence until the symptoms manifest. I just wanted her to be aware so she can watch for any changes in her physiology. How are *you* taking it?"

"I've already shoved it down into the dark well behind my heart. Figure I'll hash it over later."

Nash said nothing.

"Thank you," Cade said. "Telling me was the right thing to do. The *only* thing to do."

Nash remained tightlipped, tears forming in her eyes.

Cade placed a calloused hand atop hers, squeezed once and rose. He scooped up his carbine from the chair and made his way out of the room without uttering another word.

Chapter 41
3:45 p.m. MST

Clearly not happy to have been cooped up in the F-650 during the return trip, the second Jamie opened her door Max jumped over the seatback and sprang off her lap and into space.

The hairy missile hit the ground running, claws and paws kicking up a spray of dirt and grass, and rocketed across the clearing on a collision course with the throng of survivors. Easily overtaking Oliver, who seemed to be taking his time making his way to the RV, the Shepherd didn't hit the brakes until he was almost on top of the two girls sharing a single reclining lawn chair under the awning.

After ducking the sudden salvo of airborne soil, Raven threw aside the blanket and rolled off the reclining chair only to find herself on the receiving end of a blast of warm dog breath and sloppy licks to the face.

Brook, who was standing on her toes and waving Lev and Jamie over, saw Max accosting her girl and knelt to his level to scratch his ears.

"He's a bundle of energy," Raven said. "Aren't you, boy?" She wiped the slobber from her face and joined her mom in showering attention on the dog that had adopted the Grayson family back at Schriever in September. Now nearly November, and in an entirely different setting—trees and mountains, versus concrete walkways and airplane hangars—the multicolored pooch seemed to have adapted just fine and seemed to have adopted the entire Eden group as his pack.

Brook rose with a grimace and looked to Sasha. "Why don't you and Raven take Max down to the end of the runway and throw a ball for him. I'll call you when dinner is ready."

"Almost ready," Tran called over his shoulder.

"Go," Brook said, the underlying sense of urgency in her voice lost on the girls.

Tran motioned at the girls with the greasy barbecue tongs. "Don't go *too* far," he said in his sing-song voice.

The obvious dig at the unsanctioned excursion that almost got Raven and Sasha killed and saw them punished with ninety days dishwashing duty was *not* lost on the girls.

Raven pursed her lips and glared at Tran for a beat. Finally, she said, "Don't worry, Mom. I'll stay where you can see me."

Also regarding Tran with contempt, Sasha rose and tossed the blanket unceremoniously onto the lounge chair. "And *I* won't lead her astray."

"Bird's her own keeper from here on out," Brook said. "After what nearly happened the other day, I can't see either one of you girls making *those* kinds of bad decisions ever again."

Lev handed Raven the small therapy ball and curved, long-handled device he'd brought with him from the truck. "This will save your arm."

Raven took the items and started walking toward the airstrip. Once she made the first of the two parallel packed-dirt tracks, she turned a hard right and sprinted away with Sasha close behind and Max bounding excitedly through the narrow strip of tall grass growing up between the beaten-down tire tracks.

Brook watched the girls go. When she turned and cleared her throat to quiet the soft conversation, the air of confidence and total control she always displayed in front of her daughter was gone. In its place was a deer in the headlights stare. Her shoulders were rounded. And more pronounced than it had been in days, the stiffness and lack of range of motion in her right arm made her seem frail and aged beyond her thirty-five years.

After exchanging a knowing look with Duncan, she let her gaze walk over the assembled survivors. Everyone save for Cade, the girls, and Seth, who was currently watching the cameras, was present.

Sensing something was amiss, Glenda rose and came to Brook's side, steadying her more with her presence than any kind of physical act.

Oliver, Daymon, and Foley were already seated—the latter two chatting quietly between themselves prior to seeing Glenda's silent gesture. A half-beat later they were mute and waiting for the proverbial shoe to drop.

In the process of arranging camp chairs of their own, Lev, Jamie, Taryn, and Wilson also froze and turned their undivided attention to Brook.

As if on cue, the steady hiss of the barbecue grills died to nothing and Tran quietly closed both of the gleaming lids to keep the early evening chill out.

In the next half-beat, shattering the still that had fallen over the clearing, the door to the RV hinged open with a clatter and Heidi came bounding down the retractable stairs.

"There's my man," she called, plopping down on Daymon's lap and nearly pitching them both head over heels in the already unstable folding chair.

Pressing a finger vertically to her lips, Glenda shot a glare Heidi's way and wrapped her arm around Brook's shoulders.

"I'm glad most of you are sitting down," Brook said. She cast a furtive glance over her shoulder in the direction of the girls. Satisfied they were well out of earshot, she again cleared her throat and went on. "What I am about to tell you caught me completely flat-footed a few minutes ago. Matter of fact, I'm still processing it all, but I fear if I don't get it out in the open now, denial will set in and I'll stuff it all and maybe put my family and all of you at risk as a result." She walked her gaze around the semicircle of survivors. Save for Duncan, whose affect was flat, expectant looks had settled on each and every face.

"What's wrong, sweetie?" Glenda asked.

Heidi began to apologize for her rude interruption, but was herself interrupted as Brook relayed nearly verbatim the troubling news Cade had just broken to her over the satellite phone. Minus her husband's exact verbiage, what Brook said in a low voice was the same thing she had shared with Duncan in private moments before deciding she owed it to the group to inform them as well.

"Infected?!" Oliver exclaimed, his body suddenly going rigid.

"The lady said, '*might be*,'" Glenda corrected.

Addressing the elephant in the clearing, Oliver said, "So she may be infected and it's *OK* with everyone here that she gets to stay inside the compound? Good God, she'll be locked underground with"—he did a quick head count—"at least twelve of us. Any of you want to take a chance of her turning and eating one of us?"

"Stand down," Duncan hissed. "She hasn't turned. And there's no reason to believe she is going to anytime soon."

Daymon was leaning around Heidi and regarding the newest member of the group with a death glare.

"*Oliver*," Glenda barked, shooting a look only a mother could at her child. "You apologize right now."

Oliver said nothing as he rose and started off in the direction of the compound.

"Stop, Oliver," Brook said. "The last thing I want to do is put you or anyone else in jeopardy. I'll think of something."

Oliver stopped and turned back toward his mother.

"You can stay in the RV tonight," Daymon said, tearing his eyes from Oliver. "Consider it yours until Cade gets back. Then you two can decide on what's best for your family. Figure out where you want to go from there."

Duncan bolted up from his chair and nearly spilled his new shotgun and cleaning kit from the low table. "*Go*?" he said, incredulous, the veins in his neck beginning to bulge.

Daymon raised both hands in mock surrender. "Figure of speech," he said. "I was in no way suggesting we exile Brook. That was the *last* effin thing on my mind."

"I was," Oliver muttered as he turned and continued on his way.

Foley leaned in toward Lev. "Good riddance, motherfucker," he whispered. "That big baby was getting on my nerves."

Lev nodded. "We put him on notice today."

Addressing Duncan as he sat back down, Brook said, "It's OK. I didn't take it that way."

The flush still draining from his face, Duncan removed his Stetson and set it on the table with the Saiga.

Brook leveled her gaze on Daymon. "I'll take you up on your generous offer. But only for tonight."

Jamie asked, "What about the girls? What are you going to tell them?"

"I'll have Sasha suggest a sleepover," Wilson said.

In a funereal voice, Jamie asked, "When and what are you going to tell the girls?"

"We'll have a family meeting once Cade returns," Brook said. She swallowed hard and ran a hand through her dark hair. "I'll tell Raven the truth once Cade returns. As for Sasha, I'll leave it up to you, Wilson. You know her best."

Wilson said nothing. However, actions speaking louder than any words could, he grasped his boonie hat's worn brim two-handed and pulled it down tight so that his eyes were barely visible.

"Settled," Brook said, forcing a weak smile. "Now I hear someone wants to take a vote on going north to—"

"Bear Lake," Daymon said, finishing for her. He produced the matchbook found in the attic and proceeded to give a play-by-play account of the day's events, leaving out only the brief stop at the sprawling house east of Woodruff and the *tests* Oliver was subjected to.

Once Daymon finished, the others added their observations, the most astute among them coming from Wilson, who posited that if those people came south looking for food and supplies, chances were, they were likely to be aggressive and many in number.

Daymon scoffed first at that. "We can't let assumptions based on one dissected walker and a couple of booby traps likely set by whoever carved ADRIAN into a windowsill dictate where we go. If we do, we'll run out of food before winter is over. If that happens … we *will* be forced to find out their true nature while at half-strength and bogged down by the weather."

"I agree with Daymon," said Lev. "However, if we do wait for the weather to turn, when we do go out, the dead things will be taken out of the equation."

Duncan shook his head. "We can't wait," he said. "Goes against everything I've been taught. If Cade were here he'd say the advantage goes to the one who acts first. Or he'd pull some other Sun Tzu kind of quote out of thin air."

"I've heard him quote Churchill," Wilson said. "Can't remember hearing anything by the other two dudes."

"Sun Tzu is *one* dude," Daymon said.

"You can quote *me*," Duncan said, again rising from his camp chair. "Let's quit pussyfootin' around and put it to a vote. Those who want to go north and claim what ain't nailed down as our own please raise a hand." He stuck his hand in the air and fixed each person in succession with a steely glare.

Daymon was first to indicate his willingness to go.

"I'm all for it as long as I get to go," Foley said, raising his hand.

Tran thrust his greasy tongs into the air. "We need more food," was his reply.

Taryn and Wilson looked around and once Lev, Jamie, and Heidi threw their hats into the ring, they also added their votes to the affirmative column.

Always the voice of reason, Glenda said, "I'm on the fence on this one. Shouldn't we wait until Cade gets back so he can go with us?"

"Mother Nature is about to turn on the snow spigot. That road out there"—Duncan gestured toward 39—"it's normally closed during the winter months. Getting in and out is going to be next to impossible once it starts spitting and decides to stick around."

Daymon shifted in his chair so he could lean around Heidi's cocked elbow. "Even if we did want to travel east after the snow sticks, we'll not only be giving away our position by the tire tracks, but it's likely we'll also find ourselves clearing a bunch of downed trees along the route."

"And trucks running on snow in four-wheel-drive burn a hell of a lot of fuel," Foley added.

"My arm's getting tired," Taryn said.

After a forced half-smile, Glenda raised her hand. "You sold me."

A trio of two-way radios warbled simultaneously. Brook fished hers out and said, "Yes, Seth?"

"Why is everyone waiting for you to call on them?"

"We're taking a vote." She motioned for everyone to relax then quickly filled Seth in, assuring him his vote would have been solicited had he been needed to break a tie. That being far from the case, she still asked his opinion.

Voice tinny and marred with a burst of static, he said, "What's it matter? No one ever asks me if I want to go out on runs anyway?"

"Do you?" Brook asked.

"No way. I'm cool running the security pod. Just thought I'd bust your—." Realizing who he was talking to, he cut short his quip. "I say yay to as many runs as you want to go on. Just keep your eyes out for Cheetos, will you?"

For the first time since she'd dropped the bombshell on the group, Brook smiled. "Will do," she said. She scrolled the volume down and looked a question at Duncan.

Duncan did a quick headcount. "Eleven for going to Bear Lake. Though he's not here, I'll count Oliver's vote as against."

"Against going outside the wire for *anything*," Daymon quipped.

With a puzzled look settling on his face, Duncan singled the dreadlocked man out. "What's that supposed to mean?"

"I'll tell you later," Daymon answered. "Around the campfire. Over s'mores."

"Bear Lake it is," Brook said. She walked a few feet away from the group and whistled. "Girls … dinnertime."

Tran began heaping plates with generous portions of steaming meat and potatoes.

Instilled from years of food service, the instinct to jump into the fray struck Heidi and Wilson near simultaneously. Each balancing a half-dozen plates on their outstretched arms, they had dinner and drinks served before the girls had walked half the distance from where they'd been exercising Max at the far end of the clearing.

"Before the kids get here, I have something else to say."

Expecting the other shoe to drop, all eyes settled on Brook.

"Dregan was elated to hear that Ray and Helen were safe and sound. He just adores those two." Brook peered over her shoulder at the girls, then went on. "He told me to hug and kiss each and every one of you who went along on the welfare check."

Wilson pointed at his pursed lips. Smiling and a little flushed of cheek, he said, "Those two are tough as nails. Hard to believe anything or anyone could get the drop on them."

"I've been on the wrong end of Ray's rifle," Brook conceded. "Just crossing T's and dotting I's, that's all."

Silently solidifying the pact they had made earlier concerning their slip-up at the farm, Wilson and Taryn locked eyes.

Max cut a path through the scattered camp chairs and sat on his haunches at Tran's feet.

Tran loaded his plate last and closed the grill lids. He knelt and shoveled a third of his venison onto the ground for Max. "Good boy," he said, watching the hungry Shepherd wolf down the food. "You get anything I don't finish."

In response, Max's stub-tail thumped the ground.

From the west, a cold wind knifed through the clearing, rattling the overhead awning and making the tarps covering the Black Hawk and Humvee snap and pop.

Good decision, gang, Brook thought, staring at the darkening clouds.

She said, "Get a plate, girls." And as Raven and Sasha took their plates to their low-riding camp chairs, she added, "How's a sleepover at Sasha's tonight sound to you, Bird?"

Her mouth full of food, Raven glanced up from her plate and flashed a thumbs-up.

Brook took a bite of venison, chewed and swallowed. "Good," she said. "I'm going to stay topside and talk with the adults after dinner. Think you can tuck yourself in tonight?"

Another thumbs-up from Raven.

Tweens, Brook thought, her mood suddenly going dark. She took another bite and moved her gaze from face to face, seeing expressions on them mirroring exactly how she was feeling inside.

Chapter 42
8:09 p.m. Mountain Standard Time 9:09 p.m. Central 10:09 p.m. Eastern
Naval Station Norfolk, Norfolk Virginia
Aboard the *Lanzhou*

"Admiral on the deck," Corporal Meng said, snapping off a smart salute.

"Stand down, Corporal," Admiral Qi said, turning to the radio operator hunched over a touch-screen monitor. "Lieutenant Shou, did you intercept any military communications?"

Shou rose at once, but dropped his notepad onto the floor.

Waiting for the radio operator to compose himself, Qi shifted his gaze to the steel plating above his head and pressed his thumbs against his temples.

Embarrassed, Shou collected his notes and stood. He snapped off a salute, then, speaking rapid-fire, brought the admiral up to speed, leaving nothing out, even going so far as beginning to read the random musings of an obviously deranged HAM radio operator he had been eavesdropping on since his watch had started. He rounded out the situation report by stating that the sonar had detected no seaborne contacts and the 360-degree active-phased array radar had picked up no airborne threats since the destroyer had dropped anchor.

"A simple *no* would have sufficed," Qi said dismissively. "I didn't need to know the details of your long range radio fetish."

Wondering what had gotten into the usually stoic, yet even-keeled admiral, Shou looked to the second in command, Jow Yuan, a slightly overweight man with the rank of captain on his uniform.

Qi was also regarding Yuan with a look bordering on uncertainty. After a few seconds, he said, "Alert the rest of the fleet we are pulling anchor. I want us to be underway in five minutes and steaming north up the Chesapeake in fifteen."

Yuan nodded an affirmative then snatched up a red handset and began relaying Admiral Qi's orders to the rest of the taskforce.

Still standing at attention off of Qi's right elbow, Corporal Meng asked, "Shall I alert Captain Zhen that we are soon to be underway?"

Never one to let a subordinate have the satisfaction of knowing beforehand that he had been second-guessed, Qi shook his head. "Don't bother. Unless Zhen sleeps like a sun bear, he already knows that preparations to embark are proceeding."

***

There was a fingernail-thin band of dark purple crowding the starless black void when destroyer *Lanzhou*, multi-role frigate *Yulin,* and amphibious transport dock *Kunlan Shan*, the latter of which carried a dozen armored vehicles, nearly a hundred PLAN marines, and Zhen's special forces operators, hauled anchor simultaneously.

And well within Qi's allotted fifteen minutes, under cover of full dark, the three vessels were steaming a steady twenty knots up the Chesapeake.

***

An hour after rounding Sewell Point and entering the Chesapeake Bay, the *Lanzhou's* excursion into enemy territory took a terrifying turn. For three straight miles the three ships were forced to slow to a crawl to navigate a channel clogged with all manner of watercraft. Inside the *Kunlan Shan*, whose hull rose from the waterline at less of an angle than the frigate and destroyer, sailors reported hearing the eerie keening of fingernails transmitting through the steel plates just above the waterline.

By the time the warships were clear of the undead flotilla, dozens of the smaller boats and their undead cargo that had been anchored in the path of the much larger warships were either already at the bottom of the bay, or were taking on water and soon would be.

All through the ordeal, Qi had been focusing a pair of high-powered binoculars on the eastern shoreline, certain the enemy was training a full battery of ship-killing missiles on his tiny flotilla.

Schriever AFB, 10:09 p.m. Mountain Standard Time

As it turned out, Ari's declaration of *wheels up in one hour* failed to happen. A routine inspection brought upon by an error message had revealed that a vital component of one of the Ghost Hawk's turbines was close to failing. Thankfully, the compromised part was universal to the UH-60 Black Hawk, and Whipper's aviation techs were able to come up with a replacement part to install in the Ghost Hawk. However, all combined, the briefing, refuel, rearming, and maintenance on the turbine had grounded the bird and detained the Delta team for several hours more than expected.

In the big green machine, known formally as the United States Army, *hurry up and wait* was the norm. Having endured more than his share of the latter, Cade had learned to sleep anywhere and at any time. So he had grabbed a patch of concrete in the corner of the hangar, curled up into a ball with his head on his rucksack, and quickly succumbed to Mr. Sandman's pull.

Now, having been rudely awakened by the vibration from a strategically placed kick to his boot sole, Cade raised his head off his rucksack and fixed a death glare on Ari. For the first time in a long while he saw the aviator without sunglasses or a helmet visor covering his hazel eyes. There was a twinkle of mischief in them and the man's lips were parted slightly as if he were about to deliver a punch line. Which, when taking the man's general outlook on life into consideration, didn't seem outside the realm of possibility.

"You don't even have *one* knock-knock joke locked-and-loaded?" said Cade as he worked at rubbing a kink out of his neck.

"Saving 'em all for the long flight," Ari said, donning his helmet. "We launch in five."

***

10:15 p.m. MST Leaving Schriever

Cade had policed up his gear and was strapped into his usual port-side seat in the Ghost Hawk in a little under two minutes. Fact of the matter, he was itching to get the show on the road. The sooner the job was done, the sooner he could get back to Eden and see to Brook and Raven. Best case scenario, Brook was going to have to be quarantined until more was known. However, worst case scenario, grim as hell as it was, if what Nash had told him earlier about how the 4th ID soldier's death had any truth to it, he could be going home to a freshly filled grave. But for now, there was nothing he could do about it. And where he was going, it would be suicide to dwell on it. So he pushed it all back where it belonged. All of the emotion attached to the slim possibility of the latter had to remain in that black hole of his where a stray thought was less likely to escape. Because stray thoughts had been known to jeopardize good judgment and sound decision-making. Which could lead to him getting killed. Or even worse, someone on his team going down due to his negligence.

"You're zoning out like a Zed, mate," Axe said, waving a hand in front of Cade's face.

The turbines fired up off to Cade's right. He heard the cough and sputter then felt the slight vibration he knew was the rotor overhead beginning to spool up.

"Sometimes I feel like one," Cade said.

"You and me both," Axe conceded as he buckled himself into a seat near the internally stowed starboard minigun.

Cade nodded to Cross and Griff when they boarded.

"Launching in one mike," Ari said over the comms.

While Skipper was helping the other Delta shooters stow their gear, Cade was rehashing the last part of his private conversation with Nash. The part in which she ran President Clay's very risky, yet hugely rewarding side mission by him. It was doable, that much they had agreed upon. But the onus was on him to get the consent of the other involved parties. "All of them," Nash had said, a no-nonsense look parked on her face. Then, without breaking character, she had added, "I'm behind you one hundred per cent, Grayson. God speed to all of you." Recalling the initial look of surprise on her face when he'd accepted the task, even with the specter of Brook's condition weighing heavily on his shoulders, he cracked a little half-smile and shook his head in disbelief. Looking to his left, he saw Ari craning around in the right seat. "You working on a knock-knock joke of your own?" the aviator asked.

Allowing his smile to dissolve slowly, Cade said, "Not my style, Ari."

Ari turned his attention to the switches and gauges laid out all around him. After a moment of silence, he came back on the comms and said, "That's OK, Wyatt. I've got enough yuks for the two of us combined."

Feeling the full press of gravity on his body when the fuel-laden Ghost Hawk sprang from the tarmac, Cade honored Lopez by making the sign of the cross over his chest. Finished, he settled his gaze on the hulking silhouette Pikes Peak presented and then took in the majestic breadth of the distant Rockies as the ship, once again dubbed Jedi One-One for this mission, nosed down and swung a hard one-eighty.

By the time the Jedi ride was level and tracking nearly due east, Schriever's northern fence line was a barely visible strand of silver rippling below Cade's window and the siren's song of sleep was beginning to call to him.

Eden Compound, 11:20 p.m. Mountain Standard Time

Brook awoke with the gauze-like remnants of a nightmare clinging to the edge of consciousness and the all-too-real startled yelp that it had produced echoing inside the RV's confined sleeping area. Shivering hard, she searched for the missing blanket in the dark, which, inside the RV with the curtains pulled, was absolute and inky, like she imagined the bottom of the ocean must be.

Teeth chattering an eerie cadence, she finally snagged hold of a corner of the fleece blanket, drew the supple fabric up to her neck, and trapped the loose end to her chest with her chin.

Truth be told, being separated from Raven and Cade—not only by distance, but also the chasm of not knowing what Nash's revelation presented her—was the hardest thing she'd yet to face in this new Omega-affected world.

But she wasn't truly alone. She was wearing Cade's Army tee shirt and Raven's stocking cap. Both items radiated their individual scents, and though one was a hundred yards away under tons of dirt, and the other, hundreds of miles to the east of the Eden compound, in spirit they were right here in the Winnebago with her.

Eyes wide open and fixed on the ceiling she knew was there but couldn't see, Brook revisited the after-dinner exchanges she'd had with every one of the survivors, save for Oliver, who hadn't been seen since stalking off during her impromptu confession.

Beginning to come to her softly on the periphery of sleep, like whispers in a cavern, the conversations she had had earlier, some only a word or two in passing, most lengthy and bordering on some kind of pre-death eulogy, barged their way back into her head.

Having stuck with her at the time as genuine and heartfelt, Duncan's offer to "do whatever is necessary" in Cade's absence was the most important declaration echoing in her head. And second only to that delicately veiled, albeit morbid promise, what

Glenda, Jamie, and Taryn had said to her in no uncertain words during a private late-night huddle, left her feeling that no matter what happened going forward, Raven would not only be safe and cared for, but most importantly, she would be loved unconditionally.

A tear ran hot and fast down her cheek. More followed, wetting her pillow.

Sobbing silently, she rolled over to her left side, drew her knees to her chest, and wrapped them up as best she could with her weakened right arm. The wind subsided for a brief two-count and she thought she heard something moving outside the trailer. There was a swishing sound, like grass being parted. Then that not too unusual noise was followed by a brief rasp of metal-on-metal. She listened hard and thought she could detect a constant clicking noise that seemed to be steadily retreating. But before she could be certain, or work the courage up to arm herself, put boots on and investigate, the wind kicked back up and whistled unabated through the motor pool, making the tarps crackle like a far off barrage of heat lightning.

During the follow-on-lull between gusts, Brook rolled to the edge of the bed abutting the wall and pressed her ear hard to the wood paneling.

Nothing.

So she felt around in the gloom atop the nightstand until her hand found the satellite phone. Clutching it near to her chest, she powered it up and bit her lip in anticipation. After a short, albeit nerve-wracking three-second wait the vibrant display came alive with color. She cycled through to the message screen and, sadly, learned that there was no voice or text message from Cade. For a half-beat she considered sending a brief SMS message to his sat-phone, but quickly decided against it. He'd undoubtedly processed the information about the suspect antiserum and was back into mission mode. Busy being *frosty*, and she wanted it to stay that way. Besides, though she was feeling a little under weather—and had been since being bitten and subsequently saved with a dose of antiserum—she had no reason to fear the worst.

So for now, she decided grudgingly, until the final chapter was written and she was left with no other decision than to end her own life, a protocol of quarantine—with an electronic lifeline, of course—was the only way to see this play out. Whether it would last a day, week, month or more, she had no idea. Best to take it one day at a time was the mantra going through her head when the tiny screen on the phone still clutched in her left hand went dark.

She put the phone back and lay there for a moment, eyes closed and praying to her God that her new friends followed through on every one of their promises, whether spoken or tacit.

Five long minutes after being yanked from sleep by a boogie man she couldn't put a finger on, her breathing and heartrate slowed and sleep once again took her.

Chapter 43
5:06 a.m. EST 4:06 a.m. CST 3:06 a.m. MST Springfield, Illinois 100 miles north of St. Louis, Missouri

Cade opened his eyes and swept his gaze around the inside of the gently vibrating Ghost Hawk. Slightly disoriented after coming to all awash in muted red light, he hitched up his sleeve and triggered the light on his Suunto. Noting the time on the glowing green display, he made some mental calculations based on time elapsed since he'd dozed off over Kansas, a guesstimate at the Ghost Hawk's maintained airspeed over that time, and, finally, after adjusting for time spent refueling, he came away thinking they were over Illinois and—much to his chagrin—he was facing at least four more hours strapped to the uncomfortable fold-down seat.

No sooner had he accepted his assumption as fact than Ari came in over the shipwide coms to say they were overflying Springfield, Illinois and, to add perspective, indicated that they were roughly seventy-five miles due north of St. Louis, Missouri. Then, yammering away in full-on Night Stalker Airways mode, he said that barring any unforeseen circumstances, they should be approaching Target Alpha in less than five hours.

Taking the bad news in stride, Cade wiped the sleep from his eyes and regarded his surroundings. Across the aisle, on the starboard side of the ship, Griff and Cross were sound asleep. Heads lolling gently against the bulkhead, both shooters were clad in MultiCam ACUs with plate carriers and MOLLE gear snugged on over top of them. *All Velcro and camo*, was how Brook liked to describe Cade when he was dressed similarly and loaded down with the battle rattle, or tools of the trade he used to kill bad guys and Zs. Propped up against the bulkhead between the former Navy SEALS were two vastly different weapons. On the seat next to Cross was his stunted H&K MP7 submachine gun. A slightly curved 40-round magazine protruded from its pistol grip, and riding picatinny rails on the suppressed weapon's top and fore was an EOTech holographic sight and compact, combination targeting laser/infrared designator. Threaded onto the short barrel and balancing the weapon out nicely was a Rotex-II suppressor.

Griff, on the other hand, had come away from the armorer's shack with a cleaned and oiled H&K 416 identical to the weapon his Team 6 brethren had used to pop Bin Laden. Also suppressed, this CQB (close quarters battle) rifle was equipped with a drop down fore grip, holographic sight with deployable 3x magnifier, and similar targeting laser/infrared designator as on Cross's weapon. Chambered in 5.56 x 45mm like the M4 he favored, Cade knew Griff's weapon had reliable stopping power, but not the same concealability and rate of fire its little brother, the MP7, possessed.

To Cade's right, the affable Nigel Axelrod was slumped in the forward-facing seat Lopez liked to refer to as the "*bitch seat.*" His desert tan tactical bump helmet was on the vacant seat next to him. The sand-colored beret he'd been wearing when they boarded was now canted at an angle on his upturned face, easily covering most of its narrow expanse.

Finally, finishing off his visual sweep of the passenger cabin, Cade settled his gaze on Skipper. Seemingly oblivious to the fact he was being scrutinized, the always vigilant crew chief wore a pair of the newest four-tube night vision goggles clipped to his helmet and was scanning the darkened countryside outside his window with them.

Unsure if the other aircraft were still keeping pace with the high-flying Ghost Hawk or had already gone on ahead as planned in order to secure the only road in and out of the target area,

Cade shifted in his seat and craned to see out his port-side window.

The crescent moon was behind high cloud cover and did little to illuminate the ground scrolling by nor anything airborne in the lead craft's general vicinity.

"You pick up Jedi One-Two yet?" Skipper asked. "She's out there. Your ten o'clock. Stacked two discs left off our six."

Cade squinted and probed the night sky for the gen-3 twin-rotor SOAR bird carrying the Army Rangers, but saw nothing. Knowing the crew chief could see him clear as day, he shook his head. "I'll take your word for it, though."

"One-Three is on starboard. Same position."

Cade dipped his head and tried to find an angle past Axe.

"She's there, mate," Axelrod assured Cade. He removed the beret from his face and peered out the window to his immediate right. "Yep. Darth-Vader-black Chinook at my two o'clock. Maybe … one hundred fifty meters off our tail."

"I'll take your word for it," Cade said to the SAS operator. "Anything else interesting?"

"Not really, mate. Just the wide open expanse of your country's fly-over states. Isn't that what most of your ruling class thought of middle America before middle Americans began eating them?"

"You got that right," Cade said. "All the meddling by the powers that be in traditional military affairs was the main reason I was out of the teams before this mess started."

"Right," Axe said agreeably. "Our hands were tied as well. Whatever bloke thought it a good idea to let Parliament determine our ROEs needed to be out there eating sand with me and my mates."

"It's different now, though," Cade said. "Gloves are off. No more haggling with lawyers and waiting for them to tell us whether we can take out an insurgent on a motorbike or not."

Axe rolled up his beret and stuffed it in a pocket. "Different enemy, different rules."

Cross stirred, but stayed in the same position—head back, eyes closed—he'd been in since they launched from Schriever hours ago.

"Different leadership," Cade proffered. "In my opinion, that's the major difference between then and now."

"I reckon you know the blokes at the controls of this eggbeater?"

"I heard that," Ari said over the comms. "I may be poor, but I'm not *bloke*."

"Nothing wrong with your funny bone," Cade said. "How's the rest of Ari holding up?"

"Like a sugar cookie in Coronado surf," he said. "I could really use another of those five-hour energy drinks Skipper's been bogarting since the Kansas line."

Without a word, Skipper ripped the Velcro on a pocket and fished out four of the brightly colored bottles. He handed them forward and dropped them in Haynes' baseball mitt of a hand.

Cade remembered seeing those small pill-bottle-looking items on the counter of his local 7-Eleven. And like Tribbles of Star Trek fame, those garish-colored bottles seemed to multiply between trips there for Diet Cokes. It didn't surprise him that Ari needed one of the pick-me-ups. The man, in fact the entire aircrew, had been incredibly quiet since they'd crossed over from Colorado into Kansas. The Auntie Em and Toto cracks went on for a couple of minutes until Cross and Griff checked out. The cockpit chatter ceased shortly thereafter. And Cade couldn't blame them; it had been a long time since Ari had kicked the bottom of his Danners to rouse him, and nearly twelve hours since they'd lifted off from Camp Bastion.

A burst of static sounded in Cade's headset. After that subsided he was amazed to hear someone from Scott AFB welcoming them to Illinois. He remained silent and listened to the male voice relay details pertaining to the next aerial refueling set to happen somewhere over West Virginia. He stared at the ground, trying hard to see anything that might give the base away. Runway lights. Light spill from an improperly blacked-out window. Perhaps shielded headlights of a vehicle following a patrol route.

Seeing nothing pointing to the location of the base he knew was somewhere north of their position, he leaned into the cabin and peered through the cockpit glass. Framed by Ari and Haynes, way off in the distance, was a horizontally oriented razor-thin ribbon of light. Just a hint of bluish purple bullying its way into the vast expanse of blackness all around it. Chasing dawn was always a cool thing to experience, and this wasn't Cade's first time going into harm's way doing so.

Chapter 44
Chesapeake Bay, 89 Nautical Miles North by Northwest of Sewell Point, Norfolk, West Virginia – 4:09 a.m. EST

Qi focused on the night sky far off the destroyer's starboard side where astronomic twilight was giving way to nautical twilight. Soon dawn would be mounting its glacial-paced assault on the starless black void.

He smiled at nature's beauty, then turned his gaze to the *Yulin*. Fitted with air defense and anti-submarine rockets, the angular warship, though smaller than the destroyer *Lanzhou*, still produced an imposing silhouette when backlit by the diffuse light radiating from the distant rising sun.

The 440-foot-long Type Fifty-Four-A multi-role frigate was patrolling the waters near the mouth of Eastern Bay with its powerful Type 382 radar keeping vigilant watch over the rapidly brightening night sky. With the ability to pick up over the horizon airborne threats within a thirty-mile radius, the more maneuverable *Yulin*, Admiral Qi had decided, would best serve as a mobile picket of sorts. Having the pale gray frigate patrol the narrow stretch of Chesapeake while simultaneously watching out for air or land-based threats freed the admiral to give his undivided attention to the unloading of the slab-sided *Kunlan Shan*.

And undivided it had been. He had watched from the bridge of the *Lanzhou* as the amphibious transport dock eased into position, stern facing shore, and disgorged the four noisy LCAC (Landing Craft Air Cushioned) from her cavernous well deck. Always a sight to behold, the vehicle- and troop-laden hovercraft frothed the water as their humongous stern-mounted fans propelled them at high speed on cushions of air from ship to shore. It had taken the hovercraft four round-trips to ferry the entire expeditionary force to the beachhead.

Qi's chest swelled with pride as for the first time in his life he saw Chinese boots on the shore of one of her greatest enemies. The two countries had a history of always clashing through proxies. For as long as he could remember his desire to see this bully of a nation get her just desserts had burned strong in his belly. The calculated spread of the so-called Omega virus had been the first step in this final end game. The march to her once glorious capital would be the second. And with the information Zhen and his team were soon to extract, the third step could commence. Leaving behind manufactured evidence pointing to America's culpability in the greatest catastrophe to befall the world since the asteroid strikes that culled the dinosaurs would serve two purposes. In the near term, once the false proof was shown to the surviving heads of state the world over, China's *humanitarian* incursion into the United States mainland could hardly be argued. If all came off as planned, Qi thought, a smile parting his lips, the results of the mission would leave China looking like the savior in the eyes of history.

Qi smiled thinking of the surgical attacks the hundreds of special forces teams already spread about the country would soon be carrying out. Just like seeing the dead rise for the first time, the American dogs wouldn't know what to do nor think when the PLA ghosts showed up unannounced on their doorsteps.

It would be akin to excising cancerous tumors from a living body, he thought. A living body that would then be ripe for repopulation. And after losing untold numbers of men and armored vehicles at the hands of only a few hundred United States Marines in California, the simple act of moving the substantial force he was looking at from shore to the nation's former capital would go a long way toward restoring the confidence the nearly decimated PLA forces had recently lost.

Now Qi's binoculars were trained on a sandy and treeless stretch of shoreline east of a town on the map called Huntingtown. The four amphibious landing craft were parked abreast where they had powered ashore the fourth and final time to deposit the last of the seven hundred marines, Captain Zhen's special forces team, and their four specially modified off-road motorcycles.

"A glorious day, indeed," he said to no one in particular as the marines on shore worked their way north through a campground filled with the tattered remnants of colorful tents and what he estimated to be several dozen jiangshi. Moving from shore, bayonets fixed, the men worked methodically. Step. Thrust. Clear. This went on for a couple of minutes and when all of the jiangshi in the immediate vicinity were put down, other soldiers moved in and dragged their leaking bodies from the beachhead to clear the way for the troop transports and armored vehicles.

Always nearby, Corporal Meng said, "If only the Party's ruling class hadn't commandeered our Harbin."

"The ruling class commandeered *all* of the South Sea Fleet's helicopters to save themselves and their families," Qi replied, grimly. "Why would *Lanzhou* go unplucked?"

"No matter," Meng said confidently. "This is a glorious day for China and truly a great moment in history."

"And history favors the bold," replied Admiral Qi in a measured tone.

Chapter 45

Save for the small clusters of lights representing newly established government redoubts on the outskirts of Springfield, Indianapolis, and Cincinnati, the vast expanse of Illinois, Indiana, and Ohio the Ghost Hawk had overflown was an impenetrable sea of black. The random structure fires and burning multi-vehicle pile-ups so commonplace during the outbreak's onset were nonexistent. Headlights of vehicles fleeing the dead no longer illuminated the rural highways and byways. Aside from the flashing infrared lights on thc aircraft engaged in the first refueling, Cade's constant companions for the duration had been the three Ds: Doctor Silence perched at his window near his minigun. The millions of dead he knew owned the land below the helicopter. And darkness of the magnitude he'd only experienced at night high up in the mountains of Afghanistan.

With the veil of night finally beginning to peel away from east to west, Ari's voice boomed over the shipboard comms. "Rise and shine. Up and at 'em. Drop your cocks and grab your socks," he bellowed ahead of a wicked laugh.

Cade imagined being a younger sibling to Ari. Oh what a hellish existence that would have been. Maybe even to the point of rivaling Air Force boot camp. He grinned at the thought and looked across the aisle where Cross and Griff both came to in unison. Barely a second removed from the impromptu wakeup, both men were back to sitting upright in their seats.

Grumbling about being so rudely awakened by such low brow humor, Griff leaned against his safety harness and flashed the smartass SOAR pilot a sour look.

Having been awake since the last aerial refuel near the Illinois border, Cade had watched as the Air Force HC-130J Combat King II tanker—its flashing running lights illuminating the immediate night sky like a fireworks display—overtook the Jedi flight and settled off their port side at his two o' clock. After dousing the visible lights, the King's starboard refueling hose complete with red and white checkered drogue chute and gently strobing IR light extended and the matte-black Stealth Chinooks drank from the boom first. After Jedi One-Two received her fill of JP-8, the dual-rotor ship fell back to make way for One-Three. Once the second helo's tanks were full, the SOAR pilot backed his bird away so the Ghost Hawk could take its turn at the well.

"Jedi Lead moving into position," Ari had said, his voice loud and clear in Cade's headset.

"Copy, Lead," the tanker pilot had replied. "Make it quick, our bird still needs to drink. If we don't … you'll be making hot refuels in Indian country all the way back to Springs."

"Native American country," Ari quipped as he bled off a little airspeed to match the Hercules.

"Figure of speech," the Herc pilot had shot back blandly.

That last exchange had stuck in Cade's head. During the last hot refuel he'd been involved in, a man had died. Nothing fluke about his death: Hicks had been gang-tackled. There were just too many Zs on the apron to keep track of. And with a fuel bowser nearby, using the Ghost Hawk's miniguns to save the operator hadn't been an option.

Now, four hours removed from the last aerial refueling and with another one looming, Cade was still troubled by the memories of all the good men lost to an act perpetrated by the very nation currently invading America.

Thankfully, bringing his train of thought back to the mission at hand, through his headset, Cade heard Ari begin coordinating the current refuel order between the two new tanker pilots and Jedi One-Two and One-Three. Trying to tune out the jargon-filled exchange, he looked through his window to the dead world below. Illuminated by the first light of day, but still partially shrouded in ground-hugging pockets of fog, the fuzzy outlines of fields and barns and silos made small by distance began to pass diagonally underneath the Ghost Hawk. As Ari side-slipped the helo to port, Cade glanced up through the barely perceptible rotor blur and caught sight of the flashing lights and angular silhouette of the KC-135 Stratotanker shadowing the entire operation from a seemingly static position high above their current altitude. Though the multi-engine jet appeared small in relation to the nearby and much slower KC-130 the flight had just rendezvoused with, he knew the jumbo-jet-sized Stratotanker keeping pace carried the fuel the Hercules would need after transferring all it had to the entire Jedi Flight so as to ensure that the "multiple hot refueling stops at abandoned Z-choked airfields" the Herc pilot had spoken of would not occur.

***

Ten minutes had elapsed between the time Ari moved into position and gently coupled with the boom trailing the larger gray turboprop and their delicate dance was completed. After Ari's customary promise to buy the tanker crew beers when they next met, the Hercules serviced the other two helos and drifted up and away to a refueling rendezvous of its own.

Based on the parting chatter between Ari and the flight crew of the Stratotanker that had been stalking them, Cade drew the conclusion that it was one of the last airworthy birds of the 435th Aerial Refueling Wing operating out of Grissom Air Reserve Base in North Central Indiana, and once it had finished topping off the KC-130 it would have just enough fuel to return to base.

***

Ninety minutes after the latest aerial refueling in a string of many, the Ghost Hawk was crossing over from West Virginia into Maryland. Suddenly the shoulder straps bit into Cade's shoulder as the helicopter banked hard to starboard and entered an ever-steepening nose-down dive that saw the distance between Jedi One-One and the ground quickly decrease by half. Grateful he wasn't hearing the electronic peal of a missile lock-on warning or feeling the craft judder as flares rocketed from the airframe-mounted dispensers, he calmly peered out his window and instantly saw the distant sun, big and white and watery, nudging its way through faraway high-strata. As planned, the two black Stealth Chinooks full of Rangers kept thundering east toward their preplanned loiter location to wait as a quick reaction force to be utilized should Cade's team find themselves trapped and in need of immediate extraction.

Once the Chinooks were out of sight, Cade cast his gaze groundward and saw the same pearlescent hue of the sun reflected back at him in the Potomac River.

Delineating West Virginia and Maryland, the south-flowing river snaked its way diagonally west to east, twisting and turning within view of Arlington National Cemetery, the White House, and nearby National Mall, Ronald Reagan National Airport, and finally the Pentagon, which was blackened by soot and ringed by dozens of Humvees and various other pieces of military hardware: Abrams tanks, multi-wheeled Strykers and boxy Bradley fighting vehicles. Arranged with their barrels aiming outward, the static armor bespoke of a frantic last stand that had obviously been won by the living dead.

"What a shitshow," commented Ari, slowing the helo and initiating a gentle turn to the east.

Just thinking aloud, Cade said, "Amazing that it took an event such as this to pry the politicians from their hold on office."

"Cold dead hands," quipped Skipper. "And I can smell 'em from here."

And Cade could, too. "Thanks for the reminder," he said, peering down on the Potomac River that, from five hundred feet in the air, looked much different than he had remembered it. Maybe it was because the most memorable image of the District of Columbia imprinted in his mind had come from a grainy newscast he'd seen nearly thirty years prior. Then the Potomac had been frozen over and an airliner-sized hole had been punched into its center. A helicopter had hovered over the shattered ice, its rotor wash creating an ever-widening concentric circle in the frigid chop. The only thing Cade remembered seeing floating atop the river's black surface at the time, other than the inches-thick shards of broken ice, had been a female survivor and the one Good Samaritan who had jumped to her aid from the nearby seawall. Something had clicked inside of him, lending to his desire to help others one day.

Now, perhaps lending to his change in perception, thousands upon thousands of bloated bodies, many of them reanimated and frothing the ice-free water with their arms and legs, had become tangled in the remnants of the 14th Street Bridge jutting from the river off the helo's port side.

Taking in the macabre sight out his window, Axe said, "Isn't that the fuck all," his British accent making it impossible for Cade to discern whether it had been question or statement. "Looks just like satellite footage of the River Thames."

"Why didn't you go home?" Cade asked, still staring at the sights scrolling by below the Ghost Hawk.

"Wifey was in Japan at the time. On business." Axe shook his head. "She made it to the embassy but never made it to the waiting birds that were supposed to take all of the British nationals home."

Cade saw that they were about to overfly the National Mall. "Did she get caught up in the Z outbreaks?" he asked.

Axe said nothing for a long while.

Silently contemplating things known only to them, both Cross and Griff were staring out their respective windows when a call came in indicating that the two Stealth Chinooks had just been painted by a ground-based radar of some sort.

Immediately there was a noticeable increase in the turbine whine and the nimble craft seemed to buck as Ari nosed her toward the deck. The ground rushed up for a couple of seconds before the Ghost Hawk leveled off close to the treetops and course-corrected north by east until the Washington Monument loomed large through the cockpit glass.

Upthrust like a middle finger to the living, the granite obelisk stood tall and majestic and as bone white as Cade had ever remembered it being. Thousands of undead marched the National Park, trampling the lawn into a dark brown morass. Of the fifty American flags once flying at its base, only a dozen were left, colorful as the day they were made and snapping wildly atop crazily canted flagpoles. Many more Zs, way too many to count, were mired in the murky water of the reflecting pool. Suddenly becoming aware of the low-flying aircraft, pale faces turned to the sky and tracked the near silent helo right to left as it passed very close to the squat, Pantheon-like Lincoln memorial.

"Haynes, anything?" Ari barked rapid-fire.

"Clear so far."

Ari said, "Skipper, keep your eyes peeled for missile launches."

Skipper said nothing.

Cade added eyes to the vigil off to port and assumed the other operators were doing the same to starboard.

"Taking her down to NAP flight," Ari warned. "We won't be shot out of the sky on my watch."

With a recently consumed MRE and pint of water bouncing around in his system, Cade drew some deep breaths in an attempt to avoid earning a Puker patch.

Chapter 46

The banging on the door was loud and constant. Brook wiped a strand of drool from the corner of her mouth and squinted against the harsh bar of light infiltrating the curtains. Muttering at the caller to relax, she threw the blanket off her legs and plucked the Glock from the built-in nightstand beside the bed.

"Who's there?"

The banging stopped and there was a brief silence before a woman's voice filtered through the door.

"Oliver is missing."

"Glenda?" Brook called. She pulled the Glock's slide back an inch. As expected—the new gold standard in the apocalypse—a 9mm round was already chambered.

The knob turned, but the door didn't budge. "Open up."

Glock leveled at the thin metal door, Brook repeated her question.

The knob rattled again. It spun left and then back to the right. "It's Glenda … unlock the door."

"Give me a minute." Brook holstered the Glock and strapped the belt around her waist. She slipped her feet into her boots and laced them up. Lastly, she donned a medium-weight parka and stuck a hand in its left pocket. Feeling the raised plastic teeth on the pair of thin flex cuffs inside, she removed her empty hand from the pocket and zipped it shut.

Outside the RV, the majority of the survivors were standing under the metal awning. Glenda was at the bottom of the steps, her face screwed up with worry. Duncan was by her side. With the Saiga held loosely in hand, white Stetson pulled low on his brow and tan Carhartt jacket zipped to the neck, at first glance he resembled one of those stagecoach drivers from a century and a half ago.

"What's the matter?" Brook asked.

"Oliver has up and run off," Duncan answered, eyes downcast.

"Wasn't my fault," Daymon said, showing both palms.

"I beg to differ," Wilson said.

"We were *all* a little hard on him yesterday," Lev added.

While Daymon knew he wasn't the only one in on the trial-by-rotter Oliver had endured, he held his tongue on that matter. Instead, wisely, lest he say something else he'd likely regret, he stalked off toward his truck.

Duncan turned his body and tracked Daymon with his eyes. "Where are *you* going?"

"To my truck."

"He's probably taking a walk in the woods," said Lev.

Daymon shook his head. "I've got a good idea where he's going and how he's getting there," he said, and stalked off toward his Chevy pickup.

"Wherever he's going, he's not driving," Taryn called. "Because I checked inside every vehicle in the motor pool, and they're all accounted for. And I know for a fact he's not asleep in Dregan's eighteen-wheeler or the helicopter. I checked those, too. So where *could* he have gone to at night and on *foot*?" She said the last part looking at the others and in a voice that inferred that even saying it out loud was justification to be committed to the loony bin.

Brook was watching the round robin conversation with rapt attention when it suddenly dawned on her Raven and Sasha hadn't yet emerged from their sleepover. Probably for the best, she thought. No way they're joining an outside-the-wire search party anyway.

Tran and Foley exited the woods nearby, both shaking their heads. While Tran continued to the RV and chose an unclaimed camp chair, Foley stopped in his tracks and blurted, "I want to be part of the search party."

A V8 motor rumbled to life down by the motor pool. A tick later Daymon pulled up close to the assembled survivors and brought his Chevy to a lurching halt. The window powered down. As if he'd been reading the older man's mind, Daymon looked to Foley. "Get in," he said. "Your longing for action and adventure is about to be realized." He looked to Lev next. "You and Jamie coming?"

"You two can take the beast," Brook told Jamie.

Taryn approached the Chevy. "You really think he just up and left on foot?"

"No way," Daymon answered, the truck shimmying as Foley opened the door and slid across the seat. "He took Sasha's bike. And he's not out on some early morning joy ride, either."

"What makes you so sure?" Duncan asked.

Daymon leaned out his window and whispered, "Because his gear is gone. All of it. The makeshift body armor, night vision goggles, and that custom rifle of his, too."

"I heard that," Glenda said, rising from her chair.

Duncan looked up at the dark clouds forming overhead. His jaw took a firm set. "So where do you think he went?"

"I figure we'll find Sasha's bike at the roadblock," Daymon said. "He'll have crossed to the other side and taken one of the vehicles we left there."

"Why?" Glenda asked. "What did you do to him?"

"Called him on his bullshit," Daymon said. "Your son froze up as soon as we left the wire. Can't be having that." He went on, detailing everything that had happened the day before between him and Oliver, leaving out only the trip to the house.

"So he only traveled the PCT at night," Lev said. "Makes sense."

"I say we quit jawin' and find the kid," Duncan drawled.

"I'll get the truck," Taryn said, leaving her gear with Wilson.

Clutching Duncan's arm tight, Glenda said, "I already lost him once. I can't bear to go back to the not knowing."

Duncan fished the keys to the Dodge from a pocket. "I'm going. The more time we waste, the colder the trail will get."

"I want to go," Glenda demanded.

"Under no circumstances," Duncan said, shaking his head. "I don't want to risk losing you, too." He gave her a peck on the cheek, motioned for Tran to follow, then strode off toward the motor pool.

An engine fired to life on the other side of the RV. As the throaty rumble of the F-650's V-10 filled the clearing, the radio in Brook's hand came alive with static. "The road's clear," Heidi said, her update obviously meant for those going outside the wire.

"Roadblock first," Daymon called, as Lev nosed the F-650 close to his bumper. Singling out Wilson, he added, "Be sure to bring along extra ammunition and food. Because if the bike isn't there, we'll be heading north into unknown territory."

Chapter 47
Northeast of Washington D.C.

Though the enemy radar that had painted the two Stealth Chinooks had likely originated from some type of military vehicle traveling one of the numerous highways and byways between Washington D.C. and the Delta team's target, needing to reach the loiter position without revealing themselves to the enemy prohibited the heavily armed helos from turning back to hunt down and kill the offending parties. So after taking precautionary evasive maneuvers of their own, the co-pilot aboard Jedi One-Two had noted the coordinates where the c-band radar waves had lit them up and passed the information on to the TOC back at Schriever.

Nineteen Miles Southwest of Target Alpha

Still alive, Cade thought, swallowing hard against the rising tide of bile. Still feeling as if his stomach was lodged in his throat due to Ari's sudden dive to the deck, he met the adrenaline-charged gazes of his teammates and flashed a thumbs-up. Anticipating Ari's call of *ten mikes out*, he bent over and made sure the Velcro straps on his new ankle braces were tightened to the fullest. Satisfied, he sat up and stuck his thumbs in his ballistic plate carrier to allow some air to circulate underneath. After a few seconds of that, he patted his MOLLE gear, counting the extra magazines for his M4 and smoothing the straps holding them in place. Next, he rattled another twelve hundred milligrams worth of ibuprofen into a palm and swallowed the pills sans water. Finally, out of respect for Lopez, who he guessed was in post-op recovery by now, he capped off his egress preparations by performing another sign of the cross over his chest.

"Ten mikes out," Ari called over the comms.

Cade consulted his Suunto. *Right on time, Night Stalker.*

Across the aisle, Cross was going through the motions of checking the action on his MP7. Next, he checked the suppressor on the business end of the submachinegun for tightness. On his chest were a trio of spare magazines snugged into a MOLLE rig like Cade's that also served as a carrier for a number of ceramic ballistic plates. The thin, light-weight pieces of armor rode in sleeves front and back and served to protect his vital organs, spine, and neck from pistol and light-machine-gun rounds.

Already squared away gear wise, Griffin was sitting erect, eyes closed, back pressing the fuselage and clutching the black HK 416 two-handed, its stubby suppressor planted against the vibrating floor.

"You good to go?" Cade asked Axe.

Patting his highly modified M4, the SAS trooper merely nodded and flashed a toothy grin.

Born ready, thought Cade.

"Eight mikes," Ari called.

This brought Skipper to life. The SOAR crew chief grabbed his goody bag, unhooked the carabiner keeping it in place next to the door, and set the olive green canvas bag on the cabin floor near his feet. Having already gone over the process of arming the smaller, golf-ball-sized Screamers, he brought out a dozen of the orange spheres and passed them around, dividing them among the shooters. Next, he extracted four of the six remaining full-sized Screamers and began prepping them for deployment.

Cade peered out his window and saw that down below the devastation to northeastern Maryland was far worse than the satellite imagery was capable of conveying. In person, as viewed from barely three hundred feet above the skeletal trees, light standards, and multi-pitched rooftops, the destruction was breathtaking. It looked as if not one commercial building had escaped the widespread looting being reported on all of the cable news stations on that fateful Saturday in July that had since come to be known as Z-Day. Crumpled paper and fallen leaves had accumulated, filling up the street-facing doorways, in places, knee-high to the walking dead.

One grocery store's car-choked parking lot still held the remnants of what looked to be hundreds of cardboard boxes. Having been exposed to the elements for some time, the once three-dimensional objects had been reduced to a morass of tan sludge pounded flat by the scores of zombies still patrolling the lot. *Old habits die hard*, crossed Cade's mind as the areas of commerce gave way to a neighborhood he imagined once stood proud with stately Colonial-style homes, churches, and schools. *Not so much now.* He could look straight down into many of them lost to a conflagration that had claimed what he estimated to be hundreds of structures once standing on the twenty or so square blocks encompassing his bird's eye view from south to north.

The dead were everywhere. They were milling about side streets in small knots. They traipsed across scorched walks and drives bordering squares of blackened lawn. The cement foundations left standing were no deterrent to the creatures that, following life-long conditioning or acting on some snippet of buried memory, stood rooted in what used to be family rooms or kitchens or dens, their pasty white faces standing out starkly against the light-stealing sea of black as they gaped hungrily skyward at the passing black helicopter.

A sprawling, two-story brick-and-cement building passed by outside the port-side glass. The amber-tinted windows above ground level were all intact. Old Glory hung limply from the pole out front. And hard to miss from nearly any altitude, spelled out in huge, blocky red letters, the words "Fairmont Heights" emblazoned one end zone of the adjacent football field.

"*School's out forever*," Axe sang, sounding nothing like Alice Cooper.

"Any kids?" Cade asked.

Axe shook his head. "We were trying … I'm bloody well grateful me swimmers were on strike. It's hard enough knowing my lady is out there somewhere trolling around as one of 'em things. It'd be fuck all knowing my offspring is doddering around with her. What about you, mate?"

"A girl. Raven's twelve."

With Cross and Griff looking on, Axe made a face. "You're a Poe fan?"

"Nothing to do with it," Cade responded. "But she is a handful."

The helicopter slowed and bled speed. It swung wide left and the tops of trees, buffeted by the rotor blast, bent and whipped the air near the port-side windows as the lumbering craft passed them by.

"Bloody hard to get used to how quiet this whirlybird is when she's going slow and low," Axe observed.

"Tenth time aboard her and it still makes me think she's falling out from underneath me," Griff conceded. "Figure I'll never get used to it."

Skipper interrupted the conversation. "Six mikes out," he said, one hand on his boom mic, the other gripping the door handle to his left. Without warning, he hauled the door open, letting in a blast of cold, carrion- and jet-exhaust-tinged air.

"That's what I can't get used to," Cross divulged. "Whole world's one big mass grave."

"Screamer away," Skipper called as he leaned out the door and dropped one of the orange spheres in the center of the expansive parking lot northwest of the target building. "Get your soccer on, rotters."

"Football," Axe said forcefully, drawing the word out. "And don't you forget that, Doctor Silence."

Skipper primed the second Screamer and leaned hard against his safety strap. Flipping Axe an awkward-looking bird with the hand gripping the door frame, he let the device drop at the far end of the near empty expanse of lined blacktop.

Without warning, the helo banked and wound around the largest building on the sprawling campus. Ten seconds later

Skipper was dropping another pair of Screamers a thousand yards south of the target building near the car-choked security entrance.

"Lock and load," Ari said. "We'll give the deaders five mikes to find the screaming meemies and then we're going in silent."

While the rest of the team swapped their borrowed flight helmets for their low-riding tactical items, Cade unplugged his headset from the jack on the fuselage wall and reconnected it to his portable comms. He looked forward and saw Ari working the stick while, presumably, Haynes was cycling Jedi One-One's radio to the usual ship to ground frequency.

A tick later the monotone query *Anvil Actual, Jedi Lead. How copy?* sounded loud and clear in Cade's headset.

"Good copy," he replied to Haynes while going about adjusting his boom mic and cinching his Kevlar brain bucket a little tighter.

"That woman hasn't a creative bone in her body," said Griff. He gazed at Cade. "If my memory serves, the call signs were identical when we went to La La Land to rescue her daughter. Isn't that right … Anvil Actual?"

"That woman—," Cade began.

Cross leaned in front of Griff and cut Cade off at the pass. "Pay gruff Griff here no mind," he interjected. "He's just missing the teams. Been a fish out of water for too long, that's all."

"Well tell Flipper there that he better lock it down," Cade growled. "Because we're about to be in the thick of the shit."

"Locked down," Griff said, wearing a wide grin.

In his best deadpan, delivered as he flared the black chopper to deposit another Screamer, Ari said, "Can't we all just get along?"

"That's the worst Rodney King you've ever done," Haynes said. "And Lord knows you've used that one before."

"I concur," Axe said. "Third one isn't the charm, Ari. Your standup routine as of late has been pure shite."

"Guys, guys … take it out on the Zs," Skipper said, tossing the armed device out the door and into the midst of a sizeable, tightly packed throng of dead.

At once Ari pulled pitch, taking the Ghost Hawk out of the reach of the gnarled fingers. Clearing the nearby light standards, he said, “Let the games begin,” and nosed the helo around to find a nice copse of trees to hover behind and watch the undead soccer match ensue.

Chapter 48

The rain was coming at Daymon sideways when he exited the warm Chevy—yet again—to open the main gate. He thought about having Foley get out into the worsening weather, but quickly decided that after the way he treated Oliver the day before, delegating the task to Jimmy would be seen as a major dick move. Perceptions aside, when it got right down to it, it just seemed logical he be the one after already enduring the driving rain at the middle gate to let the other three vehicles pass through.

Now, as he stood on 39 waiting for the rigs to cross the threshold one last time so that he could close the camouflaged main gate, the ramifications of his benevolent decision had become abundantly clear. His pants were soaked from mid-thigh down and beginning to feel as heavy and ungainly as his old firefighting turnout gear. And adding insult to injury, a steady trickle of water was wicking off his stocking cap and taking a direct route under his jacket collar, down his spine, and between his butt cheeks.

The saving grace, he thought as he closed and locked the gate, was that his well-oiled cork boots and Day-Glo parka he'd taken off the mannequin at the ski hill had kept him warm where it mattered most.

Planting his feet a shoulder's width apart, he bent over by the driver's door and shook his head vigorously in an attempt to wick the beaded water off his hat and the ends of his dreads protruding from underneath it. Feeling like a waterlogged dog, he climbed behind the Chevy's wheel and led the four-vehicle convoy west, toward the fallen tree roadblock.

***

Five minutes had elapsed since getting back into the truck with Foley and still Daymon hadn't said a word. He negotiated the final turn before the roadblock and saw that they had company. Where there were usually less than a half-dozen rotters that had met the impasse and remained there milling about the road, there were now more than a dozen. So he swung the truck into a wide one-eighty and parked it a good fifty yards from the zombies, while leaving enough room for the rest of the convoy to follow suit and park single file behind him.

Foley grabbed his carbine. "I'm going," he insisted.

Daymon threw the transmission into Park and silenced the engine.

"No need to do it with that," he said. "Reach back and grab me my bow."

Foley unbuckled and twisted around in his seat. "I don't see it."

"Probably in the bed," Daymon guessed. "Here, use this." He unsheathed Kindness and handed the machete to Foley. "We save the bullets for the living."

"Or a last stand against the dead," added Foley.

Stepping to the road, Daymon said, "The man has a point." He closed his door and peered over the bed rail and saw only gas cans, the Stihl chainsaw, a worn yellow tow strap, and his Kelty backpack, which, like him, was thoroughly soaked. "Fucker took it."

"Your bow?"

"Yeah," Daymon spat. "Thing never left this truck."

"You're sure?"

"Positive." Daymon kicked the Chevy's rear tire.

"Take this," Foley said, handing the machete back. "I'll use mine." He took a long-bladed dagger from the sheath on his hip.

"That'll do," Daymon said, admiring Foley's pig sticker. "Let's get this over with." He strode to the centerline, head bowed against the stinging rain which was showing no sign of letting up.

Doors on the other trucks hinged open and soon the group was assembled in the middle of 39, all armed with blades save for Jamie, who was brandishing her tomahawk.

It took the dead some time to get oriented to the newly arrived meat. A female had become inexplicably stuck to the fallen tree blocking the road and was snarling and marching in place, the jagged bough lodged in her exposed ribs not wanting to let go.

By the time the Eden survivors had halved the distance to the rotters, the rain had slackened off and the dead were spread out across the road, each one seemingly homing in on a different survivor. The waterlogged monsters were a mixture of first turns and fresh kills, the latter of which were weighted down in soaked cold weather gear and most likely had fallen victim to attack sometime before the recent snow event, when, like now, though the temperature was only in the mid-fifties, the Zs were still mobile enough to pose a threat in large numbers.

Taking the left flank, Jamie waded into the periphery, war hawk scything the air. Responsible for dropping two first turns of her own, she stepped over their frail unmoving bodies and began calling out to the others from behind, an act that slowed their march and started them stutter-stepping, unsure which one of the survivors to stalk.

Taking advantage of the distraction, Foley approached two rotters from behind and, one at a time, quickly sank his dagger to the hilt at the base of their necks, only a couple of seconds separating each surprise attack.

Even Wilson wetted his blade, but not without tripping over Taryn's first kill of the day and finding himself draped by a rotting corpse and having to twist away from the snapping teeth while burying his knife blade in its eye socket.

When all was said and done, Daymon was standing among a quartet of headless, prostrate corpses whose blood was mixing with the rainwater and streaming in thick red rivulets to the nearby ditch.

"You're cutting it too close, Wilson," said Duncan from the far shoulder where he had already deposited his one and only kill, an awfully emaciated teenaged Z, likely a female from the looks of its tattered skin-tight denim shorts. "Watch what Taryn does. She doesn't rush in." He paused for a beat and regarded the others as they started off toward the wall of fallen trees. "Just let 'em come to you," he added, nearly whispering. "Measure their speed, then … *boom*!"—Wilson nearly jumped out of his boots—"you've got yerself a twice dead rotter. And you know what they say about rotters?"

Looking sheepish, Wilson shrugged.

"The only good rotter is a dead rotter. Don't you forget that, Wilson."

Cheeks nearly as red as his hair and thinking maybe Duncan had taken to the drink again, Wilson merely nodded in agreement. "I'll reign in my enthusiasm," he said, tongue firmly planted in cheek. Wiping away the putrid skin and flesh that had sloughed off the Z and soiled his jacket, he hustled to catch up with the others.

***

Ten minutes spent scouring the woods on either side of the road produced no bike, no Oliver, and no signs he had come this way. There were no new boot prints along the muddy trail west of the block, either. The only indication that someone had transited it were the water-filled impressions, all eastbound, and, in Daymon's opinion, all several days old.

"Nothing here," Duncan called from the north side of 39.

Lev and Jamie were standing atop a fallen Douglas Fir. It was an amazing specimen, bigger around than any one of them could reach, and bristling with upthrust needless branches. One hand gripping a stunted bough for balance, Lev pressed a pair of Bushnell binoculars to his eyes and studied the narrow, cement bridge beyond the roadblock. "The vehicles are still there," he said. "There are also thirty or so rotters." He sighed. "Unfortunately, I see no sign of Oliver or the bike."

"He went east, then," Duncan stated confidently. Shotgun slung on a shoulder and banging his hip, he approached Daymon. "Any idea *why* our resident hiker would want to go east? His childhood home is in Huntsville."

"The ski hill is there, too," added Jamie. "I've never seen a couple of guys happier than when you two returned from your disappearing act."

"They were high on pot," Taryn said flatly.

Changing the subject, Daymon said, "I have a good idea where he went. Load up."

Duncan leaned against the fallen timber. "Care to share?"

"Not really," Daymon replied. "Just trust and follow."

"Easier said than done," Duncan replied. "Good thing for you that I'm easy like a Monday morning." Humming the tune of the same name, he pushed off the tree with a guttural oomph and started a slow walk along the blood- and gore-slickened highway.

Chapter 49

Duncan watched with interest as Daymon pulled even with an ordinary-looking pasture gate. Since there had been no sign of Oliver's passage at the quarry entrances—upper and lower—he highly doubted this side trip of Daymon's was going to bear fruit. Just looking at the single-lane drive with its mohawk of tall grass growing between the two muddy ruts made him think it laughable that anyone would have a reason to go down the road Daymon was preparing to lead them.

After inspecting the ground around the entry, Daymon unwrapped a chain and pulled the steel tube gate toward him.

Duncan recognized the style: four horizontal bars intersected by more of the same running diagonal between them. Sheep gate was what he'd heard them called. He looked beyond the road and saw brambles and what could be walnut trees. Nothing he saw suggested the tree-choked acreage ever supported sheep or livestock.

"You want us all to follow?"

"I was hoping you would," Daymon answered, climbing into his pickup.

"These rigs might make it down the road," Duncan noted. "But where're we going to turn 'em around?"

Daymon closed his door. "You'd be surprised. Just follow … it'll be a quick in and out." He pointed at Lev in the F-650 bringing up the rear. "Close and chain the gate after."

"You sure about this?" Foley asked as Daymon pulled onto the feeder road.

"Positive."

***

Three minutes after pulling off of the paved single-lane and onto the gravel feeder road, all four pickups were parked in the huge circular turnaround fronting the stone and timber home.

Duncan was first out. He paced to the bottom of the first run of stairs leading up to the multi-story mini-mansion and whistled. "Snowbasin, eat your heart out." Finished ogling the structure, he turned and walked the twenty yards or so to the basketball court. He halted at center court and turned a full circle, eyeballing the pair of regulation standards sprouting from the smooth asphalt at either baseline.

Carrying a carbine one-handed and working his way toward the north side of the house, Daymon said, "Nice setup, huh?"

"Three-quarter court?"

Grinning, Daymon replied, "Full size … it's longer than the RV they had parked next to it."

Duncan nodded. "Who's *they*?"

Daymon shrugged as if to say *beats me.*

"Wish I had a ball," Wilson said.

Daymon stopped in his tracks and regarded the redhead, one brow arched. "You got game?"

"I was a high school starter. So, yeah … I'd say I have *game.*"

"We'll have to find out some day."

Still sitting in the F-650, Lev asked why they were here.

Daymon explained how he found the place and what he had planned for it.

"You two are going to be rural Utah's Bill and Melinda Gates," Duncan quipped. "If Dregan is the *Natural Gas King* of the area … what's your title gonna be?"

"Claustrophobic in recovery. Sure you can relate," said Daymon. "I'll be right back."

Suddenly gone serious, Duncan looked to Wilson and Taryn. "You two watch the road."

Hustling to Daymon's side, Foley announced he was coming along.

"Suit yourself," Daymon said, picking up his pace.

Once the pair had rounded the corner and were walking in the shadow of the massive multi-car garage, Foley cleared his throat theatrically. He removed his worn ball cap and ran a hand through his thinning hair.

"You got something to say?"

"What was up with the chained-up Z beside the road?"

"He's my watch rotter," Daymon replied as he mounted the stairs to the side door.

"You chained him up there?"

"Yep," Daymon said, running his hand around the doorjamb.

"That's kind of a dick move."

Daymon turned on the stair and peered down at Foley. *Was the guy a mind reader or some shit?*

"But it's an effective dick move," Daymon conceded. "What should I do? Put it out of its misery? It's no longer human."

"It was someone's son or brother. Some little kid probably called him Daddy before all of this."

Daymon nodded. *Time to lead by example*, he told himself. He inspected the Welcome mat then looked through the window and scrutinized the contents of the mud room.

"Well?"

"Oliver's not here," Daymon stated confidently. "And he hasn't been here, either. The door mat is exactly as I left it." Without meeting Foley's gaze, he turned and tromped down the stairs, brushing past the shorter man.

Back at the circular drive, Daymon reported his findings to the others.

Duncan raised a hand and spun it clockwise, finger cutting the air. "North it is, then. Mount up troops." He looked to Daymon. "Can I have a word with you, please?"

Sighing audibly and feeling like a kid being called out in front of the entire class, Daymon looked a question at his friend.

"The rotter by the road?"

"Yeah, yeah," Daymon replied, hauling his door open. "I'll take care of it." He climbed behind the wheel and buckled in.

"Good on you," Foley said, hauling his shoulder belt on. "Maybe Dregan knows where to get a dog."

"Maybe," Daymon replied. He waited for the others to mount up, then fired up his Chevy and dropped it into gear.

***

After driving in silence the short distance to where the Z was chained and staked down, Daymon stopped the Chevy and dismounted. Keeping to his word, he approached the snarling Z and, with one downward chop of his aptly named machete, freed one man's soul and cleansed a small portion of his own karmic slate in the process.

Chapter 50

The group stumbled upon Sasha's mountain bike thirteen miles north of Woodruff. After crisscrossing all twelve square blocks of Randolph and finding only walking corpses and houses, businesses, barns, and outbuildings with their doors either scribed with an X or hanging wide open on busted hinges, it was painfully obvious to them that whoever had picked Woodruff clean of supplies was also responsible for doing the same here. That there were a handful of virgin doors in the tiny town—probably booby trapped or hiding another Z, its flesh stripped to the bone—strengthened that first impression and made moving on with four empty truck beds and no trace of Oliver easier for all to bear.

Finding the bike had been a stroke of pure luck brought upon by three separate occurrences taking place seconds apart. First, the rain ceased and the clouds parted, allowing the sun to wash a narrow stretch of 16 that had been undergoing a minor repaving project before the world went to hell. Then, the convoy crested a rise in the road and came upon a pair of flesh eaters taking up more than their share of said stretch of torn-up state route, which forced Duncan to jerk the Dodge to the far right shoulder in order to keep from hitting the doddering duo. Lastly, two wheels riding the shoulder and kicking up gravel led to Duncan seeing a glint of sun off of chrome a hundred feet distant, which in turn led to him stopping in the general vicinity of his sighting and happening upon the girl's 18-speed mountain bike at the bottom of the roadside ditch.

With Glenda's tearful admonition for him to return with her boy echoing in his head, Duncan watched the other vehicles creep past the zombies and glide to a stop, all three trucks lined up bumper to bumper in the southbound lane.

Now, sitting in the idling Dodge with its door propped partway open and his muddy boots dangling a foot above the road, Duncan glanced over his shoulder at Tran. "Staying or coming?" he asked, hopping to the still damp blacktop.

Tran glanced in the wing mirror. Just above the words OBJECTS ARE CLOSER THAN THEY APPEAR he saw the zombies. Their heads lolled lazily and their eerie hissing carried on the wind as they trundled toward the stopped vehicles. "I'll stay here and keep watch for you," he said, eyes never leaving the macabre sight reflected in the mirror.

"Good man, Tran," Duncan replied, grabbing his shotgun and Stetson. "Hit that horn if you see anything approaching from the north."

Binoculars already in hand, Tran nodded, his brown eyes liquid and focused intently on the zombies.

Everyone but Taryn was on the road by now and advancing forward. "I'll watch our six," she called out, binoculars in hand and the upper half of her body already protruding through the truck's open moon roof.

Duncan nodded then shifted his gaze to the bike. At once he noticed that its rear wheel was bowed in considerably. *Tacoed*, is what he had heard his little brother, Logan, call it when he'd done the same to his rim while biking in Moab years ago. The knobby tire was deflated and hung limply off the rim. He bent over and lifted the twisted heap from the knee-high grass. Half pushing, half dragging, he removed it from the ditch and held it upright on the blacktop, where he saw the frame was cracked near the seat post and most of the root-beer-brown paint had been abraded from the side that had been facing down.

The bike had taken a beating. That was for sure.

Duncan laid the bike down on the soft shoulder and strode to the Dodge's front bumper, where he turned on a heel and began a slow, head-down walk to the parked vehicles. Sensing all eyes on him, he lifted his gaze from the road and regarded the others. "Maybe one of you could go search both ditches further up the road. Someone else needs to climb the fence and search the tall grass. Start on the side the bike ended up."

"What are we looking for?" asked Wilson.

"A dead body," answered Daymon, eyes already sweeping the road ahead. "Oliver's … dead … body. I'll take care of the rotters."

"No. Allow me," Foley insisted, brushing past the taller man. "About time I do a little more than set up solar panels and keep the communications shack running."

Seeing Foley win the argument, Duncan cast scrutiny on the road to the south. Though he was no crash-scene detective, he saw the writing on the wall. The mangled bike. The twin stripes of rubber on the down side of the crest. Put together, these clues told him a speeding vehicle braked a little before hitting the bike from the rear. And from the position of the bend in the rim, he guessed the vehicle had been fitted with a grill guard or some kind of bumper overriders. After the second it took him to process all of this, he looked at Wilson and reluctantly answered his question.

"Daymon's right. Oliver's body is probably somewhere around here." He sighed, his body seemingly deflating as he did so. "Look for a blood trail. Follow it and I guarantee you're not going to find a pot of gold at the end."

Lev and Wilson scaled the barbed wire fence bordering 16 to the east.

Head down and ignoring the death dance taking place between Foley and the pair of first turns a dozen yards off her right shoulder, Jamie walked the ditch north from where the bike had been resting, trampling the grass under her boots and warily eyeing the ground to her fore for anything moving—alive or dead.

"I found something," Lev called. He was facing the group and holding aloft Daymon's crossbow, which was nearly folded in half with feathery strands of fiberglass the only thing keeping one limb of the thing attached to the bent barrel.

"No body?" Duncan asked.

Wilson shook his head. "No blood either."

On the opposite side of the fence, Jamie lifted her boot off the spongy, sucking ground and said, "I found his night vision goggles. They're toast."

"Take 'em for parts," Duncan ordered. "Everyone mount up. Oliver's not here."

Still holding out hope to find Oliver in one state or another—for some closure, if nothing else—Daymon said, "What makes you so sure?"

"I think someone saw him roll through Randolph." Arm horizontal to the ground, Duncan swept it all the way around from the south, where the skid marks began just in front of the downslope, to the northbound lane behind his truck where Foley was dragging the last of the rotters from the road, the fresh blood trails glistening dark black against the nearly dry surface. "And then that someone got in their vehicle and chose this spot to run him down. The way 16 is hemmed in on both sides by fence for a mile or more prior to the repaving project, here makes it the perfect place to do so."

Having just returned and caught the tail end of the conversation, Foley halted on the centerline and gazed down the road toward Randolph. "This close to town he wouldn't have had much time to act. Especially in the dark. There would have been nowhere for him to escape to … even if he dismounted."

"Means whoever did it knows this road pretty good," Lev added, chucking the now useless crossbow to the ground where he'd found it. "Also means they probably didn't want to kill him."

"You all can interpret this any way you want," Daymon said. "I'm afraid Oliver's latest vision quest may be over before it really got going."

"That's harsh," Foley said, disgust in his voice.

"He made his bed. I'm just calling it how I see it," Daymon responded coldly.

Returning with the NVGs dangling from her hand by the strap, Jamie said, "I think they meant to hurt him just bad enough that it would be easy for them to take him alive. Which makes me think it was only one person. Maybe even the same person who was watching us back in Woodruff."

"Whatever shape Oliver's in," Duncan drawled, "he's either already a prisoner at Bear Lake, or whoever did this is taking him there now."

"That's enough," Daymon said in a low voice. "I'm partly responsible for this … so I'm the one who should go after him."

"Let's think this through a minute," Duncan said.

"No thinking necessary," Daymon shot, casting a sidelong glance at the others. "I'm going with or without you all. Whoever's going with me better say so now."

Hands went up all around. Even Taryn leaned from the Raptor's open window and cast her own vote to go.

Duncan looked over the rest of the group, meeting each person's gaze for a beat until he arrived back to Daymon. "I'm in," he said, resignation evident in his tone. "But we have to take it easy."

"We have a saying in the Army," Lev began. "Slow is smooth—"

"—and smooth is fast," Duncan finished. "Mount up. Oliver's life may be hanging in the balance."

Chapter 51

After laying the Screamers out and swinging around wide of the target building, Ari nosed Jedi One-One north over multiple parking lots and auxiliary buildings to the wide expanse of fenced-in asphalt behind a shipping and receiving warehouse. Intent on giving the Screamers twenty or thirty minutes to draw the throng of Zs away from the building, he settled the bird next to the black Chinooks, shut her down, and joined the Rangers and air crew outside for a much-needed piss and stretch of the legs.

***

Twenty-three minutes after deploying the Screamers south and north of the black obelisk of a building, Ari held the Ghost Hawk in a hover twenty feet above a copse of cottonwoods bordering a traffic-snarled freeway off-ramp half a mile northeast of the Delta team's insertion point. While Ari worked the controls to keep the bird steady, Haynes manipulated the nose-mounted FLIR pod, bracketing the nine-story glass and metal building and then piping the slightly wavering image onto the flat-panel display in the passenger cabin.

"Looks like they've taken the bait," Cade said.

"They always do," answered Cross. "I've seen the living show interest and come a looking, too."

Cade took his eyes off the army-ant-like march of the dead taking place on the monitor. "Chinese?"

"Yep. Griff and I had been following a two-man team since they crossed over into Nevada from California. We hung back and tracked them by the dust they were kicking up. Finally they just up and stopped and set up shop right outside of Vegas. Stowed their motorcycles behind a roadside sign just like the ones the cops hide behind in the movies and pitched a tent in its shadow. So we dump our bikes and while I'm praying our dust trail dissipates before theirs, I see this sign that says Vegas 3 Miles and below that is that famous tag line."

"What happens in Vegas—," Cade began, nodding and smiling.

"—stays in Vegas," Griff finished, flashing a half-smile of his own.

"Technically they weren't in Vegas yet," Cade noted.

"Technically, you're correct," Cross said. "But something *did* happen, all the same."

Griff was full on grinning now. He said, "With the sun going down we decide that going into Vegas, what with all the dead still there, was out of the question. We're almost out of MREs and water and wanting to exfil anyway when Cross sees one of them come out of the tent, edge around the sign, and cop a squat right out in the open."

"And then one of you decided to throw a mini-Screamer his way," Cade said, running the hilarious scenario over in his mind.

"That I did," Cross said, the beginning of a smile revealing his unnaturally white teeth.

"Cali boy has a hell of an arm," Griff said, nodding.

"And then one of you wankers shot the squatter *just* as he was pulling his drawers up to keep a screaming woman from seeing his manly bits," Axe added, his curiosity now piqued.

"That was Griff's job," Cross said. "I shot the other PLA puke in the face when he poked it between the tent flaps."

Ari interrupted. "And you two still owe Ripley some beers. I heard that cramming your motorcycles, the prisoner and their gear into her Osprey along with the injured heading to Bastion from the MWTC siege got her panties in a bunch." Chuckling over the comms, Ari side-slipped the helo from cover and nosed her down, beginning the first leg of a long circuitous route that would eventually have them approaching the infil location from the southeast.

"I'd have helped her get them out," Skipper intoned, a rare smile forming below his visor. "She's pretty hot."

Axe grinned at the comment.

Cross ignored it. In a serious tone, he said, "The takedown was well worth the intel we got from the Chinese captain whose name I couldn't pronounce. Once they were translated, the documents he was carrying led to us learning about their ambitious extermination plan."

"And how today's target plays into it," Ari said. "Two mikes, men. Looks like our undead friends have taken up the game of soccer."

"Football," Axe corrected, yet again. "Who's winning?"

"Manchester United, looks like. Their players are always pasty and covered in crimson, right?"

"Bugger off," Axe spat.

"Anvil Actual, are we a go?" Ari asked.

Cade leaned toward the display. Using crowd size estimation techniques Cross had taught him some time ago, he pegged the number of Zs leaving the grounds and lots around the target for the vast acres of empty parking lots where the Screamers had been deployed at a thousand or more. Thankfully, the number of Zs remaining around the target were beginning to lean in their favor. However, as he looked closer at the clutter near the base of the building, nearly lost in the debris and a little fuzzy due to distance and the fact that they were moving, he noticed dozens of corpses loitering in and around the ground-level front entry. And the longer he stared into the gloom cast by the nine-story affair, the more concerned he became. For among the shattered glass and uprooted shrubbery and hundreds of already twice-dead Zs heaped in the building's shadow, dozens of crawlers—partially incapacitated creatures—dragged themselves along the ground.

"Ari, we're going to need to loiter a bit before going in," Cade said over the comms. "Give the ones in the lobby a chance to vacate the premises."

"Copy that," Ari said. "In the meantime, someone pass another of those five-hour pick-me-ups forward."

"Ask and ye shall receive," Skipper said, handing another pair of the small bottles forward. "If it'll keep you awake and happy and this bird in the air, I'll keep them coming your way."

"Copy that, Skipper. Much obliged," replied Haynes, reaching a long arm back to receive the bottled elixir.

Chapter 52

Minutes after heaving the bent and broken bike into the ditch where they had found it, the four-truck convoy was speeding north by west on 16 with ochre-scrub-dotted flatlands blipping by on the left, and the snow-capped peaks of the Bear River Mountain Range scrolling by a few miles off their right.

While Randolph had just been a smaller version of what they had encountered in Woodruff, with doors marked with tiny chalk Xs which the group took to mean the place was already stripped of anything of value, the two-lane road beyond the blink-and-you'd-miss-it town was a different story.

Speaking to progress made days ago over the cold-affected dead by the same people likely holding Oliver hostage, every mile or so the convoy came upon head-high mounds of twice-dead zombie corpses.

Nine miles north of Randolph, Duncan was forced to slow yet again to negotiate a school-bus-sized pile of moldering bodies. Stretching from one side of 16 to the other, the drift of death all but blocked the north side of the two-lane from view.

Fuck it, Duncan thought, steering the Dodge around the twelve-foot-tall mound. With rigor-stiffened appendages scratching out a mournful dirge on the driver's side sheet metal, he wheeled his rig past the blockage, partway into the ditch, then four-wheeled up the other side.

After bringing the Dodge to a complete stop to wait for the others, Duncan turned to Tran. "Think the 650 is gonna make it?"

"We'll see in a moment," Tran said, as Daymon squeezed his Chevy by the roadblock, its driver's side wheels fighting to keep purchase on the road while the opposing pair churned the muddy snow in the bottom of the roadside ditch.

Shifting his gaze from Tran to the mirror, Duncan watched the Chevy's grille emerge from the ditch and saw the determined look parked on Daymon's face. And sitting next to Daymon, Foley had the handle near his head clutched in a two-handed death grip and his mouth forming a silent O as the black 4x4—following the same muddy furrows churned up by Duncan's passage—clawed its way back onto 16.

Wearing a wide-eyed *I thought we were going to roll over* look on his face, Daymon rolled the muddy truck around the static Dodge and flashed Duncan a double thumbs-up.

Perfect place to spring an ambush, crossed Duncan's mind as he returned the gesture. Then, acting on the epiphany, he nodded to the binoculars clutched in Tran's hands. "While the others come on through I need you to be on the lookout for anything out of the ordinary." He pointed to the small hillock a half mile ahead on the right where the road cut through twin walls of ochre dirt before veering off sharply to the left. "Start there and work your way back here."

Meanwhile, inside the Raptor, Taryn wore a grim look as the rig entered the ditch, lurching hard to the right as both wheels on that side became one with the steep, rock-and-gravel-studded wall. Glancing sidelong at Wilson and talking loudly to be heard over the macabre sound of bone and nail raking the truck's thin steel skin near her left thigh, she said, "We are *not* going to make this."

Subtly shaking his head and pressing the flaps of his boonie hat hard over his ears to drown out the awful keening, Wilson said, "You've already committed, Taryn. If you don't gun it now and stop that awful sound … you're going to have to have *me* committed."

"Those *places* are all gone, Wilson. Suck it up," she said, sounding way too much like Sasha for her own liking.

Wilson met her gaze. Not wanting this to escalate, he wisely said nothing.

"Just hold on," she said, her narrowed eyes focused on the narrow gap.

Gritting his teeth, Wilson took ahold of the grab bar near his head and braced himself by placing his other hand, fingers splayed out wide, on the dusty dashboard.

Inching forward in her seat, simultaneously Taryn tightened her grip on the wheel and stabbed the pedal to coax all the available horsepower from the growling 6.2-liter powerplant.

Two things happened as a result. First, quad rooster-tails of dirty snow and rocks exploded from under the beefy tires spinning furiously beneath the lurching Ford. Then the off-road-tuned Raptor launched up the left side of the ditch, went airborne momentarily—albeit by only a few inches—then crashed back to earth on State Route 16 a half truck-length from Foley who was staring wide-eyed from inside the Chevy.

Finally, three minutes after edging his truck past the multitudes of leering dead and their pallid tangle of stick-thin arms and legs, Duncan was about to learn if the F-650 could shoot the gap.

"Twenty bucks says we end up winching them out of there."

Tran shook his head at that. "No way. If they make it through, you have to gut and dress the next deer for me."

"What are you going to do if I win?"

"I'll do yours and Glenda's wash."

Shaking Tran's hand, Duncan cackled then said, "You, my friend, have a deal."

Tran turned in his seat as the big black grille inched into view around the blockage..

"I want my pants ironed with a hot rock," Duncan said as he watched the Ford edge out over the ditch and begin to slowly list to the right. Then he grimaced as Lev gunned it and somehow got the right side tires tracking on the narrow strip of dirt sandwiched between the yawning ditch and barbed wire fence.

"I want thin, nicely trimmed venison steaks," Tran countered as the 650's massive driver-side tires gripped the remaining ribbon of blacktop.

"Freakin' Flying Wallendas," Duncan said to Tran as the Ford squeaked through, its rear bumper starting a corpse avalanche in its wake.

Throwing a fist pump in Duncan's direction, Tran said, "I love cooking. Hate butchering."

Already imagining the stink of spilt blood, Duncan said, "No wonder Cade and Brook love that beast."

A tick after mentioning the Graysons, Duncan suddenly reflected on how many Eden survivors he had allowed to tag along. On second thought, *allowed* was a strong word. How many he had been reluctant to discourage from tagging along was more like it.

In that instant, his stomach did a somersault and he felt a primeval live wire tingling in his scrotum. In his haste to do Glenda's bidding and find Oliver no matter the cost, he'd been blinded to the fact that Cade was away and with Phillip dead and gone, the only people at the compound at this very moment were women and children and Seth, who was far from a survivor, and even less adept as a fighter. In fact, the mercurial loner was barely one notch above Oliver in that department.

What would Cade say if he knew Brook had been left behind considering the fluidity of her current situation? Duncan expected no kind of attaboy, that was for damn sure.

He looked over at Tran and caught the man, binoculars partially lowered, staring back with a confused look on his face.

"Watch the *road*," Duncan said, cheeks flushing red. "You're not going to catch anyone sneaking up on us staring at my ugly mug."

Tran's face blanched as he raised the field glasses and aimed them at the scrub-covered plain northwest of them.

Embarrassed by his lapse in judgement, Duncan averted his eyes and studied Jamie in the side mirror as the black behemoth pulled even with his smaller Dodge. A tick later the window pulsed down and she stuck her head out. After a few seconds of pained silence, voice cracking with emotion, she said, "My gut tells me Oliver is dead. But my heart says we have to keep looking for him."

That was all Duncan needed to hear. And it was reassuring to know that someone else cared as much as he did about the troubled youngest son of the love of his life. Staring up at Jamie and feeling as if a weight had been lifted from his shoulders, he used the two-way radio to call everyone over to his truck for a meeting of the minds, so to speak.

***

It took a couple of minutes for everyone to shut down their vehicles and make their way to the Dodge.

"Why the face to face?" asked Daymon, standing with his back against the F-650.

Ignoring the attitude, Duncan walked his gaze over the assembled survivors. "Does anyone have any idea why whoever is claiming the north would want to block the road here?"

Wilson said, "Because it's right before a junction?"

"I'm not quizzing you, kid," said Duncan, suppressing the urge to take him aside and tell him to toughen up and start thinking critically. But he didn't. Instead, he took the high road. "I'll take that as a statement and say that I have to agree with you."

"It's just another roadblock," stated Foley. "Only this one is physical and comes with a warning that cannot be misconstrued. The others … the tainted trap. The crucified skeleton and Oliver's bike and gear …" He paused and looked to the east where dark clouds were building against the Bear River Range. "All of those were psychological roadblocks. I'm willing to bet the next thing that gets in our way is going to kill one of us."

"That's deep stuff," said Daymon, sweeping a stray dread under his black cap. "But I ain't scared. I'm pissed. I want to make someone pay for what they've done. Let's go. *Now!*"

"I've been thinking," Duncan said, one finger held in the air outside his window as if he was testing for wind direction. "This incremental security, if you will, reminds me of something I saw on television before all of this. But I can't for the life of me dredge it up."

"I'll be waiting with my hand on the radio and bated breath for you to enlighten me," said Daymon, the last few words uttered over his shoulder as he strode off to his Chevy.

Duncan was about to say something he might regret, something that had to do with halitosis and general dental hygiene, when Tran tugged on his shirt sleeve.

"What?" said Duncan, irritably.

"There," Tran said, pointing past the bend in the road while thrusting the binoculars into his hands. "Those are buzzards."

"And I bet they're feeding on something dead," Duncan said slowly, accepting the Bushnells from his passenger.

Tran drew in a deep breath and exhaled. "Or *someone*," he countered in a low voice.

Chapter 53

Ari called out, "Wheels down in five," over the comms a split second before drawing Jedi One-One from its steep dive and leveling the ship out directly over a gently sloping hill bristling with what looked to Cade, from his port-side perch, like the last patch of living grass on the sprawling grounds. The clouds above were just starting to part, allowing the sun to paint the National Security Agency's buildings and muddy grounds of the Fort Meade complex with a muted, gauze-like light. Just off Cade's left shoulder, almost close enough to reach out and touch, barren cherry trees planted along the building's north side were bending from the rotor wash.

Outside the starboard-side window, Cade could see six Humvees parked nearly bumper-to-bumper in a bulging half-circle with their turret-mounted weapons trained on the road passing by the front of the target building. Small arms were strewn about the ground among the putrefying bodies of the dead soldiers who had once wielded them. Clearly a stand had been made here. A stand that had folded to an insatiable and ever-growing army of zombies gnashing and tearing their way outward from the nation's former capital twenty-five miles southwest of here.

Ari called out, "Three," in his short countdown.

On cue, Skipper hauled open the port-side door, letting the rotor wash infiltrate the cabin and rustle sleeves and beards and nylon rifle slings. The stowed landing gear was just locking into full extension when Ari called out "One" and punctuated the countdown by saying, "For God and country, gentlemen."

A tick after hearing the SOAR pilot utter those final uplifting words, Cade leaped from the helicopter bellowing, "Weapons free! Go, go, go!" at the top of his voice. To his fore were two dozen Zs that for some reason or another hadn't gone in search of the fresh meat promised by the feminine wails emanating from the deployed Screamers. At once he had his M4 tucked in tight to his shoulder and he was prioritizing targets in his cone of fire. Assessing the threat of each Z based on its proximity to where the Delta team would enter the looming building, he sighted on a recent turn angling in from his right and dropped it to the cement walk with a perfect head shot. After stepping over the prostrate corpse and inadvertently sending a half-dozen spent shell casings skittering ahead of his boots, he stole a split-second glance over his shoulder and located Axe, a few steps behind and left of him, rifle leveled and on the move. The Brit's gaze was focused laser-tight as he stared through the holographic sight atop the carbine. In the same snapshot in time, Cade saw that Cross and Griff, having exited the helo nearly shoulder-to-shoulder and tight on the SAS shooter's heels, were now fanning out and training their weapons on their assigned sectors, Griff's HK sweeping left, and Cross's MP7 covering the far right where monsters were spilling from the building's shot-out lower windows. And on the tail end of that lone, furtive glance, Cade also noted that Ari had let them all egress the Ghost Hawk without even settling its deployed landing gear on the body-strewn ground.

Cade's new-to-him Danners, however, weren't so lucky. The tightly cinched boots had attracted the thick sludge like a couple of leather mud magnets and were growing heavier with each successive step he took away from the quietly hovering helicopter.

"Contact left," Axe called out, his suppressed M4 belching lead.

As Cade registered the call in his ear, simultaneously the soft clatter of the carbine's bolt, throaty rasps of the nearby dead, and increasing rotor *thwop* assaulted his ears. In a state of near sensory overload, he zippered between a row of concrete Jersey barriers fronting the static Humvees and then paused for a half-second to gaze upon the NSA building to his fore where he saw the shimmery reflection of Jedi One-One rocketing away from the makeshift LZ, the helo's new flight path taking her directly over the jostling Zs and upthrust light standards due north of the building's mirrored facade.

The rest of the team was firing into the approaching knot of dead and converging with Cade at the front entry when he dropped his gaze to the ground-level windows, nearly all of which had been imploded under the crushing weight of God knew how many dead things.

With the sound of glass kernels popping and crunching under his boot soles, Cade slipped through the yawning doors ahead of the team and found himself inside the expansive main lobby to NSA Building 9.

Every wall here was home to at least one of the ubiquitous black-dome-enshrouded security cameras. Every few yards on the ceiling larger versions of the smoked half-orbs reflected the flat light from outside. And though the windows at ground level were mostly blown-out, the air inside the lobby was damp and stagnant and stunk of cordite from past engagements that had left piles of spent brass shells and bullet-riddled bodies scattered about the wide-open floor.

As Cade took everything in, two things registered at once. First off, Nash's intel about the emergency lighting being operational was faulty—at least where the ground-level sconces were concerned. Secondly, after fixing his gaze on the pitch-black bowels of the building beyond the sunlight-dappled staircase rising up behind a thick, bulletproof glass partition making up the initial security checkpoint, he came to the realization that the newest generation four-tube NVGs affixed to his helmet were going to come in handy.

Telling the rest of the team to power on their NVGs, he drew in a deep lungful of the last semi-fresh air he figured he'd be privy to for a long while, powered his on and flipped them down in front of his eyes.

Peering into the deeper recesses of the main floor, past the multi-lane security station featuring metal detectors and X-ray body scanners, Cade was able to grasp the sheer scale of the grandiose foyer. Even rendered in a dozen hues of green, the wood and stone comprising the interior design lent it the air of an upscale hotel—not the government-run security behemoth that it was. Throw in the zombies shuffling from the inky shadows beneath the staircase and the scene would be truly baffling to comprehend had he not already memorized the layout somewhat and possessed a folded and laminated map to fall back on should he need it.

Neck hairs standing on end due to the eerie moans and scratchy, dry rasps coming from the advancing dead, Cade shouldered his suppressed M4 and began culling those beyond the wall of metal detectors, magnetometers, and whatever else was contained within the phalanx of cream-colored screening apparatus bracketing the row of turnstiles in front of him.

To the left, the distinct rapid-clatter of Cross's weapon could be heard. Flicking his eyes left and seeing the immediate vicinity beyond the turnstiles clear of dead, Cade waved the rest of the team forward.

Looking like a futuristic robot with strange ambient green lights for eyes, Cade stood shoulder to shoulder with Cross and Griff and stared into the darkness at the multitudes of closed doors and narrow halls leading off into the NSA's inner sanctum. After orienting the floorplan he'd committed to memory by matching it with the distant bank of stainless-steel-skinned elevators, he quickly radioed back to Jedi One-One and Schriever to inform them that the team was going in. After hearing both Nash and Ari acknowledge the call, the transmission rendered garbled and barely decipherable because of the exotic anti-eavesdropping film applied to the building's windows, he called Axe over from the center of the lobby where he'd been keeping watch on their six.

"Nash was right," he said, looking each man in the eye. "Comms are being disrupted by the building's latent security features. Means we're going to be on our own as soon as we get past the first checkpoint." Raising his M4 vertically over his head, he climbed over the turnstile and struck out for a distant hall with the trio of silent, deadly men glued to his six.

50th Satellite Space Wing TOC - Colorado Springs, Colorado

Wearing her full uniform, cover and all, Major Freda Nash was sharing the short stage at the front of the TOC with Colonel Cornelius Shrill and President Valerie Clay. Standing stage right of the largest wall-mounted monitor in the low-ceilinged room, under the watchful gaze of two dozen airmen of the 50th Satellite Space Wing, the three had been watching the insertion at the NSA in real-time via a feed beamed down from one of the remaining Keyhole satellites temporarily parked in a geostationary orbit over Fort Meade, Maryland.

While both the colonel and President had shown little obvious concern when Jedi One-One committed to a final approach of the NSA building, Nash had drawn in a deep breath and trapped it in her lungs as the Ghost Hawk—rendered tiny and jittery due to the satellite's distance from Earth and its current optic setting—swooped in right-to-left and settled on a wide, Jersey-barrier-ringed tract of what appeared to have once been grass gracing the front of the massive state-of-the-art facility.

After exhaling sharply, Nash had ordered an airman to zoom in tight on the hovering helicopter as the ant-sized Delta team exited the craft from the port-side and began their long sprint across the vehicle- and debris-strewn no-man's land still occupied by a large number of Zs. After the feed sharpened and closed in she was able to see the sparkle of brass and licks of orange coming from the team's weapons. She smiled inwardly as the tiny figures vectoring toward the helicopter toppled one after the other as the team engaged them on the way to the entry.

Now just seconds removed from that entry, Nash was glued to the zoomed-in feed as Jedi One-One overflew the sea of gently undulating zombies that had become packed into a tight knot on the northernmost parking lot.

Happy that Mr. Murphy hadn't seen fit to intervene and screw up the insertion, Nash saw her mood tempered when approached by an airman with a grim look hanging on his face.

"Be advised, Major," he said, handing her a set of headphones. "Anvil Team is off comms. We are currently trying to reacquire."

As expected, Nash thought to herself as she shifted her gaze to President Clay, who was shifting her weight nervously from foot-to-foot.

Wasting no time, Nash donned the headphones and adjusted her boom microphone. At first she heard deafening silence that went on for a few short seconds, but seemed to have lasted much longer. Finally, communication was reestablished and she heard Cade—using the call sign *Anvil Actual*—state that the unit was *inside the target and on the move.*

Exhaling sharply for the second time in as many minutes, Nash noticed an analyst looking at her over the top of her large computer screen.

"What is it?" Nash asked.

"Two things," the airman said, an unusual measure of concern in her voice. "Because of the way the NSA building was designed, communication with the team is going to remain spotty, at best."

Nash nodded.

"Then there's this." The youthful airman's jaw took a hard set as she tapped out a command on her keyboard. "It looks like an armored column is heading for D.C."

Before "D.C." had crossed the analyst's lips, a new image captured earlier by the satellite high above Fort Meade had materialized on the large wall-mounted monitor adjacent to the President.

Clay stopped fidgeting. She glanced at the image then quickly turned to face Colonel Shrill. "Do we have assets operating in the area?"

"Negative," Shrill said. "We have a few armored vehicles scattered about a handful of nearby air bases. But not in the numbers to form a column that size."

"Throw it on Monitor One," Nash said, her eyes already glued there.

Two seconds later the image was splashed on the larger screen in full color.

"When was this taken?"

"Fifteen minutes ago," answered the airman.

"Enhance and zoom," Nash said.

While the airman was tapping at her keyboard, Nash heard Cade report that the power was out at ground level, but using NVGs they had already cleared the lobby, breached the security station, and were now pushing deeper into the building. "Damn it all," Nash said under her breath. The analyst was right. Cade's transmission had been scratchy, his words hard to understand before dropping off in volume at the tail end. Knowing that the team would soon be underneath the massive structure and unable to communicate with either their exfil bird or their eyes in the sky here at the TOC, she said a prayer for them all and turned her undivided attention to the long column of vehicles inching slowly along a Maryland state route.

"Those aren't ours," Shrill said warily. "And they certainly didn't arrive on our soil via airlift. Even with our limited ground based stations, we would have picked up the transports before they reached any viable airstrips in the area."

"I concur," said Nash. "Except for the Jedi flight and refueling package, the skies east of here have been clear."

"Those pieces are Chinese," Shrill observed. "But they're heading *away* from the target building."

"Could our intel have been wrong?" the President asked.

"Negative, Madam President," Shrill said. "The prisoner could have been lying to the interrogation team." He removed his cover and rubbed his bald head. "That's unlikely, though. The documents Cade took off the dead PLA captain corroborate the prisoner's statements."

"Maybe with the prisoner something was lost in translation?" the President proffered.

Shaking his head vehemently, Shrill added, "Those PLA Special Forces boys know their English. It's drilled into them from day one."

"After we got him to divulge the true goal of the Fort Meade mission, he stopped talking." Nash turned and jabbed a finger at the air in front of the monitor. "That's why I'm convinced this column has something to do with their interest in the NSA facility."

Shrill said, "If their mission is to get at the intel on those servers, why go to D.C. first? Especially with all the dead in that city."

"I don't think we're looking at all of their assets, here. That column had to have come from the flotilla we lost track of in the Atlantic. Besides"—Nash edged closer to the monitor and pointed to a number of the vehicles—"Those APCs are not amphibious. Therefore, they had to have been brought ashore by landing craft."

"This changes everything," Shrill said.

The President's head was panning back and forth as she followed the conversation.

Nash turned from the display and looked to her analyst. "Pull up everything you've archived since the Keyhole came on station."

"That's only about thirty minutes' worth of feed, Major."

"It's all we've got to go on," Nash said. "Enlarge and backtrack south and east from where the column is now. I want every eyeball available searching waterways and shorelines for signs of PLA activity."

The President nodded her obvious approval and folded her arms across her chest.

Nash looked to another airman. "Do we still have a presence in Dover?"

"Limited," the young airman acknowledged, absentmindedly stroking his dark five o'clock shadow with one hand.

"Better than nothing," Nash said, still under the watchful eye of the President, a full bird colonel and a half-dozen airmen wearing expectant looks and obviously awaiting new orders. "One of you get Colonel Frederick on the horn ASAP. If Kellen's no longer with us, I want to speak to his successor."

One airman nodded and began the process of placing a call that, if Mr. Murphy was still behaving himself, would be routed to the red phone at Dover Air Force Base by way of one of the 50th Space Wing's few remaining military-grade communications satellites.

Chapter 54
Dover AFB, Dover, Delaware

"Sir, you sure you want the birds readied and pulled from the hangars?"

Colonel Kellen Frederick regarded his most senior airman with a look that could freeze water.

"That's exactly what I said, Master Sergeant." The base commander raised his binoculars and scrutinized the far fence line. Hardly practicing what he preached—let alone what the rules and regs called for—he had let himself go. His uniform was thrown together piecemeal and rumpled and creased. He wore a weeks' old growth of facial hair and hadn't had his hair cut since Z-Day plus twelve. He brushed a stray gray lock behind his ear and began to count the dead pressing against the outermost ring of fencing.

"They have all worked so hard on their noise and light discipline," Master Sergeant Michael Cassidy—a hard-working cog in the Dover AFB wheel—said in a respectful, almost pleading tone. "The men and women who are still here were instrumental in getting the biters to forget about us."

"Not these twenty-seven pusbags. They're going to have to be dealt with before they attract friends."

"With all due respect, Colonel. If we launch even one sortie the Zs will be back in full force. As it stands, we barely have enough ammunition to save our asses and get out of here if they breach the wire."

"Believe me, I know." The colonel removed his navy ball cap and set it on the desktop below the east-facing windows. He performed a four-point turn, stopping at each compass direction to peer out the sloped glass windows. While he felt it would be easy to suddenly become trapped in the control tower should the dead flood onto the base, it was the one place on the entire four-hundred-and-fifty-acre plat of land where he had yet to suffer one of his crippling anxiety attacks.

"Send a team out to clear the fence," said the colonel. And though there was no reason to expect anything different from his little band of survivors, he added, "Tell them to do it fast and quiet."

"Yes, Sir." Cassidy picked up a radio handset and was about to issue the new orders. The first of which was still absolutely baffling to him, because they hadn't conducted air operations out of Dover for weeks. There just wasn't the fuel to do so. And secondly, the amount of dead the roar of a single jet engine would attract significantly dwarfed the relatively small number currently clutching the fence. So many so that the skeleton crew that was left would likely have to mount a hasty evacuation and leave one of the few remaining airstrips on the Eastern Seaboard to the undead scourge.

"And Mike," the colonel said, catching the airman before he reached the door. "This comes down from Colorado Springs. From Major Freda Nash via President Clay, no less. If it wasn't important, she wouldn't have ordered it. President Clay is a good woman. She'd never ask us to draw attention to ourselves if there was another option."

Holding the stairwell door open with a knee, the stocky, blond master sergeant asked, "So how do we keep the fences clear when the dead do come in the kind of numbers they did those first days?"

"You'll see," Colonel Fredrick said cryptically. He pressed the Steiners to his face and glassed the northern perimeter. "You'll see."

NSA Building 9, Fort Meade, Maryland

The architectural stylings from the plaza fronting the NSA building were carried over into the lobby. Lots of wood, glass, and steel, the lines curved to mimic nature, had dominated there.

Here at the far corner of the building, the designers had seemingly run out of imagination—or budgeted dollars. Square cubicles were the norm. Every few hundred feet there was a glass-enclosed, electromagnetically shielded room used for holding meetings in utmost secrecy.

Time to try and hail Schriever, thought Cade, halting the team in front of an unmarked and nondescript steel door next to a similarly bland bank of elevators—the fourth such set since leaving the lobby and dozens of twice-dead Zs behind.

Since sharing the last SITREP with Nash and Ari from just inside the front entry, the comms had been silent.

Meeting Cross's quizzical look, Cade said, "Schriever TOC, Anvil Actual. How copy?"

Nothing. Not even a faint hiss of static to confirm his comms were still powered on.

Cade moved a few feet down the hall. Standing over a female Z that he had dispatched moments earlier with a dagger to the temple, he looked at the ceiling—as if that would help the reception—and tried again.

Still nothing.

As anticipated, the team's lifeline to the outside world was down. Not only could they not communicate with the TOC, Jedi One-One, or the two gen-3 Stealth Chinooks transporting their QRF force, they were off the grid visually as well. With no politicians crowding the situation room at the White House in order to get the ubiquitous *I was there when* photo for their wood-paneled office wall, and no JAG lawyers waiting in the wings to view the post-mission video footage in order to make sure the enemies' feelings weren't hurt, the miniature body cameras that Cade used to wear on high-profile Delta missions were deemed unnecessary. Which was a good thing. The fewer people Cade had to answer to, the better. The people that mattered to him at this very moment were the shooters stacked at his back and awaiting word on what lay behind the unmarked steel slab door.

Standing there in the dark bowels of the seemingly dead building, Cade conceded to himself that there was nothing sexy about this part of the mission. There were no scientists to pluck from danger and spirit back to Schriever. There were no bad guys bent on world domination to bring to justice. And, fortunately, since the alternative would mean another one of his friends or loved ones had been harmed, no personal scores to settle as there had been with Pug, Robert Christian, and, to a lesser extent, the turncoat, former Navy SEAL, Ian Bishop.

So, following the same protocol Tice had established at the Canadian research facility, he shrugged off his pack and from a side pocket extracted the lock-picking gun, a flexible fiber optic periscope, and its four-inch color display. He handed the latter two items to Cross, who promptly began mating the small parts.

Momentarily taking his eyes off the far corridor, Axe peeked over Cross's shoulder. "That gizmo see in the dark, too?"

Griff stared daggers in the dark through his own NVGs. "Eyes on our six," he reminded Axe.

"Take it easy, mate. We'll hear the slimy buggers coming before they see us anyway."

"It's their eyesight that's compromised," Cade reminded. "Not their hearing. With the three hundred-or-so-person skeleton crew that was supposedly inside here when the place fell, one would expect more of them than we've already come across."

"Copy that," Griff said. "Let's keep our fingers crossed they're not all behind this door."

Cross said nothing to that. Instead, aiming to find out, he forced the slender flexible fiber optic stalk under the door. As if the probe was hitting some type of an airlock seal, there was great resistance beyond the flush-to-the-floor door sweep. However, after lubing the stalk with a few drops of gun oil from a tube taken from his pack, and going at the door near the bottom corner, the device made it past the jamb and the entire landing and two runs of stairs were showing up clearly and in full color on the little display.

Dover AFB, Dover, Delaware

The trio of A-10 Thunderbolt ground attack craft assigned to the 104th Fighter Squadron, now permanently relocated from Warfield Air National Guard Base, Maryland, had been gone less than twenty minutes when the Zs began arriving in droves. Colonel Fredrick watched the small knots of former human beings stagger from the trees north of the base and come up against the outermost ring of concertina-topped chain-link fencing. He panned right and paused with the binoculars trained on the Air Mobility Command Museum located almost due east of the base proper. A hundred or more dead were parading in from the nearby feeder road. They bounced off one another as they negotiated the car-width gap between the Jersey barriers placed there on Z-Day to deter waves of frantic civilians seeking refuge from the nightmare Dover had quickly become.

The sheer crush of the combined weight of the arriving dead was bowing the fencing outward as the Zs in the rear of the pack forcibly funneled the ones at the head between the abandoned vehicles, breaking off mirrors and denting body panels along the way. As the dead marched blindly toward where the continual rumble from back-to-back-to-back take offs had originated, Colonel Frederick's gaze was drawn to the steady opening and closing of their mouths. And though he couldn't hear the eerie moans and rasps he knew were creating a sonic maelstrom down below, his imagination conjured up a spine-tingling soundtrack to go with the image. Hair on his arms standing to attention, he let the field glasses drop to his chest and scanned the skies with his naked eye.

"You hear that, Mike?"

Sergeant Cassidy leaned closer to the lightly tinted glass and shook his head. "Negative, Colonel." His eyes locked on the large contingent of dead battering the fences near the main gate. "And

I'm damn grateful that I can't. Although I've always wondered how the hell something that isn't breathing manages to do that, I don't think I'll ever learn to get used to hearing that damn noise those dead fuckers make."

"I'm not talking about the rotters," said the colonel. "Listen. We have company coming in from the west."

"Should we try hailing them?"

"Don't bother. I've been expecting them."

"Who?"

Frederick looked through the binoculars. "Just watch."

As if on cue, a low-flying aircraft materialized from the ground clutter. It was moving real slow, droning on just above the trees before dropping closer to the deck and skimming the fence bordering the runway. *Lumbering* would be a good description, thought the colonel, just as a white parachute materialized in the slipstream below the gray turboprop.

In the next beat the parachute jerked the first of the two promised ammo-laden pallets violently off the canted ramp behind the airplane. Pallet number two was still making its slow roll down the ramp when the first pallet hit the runway dead center a hundred feet beyond the yellow-chevron-painted overrun area. A hazy shotgun-like blast of accumulated tire rubber blossomed around the four-by-four wooden cube and the chute went limp as it skittered crazily along the runway, slowly bleeding off forward momentum the farther it traveled.

The second pallet didn't fare as well. After coming into contact with the runway, it clipped one of the marker lights, instantly altering its trajectory and causing the drag chute lines to wrap around it. Barely a dozen yards from where it first hit the runway after leaving the airplane, the cargo pallet careened through the vibrant green infield, along the way kicking up dark clods of soil still bristling with grass.

"Special delivery from Major Nash," said the colonel. "She pulled some strings and had the flight diverted from … somewhere."

"We just took delivery of an ammo drop destined for another base?"

The colonel grimaced, but said nothing.

Wisely, Doyle changed the subject. "Shall I send the PJs out?"

Colonel Frederick tapped the control tower glass, then pointed in the general direction of the long row of airplane hangars the A-10s had rolled out of earlier. The massive floor-to-ceiling doors were parted about a third of their travel and a desert-tan Humvee bristling with guns was already rolling through with a pair of like-colored pickup trucks close on its bumper.

"They've beat you to it, Sergeant." The colonel turned, raised the binoculars to his face and tracked the cargo plane as it crossed the east end of the runway, climbing away from the tower while banking gently to port. The fuselage was still wide open out back and a human-sized figure was kneeling near the ramp. The magnified image of the Super Hercules shimmered slightly as it leveled from the short climb and settled on a northerly tack. Not a second later the tiny figure the colonel knew was the loadmaster began tossing Day-Glo orange spheres groundward. After seeing four of the objects fall to earth north of where Bayside Drive wrapped around the end of the base, the cargo plane's ramp begin its slow climb into the closed position.

"What were those?" Sergeant Cassidy asked.

"A distraction," said the colonel, letting the binoculars hang by their strap on his chest. "One that was promised by Nash and may have just saved what's left of the 436th and 512th Airlift Wings from having to evacuate this post."

Chapter 55

Duncan lowered the Bushnells and spit a couple of obscenities under his breath.

Standing on the road apart from the others and squinting in the same general direction, Daymon turned toward Duncan and asked, "What do you see that's got you so pissed off?"

"You need prescription glasses now?" Duncan asked, handing the binoculars down. "Take a look for yourself. There." He pointed. "Near that black hulk blocking the road."

Grumbling something about having perfect 20/20 vision, Daymon put the binoculars to his eyes and glassed the landscape to his left, eventually picking up State Route 30 meandering off to the northwest. After scanning the road east to west from where it intersected 16 he saw the reason for Duncan's verbal outburst. A half-mile west of the 16/30 junction the road was blocked by a large, tightly packed throng of dead. However, these corpses weren't twice-dead like the ones stacked like cordwood on the road behind the group. These dead bodies bracketed in Daymon's binoculars were mostly first turns and fully aware of the idling trucks. And in the center of 30, some distance behind the rotters, was the completely burned-out shell of what looked to have been a station wagon.

"So what's your concern?" Daymon asked, casting scrutiny on the dirt berm beside the blackened hulk.

"Yet another great place for an ambush," Duncan answered. "Hit us while we're passing the wreck and let those rotters finish the job. I've seen it before on the road outside of Boise … early on in this shit." He shuddered at the memory of the young kids burning alive in the convertible VW. How they'd flailed, bucking and straining against their belts for long seconds as they died. He imagined Rawley's SKS chattering as the thirty-something musician ended their suffering, performing that final good deed before he was shot dead by the outlaw bikers.

"What do we do then … just turn around because of a few *maybes* and *what-ifs*?" Jamie said, one hand resting on her hip. "If we let the rotters come to us… meet them where the road is at its widest, kill them there and then give the car and road ahead a closer look before moving on."

Taryn said, "At least we won't have to worry about an ambush while we've got our hands full culling rotters."

Daymon panned the binoculars away from the wreck and walked them the entire length of a feeder road running perpendicular to State Route 30. "Might not be necessary," he said. "The last part of your plan, at least."

"And you base that assumption on what?" asked Lev.

Squinting and pointing to the field to the right of the advancing zombies, Wilson said, "Does it have something to do with the birds in the field over there?"

"Very perceptive," Daymon said. "Those look like turkey buzzards, which are wary birds to begin with. No way they'd still be out there feeding if a force of any size was lying in wait for us anywhere near that charred car."

"I second that," Foley added. "I've done a lot of hunting and found that a blind has to be pretty good to fool even the dumbest of birds."

Daymon nodded. "And I don't think there's a squad of snipers in ghillie suits hiding in the hills, either. Whoever we're dealing with is far from professional. Pretty much everything I've seen so far has been done pretty sloppily."

"Not the walkers in the fix-it shop," Wilson said, his voice wavering. "That was engineered perfectly. Taryn had *no* idea they were waiting just inside that door."

"I'll give you that," Daymon conceded. "Doesn't excuse her for letting her guard down a second time. But I digress. The crucified guy and the verses in the church was a bush league message. The bleeder leaving the matchbook and cigarette smoke hanging in the air at the rectory … both rookie mistakes."

"The trap on the back door wasn't the work of a novice," Wilson said, throwing another shudder.

Ignoring the redhead's valid point, Daymon went on, "Sasha's bike and Oliver's gear … all discarded haphazardly with little effort to conceal any of it. None of *that* makes sense to me."

Hand on her tomahawk and staring at the road by her boots, Jamie shook her head subtly. Then, as if something had just dawned on her, she chuckled and lifted her gaze to the group. "Anyone remember Hansel and Gretel?"

"Yeah," Daymon said. "But what's a story about a couple of kids lost in the woods got to do with this?"

Dying to hear the correlation, Duncan inched his head farther out the Dodge's open window and looked on in silence.

"Bread crumbs," Jamie said. "Someone's leaving us crumbs to follow."

"You may be right, young lady. But let's deal with our most pressing problem first." Duncan pointed to Taryn. "I want you to get Cade's truck and pull it forward." Then, like a kid at recess picking his team for a game of dodgeball, he pointed to Wilson, Daymon, Lev, and Jamie. "You four will ride in back of the 650." Meeting Jamie's icy glare he singled her out. "Sorry to bump you from your ride, darling. We'll need our best driver at the wheel of that monster. She's going to shuttle you all into their midst and everyone needs to chalk up six or seven kills each. I figure it'll be over real quick and then we go check out the car and see what the birds are up to."

"Shooting from the back of the truck while it's moving?" Foley asked. "Aren't you even a little bit concerned about one of them catching a ricochet or friendly fire?"

"No gunplay," Duncan said, shaking his head. "Do them with your blades."

Next to Duncan, Tran whispered, "They're coming."

"What will you be doing?" asked Daymon. "Supervising?"

Nodding to Tran, Duncan said, "Me and him will be shadowing you in the Dodge. We'll intervene if things go sideways."

"All right. If you say so," Daymon said. "What's Foley going to be doing while we're all putting our lives on the line?"

Duncan got Foley's attention. Met his gaze and said, "I'm going to need you to stay behind and watch all of our backs."

Foley nodded in agreement.

Duncan cleared his throat and spat a wad of phlegm into a handkerchief. "Things are going to get real noisy on the road. Better keep your radios close and the volume dialed to ten."

Wilson turned the volume up on his Motorola and then stepped aside as the F-650 rolled to a stop and the passenger window powered down.

"I'm not driving," Taryn said, staring down at Duncan through the open window. "I didn't earn the right to."

"It's okay," Jamie insisted.

Making eye contact, Taryn set the brake and climbed down from the idling rig. "No, it's not," she insisted, closing the door before Max could jump from the cab.

Jamie stepped aside, a confused look on her face.

Daymon materialized from around the rear bumper, slapping the 650's rear quarter as if it were a stubborn horse refusing to leave the paddock. "Oh no you don't, Miss Best Driver in the group," he chided. "The dead are closing in on us. Get back in that beast."

"Give me a moment," Taryn said.

Daymon removed his cap and ruffled his dreads. "Don't look now," he said. "Taryn's getting cold feet."

Flashing Daymon a one-finger salute, Taryn withdrew her knife from the leather sheath on her hip. Glaring at the dreadlocked man through eyes narrowed to slits, she handed her knife to Wilson hilt first.

"And what am I to do with this?" he asked, brows furrowing in confusion.

Shifting her gaze to her man, she reached behind her back with one hand and stretched taut the two-and-a-half-foot length of braided, raven-black hair she'd been growing out for more years than she cared to remember.

Knife held limply in one hand, Wilson gaped down at her. Mouth hanging open, he shifted his gaze to her long locks. After a few seconds' pause, he met her brown eyes again.

"Do it," she ordered.

"All of it?"

"Did I stutter?" she said, her face tight from the tension that pulling on her pony tail was putting on her scalp.

"Do it," Daymon urged. "I did mine a while back."

Glancing up at Daymon, Taryn asked, "Do you regret it?"

Slowly at first, Wilson began to saw back and forth.

Once the sharp blade had passed the halfway mark—the point of no return, by Daymon's estimation, he said, "Every single day."

Taryn brought the bird back, slowly thrusting it in his face, even as his shit-eating grin told her he was pulling her leg.

"Just effin with you," he said. "Short hair is pretty liberating. You'll get used to it."

A tear traced Taryn's cheek as Wilson made the final few cuts. Her eyes were welling with big fat drops when what was left of her hair—essentially a jagged Pixie cut, not much unlike Jamie's—fanned out around the nape of her neck.

Nearly in tears himself, figurative tears, because he really enjoyed it when she let her hair down, Wilson handed the length of braided hair to her over her shoulder.

"I'm not driving," Taryn said, shooing Jamie towards the driver's door as she fought to keep the tears at bay. "I need to get back on the horse and ride. Earn all of your trust back."

Shrugging, Lev helped Jamie into the Ford and closed the door.

"Suit yourself," Duncan called across the road. "Whoever's getting in back better get to doing it."

Wilson helped Taryn into the F-650's bed then watched Daymon vault the tailgate and take a spot atop the passenger side wheel arch next to Lev. Finally he crawled in and plopped down next to Taryn, mentally exhausted and still in shock from the unexpected turn of events.

Chapter 56

Cade powered off his NVGs and flipped them away from his eyes. He swung his M4 behind his back, leaned over Cross's shoulder and looked at the crystal-clear image splashed on the door probe's color display. Straight away he learned that Nash had been right about the power being on in the areas that mattered. That he was looking at a full color image of an illuminated stairway meant he owed an apology for doubting her on the matter.

Cross maneuvered the probe, training the lens on the stairwell wall where shadows, long and lean, seemed to be performing an eerie dance. "We're going to have company right away," he said.

"How many?" Cade asked.

"Looks like more than one," Cross offered, twisting the stalk to the right.

"Stop," Cade said. "What's that? Can you hold it steady? Zoom in, maybe?"

Cross said nothing. He manipulated the controls and the blurry object behind the door suddenly became an overturned chair. It was a metal item from the looks of it and had come to rest lengthwise to the flight of stairs leading up, its four legs pointed directly at the camera lens.

Cade said, "Think it's close enough to block the door sweep?"

"No telling. These things weren't designed with depth of field in mind."

"One way to find out," Griff said.

"I'm running point," Cade reminded. "Cross at two then Griff at three—"

"And the Brit brings up the rear," Axe finished.

Without a word, Cross handed his lock-pick gun over his shoulder.

"No need for that here," Cade said, reaching into his breast pocket and producing the pass card Nash had given him after the briefing. There was no writing on either side of the white card. On its back side was a black magnetic strip containing the information making it a master passkey. Holding the card vertically, Cade swiped it downward over the door at waist-level with the magnetic strip facing the spot on the door where a knob or handle should be.

There was a soft click and a slight give when he pressed inward with his other hand.

A blast of air a few degrees cooler than that in the hall escaped around the door's edge. The pong of carrion, though not as pronounced as it had been in the main lobby, was impossible to miss.

Under his breath, but still picked up by the comms, Axe said, "Smells like arse."

"Based on the angle of the shadows," Cross said, "I'd bet whatever is casting them is at least one flight down."

"The chair?" Griff asked.

"No idea," Cade answered. "Maybe someone's failed attempt at barring the door from inside." He stowed the card away and swung his M4 back around front. Gripping the carbine at a low ready, he tested the door swing.

"Quit bandying about with it for bloody sake," Axe whispered. "We've got company. Three zeds on our six. Ten meters out. Shall I engage?"

"Negative," Cade said. "They can't see us yet."

Voice rising an octave, Axe pressed, "But *I* can see them *now*, mate."

As Griff kept watch down the empty hallway running away from them, he wondered to himself who, between Axe and

Lopez, would win a bitching contest if Zs were the topic of discussion.

Ignoring Axelrod, Cade continued pushing the door inward.

Six inches.

A soft rasp, perhaps the rustle of fabric on a handrail, filtered through the gap.

Twelve.

The stench of death was more evident now.

At eighteen inches all forward movement ceased when the metal door hit a chair leg and a noise like a struck gong sounded from within. As the resonant tone crashed off the walls, a second noise—a steady *tap, tap, tap*—could be heard coming from behind the partially opened door. Then, as if the initial aural assault wasn't confusing enough, the Zs down the main floor hall began to hiss and rasp excitedly.

At once, from somewhere down the stairs and out of Cade's sight, an eerie moaning drifted up from the depths. Hairs rising on the back of his neck, he came to two quick conclusions: Whatever was behind the door was the immediate threat and therefore priority number one. Then the fresh turns responsible for the telltale moaning echoing up the stairs had to be searched out and dealt with.

"NVGs up," Cade called out over the comms. "Going in. Cross, cover me."

Moving in a low crouch, Cade rolled around the door jamb moving nimbly on the balls of his feet. Once he'd negotiated the narrow opening, he backpedaled left a full stride and looked sidelong down the stairs. "Clear left," he called. "Checking obstruction."

Under Cross's watchful gaze, feet planted a shoulder-width apart on the dimly illuminated cement landing, Cade leveled his carbine at the door, reached out one-handed, and started it swinging closed.

As the door crept slowly to his right, the thick shadows behind it were chased away in degrees and fully supplanted by the pale white light being cast from the wall-mounted emergency lamps.

In a heartbeat, Cade's gaze flicked from the metal chair, crossed the gray cement landing, and locked onto the pair of well-worn tennis shoes that had been toeing the back of the door. He thumbed the switch on the carbine's forward grip, causing a stark white cone of light to lance from the tactical flashlight affixed to the M4's forward rail. He walked his gaze up the living corpse. Saw that it had died wearing comfortable clothes: blue jeans, pink Polo, and Chuck Taylor All-Stars. The makeshift noose keeping it aloft had been passed through a tangle of overhead pipes and tied off to the stair handrail with a messy knot. Wavy blond hair framed the thing's bloated, blue and purple face. There was a trio of raised bite marks on one side of its face, and like a road map of highways and byways, burst capillaries snaked every which way across its fluttering lids, on down its cheeks and continued their run underneath the skin-splitting ligature. Those bugged-out, bloodshot and jaundiced eyes consumed Cade as the corpse jiggled and wriggled silently like a prized catch on the end of a hundred-pound line.

Must have sucked to have not been allowed to leave here after Casual Friday, thought Cade as he finished his split-second processing of the death scene.

As if in agreement, the moaning down the stairs grew louder—and nearer.

"Clear right," Cade called, as he moved the chair aside and opened the door for the others.

"Suicide fail," Cross quipped, taking in the grisly sight of the male Z banging its knees and toes against the back of the door.

At once Griff padded to the left, peered down the stairs and craned over the rail. "Still clear," he called back softly.

Cheeks showing a considerable rosiness clearly visible even in the low-light, Axe made his way onto the crowded landing, closing the door behind him. "Right close there, mate," he said to Cade, the sound of nails raking the door competing with his words.

Stealing Cade's thunder, Griff unknowingly repeated one of Duncan's favorite phrases. "Close only counts in horseshoes and hand grenades." He paused for effect and aimed his HK down the stairs where the swaying shadows were growing longer. "Unless, that is, you guys don't play horseshoes across the pond."

Now Axe was the one who said nothing as, from somewhere down the stairs, amplified and more hair-raising in the enclosed subterranean confines, the moaning started anew.

Ignoring the noisy ghouls for the moment, Cade righted the chair. Left ankle feeling better than ever, he stepped onto the seat and ended the Z's struggles by plunging his Gerber into its eye socket.

"Regular Jack Kevorkian," Axe quipped as Cade shouldered his rifle and started down the gloomy stairwell.

***

With Cade running point and Axe lagging back to watch their six, the four-man team dove deeper under the towering NSA building. Three levels below the lobby, which amounted to six full switchback runs of stairs, Cade came around a right hander and spotted the source of the rising stench and disconcerting moans. Sharing the landing marked Sublevel 3 with the jumble of rolling office chairs preventing them from climbing the stairs was a recent turn and a badly decomposed first turn. The former was male, mid-thirties, and had been scratched and bitten multiple times about the arms and face. He died wearing clothes much like the failed suicide victim upstairs. Only Casual Friday for this guy, probably mid-level management, or a GS-5 in government ranks, was slacks and Oxford. The once-white button down was stained with food and bore yellowed rings under the arms that bespoke of a lengthy post Z-Day stay at good ol' Club NSA.

The first turn was female and barely clothed. What remained of her blouse and pants were shredded, bloodied in spots, and soiled greatly with dried mud that looked to have come from the Fort Meade grounds some time ago. An identification tag was still clipped to a scrap of fabric that may have been a breast pocket.

"Looks like misery loves company," Griff said over Cade's shoulder, his weapon-mounted light flicking on and painting a second pair of twice-dead Zs in a revealing light. Tucked away to the team's right, partially hidden under the stairwell, were two more female zombies in much the same shape as the first turn. Same dried mud. Same defensive wounds and blood dried to black on the arms. And the same office casual attire that all but screamed these people had no idea what was about to go down in and around the District.

Beyond the barrier and reaching hands of the agitated Zs was a closed door identical to the one on the main floor—gore streaks, card reader and all. Cade took one more step then halted, thumbed the M4 off Safe, and stuck the suppressor against the first turn's forehead.

"Check your fire," said Griff over the comms. "There's sensitive stuff behind the Zs."

Trusting his teammate unequivocally, Cade lowered his rifle and drew the Gerber. Too late. The first turn had snaked one spindly arm through the barrier and found purchase on his MOLLE rig, ripping back a Velcro strap and sending a full magazine on a slow tumble to the floor. Grabbing the thing by the wrist, Cade glanced down at the flopping ID tag and said, "Will one of you please put Miss Lockwood down for me?"

Squeezing past Cade on the right, Griff parted the top couple of leather, high-backed chairs and grabbed the walking cadaver by the wrist and throat. In one fluid and overpowering move, he twirled the undead woman around to face Axe, who was ready with a drawn dagger that slid cleanly tip-to-hilt into the thing's left eye socket.

Cade sliced the tendons in its wrist to release the dead fingers locked onto his chest rig.

"Just like we knew what we were doing," Griff said, looking at Cade.

"She *almost* got you, mate," said Axe, emphasizing "almost" as a subtle dig to Griff. "And she ain't U-shaped nor does she have a pin to pull."

"Thanks," said Cade, looking to Griff. "I owe you. Now kill the fresh one so you can tell me why you didn't want me to shoot these two in the first place."

Griff pulled a chair from the bottom of the pile, starting a fabric, leather, and chrome avalanche that freed the Oxford-wearing Z to shuffle toward him unimpeded. "Because," he said, wrapping a gloved hand around the GS-5's neck, "one ricochet could've introduced liquid under tremendous pressure to dozens of CRAY-RS supercomputers with enough electricity coursing through them to light up a hundred electric chairs. It could have ended badly for all of us."

Shooting Griff a look that said *spill the rest*, Cade regained his grip on the M4 and plucked the reader card from his pocket.

As Griff opened his mouth to elaborate, he was interrupted by something impacting the door from the other side with sufficient enough force to make it flex against its hidden hinges.

Then the keen of nails raking metal began.

So Griff cleared his throat and spoke loudly enough to be heard over the undead awaiting them on the other side of the door to Sub Level-3 where, during the pre-mission briefing, Nash had promised they would find the NSA's newest off-the-books addition to their main above-ground Data Collection Center.

Under the watchful eye of the rest of the team, Griff went into detail about the original Data Collection Center they had overflown on the way in, telling them about the first floor where the banks of computers were housed and then finishing with the stunning fact that the eight-thousand-tons of water and Fluorinert used to cool the dozens of CRAY supercomputers' very hot electronic components was housed on the floor directly above the DCC.

Working a gloved finger under his tactical bump helmet to scratch an itch, Axe asked, "What does all of that have to do with whatever the beasties are guarding beyond *this* door? And just what in the bugger is Fluorinert?"

"Fluorinert is the name for the 3M company's line of electronics coolant liquids. It's an electrically insulating, stable fluorocarbon-based—"

Cade raised a gloved hand, cutting Griff short. "All right, Bill Nye. Where's the cooling apparatus in *this* building?"

"Nash only knew this existed. As for schematics and floorplans, she couldn't access that kind of intel."

"What's your best guess?"

To keep up with the rapid-fire exchange, both Cross and Axe were shifting their gazes between Cade and Griff and back again.

After a brief pause, Griff answered, "I'd put the water pumps on Sub Level 2 then excavate deeper and run pipes down and let gravity do most of the work."

"You'd still have to pump the water and Fluorinert back up to keep it circulating," Cross proffered.

Cade shook his head. "We're here to destroy the computers and wipe data anyway. So what difference does it make?"

Cocking his head, Griff said, "I thought I was clear about water and its propensity to conduct electricity."

Cade cast a cursory glance at the walls and ceiling. He picked up something different here. Whereas the dimensions of the doorway, stair runs and landings were the same here as they were sixty-some-odd feet overhead at the main level entry, the texture on the cured cement was different. Though still constructed from poured concrete that was no doubt reinforced with rebar, there were imprints from the plywood sheeting molds as well as coarse spots showing where pebbles and a few larger quarter-sized river rocks protruded from the poorly finished surfaces. Everything about the work here was much different than the fine craftsmanship exhibited from the main floor stairway on down to Sub Level 1. He figured the same tight-lipped government contractors had done the work on both the original basement and this new, deeper addition. But going by the unusual techniques employed here, different crews must have worked each project. Easier to keep the new additions secret by compartmentalizing the task, he guessed.

Whatever the reasons for staggering crews, clearly the construction of this stop-gap facility had been rushed. Whether the haste had been spurred on by delays of the yet to be finished mega-data storage facility—strangely enough, before the dead began to walk, slated to go in near Camp Williams in Draper, Utah—or whispers of a whistleblower spy working inside the NSA here at Fort Meade, Cade hadn't a clue and didn't want to venture a guess. What he did know, however, was that this annex was finished a year ago and he had a job to do now. Water-cooling pipes and machinery and electricity were things the Chinese wouldn't waste time fretting over, therefore he couldn't afford to either.

Having finally come to a hard-fought conclusion, Cade looked each man in the eye, starting with Cross and finishing with Griff. "We better stay frosty and shoot straight and true then, men." He flicked the M4's selector to Fire, the sharp click audible to all. "Weapons free," he said, a granite set to his jaw.

More soft thuds against the door.

Suddenly the backup lighting went out, casting the well into darkness. A tick later it flickered, then remained on, again bathing the stairs in a muted veil of golden light.

"You don't want to scope the door first?" Cross asked soberly.

Having moved away from the door, Axe was now staring daggers at the wall-mounted light fixture.

Sounding as if the dead were scraping the paint off the door from top to bottom, the noise of fingernails raking metal reverberated up and down the cramped stairwell.

Ignoring the nerve-jangling racket, Cade said, "We've got to go in no matter what. Axe, you retreat to the next landing and cover us. Griff, get my back on the landing here." He paused for a second, thinking. "Cross, dig out a mini-Screamer. I'll open the door and you throw for the end zone."

"Copy that," Cross and Griff said in unison.

Incredulous, the SAS man said, "You don't even want to know how many of the buggers are in there beforehand?"

Cade said nothing. Instead, to indicate that he'd made up his mind on the matter, he took the pass card from his pocket and tapped it against his palm while Cross went about preparing for deployment a golf-ball-sized mini-Screamer.

Chapter 57

The F-650 was crawling along at walking speed when its front bumper met the jostling throng of snarling zombies head on.

Thirty to forty my ass, Jamie thought, taking in the sight. Then, shouting so the others to be heard through the open rear slider, she said, "Looks like we've got *seventy* or *eighty* rotters up here." After a split second's contemplation, with the Zs' pale, bony hands already groping the bumper and hood and fenders up front, she added nervously, "That's like … *twenty* for each of you to put down."

"We got this," Taryn shouted back, her Tanto already in hand.

In the left wing mirror Jamie saw a glint of metal as Taryn's blade flashed out and down and disappeared into the nearest zombie's eye socket. Imagining the grate of metal on bone, she saw the young, newly bobbed brunette's arm and weapon draw back and the Z fall to the road, twice dead, and about to meet the Ford's oversized rear tire.

One down, thought Foley, as he watched the action with rapt attention through the Bushnells. Rotters number two, three, and four crashed to the road in heaps of jutting elbows and knees as he stood rooted in the bed of the Raptor, his elbows planted firmly on the flat of the roof.

"Get some," he crowed. After taking a quick second to look all around his own position and seeing nothing living or undead in the vicinity, he pressed the binoculars back to his eyes and glassed the area all around the rest of the group, adding extra attention to their fore where triple-strand barbed wire fences lined the road on both sides. Concentrating on keeping the image steady, he scrutinized the ochre earthen berm to the left of the group. *Nothing but old tire tracks on the soft shoulder there.* Swinging his gaze to the pasture on the right, the things there that caught his interest were the feeding birds, a small copse of trees beyond the raptors, and, a number of yards west of the trees, the galvanized culvert running underneath the muddy road feeding the nearby state route.

Seeing nothing pointing to an ambush, Foley depressed the Motorola's Talk button and relayed the positive news to the others.

Inside the slow-moving Dodge, Duncan heard Foley's report, the good news not nearly enough to loosen the knot in his stomach. Damn if he couldn't relax when facing substantial numbers of the dead—at least not without his old friend Jack Daniels.

At the moment Foley's voice leapt from the radio's tiny speaker the knot of walkers began spilling around the F-650's squared-off rear bumper.

As he reached blindly for the Saiga semi-auto shotgun, he witnessed Daymon cull two monsters with a pair of lightning-quick downward chops of his machete. By the time Duncan's hand had found the shotgun's polymer stock, three more rotters were out of the fight. One having fallen when Taryn reached down from the truck's bed and thrust her blade into the child-sized shambler's brain, and two more that were sent crashing to the road vertically, victim to Lev's superior knife work.

Meanwhile, on the passenger side behind Taryn, it looked to Duncan as if Wilson was having trouble timing his knife strikes. As the Ford continued rolling through the crush of bodies, the ones nearest the redhead were being repelled by the rig's mass, which in turn had a domino effect on the rest causing them to fall even further away from his substantial reach.

Seeing the dead being repulsed by the Ford, some of them swiping clumsily as it left them behind while others were sent tumbling headlong into the roadside ditch, Duncan took his hand off the shotgun and snatched up the radio. "Jamie," he said. "You've got to slow down a bit. I know it's counterintuitive, but you need to ride the brakes and allow the things to surround the truck." He let up on the Talk button.

Jamie made no reply. Instead, up ahead, the Ford's brake lights flared red and its forward motion slowed considerably.

That a girl, thought Duncan, easing up on the pedal to match her speed, which was hovering just south of five miles per hour.

On his knees in the right rear corner of the F-650's bed, Lev felt the truck slow and suddenly he was facing a target-rich environment. Reciting every cuss word learned in the Army, all of them directed at the rotting flesh eaters less than a yard to his fore, he began to thrust his Cold Steel blade into the pale faces leering back at him.

Wilson called out triumphantly from the other side. "I finally got one."

"Six more to go if you want to catch up with me," Daymon said, his machete cleaving deeply into a Z's cranial bone.

"Shit, that's seven for you now," Wilson said over the sucking sound as he wiggled his knife free of a first turn's leaking eye socket.

"Less talking, Wilson," said Lev, as there came an awful *pop* and *crunch* from the Ford's left rear tire jouncing over something organic.

Taking Lev's advice to heart, Wilson pursed his lips into a thin white line, grabbed a handful of one ghoul's greasy hair, and drove his knife hilt deep into one of its wildly roving eyes.

Duncan watched the dead dropping to the road at a much faster pace. In less than thirty seconds, by his estimation, the number of dead had been cut in half. And considering the battering the Ford had taken from the flailing arms and sheer weight of the bodies pressing in on it, even without Taryn at the wheel, it had never wavered from the slow steady course he'd asked for. "Good job," he said into the Motorola. "You kids have found a rhythm. Keep it up for just a bit longer."

"A bit longer" turned out to be an additional twenty seconds. After which the rotters numbered no more than thirty.

"Stop her right there on the centerline," Duncan drawled, steering the Dodge to the shoulder to keep from running over the amassed corpses.

Amazingly, the push-back he'd expected from Jamie over being ordered to stop with close to half of the rotters still assaulting the truck never materialized. Instead, as before, the brake lights flared red and the Ford stopped completely.

In the F-650, with the remaining dead enveloping the truck, Jamie stared straight ahead, drumming her fingers on the wheel. As soon as the first pale palm slapped the glass near her head, she closed her eyes and said a little prayer for Oliver, asking that wherever he was, he wasn't suffering. Then she flashed back to her own time spent in captivity at the hands of Ian Bishop and his right-hand man, Carson. As if she was watching old jittery film reel footage, she saw Jordan's shocked expression as Bishop's men dragged them from the shot-up garage at the upper quarry. Clear as day, though the traumatic event was weeks in the past, she heard Jordan calling for help as a dirty, burlap hood was pulled over her head and she was shoved into a waiting helicopter.

It was the last time she had seen the young woman alive.

She threw a shudder. Not from the keen of fingernails raking the door by her leg. Not from the imagined picture in her mind of the contorted faces of the undead things trying to get to her. Nor was she shaken by the idea that whoever had left the crumbs for them to follow may be waiting for them at Bear Lake with more people and firepower than eight people could handle.

Nope.

None of the above.

Jamie was, in her own way, processing the fact that the night before, around the campfire, she may have set eyes on Oliver for the final time. She took little solace from the knowledge that *the crazies from the North*—as Ray and Helen had called the nameless and faceless antagonists—didn't appear to have a single helicopter, let alone a fleet of them. Because if what they had already proven they were capable of doing was their worst, then being thrown from a helicopter like Jordan had been would probably be a better fate for Oliver than the former. God, it killed her thinking about how hard a hit Glenda was going to take if she was right in her assumption.

With the non-stop screech of fingernails raking both of the truck's flanks already driving her close to madness, Jamie pushed the bad thoughts away and opened her eyes to see one particularly tenacious rotter making out with the glass inches from her face. On the brink of pulsing her window down and unloading the Beretta into Casanova to silence the incessant clicking of his teeth on the clouded side glass, she had a sudden epiphany that gave her pause.

Out of sight was easy. Just close your eyes again.

Out of mind, not so much. At least not until she powered on the stereo and two things happened. First, the LCD display lit up with a soft red glow. Then, completely drowning out all the myriad noises produced by the zombies' all-out assault on the truck, a long dead rapper began spitting rhymes about New York, high priced hos and a lifestyle filled with bling and champagne.

A millisecond after the first stanza faded, the bass line dropped and she was receiving a butt massage from what seemed like a dozen speakers hidden from sight directly underneath the front seat.

Chapter 58

A cursory glance at the jamb and sweep told Cade that this door was different than the one they had used to access the maintenance stairwell from the main floor hallway.

Cross kneeled down and pried at the bottom edge with his knife. Shaking his head, he said, "There's no room for the device."

"I have an idea," Cade said, fishing the pass card from his pocket. He ran through what he expected from each man, then turned back and waved the card in front of the gray panel where a handle should have been.

The pass card worked on the first try. As with the main level door, there was a soft click when the bolt gave way. However, unlike the door three levels up, when Cade pushed in on this one, as if a seal had been broken, there was an audible hiss followed at once by a blast of cool air heavy with the reek of death and decay.

A little more pressure from his shoulder told Cade that there were dead things pressing their rotten flesh against the other side.

"Like we discussed," Cade said, his eyes locked on Cross.

Cross nodded, then began counting down from three.

Shoulder and palms planted against the door, Cade counted down with Cross.

At *two*, Griff let his rifle hang from its sling and placed his gloved hands on the door a few inches to the right of Cade's.

On *one*, using every ounce of strength at their disposal, Cade and Griff leaned into the door, bulling it inward a few inches.

Instantly, a gnarled hand shot through the opening. The crooked, pale fingers scrabbled around the door's edge dangerously close to Cade's face. In the next beat Cross hurled the armed Screamer sidearm through the narrow opening, clearing the reaching hands by mere inches.

"You call that a Hail Mary," Griff said between grunts brought on by keeping pressure on the door.

M4 held at a low ready, Axe called down from his perch midway up the stairs. "Again with the football reference?"

Beaded sweat was forming on Griff's brow. "Says the bloke *not* shoring up the offensive line. Trade me places?" he said, only half-joking.

The half-dozen bony hands probing the opening were now joined by a single pallid face. As the thing worked its left cheek past the door's edge, its teeth clicked and clacked and a low steady hiss emanated from deep down in its chest.

"Give me five more seconds, Griff," Cade bellowed.

"Doing my best."

At ten seconds the Screamer remained silent.

At eleven, still nothing. No recorded screams of a long-dead woman came from within the DCC.

No sooner had Cade looked to Griff and ordered him to prepare a second device than the first came alive with the same high-pitched wail the larger unit had emitted inside the Ghost Hawk. Though the mini-Screamer was a fraction of the size as the ones deployed to keep the hordes busy upstairs, this little sucker packed a sonic punch—especially in the enclosed, low-ceilinged room.

The second the Screamer went *live*, the resistance on the door disappeared and Newton's Law was in full effect.

The only thing halting *the equal and opposite reaction* part and saving the door from swinging completely inward at great speed and spilling Cade and Griff into a room full of hungry Zs was Cross springing to action.

Unbeknownst to the two off-balance operators, after hurling the device Cross had slipped one gloved hand over the door's top edge. And as the cool metal slab suddenly went light against Cade and Griff's combined weight, Cross had reacted by shooting his arm between the two operators and grabbing a fistful of Cade's MultiCam blouse.

As Cross pulled Cade and Griff away from the door, he stole a quick glance at the ceiling inside the DCC. And in that snapshot in time what he saw validated Griff's earlier warning. Where there should have been drop-down ceiling tiles, he saw pipes of all different sizes crisscrossing the ceiling left to right. And intertwined with the larger conduits like spaghetti noodles on a fork, smaller hoses wormed in and out of every available crevice.

"Griff's correct," Cross stated calmly as the door slammed shut, severing four fingers off the lone Z that hadn't gone after the Screamer. "The cooling apparatus is overhead."

Taking a chance, Cade passed the card in front of the jamb and cracked the door an inch. When no clammy appendages tested the opening, he said, "Griff," and stabbed a thumb over his head.

Griff looked at the ceiling through the sliver. "Gentlemen, we cannot afford to have *any* stray rounds go high."

Cross looked to Axe on the stairs. "Can you see what the Zs are doing?"

"Can't see past the computer cases, mate."

"We'll give them a minute," Cade said, closing the door and shutting out the all-too-real screams.

***

The minute passed by slowly.

The Screamer didn't falter.

And the dead didn't resume their assault on the door.

Cade used the pass card again and, after taking a cursory glance through the cracked door and finding nothing obstructing its swing on the opposite side, he nudged it slowly across the threshold. He padded a few feet into the dimly lit room and paused at the head of the center aisle, which was one of four running lengthwise between four identical banks of computers, their cases dark red—almost burgundy—and emblazoned at eye level with the CRAY RS logo. After a quick computation, Cade determined that thirty-two of the foot-wide, rectangular items were packed into the front third of the oblong room. Head-high to him and arranged side-by-side like soldiers standing to attention, each row consisting of eight computers looked to measure about thirty feet from front to back.

Though the steadily humming electronics ran hot, the temperature here was on par with the outside world—fifty-five degrees or so, Cade guessed. Underfoot, the once-white floors were dirtied by prints left behind by bare feet, most of them muddy, some red with blood. The walls were also white and smudged with handprints and splotches of bodily fluids transferred there by the restless Zs.

Immediately after pouring into the DCC single file, gun barrels leading the way, Axe peeled off left, heading for the aisle furthest away from the door. Meanwhile, Cross and Griff went right, each hooking a left down an aisle of their own, Cross moving in a combat crouch up the one next to Cade's, while Griff hustled between the row of computers near the far wall.

Suddenly the Screamer went silent and the guttural sounds of the dead rose over the hum of computers.

Broadcast over the comms, Cade heard Axe say, "Contact," which was followed near instantaneously by suppressed gunfire and the tinkle of brass dancing across the tile floor.

In the next half-beat both Cross and Griff were calling out that they were also engaging the dead.

They're aware of us, Cade thought, his gut clenching. In his mind's eye, he saw an overhead view of the room: Axe on his far left flank, moving and firing. Then, based on the distinctive sound of the suppressed MP7 echoing off the ceiling to his immediate right, Cross working his way between his row of CRAY computers. Finally, bookending the team on the far right, judging by the satisfying hammering of the HK's short stroke piston—clearly audible over the suppressed reports from the lead it was spitting—he saw Griff dealing second death to the Zs in his sector.

"Contact center," he called, a tick after the Screamer—no doubt jostled to life by one of the dead things—resumed blaring from the center of the room. At the end of his row of computers, Cade saw the periphery of an undead scrum which consisted of at least a dozen Zs pig-piled atop each other and digging for the noise emitter at the bottom of the crush.

As Cade heel and toed it between the CRAY cases full of red and green lights blinking incessantly behind rectangular panes of clear glass, he began picking off the dead in his path, one carefully measured double-tap at a time.

Acrid gun smoke filled the air around his head while, propelled by his new Danner boots, spent brass skittered and jumped about the mud-streaked floor ahead of his steady advance.

Nearing the last computer in the bank with the room opening wide in front of him, time seemed to slow for Cade. All at once he heard Cross's MP7 go silent. *Changing mags*, he guessed. Then the steady clatter of Griff's weapon ceased and in his headset he heard the operator declare his zone clear of Zs.

No word came from Axe, just the steady, comforting chug of a suppressed M4 coming from the far left.

After dropping a pair of Zs to the floor in a bony, ashen-skinned heap, Cade changed mags and charged his M4.

Axe's M4 went mute and he called his side clear.

Cade stopped short of the waist-high swarm of Zs that had been lured away from the door by the siren's call of the Screamer. Targeting only the heads clearly visible in the squirming organic mass, he stilled the three Zs nearest him. As he shifted aim looking for clean shots, two things happened, one right after the other. First, an emaciated female zombie pushed up off the floor and fixed its milky eyes on him. Reacting instantly, he caressed the trigger twice. The initial bullet punched through the Z's septum, sending her balding head hinging backward. Speeding along at almost three thousand feet per second, bullet number two was supposed to have punched out the thing's right eye, finishing the job the first lead missile started. Instead, the second round of Cade's carefully aimed double-tap caromed off the pale white expanse of the monster's forehead. A millisecond later, its trajectory irrevocably altered, the 62-grain hunk of screaming lead was swallowed up by the tangle of pipes running across the ceiling twenty-five feet behind the female Z. After entering the overhead warren, the bullet must have ricocheted, because it made a sound like a smith's hammer striking hot metal.

Astonishingly, the errant bullet didn't have an immediate negative effect.

Circling away from the scrum, Cade looked left and saw Axe cease firing for a split second and gape upward at the pipes. To Cade's right, Cross emerged from the computers, stepping over bodies and changing his magazine. On the far side of Cross, Griff was already standing before the last CRAY tower in his row. A table had been pulled away from the nearby wall. All of the items that looked to have been on the table now lay on the floor: Papers spilled out of manila folders. Sharpie pens and legal pads containing notes jotted down in a sloppy hand. A leather-bound logbook of some sort, its pages ripped and muddy, was propped up against the wall.

Snaking across the table were dozens of multicolored wires in various gauges. Tracing the wires with his eye, Cade saw that they spilled off the side of the table, ran across the floor and climbed the nearest CRAY to which they were still connected.

Wearing a pained look, Griff said, "The effin Chicoms beat us to it."

Cade cursed under his breath. He stared daggers at the tangle of wires, not so much pissed at any one person, but mostly at Mr. Murphy for the mechanical problems grounding the helo that in a roundabout way allowed the enemy to get here first.

"We've got a leak," Cross said, gesturing to the floor twenty-five feet to his fore.

"It won't be requiring a Dutch girl," Axe said, trying to lighten the mood.

Watching the water turn into a steady stream, the initial puddle already doubling to kiddie-pool-size, Cade reminded the team to stay clear lest they get a dose of the kind of voltage Old Sparky of death row fame used to administer.

"We still have a job to do," Griff said, shrugging off his pack. He dove in and came out with bricks of C4 and detonators to set it off.

"Make it quick," Cade implored. He pointed to the floor by the table where muddy boot prints with a familiar lug pattern were interspersed with the morass tracked in by the Zs. "They might still be close. If they are, we'll catch them."

Just off of Cade's left shoulder a second hose near the initial leak let loose a new stream of liquid. It was thicker than water and began to pool a dozen feet from the CRAY tower Griff was rigging with explosives.

"Watch yourselves," Axe said, returning from collecting the Screamer from beneath the twice-dead Zs. "We now have two pipes engaged in a pissing contest."

For a long moment there was no reply, only the rustling of Griff's MultiCam fatigues as he worked quickly to wire the explosives.

The liquid from the second leak swirled and mixed with the blood and mud on the floor as it spread and merged with the first puddle, creating a wide morass creeping dangerously close to the electronics.

"Finished," Griff said, as he shrugged his nearly empty pack on and scooped up his rifle.

"This way," Cade ordered, eyes sweeping the floor as he skirted the creeping liquid and followed the retreating boot prints deeper into the vast room.

Though the dead had trooped this way recently, the Chicom-patterned boot prints stood out and were easy to follow. They led to an open door at the far corner of the underutilized room.

On the wall inside the hallway Cade saw vague shadows undulating eerily.

He stopped underneath a wall-mounted emergency lamp, looked to Griff and asked, "Time until detonation?"

"Ten minutes," Griff answered.

Cade glanced at his watch, noting the time.

"Cutting it damn close," Axe said.

For the first time since entering the building, Cade consulted the floorplan Nash had provided. He checked the compass on his Suunto then scrutinized the map for a few seconds, turning it this way and that before refolding it and stowing it in a pocket.

Looking toward the hallway with the moving shadows, he said, "That tunnel isn't on the map. Nor is this half of the DCC. If my bearings are correct, it should run underneath the road and end up below the original DCC."

Cross said, "The building with the round domes on top."

"Exactly," Cade answered. "And our data thieves might still be in the building."

Shaking his head, Axe muttered, "Elvis has left the building."

"Stay close," Cade said to Cross and Griff. "Axe, you got our six."

"Great," Axe said jokingly. "Make me the red shirt of the team."

Smiling at the Star Trek reference, Cade shouldered his M4 and crabbed toward the yawning doorway and an eventual meeting with whatever was responsible for the wavering, spectral shadows.

Chapter 59

Crouched down low in the bed, Wilson lashed out with his right, scrambling yet another Z's brain with a well-placed knife thrust to the eye. As he watched the unlucky first turn go limp and slide from his blood-slickened blade, the V-10 engine growl lessened and the truck ground to a sudden halt.

"Why are we stopping?" Taryn called over her shoulder.

"Why cut it *all* off?" was all Wilson could summon as he caught sight of the pale nape of her neck. The question had been on his lips since he'd made that first pass across the thick, braided ponytail with her knife. And he figured that if he was going to die here, at least he'd do so knowing what she had been thinking.

But Taryn made no reply. Instead she continued fending off the creatures' groping hands with her off arm while the other holding the knife worked piston-like, the blade flashing in and out with lethal efficiency. Taking a step back from the concave bed wall, Taryn drew in a lungful of air tainted by the stench of death and caught a quick glimpse of the tops of her hands and forearms. Up to where her rolled-up sleeves fell, spatters of blood and other fluids rendered the black tattoos there nearly indistinguishable.

"We're not out of the woods yet," Daymon barked. "Keep fighting."

As Wilson paused for a tick to let the next wave of dead negotiate the mounting pile of corpses and *step right up* for a proper skewering, the truck began to vibrate and a male voice he vaguely recognized could be heard clear as day through the open sliding window. As he wondered what the hell Jamie was thinking throwing what amounted to a mini concert out here in Indian country, he glanced in Taryn's direction and saw her arch forward, exhale sharply, and grab a fistful of an elderly rotter's wispy gray hair. Then, forearms and biceps bulging noticeably, she clean-jerked Grandpa, or Grandma, whatever the case may be, off the ground and drew it toward the outside sheet metal where its knees impacted with a resounding *clang*. In the next beat the thrashing monster was grasping for Taryn's hair only to have the just-shorn jet-black locks slip through its claw-like fingers. As Wilson turned back to reengage the Zs whose kneading fingers were now coming dangerously close to finding purchase on his unzipped parka, Taryn slamming the waifish monster down chin first on the side of the box bed and her knife entering its right temple registered vividly in his side vision.

Having seen enough to know Taryn's recent and all too numerous close encounters with grabby zombies wasn't affecting her adversely, he went back to work with his blade, adding yet another pair of walkers to the growing pile on the roadway.

"Almost there, boys and girls," Duncan said into the radio. *And no sniper fire whatsoever.* He put the transmission into Park and set the brake. Let his gaze roam the mirrors and focused on Foley, who appeared as just a small figure hinged over the Chevy's roof.

"Foley … what do you see?"

Foley's head jerked and he rose, exposing his body from the waist up above the roofline. "Not a thing moving," he answered. "Just the birds."

"Good news," said Duncan, seeing the light of the darkening sky reflecting off the binocular lenses. "If I was the hombre manning an ambush up there, I would've sprung it when Daymon and the gang had their hands full with the *locals*."

"I'm no tactician," Foley conceded. "But I'd have to agree with you."

Duncan turned to Tran. The man was slumped in the seat, hands covering his eyes.

"We're good, Tran, my man. The last of the rotters are about to meet Kindness." *And some slug, shot, slug treatment.* He grabbed hold of his new shotgun and, with radio in hand, exited the truck.

The stench of death was thick outside the Dodge. Save for one lone shambler on the passenger side and the trio of hissing creatures still standing on the last clear patch of blacktop by the driver's door, twice-dead corpses in all kinds of grotesque death poses were lying knee-high where they'd fallen on both sides of the F-650.

After seeing Daymon cut down the last zombie on the right, Duncan realized the remaining three were still standing because they were just out of Taryn's reach. So he thumbed the Talk button. "Leave those three for me. I want to test out my new toy."

Taryn, Daymon, and Lev acknowledged the request; however, Jamie made no response. As Duncan advanced on the remaining rotters, he cut a wide berth to his left, staying clear of the fallen Zs and stepping over the rivulets of fluids leaking from them. As he closed to within ten feet of the driver's door he heard the faint rasps of the dead and felt the low timbre rumble of bass coming from inside the Ford.

Eight feet away and still the zombies were ignoring him.

Buncha one track mind mofos, he thought.

Then the window pulsed down and the music—if you could call it that—coming from within became more pronounced. A male was rapping about things that held no relevance to Duncan before or after the outbreak. He hollered to get the rotters' attention. No result. Nothing. They were locked onto Jamie and the tunes seemed to have them in some kind of a trance. *Hell*, he thought, *a couple verses of that stuff turns my perfectly good brain to mush. No tellin' what effect it has on a walker's already short-circuited thinker.*

Suddenly there was a whirring sound and the Zs jostled with each other for first dibs on whatever was about to emerge.

Knowing what was about to take place, Duncan slung his weapon and back-pedaled slowly away from the truck.

As hi-hats and cymbals crashed over the heavy beat, the rotter that had won out on the shoving contest had its skull split front to back by Jamie's black tomahawk. Zombies number two and three stepped to the open window and in quick succession suffered identical fates.

Seeing the last of the threats that had been blocking passage on 16 fall to the wayside, the four in the truck bed started gyrating to the music, doing their own versions of a happy dance that lasted until the song ended and Jamie popped her door and leaped over her kills.

Seeing no need to clear the road entirely of the corpses, the group made quick work of opening a path wide enough for the other vehicles to follow the F-650 through, then mounted their own rides.

***

Three minutes after leaving the killing fields behind, the four-truck caravan was stopped single file on 16 within spitting distance of the burned-out wagon which bore writing in the soot marring its rippled flanks.

Duncan was on the road first, shotgun in hand, his head moving on a swivel. As he neared the left side of the hulk and cleared its front where the grill had melted away, he could see the angular engine block under the hood, but little else. Inside the vehicle only the seat frames and oval metal steering wheel ring looked familiar.

After going down on his haunches, Duncan pushed his glasses up on his nose and read the passage written on the driver's side door. It had his attention at ADRIAN and held it through the entire rambling bit of prose that was equal parts warning and declaration.

After taking the time to read similar messages scrawled on the roof and opposite side of the car, Duncan scanned the hillock, fields and scrub flanking the road, then finally the road itself lengthwise, up and down, for as far as the binoculars could reach. Satisfied they were still alone, he radioed for the others to stay put and, with a cold lump forming in his gut, set out across the field to see what was attracting the carrion feeders.

"Want some company?" Daymon called.

Duncan trudged ahead a few more steps, the mud sucking at his boots. He felt a raindrop hit his cheek. One wet his nose. Then the back of his neck was being pelted.

Shielding his glasses from the fine mist beginning to fall in wispy sheets from the darkening sky, he turned and caught Daymon's eye. He shook his head and waved casually. "No reason for all of us to get soaked. Why don't you see to getting the trucks pulled around this heap."

Since his pants were still plenty damp, there was no argument on Daymon's part. Instead, he remained tight-lipped and threw Duncan a mock salute.

As Duncan continued on to the spot in the field where the birds were congregating, the sounds of doors opening and closing and engines starting up reached his ears. He heard four distinct motors idle down as transmissions were thrown into gear. Finally, coinciding with the carrion feeders' raucous retreat—which amounted to an initial explosion of feathers followed closely by throaty cries of displeasure as the birds took to flight—he was afforded his first glimpse of what had attracted them there.

Chapter 60

Cade smelled the pair of first turns well before he set eyes on them. As he passed along the wall with the shadows still rippling across its smooth white surface, he picked up a muffled sound that reminded him of an autumn wind caressing brittle corn stalks.

When he reached the nearby T and raised one hand, silently ordering the rest of the team to halt, not only did he get an eyeful of the sorry sights responsible for the gesticulating shadows and stench hanging heavy in the wide, sparsely illuminated corridor, but he also got an up-close earful of the subtle hissing escaping the edges of the silver tape wrapped around their craning heads.

Why someone would duct tape a man and a woman to rolling office chairs like some kind of a frat house prank and leave them in a deserted hallway instead of just putting them out of their misery was beyond him. Maybe out of sight, out of mind worked for some folks. For Cade, it did not.

The tape job holding the writhing zombies at bay began at their thighs and continued wending around both torso and chair until stopping abruptly just south of their sternums. For some reason whoever did this to them left their arms outside of the silver cocoon. They both had suffered defensive bite wounds to the arms, that much was clear as they reached and strained for Cade. Time and decomposition had taken their toll, leaving the wounds resembling purple-rimmed craters oozing viscous black blood. Whether alive or dead when they were taped to the chairs and left here to turn, it was no kind of humane way to go.

"Out of sight, out of mind," said Cross, giving voice to Cade's thoughts. "Whoever left them here to turn had probably been too close to them to do the right thing."

"Cunts is what they are … or were," Axe interjected. He unsheathed his knife, then looked a question at Cade.

Cade nodded, then watched the SAS man send the Zs to a merciful second death, starting with the waifish woman and finishing with the balding, middle-aged man.

After completing each grisly task Axe bowed his head and mouthed some kind of prayer. Cade had watched him do this in the DCC after putting down the Zs there and couldn't help but admire the man for the respect he obviously held for the former human beings.

"They're at peace now," Griff said, casting a pensive glance at his watch. "We have to get moving."

After consulting his Suunto and noting the time remaining until the charges rendered the computers in both sub levels useless, Cade picked up the trail of muddy boot prints and proceeded right at the T.

Halfway down the corridor, Cade said, "We're underneath the road right now." He slowed his gait for a second and looked up at the ceiling. "And I hope these tracks lead us to a stairwell."

The hollow clomp of boots on tile mixed with the rustling of fabric chased the team as they double-timed it down the long tunnel. They slowed at another T where Cade bellowed, "Engaging," and began squeezing off shots, the muzzle flash escaping his suppressor lighting the inside of the gloomy stairwell he was shooting into.

The action lasted a second, two at most, and then he was pushing past a previously jimmied steel door.

After pausing for a beat to inspect the dents and scratches on the backside of the door where someone had used a tool to breach it, he was scrabbling over the Z corpses sprawled out and leaking blood in the stairwell going up. He scaled the steps one at a time, his rubber boot soles muffling the sound of each footfall. At the right-hand bend before the landing, M4 tucked in tight, muzzle tracking with his gaze, he cut the corner, slowly, by degrees measured in inches and on the lookout for any movement or telltale glint of light off of glass or metal.

Finding the next upward run of stairs clear and seeing nothing but muddy footprints on the treads, he forged ahead, confident that the PLA soldiers had come this way.

"Watch for booby traps," Axe reminded, his voice bouncing off the cement walls. "We're hunting breathers now, not deaders."

No sooner had the word *deaders* spilled from his mouth than a Z lurched through yet another open door on the next landing, saw the team, and came spilling down the stairs, teeth snapping and its pale, twisted fingers kneading the air in front of its face.

Stepping aside just in time to avoid the thing's gnashing teeth, Cade shouted a warning that reached Cross and Griff's ears in time for them to sidestep the cartwheeling bag of bones. Axe, however, was not so fortunate. The Z hit him while in the heels-over-head aspect of its rotation and delivered one knee to the Brit's bump helmet and, on the follow-through, from behind and underneath no less, another solid, though wholly unintentional, flailing right uppercut to his testicles.

All at once a guttural *oomph* passed over Axe's lips and he doubled over, one gloved hand going to inventory the family jewels.

The finale to the surreal chain of events saw the Z ride the half-dozen remaining stairs face first and juddering like a malfunctioning Slinky. Shards of broken teeth *tinked* against the wall like so many miniature Craps dice as the twitching body tried to right itself.

"Bollocks," Axe exclaimed. "I don't have the energy to trek back down and give him a stick to the eye." True to his words, he shouldered the M4, sighted through the holographic optic, and put a single round into the back of the monster's already misshapen head.

"Way to break a tackle," quipped Griff.

"Nice shooting," Cross added sincerely.

Practicing a little shallow breathing to soothe the *boys*, Axe shook his head at the ribbing and took the remaining stairs two at a time.

Poking his head around the jamb, Cade looked to his right, where he saw five putrefying bodies laid out neatly before a head-high stack of cardboard boxes brimming with papers and blocking a pair of double doors. As if they had been placed there some time ago, everything wore a light coating of dust.

Looking left, Cade followed the boot prints with his eyes all the way to the end of the long, windowless hall. And like the passageway running under the street, the wall-mounted emergency lights spaced every few feet here cast orange-yellow cones of light on the walls and floor.

Without pause, Cade continued following the trail to the end of the hall where he brought the team to a complete halt a few feet from yet another T-junction.

"Axe, six," Cade said, again fishing the map from his pocket.

"Comms?" Griff asked.

"Negative," Cade answered. "This building is shielded, too." He went to a knee and smoothed the map out on a patch of tiled floor less muddy than the rest. After a second spent reorientating himself to due north with help from the Suunto, he rose and tucked the map away.

"This way." M4 shouldered, Cade padded to the T, one-eyed it around the corner, then peeled off to the left. Again with the clenched fist raised, he signaled the team to stop a dozen feet down the hall where they found themselves flanked by a pair of metal rollup doors big enough to accept a full-sized semi-truck. Beside the interior rollup to the team's left was a smaller, pass-card-controlled door. All three doors were windowless and bore the words AUTHORIZED PERSONNEL ONLY, the letters blaze red and scaled proportionately to fit the larger roller doors.

"These two lead into the DCC," said Griff, adjusting his pack which still contained a brick of C4 and the means to detonate it. "Shouldn't we go in and blow the CRAYs here, too?"

"Negative," Cade answered. "There's nothing we need on them."

"If my hunch is correct," Cross said, hooking a thumb at the rollup door behind them. "There should be a secure, fenced-in loading area beyond that door. It would make for a great exfil location."

Shaking his head, Cade said through clenched teeth, "These tracks are eventually going to end with the men who beat us here. I aim to kill them, take back what's rightfully ours, and complete this mission without losing anybody. If the map was correct, the door at the end of the hall should spit us out in another main level foyer near the building's northeast side."

"In view of the soccer pitch?" Cross said.

"Close," Cade replied. "When we infilled I saw a patch of open ground near an entrance. It *was* teeming with dead. If the Zs went to hunt the Screamers, I think we can exfil there."

"Copy that," Griff said. "Two minutes until the DCC annex ceases to exist."

***

Thirty seconds after conferring in the hall before the rollup doors, Cade and the team were standing before yet another windowless door. Like the others they'd encountered since leaving Sub Floor 3, the door had been breached and stood wide open to the east entry where the NSA director and other high-level ninth-floor workers came and went. The setup here was much the same as the main entry, only on a smaller scale. There were two elevators left of the access door, not four. Instead of six security turnstiles flanked by bulletproof glass and various sniffers and metal detectors, there were three, each with its own pass-card reader. Next to the narrow turnstiles was a swinging, polished metal gate wide enough to accommodate wheelchairs and wheeled mobility carts. And lying lengthwise on the floor, its pustule-ridden arms wedging the swinging gate in its open position, was a headshot and trampled zombie corpse. Which had befallen it first, Cade couldn't tell.

The walls were paneled in rich, dark wood polished to a high shine, and the tile floors were pale, tumbled travertine home to too many dead bodies to count. Veins of semi-dried blood snaked out from under some of the corpses. A mosaic of muddy footprints painted the floor around the fallen.

With barely ninety seconds to go until the inevitable subterranean explosion, Cade wove a serpentine path toward the entry. With the footfalls of the team close on his six banging off the floor and walls and ceiling, he crabbed over the flattened Z and through the brushed-metal pass-through. On the run and picking up his pace, he altered course from the glass revolving door to his fore and charged toward the set of double doors that looked to have recently had the glass machine gunned out of their chromed frames.

Shards of green-hued glass crunched and popped underfoot as he passed from inside to outside. Finding himself standing underneath what looked to be a poured cement portico, the pavement underfoot muddy and rife with freshly culled Z corpses, he hailed Jedi One-One on the comms intent on asking for an immediate extraction.

Nothing.

He tried raising the TOC at Schriever.

Still no response. All he heard was the dark vacuum of dead air. And to his left, way off in the distance, the muted wail of the Screamers, hopefully still doing their job.

Moving from under the portico, he tried Ari again and let his gaze wander off to his left, where he saw a trampled expanse of what was once lawn. It was now mud-blanketed with dozens of twice-dead Zs. Then, just as Ari responded to his second call, he saw reflected in the mirrored glass at ground-level something that may just redeem his failed mission.

"Cross," Cade said, motioning the taller operator forward. "Watch our six."

As Cross turned and trained his MP7 on the executive personnel entrance, Cade sent Griff off to an equally muddy area of ground beside the extended part of the building in order to cover their flanks to the east and south.

Saving the best for last, he caught Axe's eye. Motioning to the northwest corner of the glass cube rising above them, he said, "I want you to go see how the undead *football* match is going. Maybe get us a score if you can."

Cracking a little half-smile, Axe nodded and was off and running, his M4 trained on the distant, blind corner.

Feeling, more so than hearing, the beat of the Ghost Hawk's noise-defeating rotors punishing the air ahead of its approach, Cade sprinted toward the camouflage-clad corpse and overturned dirt bike that had drawn his attention to the lee side of the muddy knoll abutting the main NSA building.

Chapter 61

Five miles northwest of the zombie-corpse roadblock and burned-out wagon, Duncan began to feel small pangs of regret for a couple of things. First, acting against a strong gut feeling, he'd shrugged off what he saw in the field—even going so far as to only tell Daymon and Lev the true extent of the barbarity the dead man had faced in his final moments. Second, letting his feelings for Glenda, and to a lesser extent, Oliver, dictate his next move, he had told the others that the man in the field had been murdered—*shot in the head and stripped of his clothes*–to be exact. It was a half-truth at best. Or if splitting hairs wasn't your thing, a lie by omission.

Duncan couldn't lie to himself on this one. Every moral fiber in his body was telling him the latter was the truth in this matter. When to come clean to the others was the nut that needed cracking.

Thankfully he had a few more miles before the point of no return to gather the rest and tell them about what he had seen. What he knew based on the sheet of paper found stuffed in the corpse's gaping mouth. And what he suspected they would find if and when they caught up with Oliver's captors, who seemed to have their hands in all kinds of trouble up and down the Bear River Range.

On the passenger side of the Dodge, Tran had been sitting in silence for the duration, content to watch the range level out to the north, all the while the gray smudge of another rain band making its way south by east towards them loomed larger by the minute.

Finally, after yet another mile had gone by with the man driving the rig still as quiet, and seemingly inanimate as the radio on the seat between them, Tran cleared his throat and asked Duncan what was on his mind.

The *what* on Duncan's mind, though it hadn't been left to reanimate, was far worse of a spectacle and warning than the crucified rotter could ever be. In fact, what had been done to this man was worse than anything he'd seen done to a man during his time in Vietnam. It was much worse than seeing a couple of kids burn to death strapped into a Volkswagen. And though he had no idea what could trump it, he was sure, given time, that some madman out there in the vast wasteland America had become would do it in spades.

How a man could bleed another man slowly and then strip the flesh from the bones of his still-warm body was incomprehensible to Duncan. Even the Viet Cong hadn't been that ruthless—they usually desecrated American soldiers after they had been shot dead. And they weren't cannibals, that was for damn sure.

Proof that the man had been bled slowly came in the shape of a bloody mud angel. Wide arcing wings made by the flailing arms of a person being forcibly held down. Two knees on the shoulders, no doubt. And mud where the corpse's denuded leg bones had been positioned spoke of at least one accomplice who had helped to hold the bucking man down as the lower extremities responsible for the disturbance were relieved of their flesh. None too successfully, nonetheless, judging by the trenches worn into the muck by the doomed man's losing battle to get free.

The discarded clothes—a pair of worn blue jeans and black microfiber long-sleeved shirt—had sopped up some of the blood. However, the ground had failed to accept the rest, leaving a man-shaped puddle of viscous crimson liquid an inch deep.

Speaking slowly while enunciating every syllable, the usually demure Tran repeated his question. "What's on your mind?"

Duncan started visibly, which caused the truck to veer the better part of a foot toward the right shoulder.

The radio on the seat came alive with Daymon's voice. "Looks like you hit the rumble stripes just now. Back to hitting the Jack Daniel's, Old Man?"

I wish, thought Duncan. Tightening his grip on the wheel, he looked sidelong at Tran. "*Nothing* is on my mind," he lied.

"You've been quiet," Tran added. "Real quiet. Ten minutes of dead silence … at least."

"Be grateful I'm not Phillip," Duncan shot back. Quickly realizing how callous that sounded, he signed himself out of the respect he held for the dead motor mouth.

Tran shook his head and returned his attention to the road.

Still wrestling with his newly created moral dilemma, Duncan scooped up the radio and told Daymon where he could stick that kind of discouraging talk—even if the other man did consider ribbing him about his former propensity for the drink little more than jocular, ball-busting banter.

"It's not gonna happen," Duncan declared. "Me and Jack aren't lovers no more." He chuckled at his clunky choice of words. "Hell, we're not even friends," he finished, all of it half-truth. The reality though, as of late he'd been thinking more and more about how sweet the few hours of oblivion one square, clear bottle of Old No. 7 could afford him. But that thought was fleeting. Because as Glenda had taught him to do when euphoric recall began to morph into what sounded like a good idea to a garden variety drunk like him, he *played the tape forward.* And nothing that came up on that movie reel in his mind when he did so ever ended well. Not. One. Single. Time.

"I've been thinking," Duncan finally admitted after another half-mile of silent contemplation, "that I need to come clean with you and the others … right now." He tapped his brakes to warn Daymon, who'd been running the Chevy tight to his bumper ever since leaving behind the burned-out car and dirt knoll that they all suspected would be the perfect place to spring the ambush that, thankfully, had never materialized.

Parked on the shoulder, warning flashers blinking a cadence, Duncan spoke slowly and clearly into the two-way radio and came clean about the corpse in the field.

"What do you mean he had been rendered clean to the bone?" Taryn asked over the open channel.

"Butchered for his meat. We're not only dealing with murderers … I'd be willing to bet the farm that they're cannibals, too."

This time it was Daymon doing the questioning. "You sure of that?" he said. "How do you know the birds didn't pick him clean? I've seen what they can do to a corpse if you give them a few days."

"They were still working on the meat between the joints. Even had most of his hands and feet taken apart. Lots of little bones go into making those work," Duncan said. "But last I checked, birds don't use tools."

"What are you trying to tell us?" Jamie asked from her perch in the F-650 three vehicles back.

"There were marks on the bones made by something sharp and serrated."

In the Dodge, no stranger to field dressing a deer, Tran leaned forward to get Duncan's attention. "Like traces a boning knife would leave behind?"

"That's more engaged in conversation than I've seen you in two months … combined."

Under Tran's watchful eye, Duncan pulled the crumpled sheet of lined paper from his pocket. He carefully unfolded it, being mindful not to tear it where it was still damp and creased. Keying the radio, he announced to everyone listening what he was about to do. Stressing where he had found the note, lest some of the gang hadn't heard him the first time, and making clear the words were not his, he read the thing verbatim, never pausing along the way.

"We stole and drove and ended up caught. It seemed smart at first, but in the end it was not. And for your sins, nobody ever wins, and Nancy paid the ultimate price. Most of it naughty, none of it nice. In the end, Sid, you failed us as a friend." Finished and feeling uncomfortable in more ways than one, he sighed audibly.

"Far from Rudyard Kipling," Jamie commented.

"It was signed 'The sisterhood of CB4,'" Duncan said, before quickly insisting on forging ahead before anybody read into the words any further. And much to his surprise, Daymon was on board at once, which had the effect of instantly bringing the others into the *go ahead* column. But there was one catch: Lev insisted they radio the compound and see if Brook could get on the satellite phone and ask Dregan to bring some backup north before they moved on.

"I propose a compromise," Duncan said. "If Dregan agrees to Brook's overture"—which Duncan was certain he would, blood oath and all—"I want to move as close to the lake as possible without giving ourselves away. Looks like that storm is heading right for us. Figure it'll mask our approach. Let us get close enough to see what side of the lake they've put down roots."

"Why not wait here until we know for sure what we're working with?" Jamie asked.

Duncan thumbed the Talk button. "Because I want to have a plan in place when we do meet up with Dregan and his men," he explained. "It's what Cade would advocate. If we get close enough, we can watch them and study their movements."

"*If* their AO really is Bear Lake," Lev stated over the open channel.

In the Dodge, brow arched, Tran mouthed, "AO?"

"We only have the bleeder's matchbook to go on. Better than nothing. However, if Bear Lake isn't their"—he matched Tran's gaze—"area of operation … we'll know almost immediately and can call Dregan off."

Tran nodded and broke eye contact.

"Good call," Daymon said. "That way we won't have to share any of the food and supplies we find with them."

"Calling Brook now," Duncan said. "Back in a moment."

Already one step ahead, Tran handed over the long range radio. Giving voice to the look that accompanied the radio, Duncan said, "I hope we're not out of range."

"I've been keeping track of the miles," Tran said. "I think as the crow flies we may be by a dozen miles or more."

"Damn it all," Duncan spat. "And I don't have a satellite phone. Better add one to my shopping list." Shaking his head, he rolled up the volume and thumbed Talk.

Nothing.

He tried again and released the Talk key, listening hard for anything coming through the static.

Five seconds passed.

Another sign, the first three feet of its white-painted post hidden from view by a mound of corpses, blipped by on the right. As if the corpses weren't warning enough, TURN BACK NOW was spray-painted over the UDOT-supplied information.

Another ten seconds ticked into the past and still no reply came from the Eden compound.

Just as Duncan was about to give up and curse Cade's nemesis Mr. Murphy up one wall and down the other, a wizened voice usurped the white noise. "Ray Thagon here."

Hearing the familiar gravelly intonation spring from the tiny speaker instantly started the wheels in Duncan's mind to grind out a workaround to their lack-of-satellite-phone dilemma. He took a moment to lay out his plan to Ray and then waited for an answer.

More white noise.

Conferring with the boss, thought Duncan, as a grin parted his lips. Lately, Glenda had taken to wearing the pants on occasion, and that wasn't all bad.

"You there?"

"I hear ya loud and clear, Ray."

"Helen says her Con Edison operator days are over, but she's agreed to go ahead and help out with this party line idea of yours."

***

Ten minutes after setting in motion the series of back-and-forth satellite phone and long range CB radio calls, Duncan scooped up the two-way radio and informed the rest of the group following in the three vehicles the location of the agreed-upon rendezvous point. In his side mirror he saw the headlights on all three trucks flash in acknowledgement. A moment later Daymon's strained voice broke the silence in the cab. "How is Brook?"

"I didn't talk directly to her, Ray and Dregan did," answered Duncan.

"Did they mention her?"

"Neither one of them said a thing. So I assume she didn't tell them about her *condition*."

"And you didn't?" shot Daymon.

"Not my place," Duncan replied. "And I doubt if *she* did. Hard to see Dregan honoring his lifetime pledge of allegiance to her if there was an outside chance the Omega antiserum might turn on his son's immune system and finish what that roaming rotter's bite started."

The interior of the Dodge was morgue silent for a full minute.

"I see your point," Daymon finally admitted. "When we get to the rendezvous, I'm the one going forward on foot to recon the situation."

"I'm coming, too," Lev said over the open channel. "Be just like old times. You and me and a lake."

"I'm going, too," Tran said, his voice rising over the banter coming from the radio.

"You're both big boys, suit yourselves," Duncan said, acknowledging Lev and Daymon simultaneously. He set the radio aside and looked sidelong at Tran, an unspoken question lingering on his lips.

"I'm a big boy, too," Tran said. "It's about time I started to learn what it's really like out here. So I can do more than just garden and cook and occasionally ride shotgun feeling like a trapped mime."

A shield-shaped State Route sign with **ADRIAN** spray-painted on it in red passed by outside Tran's window.

Duncan drew a deep breath and swung his eyes forward, fixing his gaze on the angry horizontal scar passing for sky. The distant Wasatch were obscured, as was most everything above treetop level for as far as he could see.

Finally, as he began to brake and pull onto the gravel lot surrounding a rundown drive-in called *Merlin's*, he asked Tran in a funereal voice, "Have you killed a man?"

"Two," Tran admitted. "Burned one of them alive, I think. The other I killed indirectly by letting the demons into a house the two human animals had broken into."

Gravel crunched under the tires as Duncan applied the brakes.

"These the guys who did the stuff to Heidi?" he asked, wheeling around the sign post and aiming the Dodge for the drive-in's covered parking.

Tran nodded.

"And they hurt you, too?"

Again with the subtle nod.

"Well I'll be dipped in shit," Duncan said gleefully, his trademark cackle punctuating his statement. "Never had you pegged as a cold-blooded killer."

"They earned it."

"And you delivered, Tran, my man. You delivered them to where they needed deliverin' … in spades."

Tran said nothing.

Duncan asked, "Do you have a two-way radio?"

"I'm quiet," answered Tran, "not stupid."

Duncan reached over and punched the glove box open. "In there … nine-millimeter Beretta. Keeping your finger away from the trigger, I want you to pull it out. And the two mags."

Tran plucked the three items out and laid them on the seat. There was a great deal of respect conveyed by the way the slight Asian handled the weapon. He had instinctively practiced proper muzzle discipline, keeping the semi-automatic pistol pointed away from him and Duncan as he set it down gingerly.

Very good, thought Duncan as he began detailing the weapon's particulars: Its rate of fire. Magazine capacity. How the double-action operated. Finished, he stilled the Dodge's engine. "There will be a test in a minute," he informed Tran.

"This is the place?" Lev asked, his voice coming out of the speaker a little garbled.

Duncan plucked the Motorola off the seat and said into it, "This is where Dregan insisted we meet him."

"What now?" asked Wilson, his pale, freckle-addled face a yard away and staring through the Raptor's open passenger window as Taryn brought the bigger rig to a slow, smooth stop underneath the drive-in's canted roof.

"You and Pixie there arm yourselves and take up positions on either end of this little oasis while I take a look inside," Duncan answered.

Still staring down at the Beretta, Tran said, "May I come?"

"Your job is to watch the Kids' six. If you see anything they don't, radio them at once." He reached into the center console and came out with a black nylon holster. "It's not made for that weapon, but it'll do in a pinch." He handed it to Tran, then turned to open his door.

Fingers wrapping around the pistol's knurled grip, Tran nodded and sat up straight.

The big Ford and smaller Chevy slid onto the lot one right after the other and parked in the two spaces left of the Raptor. In no time Duncan was entering the drive-in alone, while Lev, Jamie, Daymon, and Foley were fanning out around the building perimeter on the lookout for any rotters drawn around by the noisy engines.

***

Five minutes after pulling into the deserted parking lot, the four trucks were parked side-by-side under cover and Taryn and Jamie were sitting inside on vinyl stools before a long white counter. As if Duncan had not done a thorough enough job initially, Foley was traipsing through the restaurant and checking every nook and cranny for anything of use.

After having cleared the thoroughly looted building and put down the pair of Zs someone had locked inside the rank-smelling walk-in cooler, Duncan was back in his Dodge and dividing his attention between the state route south of them, and the trio not twenty feet to his fore sitting inside the drive-in's gloomy, but dry confines.

As the rain began pelting the windshield with soft little patters, Wilson returned from his latest recon around the diamond-shaped block Merlin's drive-in sat upon. "The perimeter is rotter-free. What do we do now?" he asked, pulling his parka hood over his boonie hat.

"Now. We. Wait," answered Duncan, kicking the wipers on and delivering the dirty windshield a five-second spritz of cleaner which allowed him to see Daymon, Lev, and Tran, who were by now distant specks on the state route heading north to Bear Lake.

Chapter 62

Though he didn't let it show as he loped from the PLA soldier's body toward the settling helo, Cade was seething inside. Rumbling the ground under his boots, the charges had gone off in the DCC as planned, but the real damage had already been done. The PLA Special Forces team that had beat them to the DCC had downloaded the cell tower ping data that could effectively lead them to the doorsteps of every surviving essential member of the United States government from the Joint Chiefs of Staff to the Supreme Court Justices on down to low-level cabinet officials, many of whom were thought to still be holed up in underground bunkers scattered about the country.

Ignoring Skipper's offered hand, Cade waited until Griff and Cross boarded and moved out of his way, then tossed his ruck in behind them and climbed aboard. After taking a spot on the starboard side opposite Griff and Cross, he uncoupled the jack from his personal comms set, plugged into the shipwide net, and was taken aback when he heard none of the usual quips or cracks being spouted by Ari or Haynes. Instead there was a heavy silence. No static. No chatter from the other members of the Jedi flight. He was alone with his own thoughts for a few long seconds.

Having been sprinting across the churned-up sod from the opposite direction as Cade, Axe tossed his ruck through the open door, turned nonchalantly toward the NSA building's far corner from whence he came, and flipped a pair of upthrust middle fingers at the two dozen Zs staggering in his direction.

"There's more of the cunts where those came from," he said, scooting clear of the closing door.

"Might be a good idea to get this bird in the air," said Skipper, panning the minigun's lethal end toward the Zs.

In his headset Cade heard a burst of static. A tick later a female airman at Schriever was relaying a set of waypoints to Ari and instantly Cade was grateful it wasn't Nash herself delivering them. As it stood, the petite major was high on his shit list for shutting down his request that they follow what he felt was still a warm trail. After all, the PLA soldier's liver still retained some warmth. A quick slice with the Gerber and two bare fingers thrust deeply into the incision had told him so. That she was letting the rest of the enemy team abscond with terabytes of sensitive information was unconscionable.

Feeling the Ghost Hawk going light on its landing gear, he craned and stole a final look at the PLA soldier, spread-eagled on the muddy ground next to his dirt bike, the damage done by the single coup de grace gunshot to the forehead impossible to miss. As were the hundreds of spent brass shell casings and the hundred or so twice-dead zombies the PLA team fought their way through to get to their rides after their successful foray inside.

Good thing his Delta team had the Screamers to deploy, Cade thought, seeing the PLA soldier's body start to spin, an optical illusion created as the helicopter rose off the ground and corkscrewed a quick one-eighty, the rotation stopping only when Jedi One-One was facing opposite the direction it had arrived.

In the next instant Cade felt the Ghost Hawk nose down and pick up speed.

Off the starboard-side, her stars and bars whipped into a wild frenzy by the helo's down blast, Old Glory stood silent witness to Fort Meade's losing battle against time, the elements, and the infected masses.

After feeling the slight bump of the landing gear snugging home underfoot, Cade swept his gaze around Jedi One-One's cabin.

Strapped into the seat near the still-deployed starboard minigun, Skipper was his usual silent, stoic self, unsmiling under the flight helmet and tinted visor.

Directly across the helo from Cade, his helmeted head and back pressed firmly against the inner bulkhead, Griff was shooting a wide-eyed *what the fuck* look his way.

Knowing the emotion was a direct result of the possibility of the mission's redemption suddenly being yanked from underneath them, Cade mouthed, "Orders," and shook his head sympathetically.

Cross, on the other hand, was already snugged into the seat next to Griff and smiling as he plugged his comms set into the shipwide net. *Not a care in the world,* thought Cade as he regarded Axe, who was holding his carbine between his knees and looking groundward while the helicopter buzzed overtop the hundreds of light standards bristling from Fort Meade's acres of parking lots.

"Who's winning the match?" Cade asked, his eyes picking up the movement of hundreds of Zs clustered near the east end of the nearest lot.

"Fucking Manchester, looks like," Axe replied.

His mood lightening up just a bit, Cade asked Ari what was so pressing that they couldn't search for the freshly churned tire tracks he was sure would lead them to the departed PLA motorcycles.

"Wait one," Ari said. "Bringing footage up on the flat-panel."

While Cade waited for the screen to light up, he shifted his gaze outside and watched the inbound pair of Stealth Chinooks bob subtly as they bled speed and formed up off of Jedi One-One's starboard-side.

"Ten mikes out," Ari said over the shipwide comms. "Feast your eyes on the boob tube, gentlemen. The *brrrt* show is about to begin."

Cade asked, "Is the footage real time?"

"Taken within the hour," Ari replied.

As the static, color image splashed onscreen, Cade settled in for the show. And what a show it was. With the other operators offering up their personal accounts of the venerable A-10 Thunderbolt II and its propensity to make life hell for even the most determined of enemy combatants, all eyes in the cabin were witness to the utter destruction wrought upon an armored column by just three of the stout, heavily armored aircraft. With its twin tail-mounted turbofans, near straight knife-edged wings, and six barreled cannon protruding from under its rounded snout, the Warthog—as it was so affectionately named because of its hard to love lines—more than lived up to its mammalian namesake both in ferocity and hardiness.

The column was taken completely by surprise, Cade decided as soon as the image started to move. A classic aerial ambush, the type of which the Hog was designed to spring on Soviet armor storming Germany's Fulda Gap. Nearly two-thirds of the vehicles were on fire in seconds, the ammunition in their magazines cooking off and sending tell-tale puffs of gray smoke into the air.

"They didn't have much of a lead over the horde following them," Cross noted as soldiers poured from one of the troop transports and took up defensive positions flanking it. "No way they could have held off the monsters *and* engaged the Hogs effectively." He looked to Cade. "I'm sure it's an effin feeding frenzy down there by now."

"It wasn't pretty," Ari commented. "Nash indicated as much."

Cade was still watching the monsters converging on the stalled convoy when the A-10s made another gun run from the opposite direction. There was no return fire. No spiraling white contrail indicating MANPADS had been deployed by the PLA troops. No winking flashes from muzzles throwing lead skyward. All of the small arms were being discharged at the approaching Zs.

It was a turkey shoot, and thankfully the image froze with the surviving vehicles frantically jockeying about on the road in a vain attempt to escape the carnage.

"Did any vehicles escape?" Cade asked.

"Negative," Ari answered.

"Personnel?"

"Doubtful," Ari said. "We will have eyes on in five mikes."

With a cold ball forming in his gut, Cade cinched his harness tighter. Expecting to again see the tell-tale puff of smoke and evasive maneuvers to follow, he cast his gaze out his window and waited.

Pray for the best, prepare for the worst, crossed his mind as the helo banked sharply and dove for the deck.

Chapter 63

As a former high school long distance runner, Daymon's first inclination was to run the entire mile-plus to the lake's edge. However, Lev had quickly shot down that idea. As a former soldier in the United States Army, Lev pointed out that the easiest way to draw attention to one's self—save for shooting indiscriminately into the air—was to go running headlong into enemy territory.

So with the rain letting up the three kept to the road and walked at a brisk pace, stopping every now and again to listen for approaching vehicles and sniff the air for the unmistakable stench that always preceded an appearance by the living dead.

Roughly a quarter of a mile from the lake, the peaked roofs of a number of houses built on shoreline property came into view. Fronted by a picket of bare trees, the colorful two- and three-story homes stood out in stark contrast to the unusually bright blue waters stretching for as far as the eye could see beyond them.

Stopping to take a pull from a bottle of water, Daymon said, "If I remember correctly, the lake is almost twenty miles long south to north and seven or eight wide at the center."

"It straddles the Idaho and Utah border, doesn't it?" Lev asked.

Daymon passed the water to Tran, then gestured to their left. "The lake is bisected almost equally. The towns of Fish Haven and Saint Charles are north of the border in Idaho. Garden City is a few miles west of us just south of the border."

Lev asked, "What's on the lake's east side?"

"Mostly campgrounds and places to boat and fish," Daymon said, as he took the water back from Tran and resumed walking the road. "Rendezvous Beach is real close. Took a couple of girls camping there senior year summer. Got lucky with both of them." He passed the half-empty bottle and cap to Lev.

Tran slowed his gait and, without saying a word, veered off across the two-lane toward the far shoulder.

Lev regarded Tran briefly, then shifted his attention to Daymon. "*Rendezvous Beach*, huh? You got lucky with *two* girls on the same trip as a *senior* in high school?"

Daymon's dreads bobbed as he shook his head. "I've never been *that* lucky," he conceded, a smile breaking out. "It was two *different* camping trips."

"Still…" Lev tipped the bottle and drank it dry. He twisted the cap on and stowed the empty in a cargo pocket.

"Daymon. Lev," Tran called, motioning urgently for them to cross the road.

The two men hustled to where he was crouched by the tall grass on the other side of the ditch.

Flanking Tran on the left, Daymon followed the shorter man's gaze across the scrub toward the hills rising up on Bear Lake's west flank. "What?" he whispered.

"Do you hear that?"

Lev cocked his head and listened hard.

Daymon tucked a stray dread behind his ear and stood motionless, his face screwed up in concentration. After a couple of beats he said, "You're hearing things, Tran."

A tick later there was a low rumble of thunder and the westerly breeze dropped off.

Hearing a steady thunking sound, like something drumming on wood far off in the distance, Lev said, "Yeah, I hear it now. Sounds like a *woodpecker*."

Still staring across the scrub-covered plain, Tran said, "That's no woodpecker. It's a machine."

"He's right," Daymon said. "Someone's working a log splitter. I could be wrong, but I think the sound is coming from the southwest shore. Maybe even the campground at Rendezvous Beach. With fuel getting harder to come by, I'd bet my left nut whoever is working that splitter is staying nearby. Doesn't make sense to burn fuel to go out and get fuel. Lugging it back in a truck over a long distance just doesn't add up."

Lev walked to the centerline and looked the road up and down. Returning his gaze north, he said, "I concur. Let's get to one of those houses by the lake. One, it'll get us out of the coming rain. Two, we may be able to see what's making that racket."

"What then?" Tran asked, all of this new to him.

Lev started walking north at a brisk pace. "If we're able to see Rendezvous Beach and a couple of miles or so of each shore south to north from one of those houses, perfect. We check in with Duncan and squat there for awhile."

"If the dirtbags that took Oliver are anywhere near here," added Daymon. "We should know as soon as we set eyes on some of the doors."

Lev looked at Daymon. "The chalk marks?"

Daymon nodded. "Stands to reason these would be the first houses they stripped of food and supplies."

Tran started off jogging, then passed Lev and Daymon at a near sprint. "We run," he stated forcefully in passing. "They can't hear anything over that machine."

Daymon looked to Lev. "Man has a point."

Without another word, Lev and Daymon broke into a slow, steady jog and eventually formed up abreast of Tran.

***

A handful of minutes after Tran had enacted his executive decision, the trio were within spitting distance of the row of lakeside houses and crouched low in the tall grass crowding the base of a roadside sign. ADRIAN VILLE - TRESPASSERS WILL BE SHOT ON SIGHT was scrawled in black spray-paint over the names of the nearby towns and driving distances to get to them.

Motioning toward the sign, Daymon said, "Doesn't get any clearer than that."

"Crystal," said Lev. He parted the grass with his carbine's barrel and regarded the homes across the two-lane. The nearest on their left was a two-story Tudor-style affair painted in two different shades of gray. Like the other three homes to its right, the driveway was empty. And on all of the houses, shadows crowded the few upstairs windows whose curtains had been left open. Clearly Adrian hadn't gotten his *Ville's* power grid back up and running.

Of the three houses right of the Tudor, two were nearly identical Craftsman-style, both painted in muted hues of brown. Fire had partially consumed house number four on the far right, reducing it to little more than charred timbers crisscrossing a blackened cement pad.

"They *all* look deserted to me," Daymon stated.

"I concur," answered Lev.

There was a ripple of soft pops as Daymon cracked all of the vertebra in his back. "What do you think, Tran?" he asked, finishing off his DIY chiropractic treatment by wrenching his neck around, first left, then right.

Tran looked to Daymon, then regarded the three intact dwellings for a tick.

"*Well* ... which one floats your boat?" Daymon pressed.

After subjecting the houses to a mental game of *eeny, meeny, miny, moe*, Tran said, "The middle one."

Daymon slipped his pistol from its holster. Checked the chamber for the gleam of brass. Satisfied, he returned his gaze to Tran. "Why the middle one?"

"Gut feeling," Tran said, smiling inwardly.

Lev shrugged. "Good enough for me."

One at a time, with Daymon in the lead and Lev bringing up the rear, the three men crossed the two-lane running in a low-crouch. Once on the other side, Lev paused on the shoulder and scanned the length of the road in both directions. Seeing nothing to indicate that they had been spotted by anything or anybody—

dead or alive—he told Tran and Daymon to start out ahead of him. After giving the pair a two-second lead, he kept his gaze locked in the direction of Rendezvous Beach. Casting glances over both shoulders, he rose and crossed the expanse of grass providing a buffer between the homes and stretch of blacktop looping behind them.

Catching the others near a low hedge bordering the driveway of the light-tan two-story Craftsman, Lev took a knee and regarded Daymon.

"We get across without being spotted?"

Lev nodded. "The hammering never stopped."

"You sure?" Daymon pressed. "If something's picked up our scent—"

"You better stuff that claustrophobia talk," Lev interrupted. "We are *not* going to get trapped in the attic in this fucking house."

Daymon said nothing.

"Follow me," Lev said. Rising into a low crouch, he made his way up the driveway to the tan Craftsman's garage and banged a fist on the multi-panel door. It was a double-wide roll-up number painted in a brown two-tone scheme and it rattled like hell in its tracks each time he struck it.

They all cocked an ear and listened hard for a long ten-count.

"Nothing moving in there," Lev said.

"This isn't Hanna," Daymon said aloud to himself. Then, without consulting either Lev or Tran, he rose and crept around the left side of the house.

During the entire exchange between Daymon and Lev, Tran had been panning his head back and forth. Now he had Duncan's spare Beretta held in a two-handed grip and his eyes fixed on Lev. "Should we follow?" he asked politely.

Grimacing, Lev pushed the muzzle aside and said, "Holster that thing."

Tran did as he was asked without complaining.

After taking a minute to contemplate Daymon's behavior, Lev finally spoke up. "We'll wait here," he said. "Daymon needs time to himself … to work through some *things*."

Just then Daymon returned from his clockwise recon of the property. "*Things* are worked through," he said, eyeing Lev. "There's a ground-level slider around back but it's locked and has a bar in the track shoring it up. The front entry"—he hooked a thumb behind him—"has a metal storm door that's locked up tight. I banged and waited and didn't hear any movement inside. Which makes sense, because there's another one of those white Xs drawn on the jamb beside the storm door."

"That's good news," said Lev, just as the sky opened up and big fat drops began slapping the ground all around them. "Means the place has been cleared of rotters already."

"Or booby trapped like the others," Tran said quietly. "I can fit through this." He pointed out the doggy door inset into one of the garage's lower panels. Making the door easy to overlook unless you were right on top of it, the plastic frame and flap were nearly the same light brown as the rectangular panel in which it was installed. Tran lifted the vinyl flap to reveal a plywood sheet blocking the entry from the inside.

"You're not going in that way," Daymon said. "Unless, that is, whoever put the board there decided to half-ass it." He gently swept Tran and Lev aside with his long right arm and backed away from the garage door a half-dozen feet. Imitating a place kicker lining up a game-winning field goal, he squared up with the doggy door, took one and a half steps to his left, and then stuck his index finger toward the sky as if testing the wind direction.

"Hut, hut … hike," said Lev, playing along.

Tran watched with a confused look on his face as Daymon performed a theatrical forward stutter step a tick before driving a powerful wide-arcing kick toward the door.

There was an explosive bang as his boot struck the plywood shoring the dog door. Immediately following the loud report, there was a clatter of something skittering across the cement floor inside the garage.

"Yep, they half-assed it," Lev said. "Nice form, Daymon."

Daymon smiled and made a show of knocking the imaginary dust from his hands. Then he lifted the flap and nodded to Tran. "All yours, Fido."

***

By the time Daymon and Lev made their way around to the front door, Tran had been on the inside for less than thirty seconds. When the interior door sucked inward, which in turn caused the outer storm door to rattle in its frame, the newly minted cat burglar had been gone for two minutes, tops.

After working the lock, Tran pushed the storm door out ahead of him and stepped aside to let Daymon and Lev pass.

Squinting against the flat light spilling in through the north-facing floor-to-ceiling windows, Daymon padded a few paces beyond the foyer and looked around the empty great room.

"Nothing dead in here?" he asked, his chest tight and mind threatening to take him back to Hanna.

Tran shook his head. "There are no demons inside," he stated confidently.

Daymon said, "Well, well, maybe our luck is changing."

There was a lull in the wind and for few beats Lev's *woodpecker* was back, the banging now crisp and clear and coming over the lake from somewhere west of the house.

M4 held at low ready, Lev padded around Daymon and Tran and moved deeper into the unfurnished house. Upon hearing Daymon's optimistic talk, he called over his shoulder, "My money is on Mr. Murphy making an appearance before nightfall."

"You and Cade and your damn Army superstitions," Daymon said, his voice echoing off the bare walls and floors. "I prefer to call it *bad luck*. And if it wasn't for that, I'd have no luck at all."

"We find Oliver alive," replied Lev, "I'll change my mind. Until then, color me pessimistic."

Daymon looked across the wide-open floor, past Lev and out the ground-level slider. The sky to the north was darker than ever and the lake's surface was wind-churned and resembled the

Pacific more so than the placid, brilliant blue lake he remembered. Down by the shore a lone, waterlogged-looking zombie was doddering toward the noisy machine.

Lev nudged a box full of dishes with his boot. "Looks like the owners were either moving in or moving out before the *event*."

Head tilted slightly, Tran shot Lev a questioning glance.

"The *event*," Lev said. "The dead rising. People eating other people. Martial Law."

Tran nodded an acknowledgement and headed for the stairs leading up to the second level.

As Tran disappeared from view, Daymon retraced his steps across the living room and slipped into the garage through the door off the foyer.

Lev had been alone for but a handful of seconds and was roaming the kitchen when Daymon called for him.

"Coming," he said, crossing the room. Pausing before the threshold to the garage, he wasn't at all surprised to see that it was half-full of boxes with the names of all the usual rooms in a house labeled on their sides in neat block letters. He descended the single stair and crabbed between the boxes until he came upon Daymon surrounded by shipping peanuts and elbows deep in a steamer-trunk-sized box marked **Pacific City Beach House.**

"What'd you find, someone's collection of priceless glass floats?"

"Better than that," Daymon replied, pulling a white cylindrical object from the box and inadvertently adding more of the green Styrofoam squiggly things to the growing pile on the floor.

"What is it?"

"It's a spotting scope. I'd guess its previous owners used it for eyeballing ships off whatever coast Pacific City is on."

"Or ogling bathing beauties from afar," Lev proffered, flashing a sly grin.

"Or," Daymon said, excited at the prospect of not having to venture out into the passing squall, "covertly ogling the first two or three miles of shoreline in either direction."

"I doubt if it has the reach in this weather."

Tran showed up in the doorway. "There's a perfect spot for it in the master suite upstairs. Let's set it up."

"With unobstructed views to the west, north, and east?" asked Lev.

Tran nodded.

Relieving Daymon of one end of the three-foot-long scope, Lev said, "Good job, Tran. As a prize you get to grab the tripod and show us the way."

***

With the spotting scope set up behind a sliding glass door in the master bedroom that featured a stunning two-hundred-seventy-degree view of the lake, Daymon started his visual recon beginning with Rendezvous Beach. Obviously once home to hundreds—if not thousands—of people fleeing urban population centers during the first days of the outbreak, the sandy beach and treed campgrounds now held only the weather-beaten remnants of the greatest human diaspora known to modern man. Colorful tents and tarps, all flattened by the recent freak snowstorm, dotted nearly every square inch of the trio of strung-together campgrounds.

Rising up from the sea of wind-whipped technicolor fabric were dozens of latrines, one for each group of tent sites, if he remembered correctly. And even more plentiful than the small, boxy johns were the trees planted among the sites to provide a modicum of privacy as well as much-needed shade during the hot summer months.

Erected near the southeast end of Rendezvous Beach and hammering away seemingly non-stop were the machines responsible for the noise Lev had initially attributed to a woodpecker. They were blaze-red, industrial-sized, and powered by gasoline. Two emaciated men were feeding each machine thigh-sized rounds of freshly cut wood. And covering the ground around each machine where they had fallen after being split by the powerful ram-driven blade were dozens of pieces of wood sized perfectly to fit into a fireplace or woodstove.

Daymon scrutinized the vehicles parked near the wood splitters. Two were ordinary pickups, both box beds containing enough split wood to have them sitting low on their springs. The third vehicle was a Ford Econoline van stretched out in back so that it could accommodate extra passengers. It was painted an industrial gray and bars covered the windows on the inside. He tried reading the writing on the van's flank, but either his eyesight needed correcting or the viewing angle was too sharp—probably a combination of both, he decided.

"What do you got?" Lev asked.

"Two men and five women … no woodpeckers," Daymon said, taking his eye off the rubber cup. "The men are working the splitters while the women stand around picking their asses. Take a look and tell me what your gut says."

Lev bent over the scope and peered into the protruding L-shaped eyepiece. After a long ten-count, during which he panned the scope from the people to the vehicles and then back, he hinged up straight. "You forgot the part about the women being armed. I think the dudes are their prisoners."

"Bingo," Daymon said. "Figured I'd leave the shotguns and pistols for you to pick up on."

Tran took a quick peek. "They're escaped convicts," he said at once. "The writing on the van says Idaho Department of Corrections. And there are two demons coming their way from the lakeside road."

"Ding. Ding. Ding. We have a winner," Daymon said. "Let's see how they deal with the rotters." He displaced Tran and watched the melee unfold. It took a few seconds for the taller of the female guards to get wind of the shamblers. Whether she really smelled them on the wind or heard their calls, over the distance it was impossible to tell.

"Chalk one up for the guards," Daymon said as he watched two of the women pick long-handled axes off the ground and begin to close with the approaching dead.

The whole engagement consisted of a little backpedaling to get to a clear patch of ground, followed at once by precisely aimed and timed swings to the zombies' heads. In fact, to Daymon, these women looked like hardened killers. They were obviously survivors to still be alive this far into the apocalypse, but their posture and demeanor told him they also gave zero fucks.

As soon as the guards dropped their axes to the ground beside their latest kills, Daymon walked the scope up the lake's southwestern shore and focused on a subdivision a mile or two south of Garden City. Even at this distance and with the gathering weather, the scope was powerful enough that he could see a half-dozen multi-pitched red-tiled roofs peeking through the surrounding treetops. And though the gauze-like curtain of rain just moving in hampered visibility, he could see that a number of concrete freeway noise barriers had been erected around the clutch of lakeside homes.

As Daymon slowly surveyed the area, he learned that the wall was still under construction. Running for several hundred feet left to right on the subdivision's east flank was a garden-variety fence constructed of a mishmash of pressure-treated cedar and chain link. Barbed wire had been strung haphazardly along the top. And clearly slated for future use, a number of cement panels lay stacked north of the unfinished compound. As he glassed the area left of the finished section of wall, he spotted a motor pool of sorts, the silhouettes of a dozen vehicles visible behind the chain-link fence.

To the right of the fenced-in vehicles and facing away from the lake was what appeared to be the front entrance. The freshly paved road leading up to the compound was blocked by a wheeled gate nearly equal in height to the cement panels flanking it.

"Copying Bear River, I see," Daymon said, as his two-way radio emitted its familiar electronic warble.

He fished the Motorola from a pocket. "Daymon," he said, keeping his eye glued to the rubber eyepiece.

"Were you going to check in *today*?" Duncan asked.

"Yes, Old Man. I was just about to before I was so rudely interrupted."

"Bad news or good?" Duncan drawled.

"We have eyes on target," Daymon said, going on to detail the nearby log-splitting operation and how efficiently the *locals* had dealt with the pair of rotters. Then he went on to describe the distant lakeside compound. Finally, eye still glued to the spotting scope, he took a breath and added, "And I think I just picked up some movement inside their perimeter."

"Do you see Oliver?" Duncan asked, sounding tired.

"Nope. Visibility sucks right now. But once this storm passes, I think, as you like to say, more will be revealed."

"Maybe I should be singing that old John Nash song," Duncan said.

"What song is that?" asked Daymon, shooting the radio an irritated look.

"Never mind," Duncan answered. "Before your time. Good work, by the way. I'm going to send this on to the Thagons and have them tell Dregan and Eden what we're up against."

"Copy that," said Daymon, a smile creasing his face as a thin, horizontal band of golden sunlight made a brief appearance below the scudding clouds.

From somewhere around the corner, Tran was singing a song whose lyrics had to do with seeing clearly once the rain had gone.

Shaking his head, Daymon tilted the scope down and trained it on the woodcutting operation. And just in time, too, because one of the guards was picking her way through the tents and dead bodies on her way to the van. Once there, she craned around its sloped front end and peered cautiously in the general direction of the main road.

Thumbing the Motorola, Daymon said, "Old Man, the bad girls are closing up shop."

The guard spent a few more seconds crouched by the van looking and listening. Just when the rain from the passing storm band began to let up, she rose and walked back to the others while talking into a large walkie-talkie-looking-thing sporting a long, black whip antenna.

Drawing in a deep breath, Daymon radioed back. "I think they might be onto us. One of the guards just eyeballed the road in your direction and called someone on a big ass walkie-talkie."

"Good eye," Duncan replied. "Stay put and keep tabs on them. I'll hail you when the cavalry arrives."

"Copy that," Daymon answered, tossing the radio onto the carpeted floor.

Chapter 64

Ten minutes after leaving the airspace over Fort George G. Meade, Maryland, roughly twenty miles by crow to the southwest near Suitland, Maryland, Cade spotted the smoke plume rising vertically into the sky. Several hundred feet over the ambush site, the prevailing winds had dispersed the roiling column into a flat gray smudge stretching east to west for a mile or more.

The closer they got to the killing field, the more Cade got a feeling that the PLA force dispatched to the middle of Maryland was either a diversion of some sort, or had been sent on some kind of sacrificial suicide mission. He watched the pair of Stealth Chinooks suddenly gain speed and bank toward the deck some eight hundred feet below the speeding Ghost Hawk.

"Three minutes out," Ari said over the comms. "Anybody bring marshmallows?"

Having been asleep and snoring for the last fifteen minutes, Griff mumbled something unintelligible and shifted in his seat.

Next to Griff, Cross rolled his eyes and shook his head.

Chuckling, Skipper said, "I don't think our customers are going to be able to get close enough to conduct a proper BDA, let alone make s'mores."

That got Cade's blood boiling again. Damn if Skipper wasn't right about this being a glorified battle damage assessment mission. Based on the footage they had watched, nothing could have survived the multiple strafing runs the Hogs had wrought on the enemy element. Even if the PLA Special Forces team had somehow survived riding a trio of motorcycles this far through Indian country, it was highly unlikely that they had escaped the hurt doled out by the Army National Guard aviators. And for that matter, they were just as unlikely to have survived the conflagration as were whatever data collection devices they had spirited from the NSA facility back at Fort Meade.

Channeling the late Mike Desantos, Cade said, "Any way you stack it, this is a goat rope of the first order."

Opening one eye and acquiring Cade with it, Griff said, "Agreed. Those boys on the bikes are long gone by now."

Cross leaned forward against his safety harness and joined the conversation. "You all need to give President Clay, Colonel Shrill, and Major Nash a little more credit. They're running the show. Therefore, only they're privy to the big picture."

"Why should I capitulate on this one?" Cade asked, placing a hand over his boom mic. "We're about to waste another Screamer and at least twenty minutes carving Maryland airspace while we wait for the Zs to clear out. Then we're going to burn twenty more minutes picking through that road to Basra reenactment down there. And after adding that forty-plus minutes to the twenty-some-odd it took us to get here from Meade, we're going to be hard-pressed to catch the PLA infiltrators and fulfill this mission."

"I heard *all* of that," Ari said. "You know … the road to Basra was a hundred times worse of a weeny roast than this one. I've heard first-hand accounts from some of the Hog drivers who were there. And it only cost me a few beers and a couple of shots. By the way, Wyatt, in case you didn't notice, I got us here in one piece."

"Just get us to the road so we can move on," Cade shot back.

"That's not like you, Anvil Actual. Problems on the homefront?"

Cade said nothing to that. No way Ari could know how close to home the quip really hit.

"Looks like we have two fellas aboard worthy of wearing the Doctor Silence mantle," Ari pressed. Then, all business, he added, "One mike out. Deploy the port minigun, Skip. Then get the Screamers prepped. While Skipper's busy with that task, I need the rest of your eyeballs on the deck looking for movement or signs of missile launch. We may still have some survivors armed with MANPADS down there."

Cade cast his gaze out the starboard-side window. The four-lane highway ran east to west, with the eastbound lanes clogged here and there with stalled-out vehicles and multi-car pileups. The westbound lanes ahead of the crippled and burning armor was crawling with zombies, but had far fewer static vehicles and pileups. However, behind the column was evidence that a Pied-Piper-like scenario had been playing itself out as the column had advanced: bodies lay in the road for as far as the eye could see. Closer in, the Zs that had been in tow had caught up with the unmoving vehicles and completely enveloped them.

Without warning the doors concealing Skipper's minigun parted horizontally. All at once the stench of carrion and smoke laden with the acrid smell of the smoldering vehicles invaded the cabin.

After unlocking the mount for the minigun, Skipper hefted it up and snugged it into place atop the bottom half of the opening. With its six-barreled snout pointing groundward, he powered it on and tested the electric motor. "The thirty-four is hot," he said, after seeing the barrel spinning without a hitch.

Still sitting in the bitch seat, all Axe could do was hold on tight to his M4 and peer straight ahead between the pilots at the rapidly tilting horizon.

"Going to the deck," Ari called. "Countermeasures hot."

"Copy that," answered Haynes. "Measures hot. I have eyes on the deck. We are clear to port."

Ari said nothing, busy maneuvering the helo behind the parade of zombies amassing around the east end of the column. "Screamers ready?" he asked, eyeing the much noisier Chinooks already hovering over Suitland Parkway a thousand yards west of the column's inert, Humvee-looking lead vehicle.

"Almost there," called Skipper.

"Jedi One-Two and One-Three report Screamers deployed."

"I'm working on ours," Skipper said, handing the first activated Screamer over to Cade. "One to go."

Cade unbuckled from his safety harness and then clicked the crew retention lanyard affixed to the helo's bulkhead onto his MOLLE gear. As the helo powered through a tight turn, he fought against the G-forces to rise from his seat as the door beside him motored open.

As if Jedi One-One's avionics were hard-wired to Ari's brain, in one fluid set of movements he snapped her back to level, increased RPMs to the rotors, and settled the black helo into an unwavering hover directly above a knot of stalled-out civilian vehicles clogging one of the parkway's eastbound lanes.

"There," Ari barked. "In the middle of the snarl-up."

As Cade depressed the arming button, he sized up the kill zone. Obviously this stretch of highway was chosen for the ambush because of the low rock formation on the north side and dense copse of trees on the other. It was a textbook-perfect chokepoint in that the terrain didn't allow for maneuver after the trap had been sprung. Respect growing for whoever decided to hit the PLA forces here, he underhanded the active Screamer out the door then craned and watched it plummet forty feet, carom off of an old sedan's raggedy black vinyl top and disappear from view, belting out the high-decibel scream that proved loud enough to be heard above the helicopter's whining turbines and baffled rotor chop.

"Is the caravan of death and tree line south still clear?" Ari asked.

Eyes still glued to the FLIR display, Haynes answered, "Still no body heat signatures. I'm only picking up hot spots from the smoldering fires and hot metal down there."

"Copy that," Ari said, as he finessed the bird's nose around to the left.

Once the helicopter finished its rotation and began side-slipping to the east, Skipper handed Cade the second Screamer. Same routine as before; Ari hovered and called out a target. This time it was the arcing copse of trees south of and paralleling the divided four-lane.

"Tree line, three o'clock," Ari called over the comms. "Then seal her up and we're going to the well for a drink."

Hanging partway out the open door, Cade activated the second diversionary device and let it roll from his fingers, watching it all the way to the ground where it bounced on the sloped roadside, rolled through the grass a short distance downhill, and became lodged at the base of a pair of juvenile dogwoods.

"Six, ten split," Cross called from his port-side seat.

"Spot on to *cow corner*," Axe exclaimed, garnering curious looks from Skipper and the Delta shooters.

As soon as Cade heard the Screamer come alive, he returned to his seat, leaving the lanyard clicked to the bulkhead next to the door. Looking groundward, he saw the undead horde immediately lower their expectant gazes and lurch for the nearby guardrail, the ones already there spilling over and rolling down the hill even before the Ghost Hawk began to slip west over the column.

"Cow corner?" Cross mouthed as the helo gathered forward momentum, pressing everyone into their seats.

"Some strange English soccer term?" Griff pressed.

"Cricket," Axe said. "It's a bloody cricket term and I'm not going to bother expounding on it. You gents wouldn't appreciate the nuance anyway."

"Greek to me," Griff said, cracking a smile.

In his headset Cade heard the pilots of One-Two and One-Three report success in deploying their two remaining Screamers. Having completed their aerial refuel during the leg from Meade to the current GPS coordinates Nash had provided, there was no need for the Chinooks to form up with Jedi Lead so they thundered off to the east to let the Screamers do what they had been designed to do.

After watching the Chinooks depart low over the trees, Ari made the subtle course corrections necessary for Jedi One-One to meet up with the tanker at the agreed-upon waypoint.

Chapter 65
Laketown, Utah

The rotter had been mashing its face against the plate glass window, barely six inches from where Duncan was seated in the red vinyl booth, for the better part of an hour. With no lower mandible to keep its tongue in place, the constant pendulum-like-movement of the seven-inch length of bloated black flesh had created on the reverse side of the window a milky cataract the size of the Vietnam veteran's wide-brimmed Stetson.

Over the course of that hour, Foley had been pacing behind the counter, stopping now and again to engage Taryn or Jamie or Wilson in inane conversation.

On the chipped Formica along with sets of salt and pepper shakers, placards declaring daily specials and bulging plastic ketchup bottles were a pair of AR-15 carbines and Taryn's unholstered Beretta.

Using a whetstone found in the kitchen area, Jamie had spent the time putting a fine edge on everyone's blade then honed her tomahawk razor-sharp.

"When are they going to get here?" asked Wilson, casting a glance over his shoulder at Duncan.

The *when are we going to get there* act wearing thin on Duncan, he tore his gaze from the Make Out Bandit and rose, the black Saiga shotgun clutched in one hand. "Just be grateful Brook … or whoever swayed Dregan to come, was able to do so in the first place."

Changing the subject, Foley said, "Sounds like the folks outside of Garden City have a pretty elaborate setup."

"Same as Bear River," said Jamie. "It's not too hard to erect a few concrete barriers."

"Then why haven't we done the same at the compound if it's so easy?" Taryn asked.

Wilson fielded the question. "They'd be a dead giveaway that someone was trying to protect some pretty cool toys and food—mostly the food—behind said recently installed barriers."

Duncan nodded, then turned toward the hideous sight relentlessly slathering up the nearby window.

"Want me to take care of it?"

"No, Foley. If more of them start showing up, we'll take measures. Until then, just keep your eyes and ears open for our Bear River friends."

No sooner had Duncan uttered the words "Bear River friends," than two things happened, one right after the other.

First the low rumble of what sounded like a dozen approaching vehicles could be heard from the state route. Then the two-way radio sitting on Duncan's table warbled to life and Daymon was calling for yet another update.

Timing is everything, thought Duncan as he snatched up the radio. "Calvary is here," he said to no one in particular as he made his way to the locked front door, inadvertently bringing the jawless zombie with him. Along the way he spoke into the Motorola. "Give me a second, Mister Patience," he said. Without waiting for Daymon's answer to that, he pocketed the radio and eyed the zombie still stalking him.

"Here," Jamie said, offering up the wooden handle of the knife-sharpening tool she'd been using on the blades. She nodded at the door. "It should fit through the mail slot."

"Smart," Duncan said, hefting the tool and eyeing its ten-inch tapered metal shaft. He crouched down on his haunches, opened the metal flap with one hand, and stuck the fingers of his other through the horizontal opening. "Hey, Gene Simmons… come and get it."

The engine noise grew louder, but didn't trump the fleshy digits wagging the air less than a yard distant. Rheumy eyes locked and tongue doing the grandfather clock back and forth swing, the undead man grabbed onto the horizontal push bar two-handed, dropped to his knees like a trapdoor had opened beneath him, and struck the door head first, starting a series of cracks running every which way from where his forehead struck the glass.

Duncan pulled his fingers from the mail slot a tick before the jawless monster set the door to vibrating in its frame. He held the knife sharpener level with the slot, its tip keeping the one-way mail door propped open.

"Come on," Duncan called. "Work with me here."

What was left of the zombie's upper teeth—mainly jagged stumps—scratched against the metal flap as its limp tongue deposited on the opening a thick rope of the same putrid excretion that was drying on the front window.

"It's not going to cooperate," Jamie said. She craned to see around the pickups parked out front. "Dregan's brought the Humvees."

Still probing the opening with the tool, Duncan said, "How many?"

"Two."

"And?" He stabbed the zombie in the cheek hard enough to send it sprawling backwards onto its butt. Then there was a hollow thud as the back of its head hit the concrete, sending a vibration rippling under the door and up through his boot soles.

"That had to hurt," Foley said. He had come around the counter and was standing next to Jamie, the two of them casting a misshapen shadow over Duncan and the dusty *Welcome* rug he was kneeling on.

Still wincing from the resonant sound of bone striking cement, Jamie cast her gaze on the road south. "I count four vehicles."

"Plus the Hummers?" Duncan asked as he rose creakily.

"Counting the Hummers," Jamie answered.

A black and white SUV slid into the spot next to Duncan's Dodge.

Wilson crawled into a booth left of the door and pressed his face to the glass. "That's Jenkins Tahoe," he said, incredulous.

Stick-on letters spelling out **Bear River Police Department** now covered the Jackson Hole PD markings.

Standing beside an unoccupied booth, Duncan said, "Who's in the blue truck?"

"That's old Ray," Wilson said.

Duncan snatched his shotgun off the floor and snicked the door lock open. "Four vehicles and what… seven bodies at the most?"

The rotter was on all fours now, holding a sort of downward dog position with the crown of its head facing the door and its tongue nearly touching the ground.

"I count five," Taryn said, as the pair of Humvees rolled onto the drive-in's lot behind the black and white.

There was a screech of metal on metal as the battered blue pickup ground to a halt on the south side of the parking lot.

Still scrabbling to stand, the rotter slapped the glass and pawed at the metal door handle.

In one fluid movement, Duncan flipped the Saiga into the air and caught it atop the barrel one-handed. Simultaneously, with his off hand he unlocked the door then yanked it inward causing the zombie to pitch face first where it said *Welcome* on the rug.

In a blur of movement, Duncan brought the shotgun's butt straight down to the back of the monster's skull, which had already been partially cratered by its earlier fall. Instantly the creature went still, a trickle of dark blood spilling from both ears.

"Help me move this thing," Duncan said to Wilson. "Jamie, greet Dregan and then sweep the lot for more rotters."

Wilson was up and helping as soon as Jamie had squeezed out the front door.

After pulling the corpse inside, Duncan fished the radio from his pocket. He thumbed the Talk key. "Still there?"

Daymon was back on at once. "How's that for patience?"

Duncan said nothing.

"The weather's lifted here," Daymon went on. "How is it there?"

"Rained enough to soften the bugs on our windshields. That's about it. What are you seeing there now?"

"You're not going to believe what these fuckers are up to."

"Did you find Oliver?"

"I think it's him," Daymon said, his voice softening. "And if it is him… he doesn't look so good. He's got road rash on his face and a broken leg ... looks like a real bad compound fracture."

"He's walking around?"

"No," Daymon said. "He's been put in one of those things. Those torture devices the Pilgrims locked people up in. You know … like in the town square, to humiliate them."

"Stocks?"

"If that's what you call 'em, sure."

"Are you compromised?" Duncan asked.

"Huh uh. The storm moved on and now I can see twice as far with this scope. Except for a couple of rotters, nothing's moving on the beach or in the campgrounds."

"Good. Hang tight," Duncan said, the gears already turning in his head. "Dregan and his guys just pulled up." What he didn't say was how few of *his guys* there really were. *Oh well*, he thought. *We'll just have to make lemonade out of lemons.* At least the Humvees Dregan brought were the two he used to briefly put the Eden compound under siege. The lead vehicle, painted woodland camouflage—mainly greens and browns with a little black shading thrown in for good measure—came complete with a turret-mounted MK-19 grenade launcher. The same launcher one of Dregan's men had used to lob the high explosive rounds at the compound, bringing Brook speeding to the gate in the F-650 all full of piss and vinegar. Duncan chuckled, recalling the story she had relayed around the campfire that night. Catching Dregan with his guard down was a hell of an achievement by anyone's standards.

The second Hummer coasted to a noisy halt beside the first. It sported the same dark camo paint scheme and was armed with a Ma Deuce .50 caliber Browning. The heavy machine gun was identical in every way to the one atop the National Guard Humvee currently parked in the motor pool at the Eden compound. *Great place for it*, Duncan mused. What he wouldn't give to have had the foresight to bring that and the three-hundred-plus rounds of .50 caliber ammunition he'd had Phillip link up for him weeks ago.

Suddenly he missed Phillip's constant nagging and calling him "Sir." But that feeling was pushed aside the moment Dregan swept into the diner, his duster-shrouded six-foot three-inch frame filling up the doorway as he did so. Then Duncan saw Gregory, oldest son of Dregan, who had received a dose of the same suspect Omega Antiserum as Brook. It was apparent the moment he saw the younger man enter behind Dregan that he was far from death. Instantly, though he didn't let it show, Duncan was awash with emotion. Maybe Brook wasn't carrying a latent dose of the Omega virus. He had burning questions he wanted to pose, but knew he had to hold his cards close to the vest.

"Thanks for coming on such short notice, Alexander," he said, extending his hand to the elder Dregan.

"Dregan," the giant of a man said as his hand enveloped Duncan's. "Call me Dregan, please. And this is my son, Gregory."

The entry Duncan was looking for. He reached out and shook Gregory's hand. It was warm and the man's grip was firm. He said, "It's good to see you under better circumstances." He sized up the bandage covering the bite wound to Gregory's neck. Inexplicably, it was clean and white. "And you look much better than when we met last."

"So much was happening the other day," Gregory answered, looking embarrassed, "what with me kidnapping the kids and nearly paying for it dearly."

"Helen said you were down for the count," Duncan said. "But you look healthy as a horse to me." *A lie*. In fact, the broad-shouldered young man was pale and gaunt and his eyes were shot through with blood.

"He was coming down with the flu before he got bit," the elder Dregan interjected.

"And the healthy as a horse thing," Gregory said. "I don't know about that … but I could probably eat one right now." He cast his gaze at the menu on the wall above the pass-through window behind the counter. It was a two foot by ten foot sheet of white plastic with horizontal slots designed to hold interchangeable plastic numbers and letters. The dust- and cobweb-covered thing offered everything from plain old hamburgers to French dip sandwiches to onion rings. Twisting the culinary dagger in his gut, colorful pictures of hot fudge sundaes, dipped ice cream cones, and banana splits framed the lunch offerings on both sides. "As a matter of fact a jumbo hot fudge sundae would fill the void."

At the tail end of Gregory's fast food fantasy the door opened and Ray entered. He paused on the blood-and-brain-matter-soiled *Welcome* rug and walked his eyes around the diner. Finally settling his gaze on Duncan, he said, "I know the kids. But you and I haven't met."

Duncan stuck out his hand. "Duncan Winters. Pleasure's all mine."

Ray reciprocated and asked, "Where's that easy-on-the-eyes lady named Brook?"

"She's back at the compound. Came down with the flu yesterday," Duncan said. "Probably the same strain that's going around Bear River."

The door opened again and Jamie stuck her head in. She matched Ray's smile, then motioned for Wilson and Foley to join her outside. "We've got more rotters coming up the state route."

"No gunfire," Duncan said.

Dregan regarded Jamie. "Cleo's in the police rig. He may not look like much, but he ain't afraid to get his hands dirty. Take him with you." Then, changing the tide of conversation, Dregan sat on a stool at the counter and stared at Duncan. "Please, fill me and my boy in on what we'll be going up against."

Chapter 66
Maryland

As Ari backed the Ghost Hawk down and away from the refueling probe, Cade's one-hundred-and-eighty-pound frame got light in the seat and the pitch of the four-blade rotors punishing the air over his head decreased sharply. In seconds, the helicopter had performed a tight one-eighty and was diving south toward the stretch of highway located roughly seven miles southeast of the District of Columbia and nearly equidistant to the Maryland cities of Suitland and Morningside.

Recent flyovers of each city by the Stealth Chinooks had returned grim news: Both were teeming with dead and even after multiple low-level passes, the pilots, crew chiefs, and Rangers aboard the helos had failed to spot a single living soul.

As the parkway and tiny vehicles scattered haphazardly on it grew larger, Cade gazed off to the west where the sun was getting low in the sky and noted the presence of clear blue sky. It looked as if the flight home across a pitch-black United States was looking good for viewing celestial bodies. But first, he reminded himself, they had human bodies to identify and, hopefully, stolen data to recover.

From his seat by the starboard window Cade saw the Chinooks come into view, flying in tight formation and gliding slow and low over the treetops. Vectoring in from the south, the two birds came within visual range of the convoy then suddenly parted ways.

As planned, Jedi One-Two banked west and came in low over the PLA convoy. After clearing the whip antenna atop a scorched desert-tan multi-wheeled personnel carrier near the head of the convoy, the hulking matte-black next-gen Chinook flew another thirty yards down the parkway, flared and settled softly on the only clear spot of blacktop in sight.

Out of sight around the slight bend roughly a quarter-mile west of where One-Two had just set down, Cade could see the mini-horde of Zs lured there by the recently deployed Screamers. The rotten mass was ten to twenty bodies deep and spread across all four lanes of oil-streaked blacktop.

Flicking his eyes right, Cade picked up One-Three just as she cleared the end of the convoy. He knew the Rangers aboard were finished tightening ruck straps and checking weapons and were chomping at the bit to deploy.

He watched the Chinook flare and hover a few feet off the deck, its wheels inches from the mangled Z corpses the passing Chinese convoy had left in its wake. Even with the ramp fully deployed, it looked to Cade as if the Bravo chalk of Rangers on One-Three were left with a three-foot drop to the road.

After watching the Rangers leap from One-Three and move into their blocking position on the east end of the kill zone, Cade's thoughts shifted to his wife and daughter. He uttered a prayer for each—the first for Brook to stay strong, the second for Raven to be a pillar of support for her mom in his stead.

Ari's voice snapped Cade back to the mission at hand. "Wheels down in five," the aviator said over the shipwide comms.

Cade peered down through the window and saw the dashed yellow centerline of the mostly clear westbound lanes rushing up. Quickly, he went through the ritual of checking his M4's magazine and chamber. Finding the rounds seated in the former and the latter empty—as expected—he charged a round and set the carbine to Safe.

"Four," Ari called.

As Skipper started the port-side door on its rearward slide, Cade unhooked his safety harness and stomped his feet to get the blood flowing. And when he moved to the front of his seat and put some weight on his bad left ankle, he was pleasantly surprised to find that thanks to the Motrin in his system, it was virtually free of pain. *Thank God for grunt candy.*

"Three," Ari called, never breaking cadence in his long, drawn-out count.

"Stay frosty," Cade said, letting his gaze sweep across his cobbled-together Delta team. And though he had already gone over the mission details twice over the course of the recent refueling—once as the team had hatched the plan, and a second time when he had shared it over the comms with all three aircrews and the lieutenant and first sergeants who would be leading the Rangers—he ran over it one last time in bullet-point fashion. "We're looking for WIAs, motorcycles, and backpacks full of data storage devices. Griff and Cross will head east and curl around the rear of the column, then work their way west toward the lead elements. Me and Axe will exfil and head west, toward the front of the column where we all meet up. Remember … don't catch a bullet and don't get bit."

"Two," Ari called.

Focusing his attention on Griff, Cade said, "We've got to locate those backpacks." Swinging his gaze around the cabin, he finished with, "And watch your fire. We've got Rangers and helos at both ends of the parkway."

Ari was calling out, "Wheels down," just as the bird settled on a patch of bare pavement in a lane adjacent to the three Humvee-looking vehicles bringing up the rear of the column.

Before the subtle vibration of the shocks sucking up the helo's weight could fully course through the ship's airframe, Cade was out the door with Axe on his six. "Weapons free," he called, fanning left while keeping his M4 trained on the soot-covered vehicles. After clearing the ship's tail boom and wildly spinning tail rotor by a dozen feet, he took a knee and peered over his shoulder, seeing that Cross and Griff had already hurdled the guardrail and were nearing the end of the column.

The usual muffled whine and uncomfortable harmonic *thwop, thwop* of the spooling rotors pummeled Cade's chest and lungs. Guarding against flying debris, he put his gloved hand over his nose and mouth and watched Jedi One-One rise slowly from the road, turn in place until its nose was pointing south, then rocket up and over the trees.

After One-One was out of sight, Cade brought up the TOC back at Schriever to alert them that his team was safely on the ground.

"Anvil Actual, Schriever TOC," an anonymous airman replied. "Good copy. Good hunting."

Cade said nothing. He flicked his carbine off of Safe, rose, and motioned for Axe to follow. With the stench of decay, cooked flesh, burning electrical, and jet exhaust assaulting his nose, he padded to the far guardrail and scrutinized the dirt on the shoulder.

Nothing.

He peered over the guardrail and let his gaze walk the shallow embankment and nearby tree line.

Still nothing. There were no tire tracks, motorcycle or otherwise.

Axe shook his head. "Nothing."

Cade hailed Cross. "Anvil Two, Anvil Actual. Be advised. No joy on any trace of the PLA tangos. No bodies. No motorcycles. No backpacks."

Immediately following their rapid egress from Jedi One-One, Cross and Griff had sprinted off to their right, keeping their helmeted heads ducked until they were clear of the helo's whirring composite, carbon-fiber main rotor blades. A few seconds later they had already hurdled the Jersey barrier dividers, curled around the tail end of the convoy, and were beginning their east to west sweep while keeping close to the guardrail bordering the parkway to the north.

Now, after hearing Cade's discouraging SITREP, Cross checked in with bad news of his own.

"Anvil Actual, Anvil Two. We're at the midpoint. No joy to report here. Still searching. How copy?"

"Good copy," Cade replied. "Proceed to rally point."

Crabbing sideways, Cross kept his stubby MP7 trained on the spaces between the dozen-plus inert vehicles. As the two operators crept forward, Griff kept his gaze fixed on the rock face and nearby copse of trees beyond the guardrail.

Nearing the third vehicle from the front of the failed expeditionary force, Cross halted and took a knee. With the first two fingers of his left hand splayed into a V, he pointed to his eyes, then did the same in the direction of the nearby troop transport.

Understanding Cross had detected movement inside the vehicle he had pointed to, Griff nodded and joined him in the shadow of the looming troop transport.

On the opposite side of the PLA convoy, Cade was turned away from the guardrail and facing the carnage. He let his gaze roam the tangle of rent steel and charred flesh. Up close, the vehicles didn't look like toys in a diorama as they had from the air. They were stopped in a ragged line, most of them facing away at different angles, having been destroyed in place when they had tried to flee the aerial attack. From a dozen feet away he could see the individual pocks and craters and paint missing on the armored vehicle's outer skin. Each vehicle sported fist-sized gaping maws surrounded by jagged metal where 30mm shells had punched through them as if they were constructed of papier-mâché. The personnel who had tried to escape the gun runs had suffered the same fate as the vehicles. There were no tidy dime-sized entry wounds with blossoms of crimson surrounding them. No dead PLA soldiers were lying prostrate on the road and staring wide-eyed at the darkening sky. The destruction to anything organic had been utter and final. Bloody hunks of charred flesh were scattered around the rear guard APCs surviving the conflagration that had consumed the majority of the column.

Save for scraps of camouflage PLA uniforms and a couple of bullpup-style carbines lying on the road, only a severed hand and a right foot still in its knock-off combat boot was distinguishable to Cade. Nothing remotely resembling a human body was left intact after catching one of the A-10's massive bullets.

"Fuck all," Axe said, staring down at the white leg bone protruding from the fire-singed leather boot. "Some of my mates were on the wrong end of one of those beasts over in the sandbox. Glad it wasn't me."

"News of those blue on blue instances hit all of us real hard."

"Fog of war," Axe responded. "These things happen."

Then something did happen. A series of gunshots rang out from the front of the column.

Four total.

Closely spaced.

Then there was silence.

Chapter 67
Bear Lake

Though he heard the low growl of approaching engines, Daymon kept his eye pressed to the rubber cup affixed to the eyepiece. Still alone in the master bedroom and hunched over the spotting scope, he raised the Motorola to his lips and thumbed the Talk button. "How far out are you?"

"A few blocks," Duncan answered, his familiar drawl strangely comforting to Daymon.

"Well, Old Man … you better think about gearing down or coasting in from there, because if I can hear you, chances are they can too."

"How many are we talking about?"

Daymon made a quick sweep of the distant compound then returned to the attractive female guard the scope was originally trained on. It appeared that she was standing on some kind of scaffolding behind the cement noise barriers. And from the fifteen minutes he'd already spent watching her, Daymon knew her pattern of movement and every detail of her anatomy from the waist up.

Narrow in the face and wearing a ball cap that cast her focused blue eyes in shadow—much like the majority of the women survivors he had gotten to know since the event—this one looked as if she knew how to take care of herself. To add to his assumption, she paid *zero* attention to the dozen or so rotters trying unsuccessfully to scale the wall a few feet below her.

As the engine growl neared, Daymon continued to watch the forty-something woman he'd labeled *Ingrid* on account of her dirty blonde hair and chiseled Nordic features. On cue, Ingrid walked to one end of the contraption out of sight behind the wall and paused there to scrutinize the road and residential area beyond the compound's southwest flank. He counted upward to ten and, sure enough, she was on the move in the other direction. If Ingrid had picked up the engines and their throaty exhaust burble nearly two miles east of her perch, she wasn't acting like it. And if she was playing coy about it just in case someone was watching her, the performance she was putting on had him fooled.

Finally, after leaving Duncan hanging for twenty seconds or so, Daymon spoke into the two-way radio. "I count six women patrolling inside the perimeter. There's also a female guard on the wall at my twelve o'clock who's watching the road coming in from the southeast. There's also another one who will now and again climb a ladder leaning against the far wall and take a look north toward Garden City."

"Which way is the wind blowing?" Duncan asked.

"I'm watching from *inside* the house," Daymon answered.

"We're a block out. Any change in her demeanor?"

"She's still pacing in my direction. And she hasn't gone to the binoculars yet. If she has one, I haven't seen her talk into a radio, either."

"She doesn't hear us," Duncan said assuredly. "No way. No how."

Still watching through the eyepiece, Daymon said, "And you know this, *how*?"

"Check the wind."

Leaning away from the scope to see out the window, Daymon cast his gaze at the juvenile pines beside the house. A couple seconds passed before a gust bent the treetops in his general direction. "The wind's coming at me," he radioed back.

"Perfect," said Duncan. "House is two-tone brown, correct?"

"Affirmative. Lev and Tran are waiting for you out front."

"No," Duncan said. "Tran is putting down a zombie all by himself. Lev is the one standing around."

Daymon said nothing. He bent over and looked through the scope, hoping that Tran wasn't going to get himself bit trying to prove he was something it was obvious he was not.

Ingrid had continued her routine and was again pacing away from him. Beyond the stocks where Oliver was still hanging limply, Daymon saw the other guard return and move the ladder away from the far wall and lay it flat in an unkempt yard in front of the middle house.

He also noticed a thin gray haze painting the air above the middle house. His first thought was that it was the result of a freshly lit cooking fire.

The engine sounds cut out. A few seconds later there was a muted rattle from the front storm door being hauled open. A beat after that the interior door creaked and loud voices and the clomping of boot soles on bare floor echoed up from downstairs.

Still, Ingrid kept up appearances.

On her way to the middle house, Ladder Guard stopped next to Oliver and checked him for a pulse. Five seconds elapsed, her face remaining placid throughout. There were no tells in her body language, either. When she finally moved on there was no change in her gait. And once she was gone from sight, Daymon still had no idea if Oliver was alive or dead.

Daymon heard booted feet scaling the stairs. There were also voices rising up, some familiar, others accented and hard to place. So he rose and fixed his gaze at the top of the stairs a dozen feet down the hall.

Duncan emerged from downstairs first, moving toward the master bedroom with purpose the second he set eyes on Daymon.

Dregan's crew spilled from the stairway next. Alexander filled up the hall first. Barely visible behind him were sons Gregory and Peter. A few seconds passed then the fella named Cleo who Daymon had met the day before—short, fifty-something and missing a few teeth—summited the stairs ahead of the rest of the Eden crew.

"Gang's all here," Duncan said.

With twelve people crowded into the open room, the master suite felt anything but.

"We've got a dirty dozen," said Daymon after a quick head count.

"I'm lucky thirteen," gasped Ray, his knuckles white from throttling the dual handrails all the way to the second floor.

"What's one more," Daymon said, leading Duncan to the spotting scope.

"Looks like we're between storm systems," said Duncan. "While it's not pissin' rain, let's set Hubble Junior here up on the deck so we don't keep catchin' this glare off the window."

Seeing no reason to argue the point, Daymon shrugged and stepped aside.

Duncan hefted the spotting scope and waddled with it cradled in his arms to the deck, where he set it up underneath the jutting eave casting a sliver of shadow on the west-facing windows. Steady drips of water rolled off the front of the gutter above him, making soft patters on the wood decking underfoot. Some of the drips spattered his glasses and more found their way into his collar.

He spread the tripod legs a generous width apart and locked them into place. After spinning a hand crank to raise the scope so that he wouldn't have to bend over too far to access the eyepiece, he cast a glance at the others behind the glass and gestured for them to join him on the deck.

Starting left, near the mouth of the cul-de-sac which was absolutely packed full of minivans, pickups, and two gray prison vans, he worked the scope slowly to his right, examining the redoubt's layout while taking inventory of the handful of vehicles, U-Haul moving trucks and women milling about inside the perimeter.

Duncan felt a tap on his shoulder, followed by the stink of cigarettes as he sensed someone looming over him.

Taking his eye from the scope, Duncan looked sidelong to his right and saw only the lapels of Dregan's parted duster and the man's barrel chest from the sternum up.

"Hold yer horses, Paul Bunyan."

"Please, let me look," Dregan said, his accent not as thick as Duncan remembered it being immediately after Gregory had been attacked.

"Fine," Duncan said. "Knock yerself out."

Without adjusting the tripod, Dregan bent way over and planted his face to the scope. After a minute spent panning the big lens over the grounds surrounding the cul-de-sac and beach fronting the half-dozen houses, he turned and stared at Duncan. Eyebrows furrowed, Dregan said, incredulous, "But they are all women. So we go *now* and save your friend."

"Not so fast," said Duncan. *Brook's all woman, and look what she did to you and your posse*, was what he was thinking.

"Yes, fast." Dregan stood up straight and backed away from the spotting scope, sharing the look of incredulity with the others.

Standing to the right of Dregan, Taryn and Jamie folded their arms and stared daggers his way.

"Helen would kick your ass with one arm tied behind her back. Brook too, for that matter," Ray said, separating himself from the statement and the man who had spouted it.

Directing the question at Duncan, Dregan asked, "Who is the big woman with attitude?"

Having no idea whom Dregan was talking about, Duncan peered through the spotting scope, walking it over the compound in tiny increments. After suddenly going rigid, he rose up and regarded Dregan. "She is a *big* girl. And she's definitely oozing attitude."

Dregan fixed Duncan with an *I told you so* stare, then did the same to everyone else standing on the deck.

Duncan tracked the woman with the scope as she plodded over to the stocks. She was nearly as wide as she was tall. This anatomical fact led Duncan to label her "Little Lotta" after the rotund comic book character of the same name. And like the fictional Lotta, this woman's legs also resembled twin tree trunks.

Lotta stopped directly in front of Oliver, leaned over and looked him in the face. The big woman began speaking to

Glenda's youngest, but she was facing away so making out any of the words by reading her lips was impossible. However, a pair of plain-Jane-looking women emerged from the direction of the cul-de-sac, zippered through the parked vehicles, and approached Lotta.

"Lots of X chromosomes down there," Duncan muttered, seeing the pair stop opposite Lotta and turn so they just so happened to be facing him full on.

Now we're cooking with gas, he thought to himself as the taller of the two women spoke. Duncan watched her lips like a cat would a canary. She was obviously relaying something pertaining to the night's dinner, but the only words he understood by reading her lips were "fire" and "dog." *Maybe they're roasting weenies*, he thought. If anything was still palatable this far into the apocalypse, surely a lips-and-asshole-filled health missile with all of its preservatives would be.

However, the breakthrough came when one of the other women spoke. The first word out of her mouth was "Adrian." Three syllables. A. Dree. Ann. And just like that, there was no denying that these people he was watching from afar were responsible for all of the atrocities they'd encountered on the way here: the vivisected man in the pasture. The reanimated skeleton left so grotesquely on display in the church. Both the booby-trapped rectory and fix-it shop. And, to add insult to injury, they were just officially confirmed as Oliver's captors.

Then, just when Duncan thought the predicament Oliver had gotten himself into could get no worse, the big woman called Adrian turned toward Oliver with a machete similar to Daymon's clutched in her meaty right hand.

There was no more talk. Adrian reared back with the blade, paused for a spell at the top of the swing, then bought it down at an angle a few inches north of Oliver's protruding femur bone.

The damage was instantaneous, flesh and sinew and bone shards no match for the blade.

As Duncan watched in disbelief, three things happened simultaneously. First, Oliver's leg from mid-thigh on down tilted away from his body as if it were a felled tree. Then he came to and let loose a scream that Duncan could see, but not hear. And finally, as the wind left Duncan's lungs in a sorrow-filled moan, Daymon and Dregan were grabbing his elbows and helping to keep him from falling in the same manner as Oliver's leg had.

His breath coming in gasps, Duncan used the deck rail for support and stood on his own while the others looked on with questioning stares.

"What's that all about?" Daymon asked.

The first words from Duncan's mouth when he fully caught his wind were, "The big woman just amputated Oliver's leg."

Instantly Taryn drew in a sharp breath.

Shaking his head and on the verge of tears, Daymon stalked the length of the deck and disappeared through the slider.

Duncan looked to Dregan. "We have to go now. Is the Mk19 and Ma Deuce loaded and ready to go?"

Dregan nodded. "What we are lacking in manpower, we make up for in firepower."

Ray stepped forward. "Me and Helen have more weaponry than we could ever use at the house. I brought something else that might help balance the scales of justice. Come with me."

Without another word, all thirteen people that had been packed on the master deck followed Ray single-file down the stairs and out the front door, where they were greeted with a much-needed dose of late afternoon sunshine.

Chapter 68

As soon as the gunfire erupted near the front of the convoy, Cade knew it wasn't coming from Griff or Cross's suppressed weapons. And he quickly decided that the trio of sharp reports likely hadn't come from either of the operator's pistols. More than likely, the weapon was firing an oddball caliber similar in size to the ammunition Cross fed his MP7 submachinegun.

"No return fire?" Axe said to Cade at the very same moment Cross's voice sounded over the comms with news that the hostile fire was coming from inside the cab of the third vehicle from the front of the column.

"I have eyes on in the side mirror," Cross added. "One body. Driver's seat of the troop transport. His angle on us is bad."

Cade craned left and picked out the third vehicle. Its front end, including the driver's side mirrors, had been chewed up by slugs from the A-10's cannons. Fire had consumed most of the cab and licks of smoke continued curling skyward from underneath the buckled hood. Most importantly, there were no whip antennas sprouting from the vehicle, making it more likely the shooter couldn't report the presence of the Jedi flight.

"Where are the Rangers in relation to the Tango?" he asked, raising his voice because he was hearing one of the distant Screamers being amplified loud and clear over Cross's boom microphone.

"They're all on the other side of the parkway. Northwest of the divider on a diagonal from the shooter," Cross answered. "Griff has already motioned for them to take cover and stand down."

"Copy that. Hold your fire, too," Cade said, lowering his voice to a whisper. "I have an idea. If it works, we may just be able to take the shooter alive." He detailed his simple plan then released his M4 from its center-point sling and laid it flat on the road. Out came the suppressed Glock 17 and he was off, moving slowly in a tactical crouch and keeping close to the vehicles where the misshapen shadows cast by the trees to the south provided him a false sense of cover.

Axe watched Cade forge ahead, picking his way through body parts and debris, black pistol held in a two-handed grip and trained on the target vehicle the entire way. Once the Delta captain was parallel with the truck's driver-side door and had flashed him a thumbs-up, Axe whispered into the comms, "Anvil Actual is in position."

Crouched out of sight behind the transport's deflated rear passenger-side tires, Cross whispered, "Anvil Actual, Anvil Two. Copy," and started moving forward, keeping his MP7 aimed at the window from which the PLA soldier had just engaged them. Gaze trained on the large vertical side mirror, he put one hand on the door to keep it from flying open into him and trained his weapon on the window where the soldier's head had appeared before.

"Anvil Two in place," Cross whispered, beginning a silent countdown in his head.

Upon hearing Cross's report, Cade also started counting down from five. Once he reached "*One*" in his head, three things happened in quick succession. First, a pair of distinctive muffled reports from Cross's MP7 sounded opposite the transport. A half-beat later a pained grunt and rustle of fabric filtered down from the open window barely a yard from Cade's head. Then, as anticipated, the soldier returned fire from the cab, three closely spaced shots that Cade prayed hadn't found friendly flesh.

Barely a second had slipped into the past before Cade was up on the rig's running board and peering into the window, the

Glock's cylindrical suppressor sweeping the cab for the enemy soldier. Time seemed to slow to a crawl as his gaze settled on the black pistol clutched in the PLA soldier's gloved hand. Finger drawing up trigger pull, Cade angled the business end of the Glock down a few degrees and squeezed off a single shot. Another pained grunt followed at once by a shrill scream filled the air even before the muffled report had a chance to dissipate.

Seeing the young soldier double forward, both gloved hands going for the bloody entry wound in the soft flesh on the inside of his right thigh, Cade reached his arm through the window and pressed the still warm suppressor to the soldier's neck.

Still balancing on the running board, free hand gripping the B-pillar, Cade screamed at the PLA soldier, telling him in English to raise his hands and keep them up.

The soldier didn't react. Face screwed up in pain, he kept both hands pressed to his wounded leg and began rocking back and forth.

A sliver of light illuminated the headliner above the wounded man's head as Griffin climbed inside and snatched the soldier's pistol off the floorboards. "Clear," he called, seeing no other weapons.

Seeing Griff take possession of the soldier's weapon, Cade hauled open the door and yanked the screaming man out of the cab. After laying the Chinese soldier flat on the road, he quickly frisked him for weapons. Finding nothing, Cade radioed an all clear to the Ranger lieutenant. Next, he ordered Griff to join him for the interrogation and told Cross to continue searching the vehicles for the data storage devices.

After seeing Cross disappear behind a shot-up troop carrier, Cade motioned Axe over. "We can't let him bleed out."

With his Glock trained on the writhing soldier, Cade watched on as Axe fixed a tourniquet on the profusely bleeding appendage.

"I'm afraid you nicked the bloke's femoral artery," Axe said matter-of-factly. "He's got two minutes left on earth … at the most."

Cade cursed, then looked over his shoulder at the open door. "Griff," he bellowed. "Hustle!"

From the head of the convoy a staccato burst of gunfire rang out.

"Rangers engaging the dead," Axe said matter-of-factly.

Seconds after shimmying across the troop carrier's bloodied bench seat Griff arrived. Without saying a word, he set his rifle aside, took a knee next to the dying man, and began talking softly to him in what to Cade sounded like Chinese, Mandarin most likely. When Griff paused to take a breath, the soldier's eyes narrowed and he began thrashing about and yelling at the top of his voice. None of what the PLA soldier had said was understandable to Cade, and judging by the tone and delivery, it was likely nothing useful.

Confirming Cade's suspicion, Griff shook his head, then looked to the sky. "He told me he knows nothing about the NSA. Then he said he wants us all to go fuck our mothers."

"The dying always have a way with words," Axe said. "Tell him thanks for the offer, but my *mum* is dead and gone."

Griff didn't respond to that.

During the uncomfortable few seconds of silence that ensued, the lieutenant leading the Ranger chalk from Jedi One-Two came on over the comms. "One of the Screamers west of us failed," he said, stress evident in his voice. "And the Zs are starting to move our way. You've got two, maybe three minutes tops before One-Two is either going to have to engage the Zs or launch and orbit until we call for exfil."

"Jedi One-Two and One-Three, Anvil Actual," said Cade. "You are cleared to exfil Chalks Alpha and Bravo. Lieutenant, Dixon … round up your men. We're done here."

"Copy that," replied the Ranger lieutenant.

Wavering on what to do next, Cade saw the PLA soldier's eyes flutter.

"Griff, hold him down."

Griff kneeled by the soldier's head and anchored the man's upper arms to the road with both hands.

Cade said, "Axe, keep him from kicking me."

The soldier's eyes went wide and a half-smile creased his sweaty face.

Axe placed one knee on the man's shins and clamped the toes of his blood-soaked combat boots together with one hand.

Cade ripped the soldier's fatigue pants, exposing the puckered flesh wound. Hand gripping the man's thigh above where the bullet entered, Cade regarded Griff with a pained look. "Repeat the question."

Without a moment's hesitation, Griff spoke to the man rapid-fire in Chinese.

The soldier said nothing, his half-smile widening.

Without warning, Cade plunged his thumb into the gaping wound. As the man wailed and bucked under the much larger Americans, he rooted around in the wound and found what he was looking for.

With a nerve definitely struck—literally more so than figuratively—the soldier began to chatter louder and faster than before.

Releasing the pressure, Cade looked a question at Griff.

"He says we're supposed to fuck our fathers, now," Griff replied, bowing his head.

Sweating profusely, the beads cascading down his face and wetting the gray asphalt around his head, the soldier looked to Griff and uttered a phrase, which he began repeating softly, over and over.

Griff lifted his head and met Cade's gaze. "He wants me to kill him."

Cade heard the turbine whine and rotor chop increase exponentially to the left and right of his position. Then, in his peripheral vision, both left and right, he saw black blurs as the dual rotor choppers lifted off near simultaneously, leaving nothing but broken vehicles, twisted bodies, and a few thousand yards of open ground between his Delta team and the hundreds of Zs bookending them to the west and east.

"Try him one more time," Cade said, increasing the pressure on the nerves running close to the soldier's shattered femur.

Still holding the soldier's legs to the road, Axe looked away, muttering something under his breath.

Nearby, Cross was pacing the road, keeping tabs on the slow-moving Zs.

Again, Griff asked about motorcycles, external drives, and where the PLA Special Forces soldiers who'd paid the NSA a visit had gone.

Again the PLA soldier begged to be killed.

And Cade obliged him. Thinking of Brook, who was currently embroiled in a life and death struggle directly resulting from the virus this man's people had released on the United States population, he set the pistol on the road and slid his black Gerber from the scabbard.

"You reap what you sow," Cade said, drawing the dagger's razor-sharp blade hard across the man's pasty, upthrust neck.

Instantly the blood spritzed and sluiced onto the road where it mingled with the pooled sweat. Then the coppery reek hit Cade's nose and he felt the man going limp, finally beginning to succumb to the massive blood loss from the two fatal wounds.

And as the light faded from the PLA soldier's brown, almond-shaped eyes, Cade felt a burning hatred for everything he represented.

Axe rolled off the dead man's feet, rose, and stared off to the west at the approaching horde.

There was a loud tearing sound as Jedi One-One materialized over the horizon, its port minigun belching a reddish-orange rope of tracer fire groundward into the Zs.

After releasing his grip on the dead man's shoulders, Griff rose and looked off to the east. "We've got Zs pressing in from this side, now."

Cade said nothing. He wiped the blood from his knife on the soldier's uniform blouse and snicked it home in its scabbard. Still mute, he retrieved the Glock from the road and holstered it.

"Here," Cross said, handing the brooding captain the M4 he'd spotted and scooped up off the road a few yards back.

Taking the carbine from Cross, Cade nodded and clicked it onto the center-point sling.

Finally, as a shiver resulting from the ebbing adrenaline wracked his body, Cade called up Schriever to report his second failure of the day. After receiving what amounted to little more than a brush off from Nash who had picked up his call, he hailed Jedi One-One and requested an immediate exfil.

"One minute out," Ari called over the open net. "Make sure you keep the LZ clear for me."

Cade watched the departing Chinooks clear the trees on both ends of the convoy. A tick later One-Three banked sharply to the southwest and powered through a big turn that put her on a course to link up with One-Two, already surging northwest and beginning to blend in with the darkening horizon.

Not used to missions going sideways as completely as this one had, Cade decided to take his frustrations out on the approaching Zs. With the pair of Chinooks nearly out of earshot, and the harmonic thrum hitting his chest making it clear without looking skyward that Jedi One-One was inbound, he called "Weapons free" to the team and aimed his M4 in the direction of the lumbering horde.

"Anvil Actual, Jedi One-One. Check your fire. I repeat, check your fire," Ari called over the comms. "You're going to need those rounds. Nash just indicated they have the PLA team under surveillance."

Cade lowered his carbine. "Jedi One-One, Anvil Actual. Come again?"

Ari repeated himself verbatim then said, "Fifteen seconds out."

"Copy that," Cade said. "You have a clear LZ."

Schriever TOC

"Bring the image out five stops," Nash called to the airman controlling the sensor suite on the Keyhole satellite four hundred miles over Alexandria, Virginia. "Right southwest corner, grid A1, bracket and zoom five."

Working silently, the airman's fingers flew over the keyboard.

After a half-second delay—if that—the image of a freeway overpass on the large flat-panel screen situated front and center of the TOC shrank drastically. There was a brief lull, during which the airman working the computer nearby hammered away at the keyboard and manipulated a white trackball. Suddenly the overpass was replaced by an area of interest somewhere southeast of D.C., where the Chesapeake encroached on Maryland from the south. Dead center on the image were a number of objects that were impossible to mistake for anything but what they were.

Colonel Shrill removed his cover and absentmindedly scratched his bald dome.

In response to the new image being beamed down from her KH-12, Nash whistled and said, "How in the hell did they sneak all the way up there without us knowing?"

"Because I'd imagine we don't have enough personnel to monitor our SOSUS array twenty-four-seven let alone SURTASS at all."

"Limited deep water sound surveillance and *zero* towed array surveillance?" Nash asked.

Shrill nodded as the President crowded in from his left to whisper something to him.

Nash fired off a quick order to Airman Ripley. "Record GPS coordinates and see about getting laser comms established in the area."

"Get Cheyenne on the red phone," Shrill said to an airman nearby. "Tell whomever answers that the President wants to speak to Chairman Two Guns asap."

Suitland Parkway

Approaching out of the west, Ari brought Jedi One-One down low to the deck and buzzed barely a dozen feet over the Zs' bobbing heads. At once faces turned skyward and the mass proceeded to stumble and stagger, a large percentage of them toppling over like so many dominos. A hundred yards out the helo began to slow and flare. With barely fifty yards to spare, the bird rotated ninety degrees to port.

Cade saw Skipper's helmet and upper body rising up from behind the deployed minigun. About the same time Ari halted the rotation, the port-side door facing the team began to slide open.

Seeing One-One's gear lock into the full-down position and the wheels settle atop the parkway blacktop, Cade struck out with Axe, Cross, and Griff close behind.

Leading the operators as they zippered through a multitude of twice-dead Zs and grotesquely twisted and charred PLA corpses, Cade's thoughts suddenly strayed and he found himself wondering how Brook was faring. Fighting the near irresistible urge to stop right there and fire up his sat-phone to call Eden to find out, he heard the major's voice on the open comms, which Ari immediately switched to a private channel.

Though not entirely necessary, but one hundred percent instinctual in nature, as Cade always did during infil and exfil by helo, he leaned forward and clamped his free hand atop his bump helmet as he hustled to the Ghost Hawk.

After surviving the imaginary low-scythe of the whirling blades, Cade stopped beside the bird and watched the rest of his team board. Once they'd cleared out of the doorway, he hauled himself into the cabin and started the door closing. Quickly shrugging off his pack, Cade stowed his weapon between his legs, then strapped himself into the forward-facing port-side seat opposite Skipper.

In no time the helicopter had launched, turned ninety degrees to port and was streaking low over the still-scrabbling pack of Zs.

Cade regarded his team. Fatigue was showing on their faces, Axe more so than the former SEALS.

"You need a pick-me-up?" Cade said, directing the question at the very capable SAS shooter.

"Red Bull, Rip It, Rock Star. I'd even tip back a Lucozade if you have one … the warmer the better," said Axe, puckering his lips at the thought of the latter.

Cade shook his head. "You want a Five-Hour Energy?"

"No, mate. I want to sleep on the way back to Bastion."

"I heard that," Ari said. "Pass one up."

"You drink another of those, mate," said Axe, "you'll be buzzing so hard the walking wankers will hear us coming from a mile away."

"That's a risk we'll have to take," Ari quipped. "On the bright side … I'll be bright eyed and bushy tailed for your upcoming infil."

"Don't tell me we're moving on to Target Bravo," Cade said, incredulous. "Wasn't that Nash calling with an intercept vector to the PLA operators?"

"Negative," Ari said. "Bravo is a go."

Exhaling sharply, Cade leaned back against the fuselage wall and closed his eyes.

Lemonade out of lemons.

Chapter 69

Duncan won the "less is more" argument by convincing Alexander Dregan that four vehicles would be easier to maneuver and keep from getting separated from each other than seven should they encounter stiff resistance from Oliver's captors. Besides, he reasoned, keeping a couple of people and vehicles in reserve at the brown house might pay off if the worst case scenario did come to pass.

Since it had been Duncan's idea to make contact with the Bear Lake group prior to taking any kind of violent approach to freeing Oliver, he was leading the caravan in his Dodge. In the passenger seat next to him sat Tran, while in the back seat was Foley, who had once again talked his way into going along for the ride.

Having volunteered to drive the F-650, Jamie tucked the bigger rig in behind the Dodge as Duncan hung a left from the drive behind the lake house. She glanced at her silent passenger. Saw his liver-spotted hands worrying the canvas sling on the scoped long gun trapped between his knees. It was strange to not have Lev in the truck. In the weeks since Logan was gunned down, the two of them had grown close.

Knowing there was good reason for the seating arrangements, she flicked her gaze to the rearview mirror where she saw the pair of Humvees pacing her while still maintaining a sensible two-truck-length buffer. In the first vehicle she saw Daymon in the driver's seat, hands gripping the wheel, short dreads framing his pinched facial features. Lev was visible from the shoulders up in the cupola atop the Humvee and in the process of sweeping the Ma Deuce to the right where a smattering of houses were gliding by. Seeing as how Lev was familiar with the Browning heavy machine gun, both Duncan and Dregan had agreed instantly that there was no one more qualified than the young Iraq War veteran to man it.

Bringing up the rear of the convoy was the second Humvee with Alexander Dregan driving, and his son, Gregory, ensconced in the armored top-mounted turret housing the MK-19 grenade launcher.

Duncan drove south on Main Street for a short distance then turned right and followed 800 North to where it became Bear Lake Scenic Byway.

The road signs along the way all bore spray-painted warnings.

GO BACK.

CLOSED COMMUNITY.

TURN AROUND NOW OR ANSWER TO ADRIAN.

Graffiti-marred signs notwithstanding, the scenic byway lived up to its name. Passing the drive leading to the Rendezvous Beach campgrounds and boat launch, the vantage was stunning. Bear Lake glimmered bright blue in the breaking sun for miles to the north then suddenly turned steel-gray where water and sky merged.

The byway soon became South Bear Lake Boulevard which snaked north along the lake's west shore for a stretch, passing a burned-to-the-ground subdivision before splitting off to the northwest. Just prior to the boulevard shooting off toward the foothills backstopping the lake's west shore, Duncan steered the Dodge into a wide right-hand turn and bounced along an unimproved road with the blue waters of the lake filling up the windshield. A quarter of a mile down the unimproved road, adjacent to a trio of homes that looked to have been built sometime in the eighties or nineties, Duncan ground the Dodge to a complete stop. As he watched in the rearview, Jamie, as planned, did the same and let Ray out beside a copse of skeletal trees.

After seeing the spry old man loop around the nearest house and disappear from view, Duncan wheeled the Dodge across a freshly graded lot, bounced over a bright white, newly poured cement curb and took his foot off the gas.

The spooled-up momentum carried the truck forward in near silence for another hundred feet or so before Duncan stopped it dead center on a thirty-foot-wide stretch of recently laid asphalt. A hundred feet beyond the truck, a wall constructed of numerous fifteen-foot-tall cement noise barriers sprang from the ochre earth. A hundred feet to the right where the cement panels ended their run, the shorter cedar and chain-link fence rambled off north toward the nearby beach. Above the textured gray barriers rose half a dozen red-tiled roofs. In the center of the two- and three-story red-roofed lake houses which looked to be the first phase of a sprawling new subdivision was the cul-de-sac Duncan had spotted from the brown house due east of the lakefront properties.

Duncan flicked his eyes to the wing mirror in time to see Jamie make the turn and bring the F-650 to a complete stop at the mouth of the newly laid feeder road.

Taking their cue from Jamie's action, the two trailing Humvees edged past the Ford. Dregan parked his Humvee on the left soft shoulder where no trees or powerlines were in the way of the grenade launcher's field of fire, while Daymon ground his rig to a halt on the right, leaving Lev a clear shot at the gate, cement panels curving away on either side of it, as well as the cobbled-together run of fence on the compound's far east side.

A dozen feet left of Dregan's Humvee, on a vacant plat of land already graded, surveyed, and marked off for future development, was the fenced-in area where the "baddies to the north"—as the Thagons called them—had stowed a number of vehicles. Parked inside the chain-link enclosure were the log splitters hitched to pickups, a pair of large U-Haul trucks, the smaller prison vans, and a lone gray school bus with the Idaho state seal and the words **IDAHO DEPARTMENT OF CORRECTION - POCATELLO WOMEN'S CORRECTIONAL CENTER** emblazoned prominently in large black letters on its slab side.

After seeing the trailing vehicles take up their pre-planned positions ahead of the F-650, Duncan wheeled the Dodge at walking-speed down the center of the feeder road another three or four truck lengths, stopping a mere hundred feet from the makeshift gate fashioned from what looked to be metal lids repurposed from institutional-sized garbage cans. With thick welds at the seams and rolls of barbed wire strung around all four sides, the gore- and blood-streaked twenty-by-fifteen-foot wheeled gate looked damn formidable. Whether it would stand up to the firepower Dregan had brought to the table was the sixty-four-thousand-dollar question Duncan hoped would not have to be answered today.

You're going to lose this one, G.I. Jane, thought Duncan, as a blonde, steely-eyed woman popped up from behind the cement partition left of the gate with Oliver's scoped, long-barreled AR-15 tucked into her shoulder.

"Looks like we'll have no problem communicating with Oliver's captors," he quipped, fishing a sheet of paper and pen from the center console.

"You going to *write out* your demands?" Foley asked, hunched over the seatback and peering at the gate through the binoculars.

"Nope," answered Duncan sarcastically, as the pair of two-way radios on the console between them came to life simultaneously. "I'm going to write her a love letter."

Ray's voice emanated from both radios. "Care if I put a bullet between Debbie Harry's eyes?"

Thumbing the Motorola nearest him, Duncan said, "Not really. But you better let Blondie live long enough to hear what I have to say to her."

Hear? thought Tran, as he watched Duncan write **13-1** horizontally in black ink across the sheet of paper. The numbers were precise, six inches in height, and took up most of the page.

"Make it quick," said Ray. "I've got her *heart of glass* bracketed in my sights."

Touché, thought Duncan. “Which house are you in?” he asked.

“Green one lined up with the road you’re parked on,” Ray said. “I’m on the second floor behind the only north-facing window in the place.”

As Duncan thumbed Tran’s radio frequency to 13-1, he told Ray to do the same to his second two-way radio.

“Already done,” Ray said. “Powered on and volume set to ten.”

“Was the house booby-trapped?”

“Nope. Just a couple of deaders hanging around the street fronting it,” Ray said matter-of-factly. “Nothing this old man couldn’t handle.”

“Watch your six,” Duncan said.

“Always do,” Ray said. “Signing out.”

As soon as the channel was free, the rest of the group chimed in one at a time over radios set to the usual 10-1. In a matter of seconds, the next phase of the plan was in motion and all of the secondary radios were switched over to 13-1, the previously agreed upon channel.

Nearly two miles away, eye pressed to the spotting scope, Taryn heard everything over Wilson’s two-way which was already set to 13-1. She scooped up her Motorola, saw 10-1 was showing on the LCD display, then thumbed the rubber Talk button and detailed for everyone listening what she was seeing at the Bear Lake compound. Enunciating the words clearly, she said, “In addition to the blonde with the rifle on the wall, you have six other people heading to the gate … I’m pretty sure they’re all women. Whatever they are, they’re armed with a mix of rifles and pistols.”

Duncan asked, “Do you see their leader? The big gal … Adrian?”

“Yes,” Taryn said. There was a brief pause. “She’s bringing up the rear. Leather jacket over blue jeans. And now there’s another fifteen or so women coming out from between the two houses farthest north of you.”

Though he didn't expect positive news, Duncan asked anyway. "How's Oliver looking?" There was another long pause he guessed was due to Taryn having to pan the big scope across the cul-de-sac to where the stocks were located.

Finally, Taryn's voice leapt from the tiny speaker. "He's white as a sheet. And there's blood pooled on the ground all around him."

Kid's bleeding out, Duncan thought to himself. Knowing that waiting for the supposed leader to make her appearance might sign Oliver's death warrant, he held the sheet of paper against the inside of the windshield with the **13-1** facing out. He held it there for a long three-count, then laid it down on the dash, numbers facing up.

"Pasty Face got the message," Lev said from his perch in the cupola atop the Humvee. "She's fiddling with a radio as we speak."

"Copy that," Duncan intoned. "Looks like she put her rifle aside."

Tran's radio belched static. "What the *fuck* do you want?" the blonde hissed.

Tran handed the radio to Duncan.

"Tee-pee, wig-wam, tee-pee, wig-wam," Foley said from the back seat, his elbows parked on Duncan and Tran's seatbacks.

Thumb hovering over the Talk key, Duncan cast a quizzical look Foley's way.

Smiling, Foley said, "The bitch is *two tents*. Get it … *too tense*?"

"Third grade joke," Tran said, still clutching the borrowed Beretta in his right hand.

"Time and place," Duncan said, depressing the Talk button. "I want to speak to your leader. You have one, don't you?"

The radio clutched in the blonde's hand slowly fell away from her lips as she glanced down and to her left. Then, a half-beat later, she was looking forward again, the radio pressed to her lips. "She's coming." There was a pause as the woman stood statue-still, staring insolently at the Dodge. "Whoever you are, motherfucker, you've made a big fucking mistake."

"Do you kiss your mommy with that mouth?" Duncan chuckled as he scooped up the radio locked on channel 10-1 and hailed Dregan.

"Yes?" Dregan replied.

"If they don't agree to my demands—"

Dregan interrupted. "What are your demands?" he asked.

"Give us our man and you won't die, works for me," Duncan said.

"They're already dead," Dregan growled. "We all are. Look around. This country is dying. What makes you think that words are going to change minds?"

Taryn broke in. "They're moving vehicles around inside the walls. Pointing them all to the northwest. Must be an exit over there I can't see."

"Thanks for the heads up," Duncan said.

Foley handed the Bushnells forward to Duncan.

Duncan took the binoculars and trained them on the wall left of the gate where the blonde was being joined by the Plain Jane twins he had spotted earlier. For a brief second the twins both rose above the parapet brandishing what looked to Duncan like Ruger Mini 14s. In unison, the women raised the rifles to their shoulders and, as if they'd been under siege before, crouched low behind the wall, leaving only their rifles, heads, and shoulders visible from below.

The woman called Adrian showed her pudgy, wind-burned face next. Then Duncan saw her neck and the word MOM tattooed there in black Old English lettering. As she emerged fully behind the wall, the scowling blonde gestured in the direction of the Humvees.

A gust of wind kicked up from the west, ruffling the head honcho's close-cropped man-do.

"Everyone, meet Adrian." Duncan said over the group frequency.

"She reminds me more of Rocky Balboa than Adrian," Daymon quipped. "How the hell does a person keep all that weight on? It's not as if there're any all-you-can-eat buffets still in business."

In the Dodge, Foley said to Duncan, "I've managed to lose a dozen pounds since the dead started to walk."

"Doesn't show," Duncan said, lowering the binoculars and cracking a rare smile.

Frowning, Foley leaned toward Tran to get a better look at the upper reaches of the wall.

Keeping the binoculars trained on the top of the wall, Duncan watched the big woman turn to the blonde and waggle her sausage-like fingers while saying something he couldn't quite make out. In turn, the blonde handed Adrian a radio and immediately retrieve Oliver's rifle, swinging its business end back on line with the Dodge.

This time Duncan clearly read Adrian's lips as she spoke into the radio. "Can't you dumbasses read?" she bellowed. "You're way out of your element. This is *my* territory and you should *not* be here."

"Understood," Duncan said into the secondary radio. "How about you release our friend and we'll grant you your wish."

Astride the Humvee with Daymon at the wheel, Lev set his radio down on the cupola rim and shifted his aim up by a few degrees, the iron sights on the Ma Deuce settling on the wall just about where he guessed the bitchy-looking blonde's navel to be.

"That *man* is under arrest for looting," Adrian spat into the radio. "We caught him red-handed."

"You already took your pound of flesh," Duncan said. "Give him to us and we'll be on our way."

"If I don't?"

The radio tuned to Channel 10-1 came alive. Taryn said, "Oliver hasn't moved a muscle. And the blood stopped flowing from his stump."

Duncan sighed. "And the rest of the *people* inside?" he asked Taryn.

"The ones who moved the cars and trucks are coming to the gate armed with what look like AR-15s."

"Thank you, Taryn," Duncan said. "Everybody hear that? If Oliver's gonna live we have go in now."

Dregan voiced his approval over the group frequency.

"Weapons free, then," Duncan said. "Ray, take your shot if you have it." After handing the binoculars over the seatback, Duncan selected Reverse and was lifting his foot off the brake pedal when Foley said, "I think Adrian just ordered the blonde to shoot."

The second the word "shoot" rolled off of Foley's tongue, the windshield spidered from a hole punched just below the rearview mirror. A millisecond later, carried on the air escaping his lungs, a pain-filled moan was making the rounds of the cab.

In his side vision, in quick succession, Duncan saw the binoculars falling to the seat, a spritz of blood paint the air between him and Tran, and Foley's arms reach for the sky. In the next half-beat, with the crack from the rifle echoing all around, Foley's limp body crashed to the floorboard behind the seats adding a resonant *thud* to the volley of gunfire coming from behind the gate.

They're just women.

Dregan's fateful words as well as everything that had just happened in less than the blink of an eye registered to Duncan at the same point in time he was seeing the blonde nearly split in half by a short burst from the .50 caliber Browning.

Unbeknownst to all who had witnessed the blonde's body jerk violently, she was already dead before the first finger-thick slug tore through her stomach and blew a bowling-ball-sized plug of bone, muscle, and flesh from her upper back. Because a split second prior to Lev letting loose half a dozen rounds from the turret-mounted .50, Ray, roughly five hundred feet away, had reacted quicker, his Winchester Model 70 delivering the 190-grain hunk of lead that pierced the blonde's sternum, shredded her beating heart, and causing that initial death spasm prior to the .50 slugs tearing into her.

The sound of bullets impacting the Dodge met Duncan's ears. "Get back there and see what you can do for Foley," he bellowed, matting the accelerator, which started the wheels to spinning and a cloud of blue smoke swirling around the pickup's bed.

Without uttering a word, Tran punched out of his seatbelt and crawled over the seatback.

Back at the brown lake house, Taryn exhaled sharply. Upon seeing the woman in yellow and the gun she was brandishing seemingly cease to exist—there one second, gone the next—she swung the scope away from the growing halo of pink mist and noted the armed *rats* scurrying from the gate to their vehicles. As she opened her mouth to report the development, to her horror she saw one of the women passing by Oliver drag something shiny across his exposed neck. "They're running," she blurted. Then, as an afterthought, though watered down on account she didn't know the facts, she added, "One of them just did something awful to Oliver."

There was no verbal reply. Just muzzle flashes coming from the good guys to the left, then return fire lancing from the rifles of the two women who were just now rising up over the wall.

Where'd you go, Lotta? thought Duncan, as outgoing tracer fire from the .50 cut the air over his wildly fishtailing Dodge.

"He's dead," was the answer he got from Tran. Out of context, sure. But nonetheless heartbreaking, because Duncan was the one who, instead of having Foley stay behind with Wilson, Taryn, Peter, and Cleo, had caved and let him come along on this ill-planned affair.

Suddenly the windshield in front of where Tran had been a few seconds ago took some more rounds, caved inward and began shedding pea-sized kernels of sharp-edged glass. Then fabric and foam exploded into the air as more bullets tore into the still-warm seat-back where Tran had been sitting.

Hollering into the radio, Duncan directed Lev to engage the shooters on the wall.

One step ahead of the barked order, Lev had delivered a second ten-round burst right after the first, hitting only the barrier's concrete lip, which sent a cloud of gray dust swirling about the shooters and sending Adrian diving for cover.

Seeing the wall absorb the rounds, Duncan stood on the brakes. As the truck came to a complete stop and was enveloped in a rolling cloud of tire smoke, in his mind's eye he was imagining an aerial view of the houses, cul-de-sac, stocks, and their relation to each other. Determining that the stocks, and thus Oliver, were well to the right of the gate on wheels, he told Lev to rake the gate with the Ma Deuce.

No sooner had Duncan asked than the .50 was punching holes clean through the gate to no great effect.

One of the twins popped up and fired off a dozen rounds.

Bullets pinging off the front of his truck, Duncan spoke into the radio in a voice devoid of the authoritarian timbre he'd used on Lev. "Dregan, I need you to put some rounds on the gate."

Dregan responded at once, letting loose a three-round volley from the grenade launcher that went *choonka, choonka, choonka.*

There was a half-second of silence as seemingly everyone paused and waited with bated breath for the 40 mm rounds to cover the short distance and find their mark.

In the back half of the drawn-out second the silence was erased when the grenades exploded against the gate in quick succession, causing Duncan to duck his head and miss the metal panels shearing apart and scattering on the ground inside the perimeter like a discarded poker hand. Duncan also missed seeing Dregan's follow-on three-round-volley land among the fleeing vehicles, which started the fire whose smoke he saw when he finally rose up from the seat and peered over the dash, thanking God he hadn't suffered the shrapnel wounds he'd been anticipating.

Daymon came on over the group frequency. "Old Man, you've got a pair of rotters at your nine o'clock. They're too close to engage."

Having been draped across the center console, there was no way for Duncan to have seen the pair of zombies as they emerged from behind the chain-link surrounding the nearby lot full of vehicles. With the trio of dull concussions still ringing in his ears, Daymon's blurted warning went unheard.

As Duncan rose up off the seat and looked ahead to assess the damage inflicted on the gate following the triple thunderclap that had sent him ducking for cover, a hunched-over female specimen reached through his partially open window and intertwined her gnarled fingers in his thinning gray hair.

Keeping his foot on the brake, Duncan powered down the window with his left hand. Meanwhile, he hefted the Saiga from the seat with his right, jammed the semi-auto shotgun's gaping muzzle against the beast's neck and pulled the trigger—*twice.*

The first deafening blast didn't do much. The slug only succeeded in shredding dermis and flesh a few inches above her right clavicle before rocketing out the back a little misshapen and with barely half the kinetic energy as when it had struck.

The second shot shell, however, was filled with nine high-caliber lead pellets. It was cycled into the chamber automatically by the escaping gasses created by the previous shot and discharged as soon as Duncan's finger caressed the trigger the second time.

Gotta thank Daymon for this new toy, thought Duncan as the newly released swarm of shot moving at thirteen-hundred-feet-per-second punished the creature's face, half of the pellets finding brain and finishing what the slug had failed to do.

Gone half-deaf from the double shotgun blasts, Tran rose up from the back seat with his face, neck, and jacket front streaked with Foley's blood. Finding himself face-to-face with a young male first turn, and unsure what to do, he locked eyes with Duncan.

"Power the window down and shoot the bastard," Duncan instructed even as he was practicing advice contrary to his own by pulsing his window up.

Hands shaking, Tran raised the Beretta level with the abomination's head, which strangely was tilted dog-like and staring at him with eyes devoid of emotion, yet still harboring a spark of recognition.

Seeing a split-second flash of his own nightmarish visage reflected back at him off the window glass, Tran instantly relived his long march surrounded by the dead leaving Jackson Hole. The mask of his own dried blood he had worn then had helped him blend in and walk among them. The same thing was happening now. So he used it to his advantage, pulsing his window down and pressing the muzzle into the demon's left eye.

Though not as loud as the shotgun, the 9mm's report still roared inside the cab. As the spent shell pinged off the back of Duncan's head, the gory blowback of blood coated the window outside and left a constellation of crimson dotting the white headliner directly above Tran's head.

Ears ringing mightily, Tran ran the window up and crawled over the shredded seatback, thankful to be alive.

When Duncan shifted his gaze from the fallen corpses to the rearview and noticed the Humvees advancing on his position, barely thirty seconds had elapsed between the first salvo from the Ma Deuce and Tran earning the right to ride shotgun in his truck.

After watching the Zs crumble beside the Dodge, Lev threw a few more rounds from the Browning at the point in space the gate used to reside.

"Well I'll be a sombitch," Duncan said, shifting the rig into Drive. "Dregan put the hurt on the gate."

"And the house is on fire," Tran added.

"So it is," replied Duncan, craning to see through the nearly destroyed windshield. "Maybe we give Foley a Viking's sendoff. He doesn't have any kin."

"No." Tran said insistently. "He must be buried on the hill. For me, the same when I go."

"Let's not get ahead of ourselves."

Up ahead, the Humvee driven by Daymon charged through the destroyed opening, passing overtop the twisted metal sheets with a hellish racket.

Falling in behind Dregan's Humvee, Duncan started to think aloud. "I hope he checks his fire. Oliver is to the right."

No sooner had he said it than the radio crackled to life. "It's mostly clear," Daymon said. "The leader is down behind the scaffolding."

"Alive?"

"Yeah," Daymon replied. "But she's got the same kind of injury Oliver *had*. Key word … *had*. Come on in. Lev is covering her and the squirters." There was a brief moment of silence, then he was back on the open channel. "Lev wants to know if he can hose down the retreating vehicles."

"Negative," Duncan said as he wheeled the Dodge slowly over the rent metal panels. "We've got their leader. That's good enough." Once inside, he saw the back gate and a number of pickup trucks speeding away, brake lights flaring as they slowed and turned onto an identical feeder road a quarter mile away. He shifted his gaze to the Humvees and noticed that they had been parked so that their weapons were covering the semicircle of homes.

The radio in Duncan's hand crackled to life again. "I see one of the lookalike girls," said Gregory. "I will dismount and take her prisoner."

"Be careful," Alexander Dregan said to the son recently spared a painful death to Omega. "Shoot her if she moves."

Pulling the Dodge to the curb next to the stocks, Duncan killed the engine and craned over his seatback. Foley was slumped sideways on the floor, staring straight up, mouth agape. The man's white tee shirt, parka, and jeans were crimson. The rear seat was awash in blood and viscera and fine down feathers from his punctured parka. The bullet's exit out his back had no doubt left a wound many times larger than the nickel-sized hole where it entered. Hearing the low rumble of the F-650's V-10, Duncan gripped the wheel two-handed and banged his head against his own white knuckles. "Stupid, stupid, stupid," he chanted as Jamie brought the truck to a halt just outside his window.

Hearing the engine cut off, Duncan sat upright and shifted his gaze back to Oliver. Let it linger, resisting the urge to run headlong across the open ground to check the man's neck for a pulse that his gut told him wasn't there. Instead, he picked up the two-way radio set to 10-1 and began issuing orders. He tasked Daymon and Lev with clearing the homes of lingering bad guys … or gals, whatever the case may be.

Since the Dregans were already securing the prisoners, Duncan sent Jamie out across the cul-de-sac to take up station near the newly discovered rear gate. Surely the dead had heard the gunfire and explosions and revving engines of the fleeing vehicles.

Then Duncan looked into the rearview. Framed by the bent gate panels still attached to the crude set of wheels, he could see the upper story of the green house Ray had chosen to set up his overwatch. He thumbed the Talk key. "Ray … you there?"

"Where am I gonna go?"

Good point, thought Duncan. He said, "Sit tight and watch the road and gate for baddies and rotters. If all goes well, we will be by to get you shortly."

"I'm good," Ray replied. "Found me a can of corned beef and hash."

Duncan regarded Tran with a raised brow. Pocketing the radio he said, "Why don't you go and help keep watch at the front gate."

Tran looked at the Beretta in his hand for a second, then exited the truck.

Duncan spent a moment alone in the truck steeling himself against what he feared was at the end of a short walk to the stocks. "Fuck it," he said, throwing his door open.

As an afterthought, he reached back inside the truck and snatched up his Stetson. Then, moving with purpose toward the pale form hanging limply from the medieval-looking torture device, he tugged the hat down low, adjusting the brim to hide the welling tears.

Chapter 70

After lifting off of Suitland Parkway, the Ghost Hawk with the Delta team aboard flew low and fast north by west, following the colorful river of static metal and glass on the eastbound Parkway all the way to its source: Washington D.C. The closer they got to the former seat of government, the more destruction and stalled-out vehicles and roaming packs of dead they overflew.

"Two mikes to Target Bravo," Ari called over the comms.

Cade checked his weapon then peered out the port window. Below the helo, the traffic jam of death gave way to a vast cemetery strangely devoid of dead things aboveground. In seconds the grave markers and overgrown green expanse was lost from sight and a brown river was snaking away to the left.

"That's the Anacostia," said Skipper. "It borders the District to the southwest and meets up with the Potomac near Ronald Reagan."

Leaning forward and craning his head, Cade was just able to make out where the two rivers intersected. And paralleling the Potomac, he saw the airport's runways, which, from this distance, appeared as pale gray lines crisscrossing each other.

"One mike," Ari said as he cut airspeed and they passed over what remained of a six-lane concrete bridge spanning the Anacostia.

"That *was* the Sousa," said Cross.

At once Axe began to whistle *Stars and Stripes Forever.*

"Reminds me of Fourth of July fireworks," Griff added. "I'm going to miss the beer and barbecues."

"They're only postponed," Cade said. "We're coming back from this."

Skipper regarded Cade, but, as per usual, said nothing. He powered down the weapons bay door and gripped the mini by its vertical handles.

Through the new opening in the fuselage, Cade could see the two Stealth Chinooks bobbing on pockets of turbulent air, but thanks to the skilled SOAR pilots, still flying in tight formation. Beyond the helos a number of Washington D.C.'s landmarks stood out against the foreboding autumn sky.

Griff jacked a thumb over his shoulder. "Capitol building's right over here. The dome has seen better days."

Cade cast his gaze across the cabin in time to see what was left of the top of the stylized, white dome pass by outside the window. Even blackened by fire it stood out in stark contrast to the ground clutter. He pulled up the contrasting mental images of the first days of the zombie apocalypse. Save for the three helicopters cutting the airspace over the District, the skies were as serene as he remembered Portland's being after the 9/11 attacks. And unlike those crazy first days after the dead began to walk, in the whole of D.C., for as far as he could see, there were no buildings going up in flames. Not a lick of smoke sullied the crisp air.

Conditions on the ground were far different today than those first days when unfathomable apocalyptic images were broadcast to the world on cable television. Gone were the crowds of frantic people fleeing the dead. Where military vehicles had been patrolling the streets, now only the dead could be seen, their movement minimal due to lack of stimuli and dropping temperatures.

"Daylight is a dwindling commodity," Ari said. "Those Rangers are raring to get into the fight. Might as well use them."

Cade said, "We're out of Screamers. Might as well unleash my brethren."

"We've got a few of the indoor Screamers left," Cross said.

"We might need them inside Target Bravo."

"On station in thirty," Ari called. "I'll orbit. Infil is at your discretion, Anvil. The President wants her shopping list filled only if there's a good chance of everyone coming home."

Cade didn't like hearing the secondary mission framed that way. He was as passionate about it as Clay had been when she asked if it was a possibility. In fact, every man and woman in the TOC stood up and clapped when she suggested it.

"Give me one pass low and slow," Cade said.

"One?"

"*One*," Cade repeated. "Scrape the ground if you want. I don't care."

"Port side," Ari said, banking Jedi One-One and flying her right down Pennsylvania Avenue with the White House clearly visible between Ari and Haynes out the cockpit glass. A couple of seconds later Target Bravo was filling up the port-side glass, its exterior still blindingly white.

"This is the back side where the research entrance is located," Cade said. "Bring us around the building real slow." He focused on the far corner of the Grecian-styled structure.

Once the building's west side scrolled by and the front façade came into view, Axe said, "Looks like the stumblers don't fancy all the stairs."

Griff said, "The wily bastards are probably hiding in Sherwood Forest and waiting for us to come waltzing by."

The twenty-plus oversized columns dominating the front elevation did indeed offer a nice shadowy place to hide a lurker or ten. However, Cade let it be known that the public entrance had been moved to the corner of the place years ago due to ADA requirements. Which was a good thing, because the original set of bronze double-doors would probably have required explosives to breach from the outside. And with what looked to be hundreds of dead per square mile in the District, anything with more punch than a firecracker was sure to bring in large numbers of them from all around.

"We're going in there," Cade said, pointing out the entrance on the final go-around. "Put us down in the fountain."

"Which fountain?" Ari asked.

"The one with no water … just across Pennsylvania," Cade said.

"That's the Navy memorial," Cross said.

"Correct," said Cade, gesturing toward Target Bravo. "We'll cross Pennsylvania and go west around the right side and enter through the southwest corner entrance. I'll pop the lock …"

"*If* it's locked," Axe said. "It's not exactly the NSA."

Cade held a hand up in the SAS operator's direction then went on, "Elevator will be a no go. So we clear the stairwell on the way up. The objective will be dead ahead from the top of the stairs. *If* the items are still there, we'll need the Ranger chalk from Jedi One-Two for extra muscle. Once they are boots on the ground, have One-Three loiter, guns hot. We use their chalk as a QRF *only* as a last resort."

"Copy that," Ari said. Then he switched channels and relayed the impromptu plan to Nash at the TOC, and finished by bringing the other SOAR pilots into the loop.

Cade sized up his team. To a man they looked fatigued, but that was when alpha predators performed their best. And he knew when the time came, they would give him no less than one hundred and ten per cent.

Chapter 71

Two seconds after laying eyes on Oliver, Duncan knew Glenda's youngest was dead. Though it looked as if he had tried to staunch the flow of blood from his crudely amputated leg by forcing the ragged stump into the muddy soil of the once grass-covered parking strip, it had been all for naught. Because of the way the stocks supported his weight—the job falling mostly on his wrists and neck—there was no way for him to fully extend downward and apply any kind of pressure to effectively staunch the bleeding. Then there was the gaping second mouth that had been cut into his neck. *No surviving that.* Where Oliver's Adam's apple should have been was a six-inch gash that went nearly ear-to-ear. And to add insult to the life-ending injury, Oliver's tongue had been threaded through the horrific wound.

Columbian Neck Tie, thought Duncan, as he looked out across the lake. *Same shit the Viet Cong perfected forty years ago.*

He didn't know how long he stood there staring with his boots fused to the blood-soaked soil. Finally, snapping him to the present, Lev and Daymon were at his side, the latter putting an arm around him and asking, "Are you going to be OK, boss?"

Duncan lifted his head and regarded the pair with eyes red-rimmed and glistening with fresh tears.

"Anything I can do?" asked Lev.

"Help me with Oliver."

"We got it," Daymon said.

"We found three U-Hauls full of food and supplies. Dregan is taking one," Lev added. "We can make room for Foley and Oliver in the back of one of the others."

Duncan nodded, then swung his gaze back out across the lake.

A trio of gunshots sounded from the direction of the destroyed gate. After the initial report, there had been a two-second lapse followed by two more shots delivered rapid-fire.

Looking over his shoulder, Duncan saw Tran standing over a pair of fallen rotters. Beretta held limply at his side, the man turned and delivered a solemn nod.

"You're done being a pacifist, Tran," muttered Duncan, as he turned to watch Lev and Daymon dismantle the hardware fastening the wooden top bar of the stocks over Oliver's neck and wrists.

Across the cul-de-sac, near the smaller gate the half-dozen trucks and vans had escaped through, Jamie was engaging a lone walker, her tomahawk flashing through the air and settling inches deep into the thing's bald pate.

Riding the wind, the hollow thunk reached Duncan's ears a half-beat after his eyes registered a sight he thought he'd never see outside of a documentary about the Middle Ages.

Wondering when all of this fighting and killing and death was going to end, Duncan trudged back to his ruined Dodge. He collected his gear and motioned Tran over. Together, they followed the all-too-familiar blood trail to the house that had briefly caught fire but was now just spewing wispy curls of smoke from an upper window. The garage door was open and sitting on the floor cross-legged were Adrian, one of the plain-looking women, and a third woman they had found hiding in a bathroom of the house above them. The women's wrists were zip-tied behind their backs and dirty shop rags protruded from each of their mouths.

From her spot on the oil-stained cement floor, Adrian looked up at Duncan and started hurling muffled epithets his way.

"Sticks and stones …" quipped Duncan in a tired-sounding voice.

Returning from the orange and white U-Haul parked beside the house, Daymon said, "Foley and Oliver are in back of the truck outside. Found a moving blanket to cover them with. Lev tied them down as best he could."

Duncan said nothing. Continued to stare at the women.

Daymon said, "We found three men in the basement of Fatty Fatterson's house. They were real malnourished and said the Pocatello prisoners beat them often and used them for slave labor. All of them were missing fingers. One had his arm amputated at the elbow. Now and again these bitches would hold some kind of bastardized religious rituals before hacking pieces off of them … to *eat*."

Eyes bugged, Adrian spewed something unintelligible while straining against her bonds.

Duncan put his hand on the big woman's shoulder and forced her to be still. Loosening his grip, he fixed his bloodshot eyes on Daymon, then flicked the gaze to Lev.

Lev said, "I bandaged the survivors best I could. Gave them food, water, and a truck and let them go."

Duncan nodded.

Daymon said, "They weren't just eating men."

Duncan arched a brow.

"We found dog bones mixed in with the human remains out back. Oliver's missing leg was still cooking on the grill."

A half-dozen gunshots rang out from the rear gate. Then Jamie's voice emanated from the radio to let everyone know she had put down three rotters and all was well.

Resuming the conversation, Daymon said, "I let the men go because I figured we didn't need three more mouths to feed at the compound. It was all I could do to keep them from coming back to kill *Mom*."

Duncan nodded. "Did you give them weapons?"

There was a pained moment of silence. Lev and Daymon met eyes.

Lev looked at the floor.

Finally, Daymon spoke up. "Nope," he said, tucking a stray dread behind his ear.

"Good," Duncan said matter-of-factly.

"What do we do with these three little piggies?" Daymon asked.

"Put them in the stocks. Leave them for the rotters to eat."

Adrian listed to the side and hit the concrete with a solid thud. She lay there struggling against her bonds like a failed Houdini act.

Duncan tossed his gear into the U-Haul and returned and stood next to Tran, who had just arrived from the front gate.

"We'll gladly take care of these three," Lev said. "Least we can do for Foley and Oliver."

Daymon locked eyes with Duncan. "Before we go, I have something I need to get off my chest."

Duncan told Tran to sit tight. "Let's walk," he said to Daymon.

As the two men made their way out of the garage and around the corner to where the U-Haul was parked, Daymon came clean about his attempts at toughening Oliver up. Spilled about the two instances when he actually put the dead man's life in danger. Then he told Duncan how he planned to atone for it.

Duncan looked behind him, then leaned against the garage.

"Foley's blood is on my hands. I guess I let Dregan's attitude rub off on me. I underestimated those hags. That's a fact." Duncan pushed off the wall and stood inches from Daymon, looking up into his eyes. "What you did isn't the same. Oliver's always been a loner. Glenda told me as much. So in my eyes, there's no need for atonement."

"When we get back to the compound, me and Heidi are leaving. I found a place for us outside of Woodruff."

"You're a big boy. Know that I don't hold you responsible," Duncan said, backing off a pace. "I still have to tell Glenda what went down."

"All the better I'm leaving then."

Duncan closed his eyes and rested his chin on his chest for a second. When he looked up, Daymon was gone. So he climbed behind the wheel of the U-Haul and radioed Taryn to tell her they were moving out in a few minutes and to be ready to go.

A moment later Tran climbed into the passenger seat, a hangdog look on his face.

"They weren't humans," Duncan said, heading him off at the pass. "At least not anymore. And fella, if you keep that Beretta you better be willing to use it against both the dead *and* the living."

Tran said nothing. He kept his gaze locked outside the window as Duncan started the engine.

Waiting for the U-Haul's rough idle to steady, Duncan called Lev over. "Burn the place," he said. "To the ground. Then knock the side fence down so the dead can see Adrian and her evil friends."

Lev nodded and strode over to help Daymon with the prisoners.

Sitting in silence, Duncan let the engine warm up for a couple of minutes. When he finally pulled away toward the gate, he saw the stocks newly filled with the three women, the leader of the group, Adrian, acting as the meaty center of the soon-to-be rotter sandwich.

Maneuvering the ungainly box truck around the destroyed gate, Duncan picked up the Motorola and radioed Ray to say he was coming to pick him up. Then, as the U-Haul's tires hit the smooth pavement, he glanced in the side mirror and saw the licks of fire and black smoke that told him Daymon and Lev were taking care of business.

Chapter 72

After skimming the mast-styled flag poles in front of the dried-up fountain directly across Pennsylvania Avenue from Target Bravo, Jedi One-One was wheels down for a scant three seconds before the turbines spooled back up and she was lifting off minus the Delta team.

By the time Cade and his team were away from the rotor cone and sweeping their weapons toward the center of the expansive United States Navy Memorial, the near-silent stealth helo was climbing away to the west over their heads, the tricycle-style landing gear already retracting into its smooth underbelly.

"Schriever, Jedi One-One," Ari called over the comms. "Anvil Team is boots on at Target Bravo."

"Copy that, Flight Lead. Stand by for SITREP," came a female voice from the TOC.

Hearing the exchange between Ari and the TOC at Schriever, Cade rose and led the team off in the same direction the helicopter was retreating. Weaving between the jam of cars choking Pennsylvania Avenue with his M4 leading the way had looked to be less of a challenge from the air. On the ground, he and the team were forced to step up on bumpers and scramble over grimy hoods and trunks to get across the westbound lanes.

Once Cade made it to the yard-wide expanse of concrete separating Pennsylvania Avenue's westbound lanes from the eastbound, he paused and regarded the rest of the team coming up on his six. Satisfied with their progress, he walked his gaze north across the tops of the traffic snarl. On the far side of the Naval Memorial, dozens of Zs attracted by the black helicopter were making their way across the plaza. He watched Griff and

Cross slide across the trunk of a dirt-streaked Mercedes one right after the other and take a knee, each training the deadly end of their suppressed weapon a different direction down the narrow cement island splitting Pennsylvania Avenue lengthwise.

In the rear of a nearby city bus something dead was clawing at the clouded windows. Ignoring the monster's interest in him, Cross said, "That landing zone isn't going to work for exfil."

Cade nodded, his eyes tracking Axe as the SAS operator clomped across a Crown Victoria's flat hood and hurdled the rear end of a Yellow Cab. "I think I'd rather wade through three lanes of shamblies than go bonnet, boot, bonnet, boot like that again."

"Be grateful for the jam," Cade said to Axe. He gestured toward the LZ. "It's all that's keeping them from us."

Axe rose and made a slow turn to the north. Seeing the excited throng, he whistled and said, "I stand corrected."

"Let's move," Cade said, striking out between a narrow gap separating a Prius cab from the city-bus-cum-tomb whose shadow they'd been crouched in.

The going got a little easier as the team crossed the fifth and sixth eastbound lanes. Leading them across the sidewalk and angling for a triangle of tall grass on the northwest corner of Pennsylvania and 14th Street, Cade heard Nash break in over the comms to tell Ari about developments in their search for the PLA team. But before any details were exchanged, Nash said something to the effect that the satellite footage would speak for itself and then signed off.

Encouraged by what the cryptic snippet of conversation alluded to, Cade led the team charging south down the sidewalk with the entrance to the looming target building in his sights.

As he neared the recessed doors leading to the marble structure's lower level, Cade found his path along the litter-strewn sidewalk blocked when a lone shambler emerged from between a pair of static cars to his right. Slowing his gait, he leveled the carbine to take aim, but was confronted by two more child-sized first turns spilling through the same opening. After putting a Danner to the lead undead kid's chest, Cade sidestepped the pair as they fell and fired two rounds into the first shambler's balding skull. Seeing the thing's forehead implode from the double tap, he went to a knee in front of the alcove shielding the building's entrance and motioned for Griff and Cross to engage the kid walkers. Next, he caught Axe's eye as the operator was coming to a halt on their six and mouthed, "Cover me." He turned from the action and removed the lock gun from a cargo pocket.

After a quick visual sweep of the ten-by-twenty entry, which was thankfully occupied by only ankle-high drifts of orange and red fallen leaves and a yellowed Washington Post front page emblazoned with the headline **Super Flu Outbreak Hits China**, Cade kneeled before the steel door and worked the pick gun into the first lock.

Immediately following a flurry of suppressed gunshots, Cross called, "Get us inside, Wyatt. We're drawing a crowd."

After popping the first lock, Cade moved to the upper deadbolt, which took him just a handful of seconds to thwart.

Having alternated between watching Cade's progress and scanning 14th Street for more unwanted visitors, Axe saw the second lock fall and in his headset heard Cade call for Cross and Griff to disengage and rally at the entrance.

Motioning Axe forward, Cade said, "Cover me while I go in."

"Roger," Axe said, raising his M4 from its low ready position.

Slowly easing the door inward, Cade one-eyed it around the corner and saw a wide run of white marble stairs going up and a set of brushed stainless-steel elevator doors to his right. Casting a glance at the floor, he noted the fine coating of untracked dust. "Clear," he called, rising up and shouldering the door open.

Once everyone was inside and the door was secured, it was evident their NVGs wouldn't be needed. A diffuse light was spilling down the stairwell, painting the foyer a soft golden color.

Taking point, Cade scaled the stairs one at a time, keeping wide left and his M4 trained on the turn as he approached it.

Three more turns and a landing crossing later they found themselves in an equally dusty and identical foyer. On the wall in front of them was a sign directing them to the Rotunda Room.

Seeing the sign, Cross raised a brow and pointed it out to Griff and Axe, both a few steps to his rear.

Continuing on through the doorway, Cade noted that the air in the building's interior was cool and musty. With the computer-controlled HVAC units that usually scrubbed the air and kept the humidity in check not running, it didn't surprise him that the elements were already taking a toll on the building and its contents.

As Cade entered the rotunda, he was blown away by its sheer scale and complexity of design. Underfoot, the marble floor was decorated with dozens of large circles inlaid with red marble. Each of the circles were bordered with black marble. A fine sheen of dust coated everything under the dome. Motes danced in the light shafts bisecting the room from the front dais to the retired grand entry.

At the fore of the great room opposite the entry was a quartet of columns, the smaller two honed from black marble similar to that used on the floor, while the larger outside columns were the same red marble as the circles on the floor. Between the columns stood a pair of United States flags. Roughly thirty feet above the dais, supported by the smaller two columns, was a white marble arch. Intricate inlays of black marble and carved dentil details were used liberally in the grand arch's design. And bookending the columns and arch—rising from just below the base of the columns and ending where the dome began—were beautifully painted murals, one depicting men in powdered wigs and shawls attending the formal reading of the Declaration of Independence and the other showing the nation's forefathers observing the presentation of the United States Constitution.

After sweeping his gaze from left to right and determining that he and his team were alone, Cade padded across the room and stopped beneath the arch, peering down at the first of five glass cases. Inside was a leaf of worn, yellow-brown paper. He read the words *We the people* and instantly felt an electric current race along his spine.

Cade turned and directed Cross and Griff across the room to where natural light was spilling in from a huge multi-paned window and casting a grid-like pattern across a series of cases rising up from a marble dais. "Start there," he said, pointing at the cases. "And put them next to those." He hooked his thumb over his shoulder. *Those* he was alluding to were a pair of bronze doors taking up nearly a third of the rotunda's south-facing wall.

Working the screwdriver's star-shaped tip into the flush fastener on the argon-filled panel he was hunched over, Cade looked sidelong at Axe. "Are you okay with this?"

"Earl Grey under the bridge," Axe replied. "But that's ancient history. I know I would have been a Minuteman had I been alive back then."

"You and me both, brother," Cade said, drawing out the fastener. Moving to the next corner, he called up Ari and detailed how they were going to get the priceless artifacts aboard Jedi One-Two.

***

Ten minutes after entering the National Archives building, the team had secured the documents the President had requested, breached the largely unused double doors on the Rotunda Room's south side and were handing the glass-encased artifacts through the doors to the waiting hands of the Rangers from One-Two. Having just delivered the chalk to the stairs fronting the Archive building's south side, the stealth Chinook was now waiting a stone's throw away on Constitution Avenue, performing what was essentially a pinnacle maneuver, nose up at a fifteen-degree angle with the back wheels perched atop a pair of yellow taxi cabs, their roofs buckling a bit under its weight. One-Two's wide rear ramp was down and barely minutes after disgorging the Ranger chalk she was already receiving the first of five glass cases containing individual pages of the Bill of Rights.

Cade handed the Declaration of Independence through the yawning bronze doors to a Ranger and watched the master sergeant from the 75th Regiment pass it to another Ranger. Bucket-brigade-style, the documents a proud nation was founded on made their way down the stairs, overtop the snarled traffic, and were handed off to the crew chief on the ramp of the helo expertly piloted by an unknown aviator from the 160th SOAR.

As the last case containing the United States Constitution left Cade's hands and started down the stairs, there came a ripping sound as the minigun on One-Two's port side opened up with a short, three-hundred-round burst.

One by one the empty-handed Rangers descended the stairs to the sidewalk, negotiated the static cars, and boarded the helicopter tasked with bringing home the Charters of Freedom.

In his earpiece Cade heard Ari warning the Chinook pilot that he was in danger of being overrun from his blind side.

As One-Two responded by going light on her gear, the Rangers on the ramp began firing their carbines at the Zs slithering through the jam on the helo's six.

To Cade's right, Cross and Griff were busy engaging the monsters coming into view off of 14th Avenue. On his left, Axe was firing and changing magazines faster than Cade had ever seen. At the SAS trooper's feet was a growing pool of body fluids and a mound of twice-dead Zs nearly waist-high to him.

The increasing turbine whine drew Cade's attention back to the Chinook. The ramp was motoring up and the rear wheels were no longer resting on the car roofs.

"Jedi Lead, Anvil Actual. Requesting immediate exfil. We're about to be surrounded on three sides."

"Copy that, Anvil Actual," Ari answered back. "Hold onto your bonnets. Coming in hot."

After calling the rest of the team to his position on the sidewalk paralleling Constitution Avenue, Cade dumped his empty mag and reached for another, all while looking skyward at the black obelisk blocking out the flat light.

The harmonic tremor of three sets of rotors bashed Cade's chest as One-Two and One-One crossed paths at different altitudes, the former launching with the mission's objective and full complement of Rangers safely inside, the latter coming in at a steep angle, the minigun laying down a curtain of lead a dozen feet in front of the soon-to-be-compromised Delta team.

"Go, go, go," Cade bellowed, pushing Axe ahead of Cross and Griff. He watched them negotiate the chewed-up concrete and body parts of the Zs Skipper had just decimated with the mini. He was relieved to see them scale the same cars the Chinook had used as a platform. Then he dumped the remaining rounds from his magazine to cover them as Jedi One-One, its wheels still stowed internally, filled up the airspace Jedi One-Two had just vacated.

Like the last man off a sinking ship, putting his trust in both Skipper on the mini, and the brace on his still-healing left ankle, Captain Cade Grayson broke into a sprint for the hovering Ghost Hawk. Once he reached the car Griff had just scrambled atop, he bashed the M4's semi-collapsed stock into a first turn's head, put a boot on the car's rear tire, and performed an improvised half-barrel roll onto its dented roof. With gnarled fingers tugging at his fatigues, Cade rose to a knee and lunged for Cross and Axe's outstretched hands.

The rest was a blur of black blades overhead and colors of the rainbow spinning below as he was yanked forcibly inside the cabin. There was the metallic click of his M4 being unclipped from its sling and then hands were guiding him to a seat as the door began motoring shut.

"I'd say that's one for the *close* column," Axe said, wiping hair and rotten dermis from Cade's still-smoking carbine.

Cade nodded at the quip, but couldn't conjure up a smile, because, like the ring of Tolkien lore, the satellite phone in his pocket was calling to him.

Chapter 73

The parking lot and road out front of Merlin's Drive-In was crowded with vehicles. The two U-Haul trucks and Dregan's Humvees were lined up on 30 pointing south. Parked side by side next to the restaurant were the Raptor, F-650, Bear River patrol Tahoe and Daymon's black Chevy. Laden down with supplies stripped from Adrian's compound, all four vehicles sat low on their springs.

Traveling order was established and with a low rumble and puff of diesel exhaust the Humvees driven by the senior Dregan and his oldest, Gregory, grabbed gears and slowly pulled away. Next in line with Cleo at the wheel was the fully loaded seventeen-foot U-Haul package truck bound for Bear River. And after figuring how to get his new set of wheels into gear, Ray pulled the patrol Tahoe off the lot and formed up on the U-Haul's bumper.

Once the first group was underway, Duncan struck out after them driving the U-Haul containing the bodies of their fallen. Close behind was the Raptor with Taryn at the wheel and Wilson riding shotgun. The seventh vehicle in line was the F-650 with Lev at the helm and Jamie navigating. The black Chevy pickup being driven solo by Daymon brought up the rear.

The multicolored convoy rumbled along on 16, radios quiet, the conversation inside the individual vehicles practically nonexistent.

Randolph proved to be quiet and free of rotters when the vehicles motored through.

A few miles farther south not a thing was stirring in Woodruff.

Forty-five minutes after leaving Merlin's behind, the convoy parted ways at the 16/39 juncture.

The orange glow from the burning lake houses was still on Duncan's mind when he watched the U-Haul, two Humvees, and the patrol Tahoe—gifted by the elder Dregan to Ray as a replacement for the rickety blue pickup—roll on south down State Route 16 towards the Thagon farm.

After steering the U-Haul onto westbound State Route 39, the dam broke inside of Duncan and suddenly he was awash in emotion the likes of which he hadn't experienced since the Sunday in July when his best friend in the world, Charlie Hammond, took his own life. As the road began to climb and the package truck began to bog down under weight of the full load in back, hot tears rolled down his cheeks. Starting with Charlie and ending with Foley, the faces of the dead scrolled through his mind like an old silent film.

"Want me to drive?" Tran asked as the road crested and leveled out.

Startled by the sudden inclusion of sound into the cab, Duncan jerked involuntarily, causing the truck to cross the centerline as 39 swept into a blind right-hander a few hundred feet before the quarry entrance. Then, coming at the worst possible time on the heels of Duncan's course correction, Daymon's voice emanated from the Motorola in the center console. "Drinking again, Old Man?"

Muttering an expletive under his breath, Duncan's gaze was momentarily drawn from the road down to the radio.

"Look out, demons," said Tran.

Looking up and seeing a dozen rotters draped over a tiny green compact, Duncan blurted, "Shit." In the next beat he realized the things Tran had taken to calling demons were about five seconds from making violent and destructive acquaintance with the seventeen-foot U-Haul's squared-off grill.

Before Duncan could get his right foot to the brake pedal, his arms were acting as if they had a mind of their own. Hauling hand over hand to the left started the rig to slew crazily.

Thankfully, as the vehicle went up on two wheels, the brakes grabbed, slamming them back down, which started the vehicle slewing in a serpentine pattern for another thirty feet before coming to a screeching halt with Tran staring at the dead things and Duncan staring straight at the Raptor's rapidly approaching grill.

Because throwing his arms up in front of his face seemed to be his last mortal defense against several tons of hurtling American iron, Duncan missed seeing Taryn jink the wheel at the last possible moment. Instead, when the anticipated meeting with St. Peter didn't materialize, he opened his eyes, dropped his hands, and saw a flash of white in his right side vision as the Raptor's bed hit a glancing blow off the U-Haul's front bumper. Turning his head instinctively he watched the white Ford roll another fifteen feet and come to a sudden and grinding halt balanced precariously on the soft shoulder.

With the Raptor still rocking on its springs, Duncan remembered there had been two other vehicles following behind the Raptor.

As the monsters started raking the sheet metal on Tran's side, Duncan turned his head left just in time to see the hurtling F-650's front end nose down hard. Then, for the second time in a handful of heartbeats, he watched his life flash before his eyes as the rig went from forty-five miles per hour to a complete stop in less time and distance than he fathomed possible.

Thank God for adequate following distances, he thought, eyes flicking from the looming grill next to his door to his oversized side mirror, where he witnessed Daymon swerve his Chevy pickup around back of the U-Haul, its off-road tires leaving a spray of gravel in its wake.

Prying his hands off the wheel, Duncan looked to his right and took in the aftermath from Daymon's evasive maneuver. Zombies were scattered like bowling pins across the road. The left front end of the Chevy had clipped a rotter and sent it airborne like a meat missile straight into the little Toyota Tercel's rear window.

"There's someone in the car," Tran said, his voice rising an octave. "It's a woman, I think."

"So close to home," Duncan said, shouldering his door open, shotgun in hand.

Meeting Lev and Jamie on the road, Duncan hurriedly told them about the breather. Next he radioed the others and told them to stand down, lest the thing moving in the car really was a breather. From experience, he had reason to believe Tran had seen what he had. During all of his travels after that day in late July when the dead began to walk, he had never seen a rotter interested in one of its own. Especially not one trapped in an automobile in plain view.

"There's a woman in there, all right," Daymon said. "We'll take care of the rotters."

Tran flinched when the machete scythed the air in front of his face. Blood spritzed the window and one rotter collapsed vertically.

Wilson spilling out of the Raptor a dozen feet to his right caught Tran's attention. In the redhead's hand was a lock-blade knife. On his face was a look of determination as he waded into the dead from their blind side.

In less than a minute the zombies were prone on the road, legs and arms akimbo, faces frozen masks of true death.

"Nine," Daymon crowed.

"You got eight. I got four," Wilson insisted.

"Quit arguing," Duncan bellowed, as he split the two men and leveled his shotgun at the compact car's drivers-side door.

Hands raised in surrender, the person behind the wheel yelled something that sounded to Duncan like "Bee hive."

Duncan looked a question at Daymon.

"She said *she's alive*," Daymon said matter-of-factly. He sidestepped a corpse and approached Duncan. "What do you want to do?"

"Let her say her piece." Keeping the shotgun aimed at the window glass, Duncan motioned for her to step out. "Slowly," he said, as soon as she lowered her gloved hands.

The woman nudged the door open and stepped onto the road. She looked to be in her mid-forties. Close-cropped blonde hair framed a full face, marred with crow's feet and frown lines. The apocalypse hadn't been easy on this one, Duncan decided. Craning past her, he saw that the car was full of belongings, mostly clothes from the looks of it.

"Hands up," Duncan ordered. "What's your name?"

"Bridgett," she replied.

"Well, Bridgett. We're not going to reciprocate," Lev said. "That's just how it is these days."

Holding her hands up at shoulder level, the woman regarded Duncan. "I ran out of gas."

"Poor planning can get you killed," Daymon said, moving her aside to get a look inside the car.

"I was trying to get to Huntsville before dark. Planned on siphoning gas and moving on to Eden," she said, still looking at Duncan, who was half a head taller. "Though I might stay the night at the ski resort. But some *assholes* dropped a bunch of trees across the road a few miles west of here. So I had to turn back."

"Asshole … right here," Daymon said, raising his hand. "Guilty as charged." He looked to Duncan. "She's telling the truth. Gas gauge is on E. There's garden hose and a gas can in back, too."

Duncan saw a mental image of a coin in his head. *Heads she gets mercy*, he decided, closing his eyes briefly. The imaginary coin spun end over end and landed on heads. "Jacket, shirt, pants, shoes … take them off, now," he said, all business.

The woman stripped down to her bra and panties as ordered.

Taryn and Jamie moved in at once, checking her for weapons and bites.

"What are all of these from?" said Jamie, gesturing to the crisscrossing red welts running up and down the woman's arm from knuckles to elbows.

"Last time I tried to get some gas … back by Woodruff, I got jumped and had to hide from the gawkers in some roadside brambles."

Jamie looked to the others. "What do you all think?"

"Seems legit," Wilson said.

After a second or two, Lev nodded in approval.

"Nice tattoo," Taryn remarked, eyeing the multicolored, tri-petal flower snaking around the woman's bicep. "What is it?"

"A flower," replied the woman.

"What kind?" asked Wilson, inching past Taryn to get a closer look.

"An iris," said the woman, as she threw a shiver. "Can I get dressed now?"

Duncan nodded to the woman. Then, looking to the girls, he said, "When she's decent, blindfold and zip-tie her." He thought for a second. "Go ahead and stick her in back of the 650 with Max."

While Daymon and Wilson cleared the road of the dead and the stalled car, Jamie and Taryn were tying fabric around Bridgett's eyes and binding her wrists together with plastic cuffs. The woman didn't fight. She simply let it happen then allowed Jamie to lead her to the waiting truck.

Chapter 74

The TOC at Schriever was a beehive of activity. Airmen of the 50th Satellite Space Wing sat hunched over their workstations, some banging away at their keyboards sending instructions to their birds orbiting high above the United States, while others sat, eyes riveted on images splashed on the humongous monitors to their fore.

The color image on the sixty-inch plasma display at the front of the room was of a tributary of the Chesapeake. Three warships sat at anchor off a curving white stretch of zombie-covered beach while a landing craft of some type, a white wake spreading slowly from its bow, motored away from the gray vessel nearest to shore.

On the smaller screen near where Nash stood, rendered in black and white, was an overhead shot of open ocean complete with white caps and angry rollers giving off intermittent puffs of spray.

"Five steps in on Two," Nash said.

An airman nearby repeated the order, hit some keys in front of him making the image on the smaller screen change, the waves and spray becoming more noticeable as they contrasted against something sleek and shiny.

"Eight steps on One," she ordered.

Again the verbal confirmation and key tapping which resulted in the color image on the main screen going slightly grainy as everything on it grew larger.

On the top right corner of the screen were the three motorcycles the men and women of the 50th had been tracking for the better part of an hour. Using four separate satellites, each one handing off the job to the other as it passed out of range, they were able to follow their movement from an overpass south of Fort Meade all the way to where they were now. Tiny as ants in relation to their surroundings, the three soldiers dumped their bikes on the beach and sprinted for the approaching landing craft.

A ripple went through the dead crowding the beach as what looked like several hundred of them reacted in unison to the rendezvous taking place a short distance northeast of them.

Looking rested compared to Nash and Shrill, both of whom had been awake for more than thirty hours, the President rose from her chair and stood next to Nash.

After doing a quick mental calculation that took into account two converging objects both moving at different speeds, Nash nodded to the President. "On your command."

Her face conveying not one iota of emotion, President Clay said, "Do it."

Acting on the verbal command, the same airman responsible for changing aspects and magnification on the moving satellite images spoke into the red handset pressed to his ear.

On Screen Two the water directly above the sleek object churned and the image was momentarily wrought blurry. In a sort of ripple effect walking left to right on the screen the action was repeated sixteen times, once every couple of seconds, and then suddenly the ocean was back to normal, the sleek object having disappeared entirely.

The President turned to Nash. "What now?"

On the larger screen, the motor launch had seemingly swallowed up the three men and was already backing away from the encroaching zombies.

"Now we wait," said Nash.

"And root for the landing craft," added Shrill, as the color image on the screen became distorted, flattening somewhat and seeming to stretch at the edges.

"Pass it off to the next bird," Nash said, her eyes never leaving the bank of screens above the dais.

"Passing to KH-11 Misty," she heard a disembodied voice say.

Suddenly the image on the center screen switched to one being taken from a slightly different viewing angle. Nash picked up the landing craft and saw that it had turned itself around and was steaming away from shore, the water at its stern frothy and white.

Now we wait.

Chapter 75

Standing on the bridge walkway of the destroyer *Lanzhou*, Rear Admiral Qi watched the jiangshi milling about on shore through a pair of high-power binoculars. A slight offshore breeze ruffled his wispy gray beard, bringing with it the gut-churning stench of death. The dead were packed mostly into a strip of white sandy beach near where the expeditionary force had gone ashore. Since dropping anchor in the early morning hours and ferrying hundreds of soldiers and a dozen vehicles from the amphibious transport dock *Kunlan Shan* to shore via four incredibly noisy LCAC hovercraft, their numbers had exploded exponentially, going from hundreds to thousands in the span of a few hours. So Qi had ordered the handful of sailors to pull the LCAC from shore and loiter in case the expeditionary force faced stiff resistance inland and was forced to another beachhead somewhere up or down the waterway for emergency extraction. But that had not been the case. The aptly named Tiger Force had found inroads to most of the rural areas—if cities full of box stores and strip malls dare be called rural—and had made good time prosecuting the PLA Navy's first ever incursion deep into the eastern half of the United States. However, when word had come that the Tiger Force went radio silent and all attempts to contact them had gone unanswered, Qi had ordered all four LCACs to pull anchor and return to the *Kunlan Shan's* well deck to be stowed for travel.

A young officer approached. "Admiral Qi," he said, saluting, then standing stiffly at attention.

"Yes, Lieutenant Shou?"

"The Cobra force is returning." Eyes downcast, he added, "But they are only three."

Acceptable, thought Qi. "Send the motor launch. Have them wait off shore to the south and sprint north as soon as Zhen and the rest of his team makes the agreed-upon extraction point."

The lieutenant nodded and returned to the warmth of the bridge.

Returning the binoculars to his eyes, Qi saw movement in the ranks of jiangshi. Barely perceptible at first, but soon the entire mass of them were turning north in unison. No longer were the pale faces fixed on the ships off shore. Now the whole lot of them were moving almost as one toward the sounds made by the approaching Cobra team.

Panning the binoculars right, Qi left the marching jiangshi behind and focused his attention on a spit of land a quarter-mile north where the tree line seemed to merge with the dark green water.

A minute passed and still the dead were moving up the shore, a good number of them forced into the water where they fought to remain upright and continue their march. The hardy grasses near shore were trampled flat. Smaller trees in the way of the unstoppable surge of flesh and bone were bowed down under the press, some snapping off entirely leaving behind upthrust splintered trunks.

Barely two hundred yards separated the jiangshi from the spit of land by the time Zhen and his men, loaded down with heavy packs and still carrying their bullpup rifles, emerged onto the narrow half-moon of sand in view of them.

Shifting the binoculars again, this time beyond the end of the jiangshi column, Qi picked up the noisy motor launch racing south to north toward Zhen and what remained of his team. It was hugging the shoreline and creating a frothy wake that was making it difficult for the struggling jiangshi to stand.

The launch reached the spit just as the team of commandos began to engage a group of jiangshi that had no doubt followed them from where they had ditched their motorcycles on the far side of the beach. Fire lanced from their rifles and jiangshi fell in droves as the three men waded into the surf, the taller Captain Zhen in the lead.

Qi drew a deep breath as the backpacks containing the electronic devices filled with sensitive information were finally handed off to a seaman aboard the launch. Only once the team was aboard and the launch was spinning away from the knot of jiangshi that had pursued the team into the water did he exhale.

Qi waited until the launch was a hundred feet from the *Lanzhou* then went inside the bridge where it was warm. Celebration was in order, and who was going to tell him he couldn't do it on the bridge? He pulled the cigar Zhen had given him from his breast pocket. Ran it under his nose, enjoying the earthy smell of one of Cuba's finest. "Corporal Meng," he barked. "Fetch my finest spirits from my stateroom. Warm it first." *Who knows*, he thought, smiling. *Perhaps the entire bridge crew will get a taste of the exquisite elixir.*

"Admiral. I'm picking up multiple low-level contacts inbound, due south, two kilometers, four hundred sixty knots," said the officer manning the over-the-horizon radar display.

Two kilometers, thought Qi, his gut clenching. He quickly did the math and came to the conclusion that even if the bogeys were closing at subsonic speed, he had less than fifteen seconds to act. But instead of immediately issuing orders, he burned three seconds getting over the river of denial created by his own hubris.

A couple of hundred yards off the *Lanzhou's* starboard side, *Yulin's* running lights went out and a half-dozen HQ-16 medium-range air defense missiles spewed from her vertical launch cell mounted amidships.

Qi was issuing orders when a frantic call came in telling him the rest of his small fleet ninety miles to the south near Norfolk, Virginia was also under attack.

Submarine-launched Tomahawks, he thought to himself as two things happened simultaneously. First, the *Yulin's* port-mounted Type 730 autonomous close-in weapon systems—a seven-barrel Gatling gun capable of firing fifty-eight-hundred 30mm rounds a minute at inbound threats out to three kilometers—went active, spewing rounds at an unseen enemy, the orange-white fire lancing feet from the barrels impossible to ignore. Then there was a blinding flash off in the distance as the 730 destroyed an inbound threat. A split second later the *Kunlan Shan* was struck just above her waterline.

A thunderclap rolled over open water, rattling the *Lanzhou's* bridge windows. Qi took a seat, waiting for the inevitable even as his crew followed orders to get away from shore and deploy countermeasures he knew were too little, too late. He'd been fixated on the brass ring and had discounted America. Even in her darkest hour she had proven to be a worthy opponent.

More flashes of light, this time coming from *Yulin* as she fired another salvo of outbound missiles. Then there was a trio of explosions as a pair of incoming missiles struck her simultaneously, igniting her magazines in the process.

Qi felt the *Lanzhou* shudder and begin to move in reverse while swinging to port. An easy thing to do in open water. In the narrows she was currently in, not so much. Mid-turn, a flurry of HHQ-9 anti-air missiles leapt from the *Lanzhou's* vertical launcher, making him squint.

We may just live to see another day, Qi thought as a trio of explosions lit up the horizon like New Year's fireworks.

"Zhen is aboard," called Corporal Meng, a phone handset pressed to one ear. His eyes darted to the radar officer's screen and the handset fell from his grip. A second later there was a tremendous explosion and he was ripped into by a thousand shards of glass. A millisecond later, before the pain from the damage caused by the shrapnel could register, he simply ceased to exist as a wall of fire infiltrated the bridge, incinerating Rear Admiral Chan Qi and everything else in its path.

60 Miles West of Washington, D.C.

"Night Stalker Airways always strives to bring you, the customer, the best in inflight entertainment," said Ari in a cheesy voice. "Tonight's feature is brought to you by the folks at 50th Space Wing Studios. Directed by Major Freda Nash and produced by President Valerie Clay, Chesapeake Chum has received the highest Rotten Tomatoes score of the month. So sit back, relax, and enjoy."

Cade's hand hadn't left the raised outline of the satellite phone in his thigh pocket since the Ghost Hawk whisked him and his team out of harm's way thirty minutes' prior. As he watched the pre-recorded footage roll on the cabin flat-panel, his mood remained guarded. He saw the tiny figures dismount the three motorcycles. Recognizing the full packs worn by the soldiers and seeing them make it to the awaiting launch only soured his mood further.

Seeing the launch slip by a smaller frigate and reach the gray destroyer made his eyes narrow and temples throb.

"Wait for it," Ari said, over the comms. "USS Georgia was nearby. She's one of the newer converted Ohio Class subs. Lady has claws."

Axe leaned forward in his seat, eyes glued to the panel.

The missiles, just streaks of gray against the dark water, streaked in from the right. Simultaneously two of the three ships launched missiles of their own and there were multiple explosions—just blooms of light as seen from space—and the three ships were momentarily blurred from view.

"Miss Georgia just redefined close," Cross said, smiling at Axe. "No way the guys on the launch could have survived those kind of danger close explosions."

Don't bet on it, Cade thought, dwelling on his many experiences with danger close air support.

When the light flares dissipated on screen the previous image had been altered irrevocably. The larger of the three ships—an amphibious transport by the looks of it—was afire, its stern jutting skyward at a shallow angle. Farther out into the waterway, flammable liquid floating on the surface was burning.

The destroyer was sunk, that much was clear. Gaping holes were visible in her starboard side which was presenting itself to the eye-in-the-sky satellite. Her bridge and masts were completely submerged. The helicopter hangar was still closed, suggesting nobody aboard had escaped via the helicopter normally stowed there. Nearby, all that was left visible of the smaller frigate was a black slick of oil, fire beginning to lick at its edges. Soon to be consumed by flame or the dead waiting on shore, man-sized figures bobbed on the surface.

"Utter destruction," crowed Griff, offering high-fives all around.

Declining the overture, Cade peered out the port-side glass at the approaching dark band of night to the east.

"What's the matter, Wyatt," Ari asked, "cat got your tongue?"

Busy working the buttons on the cargo pocket the phone was in, Cade said nothing.

"Sixteen Tomahawk cruise missiles," said Axe. "That's a bit of overkill, don't you think?"

"Hell no! That's a strongly worded message," Cross quipped.

"Don't tread on our soil in an easy to understand language," added Griff as he peeled off his tactical helmet.

Ignoring the banter, Cade thumbed the phone on and held his breath as the screen lit up. It took a two-count to refresh, and once it had, he saw that he had an SMS message from Duncan and instantly his stomach sank.

No gnus is good gnus, had been his mantra at times. It came from some old live-action cartoon he'd watched as a kid. He'd never researched what a gnu was, and never planned on it. This time Murphy had thrown a wrench into the mix, and he was about to find out how effed up things really were back home.

After opening the message and reading it, he knew the ride home was going to be a difficult one, the two accomplished missions notwithstanding.

As the flat-panel on the bulkhead went dark, Cade took one last look at the countryside below, then closed his eyes in hopes he'd wake up to find that all that had happened from that day in July when he'd dropped Brook and Raven off at Portland

International Airport would have been just one continual nightmare.

Epilogue
Eden Compound, State Route 39

Cade awoke with a start to find the nightmare he had been living since late July was the real deal. Bathed in the red glow of the cabin lights, tinted visor retracted and eyes narrowed, Skipper was gripping his shoulder and shaking him lightly.

The crew chief said nothing.

No words were necessary. Cade knew he was home. He felt it in his gut. And with that knowledge came the realization that he was moments from finding out if his world was indeed about to be turned upside down, or if the precautionary measures Brook had taken the day before were just that and nothing more.

Depressing a button on his Suunto to light the display, he learned he'd been asleep for more than ten hours, through two aerial refuels and the star show he'd been anticipating before reading the sobering SMS message from Duncan. Two deaths were going to hit the little Eden community hard. A third might just fracture them for good. News that Daymon and Heidi had already pulled up stakes and moved on had come as a complete surprise. And considering all of the tumult the group had experienced over the previous twenty-four hours, taking in a new survivor was wholly inconceivable.

Feeling the Ghost Hawk decelerate and begin a wide, sweeping turn, Cade peered out the window. Down below in the inky black flickered the flames of a solitary campfire. It cast an eerie yellow-orange glow on the lone figure seated beside it. On the side of the nearby Winnebago was a man-shaped shadow, the outline of a hat that could only be a Stetson impossible to miss.

Turning his attention away from the inky void, Cade saw Griff and Cross give him a long-distance fist bump from across the cabin. To his right, Axe was wearing a big smile and flashing him a thumbs-up.

After reciprocating the gestures, Cade punched out of his safety harness and slid forward on his seat, clutching his M4 and rucksack to his chest.

"Next stop, Grayson Casa," said Ari over the shipwide comms. "Thanks for flying Night Stalker Airways."

"I don't want everyone waking up," Cade said, all business. "So I'll need you to put down at the end of the airstrip as far away from the Winnebago as possible."

"We aim to please," Ari said, flaring the helo and beginning a slow descent to the moon-splashed clearing where the tall grass was bending and whipping in the rotor wash.

"Until next time," Haynes called from the left seat. "Stay safe, Wyatt."

Cade had no words. He honestly didn't know if there would be a next time. So, hoping Ari and Haynes would see it reflected in their small cockpit mirrors, he flashed a thumbs-up and disconnected the coiled cord from his personal comms pack.

The Ghost Hawk's landing lights suddenly snapped on a dozen feet from the ground and a blast of cold air tinged with kerosene infiltrated the cabin when Skipper opened the port-side door.

The helo settled with barely a bounce and Cade was out the door, taking with him a slap on the back from Skipper.

Cade didn't look back when the turbines ratcheted from a low growl to a high-pitched whine. He kept trudging toward the light at the far end of the makeshift airstrip even as the harmonic punch hit his lungs and the bird launched into the dark night sky, its landing lights stretching his shadow into some kind of grotesque monster.

As the Ghost Hawk's harmonic rotor sound dissipated to nothingness, he heard a series of hollow thuds coming from the direction of the RV. By the time he made it to where Duncan was sitting, shotgun resting across his thighs, it was clear that the Ghost Hawk's arrival and hasty departure had gone unnoticed by everyone save the man who had quickly become his best friend.

Cade dropped his rucksack and M4 in a heap on the crushed grass in the light of the fire. He dragged a camp chair around and sat so that he was facing Duncan.

Duncan said nothing. Just stared straight across the fire at him. On his face was a look conveying a thousand words, none of them good.

A strong wind gust made the tarps covering the Black Hawk and Humvee crack and pop.

Suddenly the noise was back. Only this time it wasn't muffled by distance. Clearly it was coming from *inside* the Winnebago.

Ignoring the commotion, Cade flicked his gaze to the fifth bottle of Jack Daniels on the ground by Duncan's boots.

"It's still sealed," Duncan growled.

"You drinking again?"

"I'm still deciding," he drawled.

Cade removed his helmet and tossed it along with the attached NVGs onto his gear pile. Wispy fingers of steam rose from his head.

Duncan cleared his throat. Setting the shotgun beside his chair, he asked, "Do you want me to do it?"

Cade was silent for a long while.

"If I do," Duncan said, "I'll only have to live with it for another decade or so. You, on the other hand, have a solid three or four decades ahead of you. If you can keep from getting bit, that is."

Cade shook his head. "We made a pact, Brook and I. It's my duty." Then the denial he'd just about broken through built up again. "What makes you sure she's gone?" he asked, voice wavering.

"Raven saw through the bullshit real quick," answered Duncan. "Around noon she found the door to the thing locked and went into a tizzy." He removed his Stetson. The fire reflecting off his glasses, he went on. "Sasha calmed her down.

Come supper time Raven took Brook a plate. Got her to open the door. I saw them hug. Brook was starting to look like old Phillip did when I found him. Then I watched your wife give your daughter an envelope and hand over her little Glock." He wiped a stray tear and buried his face in his hands.

"How did Raven take it?"

Voice muffled because he was talking into his palms, Duncan said, "She lost it right then and there."

"Where is she now?"

"Glenda gave her a sedative. I'd guess she's out like a light in our room."

"What kind of sedative?"

Looking up, Duncan fixed his red-rimmed eyes on Cade and said, "I've no idea. Glenda's the nurse."

As Cade rose and took a few tentative steps in the direction of the RV's door, his shadow darkening the covered windows caused a new round of slamming and banging to emanate from inside. Then a pale and twisted hand ruffled the horizontal blinds, bending a number of them in the process.

Cade opened the outer door, mounted the single step and fished the lock-pick gun from a pocket. After defeating the lock, he looked back and saw Duncan hefting the Jack Daniels bottle, one hand on the long neck, the other about to twist the cap.

"Better not," Cade said, hot tears streaming down his face. "Because we're going to need you, Old Man." At that he drew his Gerber and crabbed through the door.

###

To be continued in a new *Surviving the Zombie Apocalypse* novel in 2017.

Thanks for reading! Reviews help us indie scribblers. Please consider leaving yours at the place of purchase. Cade and the gang will be back in a new *Surviving the Zombie Apocalypse* novel in 2017. Look for books in my bestselling series everywhere eBooks are sold. Please feel free to Friend Shawn Chesser on Facebook. To receive the latest information on upcoming releases first, please join my no-spam mailing list at www.ShawnChesser.com.

Shawn's Facebook Author Page:
www.facebook.com/SurvivingTheZombieApocalypse/

Shawn on Twitter: http://twitter.com/@sdchess

ABOUT THE AUTHOR

Shawn Chesser, a practicing father, has been a zombie fanatic for decades. He likes his creatures shambling, trudging and moaning. As for fast, agile, screaming specimens ... not so much. He lives in Portland, Oregon, with his wife, two kids and three fish. This is his eleventh novel.

CUSTOMERS ALSO PURCHASED:

JOHN O'BRIEN
NEW WORLD
SERIES

JAMES N. COOK
SURVIVING THE DEAD
SERIES

MARK TUFO
ZOMBIE FALLOUT
SERIES

ARMAND
ROSAMILLIA
DYING DAYS
SERIES

HEATH STALLCUP
THE MONSTER
SQUAD

CPSIA information can be obtained
at www.ICGtesting.com
Printed in the USA
LVHW081340050920
665181LV00033B/522